Myths, Gods & Immortals
The Valkyries
New & Ancient Norse Tales

This is a FLAME TREE Book

Publisher & Creative Director: Nick Wells
Editorial Director: Catherine Taylor

Special thanks to Karen Fitzpatrick

FLAME TREE PUBLISHING
6 Melbray Mews, Fulham,
London SW6 3NS, United Kingdom
www.flametreepublishing.com

First published 2026

Note: unless otherwise stated, translations in 'Introducing the Valkyries' are by the author.

26 28 30 31 29 27
1 3 5 7 9 10 8 6 4 2

ISBN: 978-1-83562-790-7

Publisher's Note: The stories within this book are works of fiction. Names, characters, places, and incidents are a product of the authors' imaginations. Locales and public names are sometimes used for atmospheric purposes. Any resemblance to actual people, living or dead, or to businesses, companies, events, institutions, or locales is completely coincidental.

Content Note: The stories in this book may contain descriptions of, or references to, difficult subjects such as violence, death and rape, but always contextualized within the setting of mythic narrative, archetype and metaphor. Similarly, language can sometimes be strong but is at the artistic discretion of the authors.

Cover art by Flame Tree Studio based on elements from Shutterstock.com/FXQuadro.

A copy of the CIP data for this book is available from the British Library.

Printed and bound in China

Represented in the EU for product safety and compliance by
Authorised Rep Compliance Ltd, Ground Floor, 71 Lower Baggot Street,
Dublin, D02 P593, Ireland. Contact at www.arccompliance.com

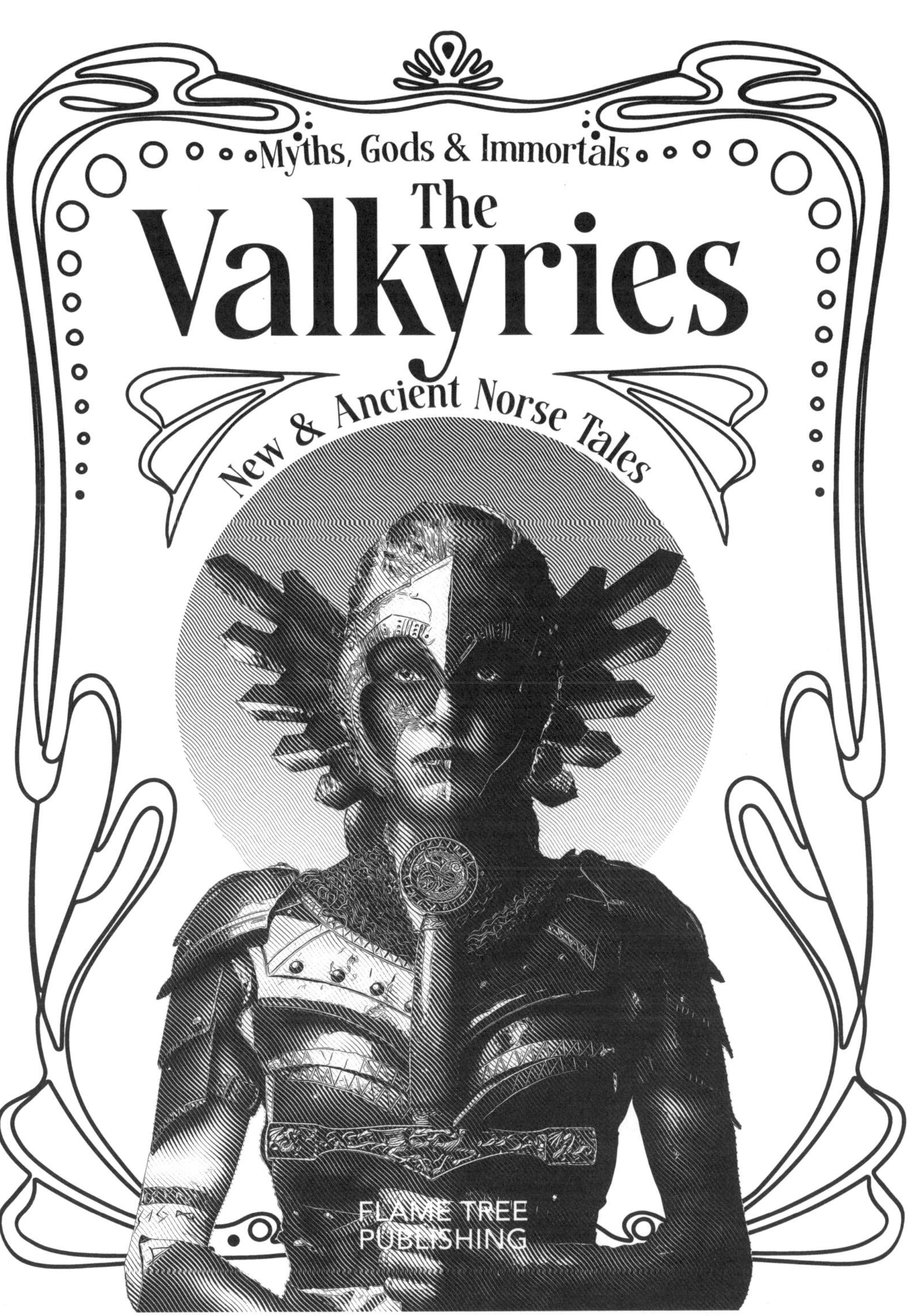
Myths, Gods & Immortals
The Valkyries
New & Ancient Norse Tales
FLAME TREE
PUBLISHING

Contents

Foreword

Dr Jóhanna Katrín Friðriksdóttir

What happens to us when we die? Each society had its own answers, but Norse pagans living in the Viking Age envisioned an afterlife in which Valkyries – supernatural armed women – carry those who have died in battle to Odin's hall Valhalla (Valhöll in Old Norse), while everyone else goes to the goddess Hel's realm. In Valhalla, an existence of feasting and fighting awaits, and the dead warriors are served at table by the same Valkyries who spirited them away from Midgard, the human realm. These warlike women have names related to weapons and war, such as Geirskögul (Spear-shaker), Brynhildr (Battle armour) and Herja (Devastate), and during battles they ride through the sky, controlling the trajectory of the spears and arrows raining down on the fighters below. Valkyries decide who lives to tell tales of great battles, and who will be taken to this new existence in Valhalla.

It is easy to see the attraction of Valhalla for a warrior – it's a place where there is no lack of food or drink, combat is a form of entertainment rather than something leading to injury or death, and Odin's girls cater to his every need. The logic of this narrative for the warriors' leaders is also relatively simple. In a time of Viking military activity overseas, men aspiring to grab or maintain power needed to recruit men for their armies, and Valkyries were one part in an ideology that offered the Valhalla afterlife as a reward. It provided a viable alternative to returning home with the treasures and status that participating in raids could yield for those who survived.

The idea of the Valkyrie as Odin's horse-mounted assistant/waitress seems straightforward: although they nominally decide on each warrior's fate, they usually carry out Odin's will rather than their own. Once the warrior is delivered to Valhalla, they enter a subservient role, perhaps a disappointing development to modern readers. On the other hand, the Valkyries' servility in Valhalla seems at odds with their astonishing power and warlike aspects – it somehow doesn't chime with the awe-inspiring women in byrnies on their powerful horses, splattered in blood and gleefully chanting war songs. Indeed, when we begin to delve into their different manifestations across the written sources, there is a remarkable breadth in the way in which people in the Viking and medieval period imagined Valkyries. Some were more interested in their otherwordliness: the poet who composed *Eiríksmál* ('Words about Eiríkr') depicted their Valkyries as fair and ethereal, possessing the language of birds. Others imagine them as impersonal and businesslike, almost like judges. In *Hákonarmál* ('Words about Hákon'), a dead warrior – in this case, the ninth-century Norwegian king Hákon – is shocked to learn that he is on his way to Odin, but the poem's Valkyries matter-of factly tell him that this is their final decision. Even a king has no scope for manoeuvre when up against the powers of a Valkyrie.

One aspect of the Valkyrie is her role as the warrior's sexual and romantic partner. The Valkyrie Sigrún (whose name means victory-rune) chooses the hero Helgi Hundingsbani (slayer of Hunding) as her lover, and in one of two versions of their story, she appeared as little more than an adoring fangirl. However, the same events are narrated in a second poem, which emphasizes Sigrún's independent will: she disobediently puts Helgi up to killing the suitor her family has chosen and later has a furious argument with her brother about the matter. The brother eventually kills Helgi, who is placed in a burial mound where the lovers spend a final night together before he goes to Valhalla. No reader can forget the Valkyrie's morbid excitement about touching and sharing a bed with Helgi's bloody, battle-scarred body. The fascinating image of a woman's sexual attraction to a corpse we encounter in this story might seem off-putting or ridiculous, but it arguably gives us an insight into how warriors might have coped with going into battle. It opens up the possibility that at least some warriors found comfort in the idea that death was to fall into the warm embrace of a beautiful Valkyrie lover.

Valkyries have freedom of movement and control over life and death, aspects that have stimulated the imagination of storytellers for centuries. Their independent will becomes a central theme in some medieval narratives: in the legend of the Valkyrie Brynhildr, who goes by the name of Sigrdrífa in her early life, her strong sense of self leads to devastating bloodshed. In a prior phase of her life, Brynhildr (Brünnhilde in Wagner's operas) pledges herself to the only man alive who has no fear, whom she believes to be the hero Sigurd the dragon-slayer. However, events pan out differently, and after marrying another man, Gunnarr, she discovers that a disguised Sigurd had wooed her on Gunnarr's behalf, and that she has been deceived into thinking that Gunnarr was worthy. Brynhildr's betrayal and subsequent furious insistence on revenge leads to a chain of events in which both Sigurd and Gunnarr die violent deaths, while she commits suicide. The dramatic story of Brynhildr and Sigurd was clearly a popular story across the medieval Northern world, and it is still a fountain for modern retellings.

In the twenty-first century, audiences expect narratives with 'strong women' and Valkyries have been useful to fulfil this expectation. Although Valkyries usually do not fight in the Norse myths, instead hovering above the fray, their warlike side finds resonance today when there is a tendency to draw a line between power and the use of violence. For example, in the popular videogame *God of War: Ragnarok* (2018), the player must defeat nine fierce Valkyries in combat, while in the Marvel cinematic universe, the character Valkyrie is a battle-hardened veteran of Odin's wars and the last surviving member of a group of Valkyries who once formed an elite band of female warriors. In the world of sport, the Golden State Valkyries basketball team, based in the Bay Area in California, is the counterpart to the male Warriors team, incorporating the Norse Valkyries' swords and wings in their V-shaped logo, and highlighting their boldness, strength and courage in their marketing. Valkyries are thus potent symbols that have been harnessed for female empowerment in a multitude of ways. Some of the stories in this collection, too, are preoccupied with the question of gender equality, but at the same time, other stories show that now, no less than in the medieval past, Valkyries are a way into exploring a plethora of themes, from universal questions about the core of human nature to the burning issues of today.

Dr Jóhanna Katrín Friðriksdóttir

Ancient & Modern: Introducing the Valkyries

by Nancy Marie Brown

1.
The Myth

Winding, winding / the web of war,
weaving banners / through the host:
We won't let / his life be lost.
Valkyries choose / who will die.

– from 'The Valkyries' Loom Song', stanza 6,
in *Njál's Saga*

THE VALKYRIES IN OLD NORSE POETRY AND SONG

On a cold winter's day in 2012, an amateur archaeologist using a metal detector near the village of Hårby in Denmark made a spectacular find: nestled in a lump of frozen mud, looking eerily up at him, were two tiny fierce eyes. Careful cleaning by a museum curator revealed an intricately detailed amulet, small as a fingertip, made of gilded silver in the shape of a woman with her long hair twisted into a ponytail. She carried a sword and shield.

She was immediately dubbed a 'valkyrie'. Why?

Because the ambitious Icelandic chieftain Snorri Sturluson (1179–1241) described valkyries as demi-goddesses with shield and sword (or spear) who accompanied dead heroes to Valhalla, the feast hall of the Norse god Odin, and there served them mead.

Snorri included the valkyries, alongside other Norse gods and goddesses, in a book that is known as Snorri's *Edda*, or the *Younger Edda* or, most often, the *Prose Edda*. It is called 'Edda' in one of the earliest manuscripts we still have. But no one knows what 'Edda' means. It could mean 'of Oddi', after the school Snorri attended in Iceland. It could mean 'great-grandmother'. It could derive from an Icelandic word meaning 'wits, poetry or song', or from a Latin word meaning 'the art of poetry'.

Put all those meanings together, and you get 'the art taught at Oddi of great-grandmother's old-fashioned songs', a title that aptly describes the *Prose Edda*. Snorri wrote it, we think, as a handbook to teach a young king of Norway how to appreciate Viking poetry.

Snorri and the King

King Hakon IV (1204–63) was 14 when Snorri, age 40, sailed from Iceland to meet him in 1218 and tried to impress him with his knowledge of ancient poetry and lore. He failed.

King Hakon had been raised by Christian bishops. He knew nothing about Odin or Valhalla or the valkyries – except, perhaps, that they were pagan and, therefore, evil. King Hakon would be taken by angels to Heaven when he died, not carried to Valhalla on a valkyrie's flying horse.

In his day, Norway and Iceland both had officially been Christian countries for more than 200 years. The Viking Age itself is commonly thought to have ended around 1066, when the Normans – descendants of the Vikings who settled in northern

France – conquered England. Though the sea-raiders that had begun coming from Scandinavia to attack other parts of Europe in the late 700s continued doing so after 1066, these were no longer raids by adventurous bands of Viking warriors. Instead, they were attacks by one Christian nation on another, led by Christian kings.

Young King Hakon was marginally more interested in the old poems Snorri knew that spoke of his ancestors, the ancient kings and sea-kings of Norway. These and other Viking poems often allude to myths and legends, so Snorri included many such tales, alongside excerpts from the poems, in the *Prose Edda*. He recorded more myths in his collection of sagas about the early Norwegian kings, known as *Heimskringla* from its opening words, 'The round world'.

In neither case was Snorri writing a comprehensive account of Norse mythology for posterity. He had a more immediate purpose. He was a politician, not a scholar. He wanted riches and power. He wanted the young king to appoint him Earl of Iceland or, at least, to name him King's *Skáld.* While a *skáld* was a poet and storyteller, the King's *Skáld* was considered the king's chief advisor, mouthpiece and ambassador.

Norse Mythology

Snorri got neither of those titles. In fact, King Hakon may never have seen either *Heimskringla* or the *Prose Edda*, which seems to have been left unfinished when Snorri was murdered in 1241 – by order of the king.

His books earned Snorri neither riches nor power. But they did gain him everlasting fame. Almost all the stories we know today of the Vikings' gods and goddesses come to us via Snorri. Introducing a 1954 translation of the *Prose Edda*, Icelandic scholar Sigurður Nordal (1886–1974) remarked that no one now read it 'as a textbook on mythology'. He was wrong. All textbooks on Norse mythology rely on Snorri.

We don't have much else to go on. The poems that mention the Norse gods and goddesses are very hard to decipher: two English translations rarely match. The images on jewellery, textiles, wood and stone are even more elusive: over the years, art experts have widely disagreed on what they depict.

Only Snorri gives us clear, memorable stories. Our modern understanding of Norse mythology, and especially what Helene A. Guerber in her 1909 translation called its 'peculiar grim humour', is a product of Snorri's imagination.

We have Snorri to thank for teaching us the Norse myths of the valkyries and Valhalla, of one-eyed Odin and the well of wisdom, of red-bearded Thor and his hammer of might, of two-faced Loki and the death of beautiful Baldur, of lovesick Freyr and lovely Freyja, the rainbow bridge, the great ash tree Yggdrasil at the centre of the Nine Worlds, the world-wrapping Midgard Serpent, Heimdall's horn, the eight-legged horse Sleipnir, and Ragnarok, or the Twilight of the Gods.

For all of these stories Snorri is our main source – and sometimes our only one.

The Truth of these Tales

Snorri lists his own sources in the beginning of *Heimskringla*. First, he used 'ancient lore', stories he was told by learned men and women whom he had met on his travels around Iceland, Norway and Sweden.

Second, he used genealogies. These could be rather fanciful – kings (even Christian kings) liked to trace their ancestry back to the old gods.

Third, he used poems that had been recited to entertain the kings themselves or their sons. The poems were his best sources, Snorri argued. Though before his time few, if any, Viking poems had been written down, 'people still know these poems', he insisted, even those that were hundreds of years old.

Like sonnets or haiku, Viking poems had elaborate rules for rhyme, rhythm and alliteration. These rules made them easier to memorize than prose. 'If a verse is composed correctly,' Snorri asserted, 'the words in it will remain the same, even as they are passed down from mouth to mouth.'

Modern scholars tend to agree with him: much of what we know about the Vikings comes from Viking poetry.

Snorri loved poetry. He memorized a great deal of it. In the *Prose Edda*, he quotes 373 verses by 64 different *Skálds*, including himself, who lived from the ninth century to the thirteenth. *Heimskringla* includes nearly 600 verses. And that is not all the poetry Snorri knew. In his books, he often quotes only a line or two, not the complete poem.

To help us (and that young king) understand these poems he so loved, he untangles their tricky wordplay and explains their obscure allusions to pagan myths as well as he can. Though sometimes, to make an explanation clear, he contradicts himself. At other times, it seems, he simply makes things up.

He warns us that poets do exaggerate: 'It is the way of poets to praise most the ones to whom they are speaking,' he said. But no poet would dare praise rulers for things that they – and everyone listening – knew were false. 'That would be mockery, not praise.'

How Snorri applied this rule to mythology, not history, we cannot say. Perhaps the best way to look at Snorri's tales is to apply what he says of his own sources: 'Though we do not know the truth of these tales, we know that wise old people have sometimes held them to be true.'

Choosers of the Slain

Introducing the goddesses in the *Prose Edda*, Snorri says they were 'no less holy and no less powerful' than their male counterparts. Beginning with Odin's wife, Frigg, Snorri mentions 14 of them before adding, almost as an afterthought, 'There are also others who serve in Valhalla, bringing drinks and taking care of the cups and ale casks'.

He backs up this claim by quoting a few lines of a poem called *Grímnismál*, or 'The Song of Grimnir'. Grimnir means 'the cloaked one' or, as translator and scholar Jackson Crawford construes it, 'Shadowed Face'. It is a pseudonym taken up by Odin, as he visits Middle Earth in disguise to win a bet with Frigg. He loses the bet. He is captured and tortured by being set between two bonfires. Before he loses his temper, he shows off his knowledge of Asgard, the world of the gods, by naming the people and places there.

At one point, Grimnir wishes for two women, Hrist and Mist, to bring him a drink. He names 11 others whom, he says, 'carry ale to the Einherjar', the host of dead heroes in Valhalla. These supernatural barmaids, Snorri explains, 'are called valkyries. Odin sends them to every battle. They choose men's fates and determine victory.' Along with Skuld, the youngest of the three Norns (equivalent to the Fates), they 'choose the slain and decide who will be killed'.

'Chooser of the slain' is a literal translation of the Old Norse word *valkyrja. Valr* means 'corpse', particularly someone slain on the battlefield; *-kyrja* comes from the verb *kjósa*, 'to choose'.

That the valkyries wear armour and carry weapons is clear from the way their names are used in the extended metaphors, or kennings, that make Viking poetry so hard to translate. Snorri defines the term in his *Edda*: 'It is a simple kenning to call battle "spear clash" and it is a double kenning to call a sword "fire of the spear-clash".'

In kennings based on valkyries' names, 'Hild's sail' is a shield and 'Gondul's crashing wind' means battle in one poem. In another, 'Skogul's wind' is battle and 'Hild's resounding storm' is a rain of spears and arrows. In other poems, 'Skogul's shirt' is a ringmail byrnie and 'Mist's frost' is a sword.

The Poetic Edda

'The Song of Grimnir' is one of Snorri's sources that we have in full – not just the few lines Snorri quotes in the *Prose Edda*. It is one of 31 poems about gods and heroes preserved in a collection known as the *Poetic Edda* or *Saemund's Edda* or the *Elder Edda* (though it is not any older than Snorri's *Edda*). The oldest manuscript we have dates to about 1275 – well after

Snorri's death in 1241, but around the time his nephew Sturla Thordarson (1214–84) was writing the sagas of King Hakon IV and his son, King Magnus VI (1238–80).

This manuscript, called the *Codex Regius* or 'King's Book', is a copy of something older, but not very much older. Scholars believe Snorri inspired it – or maybe even commissioned it. One expert has suggested that Snorri sent out teams of poetry collectors on field trips throughout Iceland, to locate poems he himself did not know. Another theory is that Snorri and his friends wrote some of the poems themselves.

That this collection is confusingly called an Edda is the fault of Bishop Brynjólfur Sveinsson (1605–75) of Iceland. Reading the manuscript, he was struck by how similar the poems were to those quoted in Snorri's *Prose Edda* – so he gave it a similar name, which stuck. He attributed the *Poetic Edda* to the founder of the Oddi school, Saemund the Wise (1056–1133).

The manuscript got its name, 'King's Book', because the bishop sent it to King Frederik III of Denmark (1609–70) to be kept in the Royal Library in Copenhagen. To make things even more confusing, the bishop also sent the king a fourteenth-century manuscript copy of Snorri's *Edda*; this manuscript is also called the *Codex Regius*.

Both of these 'King's Books' were returned to Iceland with great fanfare, the *Poetic Edda* in 1971 and the *Prose Edda* in 1985. National treasures, they are now kept in the Árni Magnússon Institute for Icelandic Studies in Reykjavík, where you can often see them on display.

Valhalla

'The Song of Grimnir' gave Snorri his picture of Odin's feast hall, Valhalla. The name means 'Corpse Hall', or 'Home of the Dead'. It is an enormous building with 540 huge doors; 800 warriors can pass at once through each doorway. Its roof tiles are shields – which Snorri says shine with gold. Its rafters are spear-shafts. The benches inside, where the warriors eat and sleep and – especially – drink, are littered with ringmail byrnies. Instead of torches, the hall is lit by bright swords.

'Do the dead heroes drink water?' asks Snorri's alter ego in the *Prose Edda* (like many medieval books, it is organized as a dialogue).

'That's a strange question,' the High One (Odin) replies. 'Would All-father [Odin, again] invite kings to his house and give them water to drink? They'd think they'd paid a high price for the honour.' Beside the hall, he explains, grows a tree. A goat stands on the hall's high roof to graze on the tree branches. Instead of milk, that magic goat gives mead. Each day it fills a vat so big that all the heroes can drink all they want from it.

A magic boar provides their meat. Each day it is butchered and cooked; each morning it comes back to life.

Mead and bacon. That's what heroes eat while they're waiting for the world to end at Ragnarok, when the gods and their human companions will fight against the giants of ice and fire.

Except that both Snorri and his source have already said the valkyries serve the heroes beer or ale, while in another poem the valkyries serve them wine. Don't expect these myths to be consistent!

Eirik Blood-Axe Comes to Valhalla

Another thing you should not expect is for Odin, the chief god of the Norse pantheon, to always be treated with respect. One of the chief delights of Norse mythology is its humour.

In the *Prose Edda*, Snorri quotes the anonymous death song of King Eirik Blood-Axe (*c.* 930–54), who with his wife, Queen Gunnhild Mother-of-Kings (*c.* 910-80), briefly ruled Norway – and, later, the city of York in England – before being killed on a Viking raid. It begins, in my translation:

What did I dream? / Just before daybreak
I readied Valhalla, / or so I imagined,
for a host of the slain. / I woke up the Einherjar:
Get up! Scatter straw / on all the bare benches,
wash out the beer-cups! Valkyries! Bring wine,
for a war leader arrives! [...]
Sigmund! Sinfjotli! / Arise and swiftly
welcome the warrior. / Bid him enter,
if it is Eirik: / He's the one I expect.

Here, Odin comes across as a frazzled innkeeper, calling out to the warriors, the valkyries and the heroes Sigmund and Sinfjotli to wake up and get to work. He's not even sure that Eirik Blood-Axe is really coming – which is understandable if, as Snorri says, half of the slain warriors the valkyries collect on the battlefield go instead to the goddess Freyja and live in her hall, *Fólkvangr* ('Warriors' Field'). Another poem Snorri quotes in the *Prose Edda* implies that Freyja gets first choice.

King Eirik's death-song also explains why the best warriors lose their earthly battles. Bragi, the god of poetry, asks Odin, 'Why expect Eirik, not some other kings?' Odin replies, 'He's reddened a blade, a bloody sword borne, in many a land.' Says Bragi, 'Why then deny him the victory in war?' Because, Odin answers, 'No one can guess when the grey wolf will attack the gods' home.'

The grey wolf, Fenrir, is one of the giant monsters the gods will face at the last battle, Ragnarok. This wolf, the seer has foretold, will defeat Odin himself. So he commands the valkyries to gather a great army, bringing to Valhalla all the best warriors who fought on earth, hoping to delay his own doom.

Hakon the Good is Called Home

King Eirik Blood-Axe was already on his way to Valhalla when his death song opened. But another poem Snorri quotes gives us an idea of what it was like for a king on the battlefield to see the valkyries swoop down upon him.

This poem was written by Eyvind Skaldaspillir (*c.* 915–90; his nickname means 'the Plagiarist') about the death of the Norwegian King Hakon I the Good (*c.* 920–60). Although Hakon I was a Christian king, Eyvind pictures him, not making ready to meet Saint Peter at the Pearly Gates, but waiting to be carried off by two valkyries. In my translation, the poem begins:

Gondul and Skogul / were sent by Odin
to choose which kings, / which of Yngvi's line,
would go to Valhalla / and dwell with Odin [...]

The two valkyries joined the battle at the very beginning, watching as Hakon put on his mail shirt and helmet and raised his banner. He marched bravely into battle, cheerful and joking with his troops. The next several stanzas describe the battle:

Spears clashed, / shields shattered,
swords battered / warrior's skulls [...]
The shield-rim's sky / was bathed blood red;
Skogul's storm / beat the shield-boss.

Hakon's army fought hard, but the tide turned against them:

His warriors sat / with swords unsheathed,
their shields scarred, / their byrnies broken.
His host was no longer / in high spirits:
It was on its way / to Valhalla.
Gondul leaned / on her spear and said,
'The gods' army grows, / now Hakon and his
great war host / are all called home.'
This Hakon heard: / the valkyries' speech;
women on horseback, / wisely they acted
and helmeted sat, / shields held before them.

Note that, while Eyvind calls these battle maids wise, he doesn't say they are young and beautiful. Snorri doesn't either, in so many words. But by being served mead (or beer or wine) by a valkyrie, one of the perks of dying in battle, he makes it easy for later readers to make that assumption.

Weaving the Web of Battle

In neither of these kings' death songs do we learn how the valkyries actually go about choosing the slain. A poem not included in either of the Eddas, however, paints an indelible image of 12 women weaving at a grisly loom. It goes, in part, in my translation:

See the warp / of spilled intestines,
loom-weights made / of severed heads,
the shafts are / blood drenched spears,
the rods are / arrows, iron-bound;
with swords we weave this victory web [...]
Winding, winding / the web of war,
weaving banners / through the host:
We won't let / his life be lost.
Valkyries choose / who will die.
Now it's gruesome / to look out:
blood red clouds / fill the sky.
The air is dyed / with blood of men
while the valkyries / sing their song.
Learn it well / and tell the others,
when you hear / the valkyries' song.
Let's ride out now, / hard from here,
with naked swords / held high.

This poem was included in *Njal's Saga*, which was written by Snorri's nephew Sturla or one of his contemporaries in the mid-1200s. It is called *Darraðarljóð*; *ljóð* means 'song' or 'lay'.

Darraðr is harder to decipher; the author of *Njal's Saga* took it to be a man's name, but scholars now think it means a kind of battle flag or pennant.

Neil Price, in his book *Children of Ash and Elm: A History of the Vikings* (2020), refers to the poem as 'The Web of Spears', while Eiríkur Magnússon in 1910 called it 'The Weaving of the Spear'. When he wrote his version in 1768, the poet Thomas Gray (1716–71), famous for his 'Elegy Written in a Country Churchyard', named it 'The Fatal Sisters'.

I think of it as 'The Valkyries' Loom Song': According to textile specialist Else Østergård in *Woven into the Earth* (2004), 'The description of the Valkyries' loom is the most complete source for the weaving terminology of the Middle Ages.'

What are the valkyries weaving on their grisly loom? The battle itself.

Imagine you are weaving at a standing loom: The warp threads (intestines) hang vertically, bounded by the shafts (spears) to right and left, and stretched taut by weights (the heads). The weft is a skein of thread, unwinding as you move it back and forth through openings in the warp created by moving the rods (arrows). At intervals, you beat the weft up against the preceding rows using a tool called a sword.

Think of a battle seen from afar: the heroes' colourful battle standards weave back and forth through the battle lines, as if guided by the valkyries' hands.

Shield-maids, Not Maidens

These bloody-handed, bloody-minded battle-weavers are a far cry from the valkyries Helene A. Grueber describes in *Myths of the Norsemen* (1909) as 'young and beautiful, with dazzling white arms and flowing golden hair', or Ingri and Edgar D'Aulaire in *D'Aulaire's Book of Norse Myths* (1967) – a childhood favourite – as 'tall and handsome warrior maidens clad in shining armor, with winged helmets' and 'lovely white cloaks of swans' feathers' or even the 'warlike virgins' of *Bulfinch's Mythology* (Thomas Bulfinch,1855).

One reason the vision of the valkyries as beautiful young girls has taken hold is our inability to translate the Old Norse word *skjaldmær*, which is used in the poems and sagas interchangeably with *valkyrja*.

Skjald is easy: 'shield'. But *mær* can be interpreted in several ways. In Richard Cleasby and Gudbrand Vigfusson's *Icelandic-English Dictionary*, the dictionary most translators have used since it first came out in 1874, the word *mær* is glossed as 'girl', 'daughter' or 'virgin'.

But a similar Viking term for a warrior woman, *skjaldkona*, 'shield-woman' or 'shield-wife', makes it clear that a woman's youth or sexual experience has nothing to do with her status as a shield-maid: She is a female carrying a shield.

The comparable word for males is *drengr*, 'a young unmarried man', a 'bachelor', a 'youth' or in modern usage, a boy.

Drengr is occasionally applied to women in Old Norse texts as well. Judith Jesch, in *Ships and Men in the Late Viking Age* (2001), defines the word as 'the follower who fights by the side of his leader in battle, and who is richly rewarded in turn'.

The issue is not sex, but status. These warriors are not householders. They have no families and no economic responsibilities.

They have no obligations except to their war leader. They are professional fighters.

A Third Gender?

Some readers question whether the valkyries and shield-maids should even be called female. By behaving as warriors, the argument goes, they are taking up a male role in society.

In some sagas, as we will see in the next chapter, they clearly dress as males. They give themselves masculine names and even change their pronouns. They do everything in their power to avoid being saddled with marriage and children.

Depending on the translator, the valkyrie in the poem *Hrafnsmál*, 'Song of the Raven', could be considered queer. This poem, preserved in Snorri's *Heimskringla*, celebrates King Harald Fairhair (King Harald I of Norway, *c.* 850–c. 932). It is framed as a dialogue between a raven, introduced as the one who picked the brains out of the giant Hymir's skull, and 'a white, bright-haired' (or possibly, 'bright-helmeted') valkyrie:

Wise, she knew herself: / She understood bird-speech;
this valkyrie, first in battle, / was no shy maid
around fighting men. / White-throated, she greeted,
with shining eyes, Hymir's / skull-picker on the cliff.

What I translate as 'no shy maid / around fighting men', Lee Hollander in his translation of *Heimskringla* (1936) notes is a difficult passage to untangle. He reads it as, 'were welcome never / men to the bright-eyed one', while R.D. Fulk in *Poetry from the Kings' Sagas* (2012) says, 'men were not pleasing to / the aggressive maid'.

Kathleen Self, writing in the journal *Feminist Formations* in 2014, notes that most discussions of the valkyries 'tend to insert them into a binary of masculine and feminine, wherein they sit somewhat uneasily in the feminine category'. While Old Norse laws (also written down well after the Viking Age ended) claim that women were punished for wearing men's clothes and carrying weapons, the valkyries and shield-maids in the stories 'are met with admiration', Self observes, 'though not as paragons of femininity'. She believes 'these figures are best understood as a third gender – a hybrid of masculine and feminine characteristics that were dominant during the time period'.

Winners and Losers

Other scholars think we should apply the modern term 'transgender' to some of the characters in these stories and poems – or at least to the warrior graves, which I discuss later in this introduction.

Jóhanna Katrín Friðriksdóttir in *Valkyrie: the Women of the Viking World* (2020) writes: 'Although it is clear that Norse society had two binary categories, a few sagas raise the question whether someone born with a female body could take on a male role with the correct clothing and behaviour, as we know people have successfully done throughout history.' She concludes, 'We can't simply equate chromosomes with social gender.'

But neither adding a third gender nor applying today's concept of transgender seems to me to explain the worldview that includes the valkyries.

I remain convinced by Carol J. Clover's ground-breaking study from 1993, 'Regardless of Sex: Men, Women, and Power in Early Northern Europe'. Viking society, she argues, was binary – just not in the way we're used to thinking about it.

In Clover's view, the world of the valkyries was one 'in which maleness and femaleness were always negotiable, always up for grabs, always susceptible to "conditions"', some of those conditions being age, ability and ambition. 'Actual genitals were pretty much beside the point,' she adds.

In the poems and tales of the Viking Age, a character was not male or female, but on a spectrum ranging from strong to weak, aggressive to passive, powerful to powerless, winner to loser or, in the Old Norse terms, *hvatur* to *blauður*.

Hvatur, always a compliment, means 'bold, active, vigorous'. It appears to be related to the verb *hvetja*, a cognomen for our verb 'to whet' – to sharpen or put an edge on. Its opposite, *blauður*, always an insult, means 'soft, weak'. It is, says the Cleasby-Vigfusson dictionary, 'no doubt a variant of *blautur*', which means 'moist'.

Hard, sharp and vigorous versus soft, yielding and moist. Think dirty and you've got it.

'What finally excites fear and loathing in the Norse mind is not femaleness per se,' says Clover, 'but the condition of powerlessness.' Likewise, she adds, 'what prompts admiration is not maleness per se, but sovereignty'.

Ash and Elm

Else Mundal, in a chapter in the collection *Gender and Religion: European Studies* (2001), notes that in Viking times 'gender transgressions were taboo, but in reality only for men. If the situation demanded that a woman had to take over the man's tasks, she could gain honour if she managed to fill the male role.' No woman in Old Norse literature is ever rebuked for showing 'courage, strength of purpose, wisdom, etc.'.

The idea that a woman should be passive and submissive – should know her place – was introduced to the Norse world by Christian clerics. It's a Christian concept that 'differences in character, abilities and intellectual competence between women and men were unequivocally tied to biological difference', Mundal notes. For Christians, 'the male represented the perfect human, the female was inferior to the male'. She was less 'God-like'.

That was not true in the world of the valkyries.

Unlike the Christian creation myth, where Eve is an afterthought, fashioned out of Adam's rib for his comfort and pleasure, in the Norse version of the creation of the world, *Embla* ('Elm', the first female) and *Askr* ('Ash', the first male) are equal.

The story of Ash and Elm is told in *Völuspá*, the 'Song of the Seer', which is found in the *Poetic Edda*; Snorri paraphrases the poem in his version of the creation story in the *Prose Edda.* According to the story, in the beginning two driftwood logs are found on the seashore by three wandering gods. These gods give the wood human shape and bring it to life with blood, breath and curious minds.

Unlike Adam and Eve, Ash and Elm are made at the same time out of nearly the same stuff. As different as an ash tree and an elm, they make a good team.

Ash wood was used for spear shafts and oars. A good rower was sometimes called an 'ash-person'.

Elm was used for wagon wheels. It was also the preferred wood for short, powerful bows: an archer might be nicknamed 'elm-twig'.

Both woods had roles in peace and war: oars and wheels, spears and bows. Their uses were determined by their size and strength, their resistance to rot or tensile stress, the denseness of their grain and where they grew.

The same was likely true for the men and women of the pagan North, before Christianity arrived around the year 1000: men and women were equals, their roles in society being decided not by biology, but based on ambition, ability, family ties and wealth.

Skadi Avenges Her Father

An example Snorri Sturluson relates in the *Prose Edda*, of a woman who gained honour by taking over a man's task, is the story of the giantess Skadi, who became a goddess.

When her father was killed as a result of one of the god Loki's tricks, Skadi 'took up her helmet and ringmail byrnie and weapons of war' and, like a valkyrie, set off to avenge him. Ordinarily a daughter would not be asked to avenge her father's death. That was a son's job. But Skadi's father had no sons.

So Skadi travelled from Giantland to Asgard, the home of the gods, and, surprisingly, was allowed to enter. No one dared accept her challenge to fight.

Instead, Odin offered her compensation: in lieu of blood money, he would turn her father's eyes into two stars in the sky and Loki the Trickster would make her laugh (unforgettably, by tying a rope around the beard of a goat and the other end around his own testicles).

Finally, Skadi could choose a husband from among the gods. Skadi wanted to marry Baldur; she had heard he was the most beautiful of all the gods. Odin said she could have him, if she could pick him out from a line-up looking only at his feet.

Njord, the god of the sea, it turned out, had prettier feet.

But he and Skadi didn't get along. He hated the mountains, she hated the sea. He hated the night-time howling of the wolves, she hated the early morning ruckus of the gulls. So they divorced.

Afterwards, Skadi was honoured as the goddess of winter, of skiing and the hunt. Though she lived alone on her mountain, ruling her father's estate, she and Odin took up together and had several sons, including Skjold, the founder of the Danish dynasty – known to the writer of the Anglo-Saxon epic poem *Beowulf* as Scyld Shefing.

Grinding Peace and War

Another story Snorri tells about valkyrie-like giantesses comes from the poem *Grottasöngr*, 'The Song of the Millstone'.

A man named 'Hangjaw' (a name for Odin) gave the legendary King Frodi of Denmark an enormous magic millstone that would grind, not only flour, but whatever you wished for.

To work it, Frodi bought from a man named 'Spell Caster' (also Odin) two strong women, Fenja and Menja. He ordered them first to grind out gold, then peace and plenty. The women began their task cheerfully. They sang a working song – *Grottasöngr* itself – and made the millstone whirl around. The 'Peace of Frodi' became a byword for a Golden Age.

But the king worked Fenja and Menja too hard. 'Sleep no longer than it takes me to recite a poem!' he ordered.

The women got angry. 'You were not very wise,' they told Frodi, 'when you bought your slaves. You chose us for strength and looks and asked nothing about our background.' Before they were captured and enslaved, they had been warrior women: They killed berserks, broke shields, killed one king and aided another. They said,

This went on / for many years:
As heroes we / were widely known—
with keen spears / we cut
blood from bone. / Our blades were red.

They made the millstone grind out an army. Said Fenja, 'Turn the mill-handle harder! We're not yet covered in corpse-blood.' King Frodi was killed in the battle.

Discussing this poem in her chapter in *Revisiting* the *Poetic Edda* (2013), Judith Quinn argues that we shouldn't be surprised that Fenja and Menja morph between giantesses and valkyries: They are 'fundamentally personifications of fate', she says. Only as valkyries can they choose which king lives and which dies, for, as Quinn says, 'It is valkyries who are qualified, according to the mythology, to discriminate between the best and the rest.'

Helgi, Beloved of Valkyries

The romantic vision most people hold of the valkyries, as lovely (and lovelorn) battle-maids, high-hearted, helmeted, on horseback, is best expressed in three poems about a hero named Helgi. These poems appear in the *Poetic Edda*; when they were composed and by whom, nobody knows – Snorri doesn't mention them.

In one poem, Helgi is the son of Hjorvard. In the other two, he has been reincarnated, the poet claims; now he is the son of Sigmund the Volsung and is known as Helgi Hunding's Bane.

Helgi was a warrior grown before he had any name at all. He'd been an unpromising lad. Though big and handsome, he was 'quiet', the poem says. Carolyne Larrington, in her 1996 translation of the *Poetic Edda*, interprets that to mean he was a coal-biter or an ash-lad – a common type of Norse hero. Such a boy stayed cosy by the fire, rather than rushing out to make a name for himself as soon as he could swing a sword. He was so unpromising, the poem says, that no name ever stuck to him. Apparently, he went by 'Boy'.

Boy was lounging and loafing one day, not by the fire, but on top of the burial mound of one of his ancestors, probably chewing a blade of grass and daydreaming in the evening sun, when a troop of valkyries rode by. He counted nine of them, but one in particular caught his eye: Larrington says she was 'the most striking'; other translators call her the noblest or simply say she stood out from the others. Again, no one says she is beautiful.

The valkyrie spoke to Boy sharply, saying a ring-giver – a king – couldn't afford to be silent. She called him Helgi, which means 'Sacred One', and the name stuck.

'What will you give me as a name-gift?', Helgi demanded.

The valkyrie told him where he could find a ring-hilted sword, gold-inlaid, with 'courage in the blade and terror at its tip'.

It wasn't enough, he said, unless he got her too – as a guide? a protector? a wife? It's not clear. Not much, in fact, about Eddic poems is clear, especially when they talk about valkyries.

The Swanmaidens

The valkyrie in this poem is named Svava ('Killer'). She is said to be the daughter of King Eylimi, who is apparently human. We're also told she 'rode on the wind and the sea'. What does that mean? Given she's a human princess, it could mean she was a great horsewoman, who rode like the wind, and a great sailor, who rode the sea-road in her dragon ships. Or it could mean what most readers take it to mean: she rode a horse that could fly and walk on water.

In some stories, valkyries can fly and swim in the shape of swans. Just as the goddess Freyja owns a cloak that allows her – or Loki the Trickster, when she lends it to him – to transform into a falcon, some valkyries have magic cloaks of swans' feathers. 'The Lay of Volund,' in the *Poetic Edda*, for example, prefaces the story of Volund (or Wayland) the Smith, and the terrible vengeance he took, with Volund and his two brothers coming upon three women spinning linen on the shore of a lake. The poem only hints at their identity. They had flown from Mirkwood in the south; valkyries are often referred to as 'southern' and several are associated with a place called Mirkwood. They are young and 'wise' (another translator says 'strange') and govern fate. Finally, one of the three is nicknamed Swan-White and is wearing swans' feathers.

A prose introduction to the poem, in the Codex Regius manuscript, is more specific. When the women were found by the lakeside, 'their swan-shapes lay beside them', it says: 'They were valkyries'. They lived happily with Volund and his brothers for seven years. 'Then they flew off to visit battlefields and did not return.' Volund's two brothers went off in search of their lovers. Volund, instead, stayed at home making beautiful jewellery to surprise her with when she came back.

On the Wind and the Sea

Returning to the story of Helgi, whether Svava the valkyrie was a real warrior woman or a supernatural demi-goddess, she took a liking to him and later helped him in battle.

In one of his adventures, Helgi killed a cliff-troll. The troll's daughter, Hrimgerd, demanded he pay compensation: he must sleep with her that night. Unwilling to do so, and unable to get at her with weapons, Helgi applied a trick J.R.R. Tolkien (1892–1973) learned from Norse lore. Like Gandalf, facing the three trolls in *The Hobbit* (1937), Helgi and his companion kept Hrimgerd talking until dawn, when the first rays of sunshine turned her to stone.

Before she became a sea-stack, standing picturesquely offshore, however, Hrimgerd revealed what Helgi and his crew, apparently, could not see. Helgi, she sniffed, would prefer sleeping with that one,

who by your men all night / kept sea-watch; bright
herself as sun-flecked sea, / she took away my strength.
Here she stepped ashore, / made fast your fleet:
She alone kept me from killing / you and all your men.

Svava had not come alone this time, either, though now she rode not in a group of nine valkyries, but, the poem says,

Three times nine the women were,
though one rode first, white-helmeted.
Their horses shook their manes
and dew fell, down to the dales,
and hail, on forested hills,
bringing folk good harvests.

This time there's no question: Svava and her valkyries were riding in the sky, dropping dew and hail on the lands they crossed, just like the mythic horse of the Sun, *Skinfaxi* ('Shining Mane'), and the horse of Night, *Hrímfaxi* ('Frosty Mane') do: the brightness of the sun, says Snorri in the *Prose Edda*, was the glow of the day-horse's mane, while dew was the saliva dripping from Frosty Mane's bit.

These descriptions led Grueber in her *Myths of the Norsemen* (1909) to interpret the valkyries and their steeds as 'personifications of the clouds, their glittering weapons being the lightning flashes'.

Clouds, or the Northern Lights?

Rather than clouds, many people today associate the valkyries with the Aurora Borealis, or Northern Lights. Search the internet and you'll find dozens of accounts that leave no room for doubt that the dancing, shimmering display of colours in the Nordic winter nights mark the ride of the valkyries. The Vikings, states the website www.norwegian.travel, 'believed that the aurora was light reflected from the Valkyries' battle armour'.

In their 1983 book, *The Northern Light: From Mythology to Space Research*, Norwegian physicists Asgeir Brekke and Alv Egeland trace that idea to the Icelandic scholar Finnur Magnússon (1781–1847), who published a Danish translation of the *Poetic Edda* between 1821 and 1823. Magnússon's opinions 'were strongly coloured by national romanticism', they note. 'He was looking for influences of a special Nordic nature in the poems' – and what could be more Nordic than the Northern Lights?

Brekke and Egeland cite the poem *Völuspá*, or 'The Song of the Seer', as an example. In the lines they quote, however, I find no references to colours in the sky:

I saw valkyries / come from away
to the gods' host, / those hard riders.
Skuld held a shield, / and Skogul another;
Gunn, Hild, Gondul, / and Geirskogul—
here are named / those hard riders,
the war-leader's women, / the valkyries.
I saw the fate / of Odin's son,
the bloody end / of Baldur.

Commenting on these lines, Magnússon wrote: 'Originally the Valkyries were certain meteors or phenomena in the air like fireballs, flaming northern lights, etc. [...] Still the plebeians in many countries believe that such phenomena signify coming wars and calamities. Here the death of Baldur is announced.'

The Northern Lights Myth Debunked?

Christie Ward, who blogs as 'The Viking Answer Lady', thinks the link between the valkyries and the Northern Lights came to the modern internet via the oft-reprinted *Bulfinch's Mythology*. Thomas Bulfinch first published his work in 1855; a 2010 reprint calls it, 'essential information for anyone interested in the study of mythology'.

Describing the valkyries as Odin's messengers, Bulfinch writes: 'When they ride forth on their errand, their armour sheds a strange flickering light, which flashes up over the northern skies, making what men call the "Aurora Borealis".'

The problem is, there are no clear references to the aurora in any Old Norse text about the Vikings. While the valkyries are often referred to as bright and shining, or associated with blood red skies, these descriptions also apply to sunbeams breaking through clouds or to sunrises and sunsets. Remember, too, that the valkyries arrive during the battle: Viking battles were not fought at night, when the aurora can be seen.

Only in Arabic does the aurora appear in a Viking context: in the northern kingdom where Ibn Fadlan met the Vikings, or Rus', the king told him the Northern Lights were armies of Jinn (spirits or demons) fighting each other.

The aurora enter Old Norse literature, vaguely, in the 1200s. A paragraph of *Konungs Skuggsjá* ('The King's Mirror'), a handbook on kingship probably also written for King Hakon IV (1204–63), reports: 'about [...] the Northern Lights, I have no clear knowledge. I have often met men who have spent a long time in Greenland, but they do not seem to know definitely what those lights are.' The author himself seems never to have seen them – though other details tell us he lived in northern Norway.

How could he not know much about the Northern Lights? Why didn't the Viking poets mention them? Physicists Brekke and Egelund have a scientific answer: the aurora forms when sunspots interact with the earth's magnetic field. But the earth's magnetic pole wanders. It waxes and wanes in strength, while sunspots come and go.

Data from tree rings and glacial ice cores, among other sources, tell us the band on which the Northern Lights can appear did not reach Iceland or Norway during the Viking Age, nor was there much sunspot activity. Colourful night skies remained quite rare from the 700s through the 1200s. Most Vikings may have never seen an aurora.

Like a Lightning Bolt

To return to our three poems about Helgi, when our hero was reincarnated, so was his valkyrie lover. Now her name is Sigrun and, although she is again the daughter of a human king, Hogni, she comes across as a bit more threatening. She first appears in these two poems, not calmly riding by a grassy mound to chastise a lazy boy, but out of a stormy sky in the midst of battle:

Light broke out / over Logafell,
and from that light, / lightning flashed
off helms shining / on Heaven's field,
off shining byrnies / soaked in blood,
off spear points, / striking sparks.

Seeing the valkyries appear over the battlefield, Helgi, at first, thought he'd been called to Valhalla. By her answer, you'd think Sigrun was a simple warrior woman – her mind is on marriage, not battle:

Asked the king / from the wolves' lair,
if these goddesses / from the south lands,
had come to take / his warrior band
home that night? / (Elm bows thrummed.)

But from her horse / Hogni's daughter
(as the din of shields / died down) relayed:
'I think we might / have other business
tonight than drinking / beer with ring-breakers.'

When they'd won the battle, Sigrun told Helgi she needed him to hustle back south to defeat a suitor she did not want to marry. Helgi immediately set off, but soon got into trouble, and Sigrun had to appear out of a stormy sky again to save him.

Sailing south, the poem says, Helgi ran into a terrible storm. Lightning lit up the sky, and lightning bolts began striking the ship. Then he saw nine valkyries riding in the sky, and recognized Sigrun among them. It had seemed the sea-goddess, Ran, would claim him and his crew,

but valiant Sigrun / from on high,
wrested their sea-steed / and they themselves
from Ran's fingers, / saved the king's ship
and his war-host / off Gnipalund.

Helgi continued on south and defeated Sigrun's suitor in battle. He won the battle maid for his own wife, but as the poem closes, the reader's left wondering: Is this what Helgi truly wanted?

Sigrun the Wolf-Rider

For the valkyrie who comes down from the sky at the battle's end to congratulate Helgi and grant him his reward is riding a wolf. And that wolf, while Sigrun is praising the hero's deeds and promising to marry him, is eating the corpses lying on the battlefield.

There's another scene in this poem-sequence that hints that the valkyries of Norse myth are not as we imagine them today, beautiful and terrible, fierce horsewomen with spears and often anachronistic armour – think of Brünnhilde's metal bustier and horned helmet in the opera *The Valkyrie* by composer Richard Wagner (1813–83).

In a strange interlude in the Helgi-Svava love story, Helgi's half-brother Hedinn was travelling home by himself through the woods one evening during the feasts of Yule when he met a troll-woman. She was riding a wolf, with snakes for reins. She offered Hedinn her company, but he turned her down. She cursed him, causing him to make a foolish vow during the usual Yuletide boasting sessions that he would marry his brother's beloved, Svava. Sick with regret, Hedinn sought out Helgi, who promptly forgave him and said it would, in fact, be a good thing if Hedinn married Svava. He said this because he suspected he was fey; it was his fetch, his guardian spirit, that Hedinn had met in the woods when he saw the troll-woman riding the wolf, he said. That meant he was fated to die soon.

And yet, Helgi's guardian spirit is Svava, isn't it? So is Svava the wolf-rider here, too?

There are other times in these three poems when valkyries and trolls (or giants or ogres) are blurred. Before one battle, Helgi's men and their enemies engaged in an insult match – a flitting. Helgi's half-brother Sinfjotli said to his foe,

You were the hideous / ogre, the valkyrie,
fierce and loathsome, / of All-Father Odin;
the Einherjar / fought against each other,
fickle woman, / for your sake.

The Einherjar, again, are the honoured dead in Valhalla, where presumably they are served drinks by the valkyries. They're not supposed to be fighting over the serving maids!

Demons of Carnage

And why would they fight over women described as hideous, fierce, loathsome and fickle – some other translators have used the words filthy, vile, dread, hateful, horrible, huge, unnatural, obstinate, foul, faithless and false, or translated 'ogre' as 'witch'. Is that the picture in your mind of a valkyrie? If not, you may have been led astray.

Neil Price in *Children of Ash and Elm* (2020) writes: 'An internet image search reveals "Valkyries" endlessly recycled today through the male gaze, usually depicted as voluptuous young women with big swords and minimal clothing. These dreary tableaux bear little resemblance to the demons of carnage in Norse mythology.'

Combing Old Norse literature, Price has gathered 52 valkyrie names. Translating them – a task most scholars have skipped – he concludes that most of them mean 'war'. There's Bright Battle, Battle-Weaver, Devastate and Disorder.

'The noise and chaos of combat is invoked in 11 names', he notes in *The Viking Way* (2019), such as Helmet-Clatter, Sword-Noise, Teeth-Grinder and Howling.

Eight incorporate the word 'spear'.

Two refer to pushing down a shield; in the name 'Shield-Scraper', Price says, 'We can almost hear the valkyrja's nails rake the wooden board.'

Other names that refer to actions the valkyries might perform in battle are: Helper, Pusher, Cloud (who 'presumably fogs a warrior's mind', Price says), War-Fetter and Chain ('who brought the freezing hesitation that could be fatal'), and Sleep-Maker (i.e., Killer). The name Silence, Price says, 'graphically represents the end of the fighting'.

Only two valkyrie names out of the 52 refer to their 'role as hostesses of the dead, perhaps with a slight sexual charge'. Price concludes: 'There is only minimal evidence to suggest they were physically attractive, but plenty that implies they were terrifying.'

Troughs of Blood

Even dismissing the valkyrie-as-love-interest type, the dignified horsewomen presented in Eyvind the Plagiarist's encomium on the Christian King Hakon I the Good remain in the minority. We believe that version of the valkyrie myth because Snorri Sturluson said it was so.

Poems and sagas written before – and after – Snorri's time describe the valkyries as monsters. They are troll-women of gigantic size who ride wolves and pour troughs of blood over a battlefield. They row a boat through the sky, trailing a rain of blood, or sit in a house with a leaky roof and blood raining down on them. They are known by their 'evil smell'.

In the part of *Sturlunga Saga* written by Snorri's nephew Sturla Thordarson in the 1270s, we learn of the dream of a man named Haflidi. He thought he saw two groups of warriors meet and fight. In one company rode an evil-looking giantess. She carried a tattered cloth dripping with blood. She whipped and snapped it at her enemies – if it touched one, his head popped off.

These valkyries resemble the Old English *waelcyrge*; both words mean 'choosers of the slain'. An Anglo-Saxon charm – recited to ease the pain of a side-stitch caused by running too hard – describes them as 'mighty women' with 'screaming spears', loud and bold.

To Latin writers of the time, the Anglo-Saxon *waelcyrge* were the equivalent of the Furies, the goddesses of vengeance in Greek mythology. Others equated them with witches. In his *Sermo Lupi ad Anglos* ('Sermon of Wolf to the English'), Archbishop Wulfstan of York (d. 1023) accuses *waelcyrge*, along with murderers, kin-slayers, and fornicators, of destroying England.

They are also quite like the bloodthirsty Celtic goddesses, the Morrigan and the Babd, who appeared on the battlefield as great birds of prey. In the Irish epic, *Táin Bó Cuailnge* ('The Cattle Raid of Cooley'), in Thomas Kinsella's 1969 translation, the Morrigan stood between the two armies, on the morning of the last battle, chanting about 'ravens gnawing / men's necks', 'blood spurting', 'hacked flesh' and 'battle madness'.

Snorri didn't care for that kind of monstrous valkyrie. It's a reflection of the popularity of his works over those of his nephew Sturla, among others, that the image of the valkyrie we hold in our heads today so closely matches that of the little gilded silver amulet found in Hårby, Denmark in 2012.

2.
The Legend

Among them was Ladgerda, a skilled amazon, who, though a maiden, had the courage of a man, and fought in front among the bravest with her hair loose over her shoulders. All marvelled at her matchless deeds.
– from *The Nine Books of the Danish History of Saxo Grammaticus,* translated by Oliver Elton (Norroena Society, 1905)

VALKYRIES AND SHIELD-MAIDS IN HISTORY AND SAGA

he shield-maid Lagertha, played by the Canadian actress and martial artist Katheryn Winnick, is my favourite character on the *Vikings* TV series, which premiered in 2013. The very first episode had me hooked. As a student of the Viking Age, I was expecting to be disappointed, but writer Michael Hirst expertly upended those expectations. He began with the cliché: big, bearded men with swords beach their dragon ships and ransack a peaceful village, slashing at people and setting houses on fire. The camera singles out a beautiful blonde and her beautiful children. Two hulking men advance on her, and I'm thinking, 'Oh, great, we begin with the rape scene.'

And then this vulnerable-looking mother whips the poker out of the fire and beats the crap out of these two men. It's an awesome fight scene. She's obviously a trained warrior, and they are not. All they have is raw strength, and she very clearly shows that practice and technique are more important than size or weight.

'She's become a feminist icon around the world. I get emails about her from *everywhere*,' Hirst said of Lagertha in a February 2015 Q&A on Reddit. 'She is a wife, she's a mother, and she kicks ass. And there are no other women characters like that on TV. And I am so proud of being a part of creating her.' He added, 'She faces a lot of issues that women still face today, the only difference being that she also carries an axe, haha!'

Interviewed by Christina Radish of *Collider* in April 2015, Kathryn Winnick agreed that her character had 'turned into a role model for a lot of young girls'. She added, 'What's great about playing Lagertha is that she's a strong woman, but she's also a feminine woman. She can be strong and sexy, at the same time. I feel that she's very much a modern woman, or modern for her time. She's able to incorporate both. You don't have to be just the sex kitten. You can be a sexy, feminine woman, but also have a strong voice and be a warrior, at the same time.'

Modern Valkyries

Kathryn Winnick's Lagertha, the sexy, feminine, bad-ass fighter, is the kind of valkyrie marketers and advertisers had in mind when they named the new Women's National Basketball Association team based in San Francisco the Golden State Valkyries. (The matching men's team is the Golden State Warriors.)

It's the image sought by the muscular-looking Aston Martin sports car named Valkyrie (with its motto, 'Impossible. Driven.') and the Highland Park Valkyrie Scotch (with its 'aroma of faraway campfires').

There are romance novels and video games named Valkyrie, Valkyrie Alliance, Valkyrie Elysium and more, all featuring kick-ass heroines.

There are defence contractors and venture capitalists, crypto-currency investment bankers and artificial intelligence firms, software applications, laser systems, robots, sailing ships and fishing boats, racing bikes and motorcycles, semi-automatic weapons, a nuclear-strike bomber, oil fields, ice domes in Antarctica, a mollusc, a crater on Venus and – my favourite – a trainer of Icelandic horses, all named Valkyrie.

In none of these cases (except, perhaps, for the guns and the bomber) is the name 'valkyrie' meant to evoke blood or evil smells or the shrieking of weapons (or fingernails) against wooden shields, battlefield chaos, the fog and paralysis of fear, or the silence of death. 'Demons of carnage', as scholar Neil Price defines the valkyries in *The Viking Way* (2019), is not the image intended here. What the marketing teams had in mind was sexy, strong Lagertha.

An Amazon, or a Valkyrie?

But this TV valkyrie is also, as Michael Hirst claimed, 'a historically accurate character'.

A woman named Lagertha (or Ladgerda or Lathgertha) is mentioned by the Danish historian Saxo Grammaticus (or 'the

Grammarian', *c*. 1150–*c*. 1220) as having lived in Norway in the ninth century. In Saxo's original Latin, she is described as *perita bellandi femina*, or an expert fighting woman, a woman who has gained her skill in warfare through experience. None other than the famous Viking hero Ragnar Lothbrok, whom she marries in Saxo's history as well as on TV, credits her with winning his battles for him.

Calling her an 'Amazon', as did translator Oliver Elton in 1905, is an interpretation of the Latin text, not a direct translation. It applies, a bit clumsily, a concept from classical Greece to the medieval Norse world. Unlike the Amazons, Lagertha did not disdain marriage or family life – or cut off a breast to make it easier to shoot a bow.

In her 1979 commentary on Saxo, Hilda Ellis Davidson says that, rather than being an Amazon, Lagertha 'behaves like a valkyrie', adding that she is 'acting as a supernatural protectress' to Ragnar. The idea that she is supernatural is, once again, an interpretation. For Lagertha to protect Ragnar, or to win his battles for him, she merely needed to be a superior fighter. Yet as late as 1979, it was thought impossible – unnatural – for a woman to fight as well as (or better than) a man.

Explains Pamela D. Toler in *Women Warriors: An Unexpected History* (2019), 'In the modern world, the idea that mother and warrior are biologically ordained opposites has been expanded into a recurring theme of feminist theory, first formulated during the early days of the organized women's movement at the end of the nineteenth century: the idea that if women ran the world there would be no war. The proponents of this theory argue that traditional "women's work" is devoted to life: feeding, sheltering, nursing, tending the elderly, and, most importantly, bearing and raising children. The violence of war not only destroys that work but is antithetical to it. [...] At its simplest, this argument is based on a series of assumptions about the relative natures of men and women that is unflattering to both. It is also counterhistorical.'

Lagertha and Ragnar Lothbrok

In Saxo's history, Lagertha is one of several warrior women who joined forces with Ragnar Lothbrok, when he came to Norway to avenge his grandfather's death. The women sought vengeance for the old king's wife and daughters, who had been taken captive and gang-raped.

Ragnar was impressed by Lagertha's fighting prowess. Declaring 'that he had gained the victory by the might of one woman', in Elton's 1905 translation, he wanted to marry her.

Lagertha was not equally impressed. She would rather return to her farm in Norway and live life her own way than be shackled to a minor Danish king's son. She gave him 'false answers', letting him think she desired him. When she reached her home, she 'ordered that a bear and a dog should be set at the porch of her dwelling'.

I can imagine the scene when Ragnar arrived.

'Release the dog,' she said, as he entered the courtyard – alone, as she had coyly suggested.

An enormous bear hound burst from a pen; Ragnar throttled it as it leaped for his throat.

'Release the bear,' said Lagertha.

'You are an exceedingly perverse woman,' Ragnar yelled, as he struggled to hold an enormous brown bear at bay with his spear.

'You could have just told me to leave you alone.'

Lagertha laughed. She raised one hand, and arrows flew from all sides of the courtyard. The bear fell dead.

'And you are an exceedingly persistent man,' Lagertha said.

They stayed together for three years. Long after he had left her and both had married again, she learned he was losing his grip on his Danish kingdom. He'd armed the young boys, he'd armed the old men, but still the rebels were winning. Lagertha – now a middle-aged mother of three – sailed south to his aid, gathering forces along the way until she led 120 ships. She swung behind the enemy's lines. Outmatched, they fled in panic towards Ragnar, whose warriors, rallying, let few escape.

Saxo Disapproved

Saxo Grammaticus disapproved of women like Lagertha. He wrote his *Gesta Danorum*, or 'Deeds of the Danes', sometime between 1185 and 1216 at the request of the archbishop of Lund (then in Denmark, now in Sweden). Like most Christian clerics of his time, Saxo believed the ideal woman was chaste, shy and submissive. The best, in his opinion, 'sacrifice themselves – to the point of complete self-destruction', notes Birgit Strand in her chapter of *Saxo Grammaticus: A Medieval Author Between Norse and Latin Culture* (1981).

When he could not avoid mentioning 'strong, resolute, and independently-acting women' like Lagertha, Strand adds, Saxo denigrates them, taking 'a malicious joy' in seeing them degraded and their honour besmirched.

For example, Alfhild put on men's clothing and ran away to lead a Viking band, rather than marry Alf. When he eventually met her in battle, rather than killing her, he 'handled' her 'with gentler dealings' (or, in another translation, 'laid hands on her more lovingly') – a chilling euphemism for rape. Afterwards, Saxo blithely states, she gave birth to his daughter.

Likewise, when King Asmund of Vik was dethroned by his sister, the hero Harald Wartooth was 'angered by such presumption on the part of a woman'. With Harald's help, the sister was killed.

Later, this same Harald heard that King Olaf of Trondheim was under attack by two shield-maids. 'Much angered at this arrogance on the part of women', Saxo writes, Harald came to Olaf's aid and the shield-maids were defeated.

Suspecting he might not be believed, Saxo insists that 'There were once women among the Danes who dressed themselves to look like men, and devoted almost every instant of their lives to the pursuit of war'. They were women with 'force of character', he writes in Elton's 1905 translation, and often were 'tall and comely'. They 'offered war rather than kisses' and 'assailed men with their spears whom they could have melted with their looks'. They 'devoted those hands to the lance which they should rather have applied to the loom.'

In doing so, Saxo claimed, they 'had forgotten their natural estate'; they had 'unsexed themselves'. As Saxo and his fellow Christian clerics saw it, Strand explains, 'Woman must be subordinate to man – or else she constitutes a menace to man – and consequently to the established order of Society.'

The Valkyries of Bravellir

Much as he disapproved, Saxo saw no way to omit warrior women from his 'Deeds of the Danes'.

Just as he could not tell the story of Ragnar Lothbrok without Lagertha, he could not write about the Battle of Bravellir, fought between the Danes and the Swedes in about 770, without Hetha, Visna and Vebiorg. Each woman led her own warband. Hetha, for example, was followed by the champion Hakon Cut-Cheek and seven other named warriors, along with a hundred who go unnamed.

These women's military skill is revealed by the Danes' battle plan. The king's deputy, Saxo writes (again translated by Elton), 'made the front in[to] a wedge, posting Hetha on the right flank, putting Hakon in command of the left, and making Visna standard-bearer', which meant that Visna led the charge alongside the ageing Harald Wartooth – who had apparently gotten over his dislike of arrogant and presumptuous women.

Bearing the king's banner was a key responsibility, assigned to the bravest warrior, for if the flag fell it signalled the king's defeat. It also meant the warrior could not carry a shield. Visna was up to the task. She was 'filled with sternness, and a skilled warrior', Saxo admits. The Swedish champion Starkather targeted Visna. She did not drop the banner until he cut off her hand. Starkather himself was forced to leave the field 'with his lung protruding from his chest, his neck cleft to the centre, and his hand deprived of one finger'.

The shield-maid Vebiorg, meanwhile, killed another of the Swedish champions. Afterwards, 'while she was threatening to slay more champions,' she was brought down by an arrow.

Only Hetha leaves the battlefield unscathed; she later becomes the ruler of Jutland.

This story of the battle between Sigurd Ring and Harald Wartooth at Bravellir – valkyries included – is also preserved in the 'Fragment of a Saga about Certain Ancient Kings', a much-damaged Icelandic manuscript written in about 1300.

The Red Girl

Saxo's Rusla, described as an 'amazon' whose 'prowess in warfare exceeded the spirit of a woman' – is also known from another source.

According to Saxo, Rusla was raiding alongside other Vikings in the Irish Sea when she learned her brother had proclaimed himself sole king in Trondheim. Sailing east to challenge his right to rule, she met his Danish allies at sea and, initially, defeated them. Drunk on victory, she headed south and attacked Denmark itself. She overreached. On the Danes' home ground, Rusla lost. She was forced to flee with only (*only!*) 30 ships. Still she bested her brother and took over Trondheim, briefly.

But the Danish king persisted. In a second sea battle, Harald Wartooth 'utterly destroyed' her fleet. Even so, Saxo writes, 'Rusla escaped with a very few ships, and rowed ploughing the waves furiously'. But her luck was gone, and she ran into her brother again. This battle she did not survive. When news of her death reached Ireland, two of her (male) comrades set out to avenge her.

Most modern historians have relegated Saxo's Rusla to the mists of legend. But Hilda Ellis Davidson, in her 1979 commentary on

Saxo, connected her to Irish reports of the Viking raider known as the *Inghen Ruaidh*, who harassed Munster in the mid-900s. Rusla means 'red'; Inghen Ruaidh means 'red girl' or 'red daughter'. Both were Viking sea-kings.

There's no story of the Irish Red Girl: she is simply a name in a list of 16 Vikings roving the Irish Sea. 'The evil which Erinn had hitherto suffered was as nothing compared to the evil inflicted by these parties,' says the twelfth-century Irish chronicle called *Cogadh Gaedhel re Gallaibh* ('The War of the Irish with the Foreigners'), as translated by James H. Todd in 1867. The whole of Munster 'was plundered by them, on all sides, and devastated'. Among the Vikings slain at the Battle of Clontarf, fought outside Dublin in 1014, the chronicle later states, were two sons of the Red Girl.

The Icelandic Sagas

Legendary valkyries like Lagertha and the Red Girl also appear in the Icelandic sagas.

The sagas are read today as fiction, but like modern historical novels they contain a core of truth. Saxo himself thought so. Of the Icelanders, he wrote (in Elton's 1905 translation), 'They account it a delight to learn and to consign to remembrance the history of all nations, deeming it as great a glory to set forth the excellences of others as to display their own. Their stores, which are stocked with attestations of historical events, I have examined somewhat closely, and have woven together no small portion of the present work by following their narrative.'

The Icelandic sagas are written in prose, though they often contain poetry. Many of the stories they tell were told orally for generations before being fixed in ink on calfskin, a technology that came to Iceland with Christianity. A missionary created the Icelandic alphabet in around the year 1030; no sagas were originally written in runes. The idea of organizing a story chronologically, rather than by place or family, was also imported from Christian lands.

Writing caught on in Iceland in a big way. Many people – not just churchmen – learned to write. From the twelfth through the fourteenth century, Iceland's literary output was prodigious. First came a lawbook; next, a history of the island. After those came chronicles of the kings of Norway and Denmark and the earls of Orkney; stories of Iceland's first families; books on grammar, astronomy, medicine, poetics and mythology; annals; saints' lives, sermons and collections of miracles; biographies of bishops and the history of Christianity in the country; translations from Latin and French; romances and fantastical tales; stories of Greenland, of Viking raids, of voyages to Constantinople or to the New World, of famous feuds and love affairs, of poets and outlaws; even a *Guide to the Holy Land.* More medieval literature exists in Old Norse than in any other European language except Latin, and almost all of it was written by Icelanders.

Sagas of Ancient Times

Confusingly, 140 of these texts are called 'sagas'. Derived from the Icelandic verb 'to say', *saga* implies neither fact nor fiction. Modern readers like their genres clear-cut. We like to know what shelf to put each book upon. Is it history? Is it fantasy?

During the sorting frenzy of the nineteenth century, the sagas were classified into genres: Contemporary Sagas (about the thirteenth century), Family Sagas (about Iceland's settlers), Kings' Sagas, Saints' Lives, Tales of Chivalry (mostly translated from other languages), and Sagas of Ancient Times. Some, especially the Contemporary Sagas, are accepted as history. Others, especially the Sagas of Ancient Times, are dismissed as fantasy.

But medieval people didn't organize their bookshelves like we do. Like any medieval source, Icelandic sagas have to be read critically to sift fact from fiction. Some authors were witnesses to the events they relate; others retell stories from hundreds of years in the past. The stories are generally more reliable the closer they were penned to the era they describe. When the authors' names are known, or when they cite their sources (folktales, poems, genealogies or interviews with their grandmothers), we can better assess their biases.

Dialogue, of course, is always fiction. Rituals and customs are shaded by those of the writer's own times. Poems likely preserve more ancient ways – if we can understand them.

Then there are the dragons.

The *Anglo-Saxon Chronicle* has dragons. Geoffrey of Monmouth's *History of the Kings of Britain* has dragons. Discard every text that mentions dragons and we'd have no medieval history at all.

The legends of valkyries appear mostly in the Sagas of Ancient Times, in stories rife with dragons, trolls, ghosts, werewolves and the walking dead. The warrior women in these texts are portrayed as human, semi-human or supernatural. But so are their male counterparts: the berserks (or 'bear-shirts') whom iron cannot bite, the half-trolls and dragon-slayers, the shapeshifters who turn into wolves. Male or female, many warriors in these sagas talk to gods, use magic, have inordinate luck or strength that increases after sunset, are matchless athletes, outlive a normal lifespan and serve drinks to heroes in Valhalla. Only the females are explained away by modern scholars as fantasy. Only the females are considered as fabulous as dragons.

The Saga of Hrolf Gautreksson

Hrolf's Saga is a good example. Though named for a man, this saga's true hero is a warrior woman. 'She bears an obvious resemblance to the great valkyrie-type heroines of the Eddic poetry', write translators Hermann Pálsson and Paul Edwards in 1972. For this reason, among others, they labelled *Hrolf's Saga* 'unacceptable as history'. Some scholars describe it as a Bridal-Quest Romance, reducing the saga's strong women to prizes for the men to win. It's been dismissed as 'late', 'popular' and 'entirely frivolous'.

Hrolf's Saga is not, perhaps, a literary masterpiece like *Egil's Saga*, a Family Saga about the descendants of berserks and werewolves. But it may be no later than this example of what Pálsson and Edwards call 'realistic fiction in the classical saga tradition'. The oldest manuscript of *Egil's Saga* is dated about 1250; that of *Hrolf's Saga*, about 1300. In a collection of sagas penned between 1300 and 1325, copies of both *Hrolf's Saga* and *Egil's Saga* appear.

And it's true that *Hrolf's Saga* was popular in the Middle Ages. While *Egil's Saga* appears in 13 copies, more than 60 manuscripts contain *Hrolf's Saga*.

As if responding to the criticism that it is 'frivolous', the saga author says (in my translation), 'It may be so for this saga as for many another, that not everyone tells it the same way. But people are of many kinds, and some travel widely. One hears this and one hears that, and each may be true, though neither is quite the whole truth. [...] Whether it's true or not, let those who enjoy it do so, while those who don't can look elsewhere for entertainment.'

The Wise Queen

Compared to other Icelandic sagas, *Hrolf's Saga* is powerfully feminist: its women are equal, if not superior, to men on all levels. In five examples, it shows that, while a kingdom ruled by a woman alone can function perfectly well, one without a wise queen – or with a king who doesn't listen to her – is 'like a ship with no one steering'.

These queens use logic and political skill to advise the men. They show compassion and kindness, reward courage and honourable behaviour and are loyal even to kinsmen who betray them. In addition to these good qualities, the central queen of the saga, Thornbjorg of Sweden, has also mastered the martial arts. Says one character, 'As far as her womanly accomplishments go, you could not find yourself a finer match anywhere in the North, while in some things, like jousting and fencing with shield and sword, she equals the hardiest knights. In that way she surpasses all other women I've heard of.'

The terms 'jousting', 'fencing' and 'knights' show that *Hrolf's Saga* was written down after 1226, when King Hakon IV began commissioning translations of chivalric romances from French.

One of the kings in the saga, however, is the legendary King Aella of England, who died in about 867. Earlier saga-tellers would have described Thornbjorg's skills in horse riding and sword-fighting in quite different terms.

Thornbjorg Becomes Thorberg

While she was yet unmarried, the saga says, Thornbjorg asked her father to give her a kingdom to govern, so she could learn to rule while he was still alive to advise her. She pointed out, 'Given that you have no more than one lifetime to rule this kingdom and, as your only child, I will inherit everything after your death, it's likely I will have to protect the realm from other kings and their sons, once I have lost you.' Her father was so impressed by her logic that he agreed to give her a third of Sweden.

Thornbjorg then held an assembly. She presented her case and asked the local landowners to vote. When she was elected king (not queen), she began using the masculine form of her name and changed her pronouns and way of dress.

King Thorberg reigned from a walled town near Uppsala that, as described in the saga, looks very much like the town of Birka, as excavated by archaeologists. Birka was founded in 750 and lasted for about 200 years; its fortress burned down and was abandoned sometime between 970 and 985. This fortress, protected on one side by a steep cliff, had a stone rampart and a wooden palisade surrounding a great Warriors' Hall and several outbuildings, including four smithies. A barricade of pilings, studded with sunken boats, protected the harbour, with its many jetties. The busy market town – remarkable for the number of rich, female merchants buried in its graveyards – was further protected by an earthen rampart over 20 feet wide. Above the rampart rose a wooden palisade with towers guarding the three city gates.

King Thorberg's city was fortified similarly, after the hero of the saga, Hrolf Gautreksson, king of Gautland, rudely insisted that the Swedish king, being merely a woman in disguise, should give the town – and herself – to him.

The Battle

'You'll be goat-herds in Gautland before you get control of this town,' Thorberg said, when Hrolf returned with an army.

The Swedes beat their shields to drown out his reply. They had prepared for Hrolf's coming by hiring smiths to build a rampart around the town, as strong and sturdy as they could make it, and to equip it with devices 'so that no one could breach it, either with fire or iron'.

The saga continues, 'They attacked with fire, and water ran from pipes set into the walls. They attacked with weapons and by digging under the walls, and the townsfolk poured burning pitch and boiling water on them, along with huge stones.' When Hrolf's army retreated, 'some wounded, the others exhausted', Thorberg and the townsfolk came out 'onto the wall, laughing at them and mocking them and questioning their courage. They paraded around in silks and furs and other treasures, showing them off, and dared them to try and take them.' Said Hrolf's brother, Ketil, 'It seems to me the Swedish king pisses rather hot.'

It took them two weeks to break in, by erecting wooden shelters and tunnelling under the walls. They found the city empty, but 'food and drink was laid out in every house; clothes and treasures were all there ready to go'. Ketil said, 'Let's have a drink and something to eat, and then we can divvy up the loot.'

Replied Hrolf, 'Now you're taking the bait, just as they wanted.' Searching the town, he found the escape tunnel and chased King Thorberg and the townspeople into the forest.

Thornbjorg Defeated

The deciding fight is a bit of a farce. Having been warned by his brother not to injure the Swedish king, Ketil slapped Thorberg on the buttocks with the flat of his sword.

Thorberg retaliated in the same fashion, turning his axe so the blunt end hit Ketil under the ear. Scholars highlight the sexual overtones of that slap on the ass, but fail to react equally to the way Ketil was shamed: 'He was flung head over heels. "We beat our dogs like this when we're tired of their barking," Thorberg said.'

Nor do scholars generally condemn Hrolf's dishonourable behaviour: while Thorberg was proving himself an equal fighter to Ketil, Hrolf snuck up behind them and wrestled Thorberg to the ground. To Hrolf's credit, he did not then 'lay hands on her more lovingly', raping her as Saxo's Alf did when he captured the valkyrie Alfhild. Hrolf merely pinned his opponent and called for a truce. He would leave it to Thornbjorg's father, he said, to decide if she must now marry him.

King Thorberg accepted this offer and rode to Uppsala, where he again changed gender. 'He went before his father, King Eirik, lay his shield by his feet, took his helmet off his head, bowed to the king and said: "My dear father, I have been overcome by strong fighters and exiled from the kingdom that you gave into my hands, and for this reason I ask that you make those plans for my marriage that are most to your liking.'"

Submission?

After Thornbjorg married Hrolf, she devoted herself to embroidery, not fencing. She had two sons, and – according to Pálsson and Edwards – her 'submission to her husband is complete'.

Jóhanna Katrín Friðríksdóttir in *Women in Old Norse Literature* (2013) disagrees. She writes that Thornbjorg 'by no means becomes subservient or oppressed, and it is impossible to imagine her ever becoming meek and passive'. While her 'masculine masquerade', in Friðríksdóttir's term, is temporary, she is like other legendary valkyries whose 'retinues accept that their leaders, as biological women, can break out of the confinements of their traditional female role and "become" men for all intents and purposes, to perform a masculine role, regardless of what they once were. Whether physique plays a part in enabling this process is unclear as these characters are never described; a more important factor seems to be their mental qualities, the sheer determination to successfully live as males.'

Thornbjorg's 'submission' to Hrolf is similar, in fact, to that of a Scottish (male) Viking named Asmund in a later passage in the saga. In a sea battle, Asmund was badly wounded, but he continued to fight. Impressed by his enemy's bravery, Hrolf offered him a truce if he would become his blood brother. Asmund agreed, 'if you lay no burden of shame on me or my followers'. Like Thornbjorg,

Asmund gave up his independence and submitted to Hrolf's leadership, but the saga is clear that he was treated afterwards as an equal.

Thornbjorg Rescues Hrolf

It was to help Asmund win the Princess Ingibjorg as his bride, in fact, that sent Hrolf to Ireland, where he was captured and imprisoned by Ingibjorg's father. When he did not return home as expected, Thornbjorg gathered an army of Swedes. She called upon Hrolf's brother and another blood brother to join their forces to hers, until 'the queen had the rule and command' of 60 ships.

Reaching the Irish kingdom, they saw Hrolf's ships deserted by the shore. Angry, Hrolf's brother, Ketil, impulsively set fire to the town. Thornbjorg tried to stop him, warning – logically – that Hrolf could be killed in the fire, if he were there, but Ketil wouldn't listen. Hrolf was, indeed, in the town, having escaped from prison with Ingibjorg's help.

He and his men 'took a log and rammed the door of the women's bower, burst it in pieces, and rushed out. King Hrolf quickly recognized Gauts and Swedes among his attackers. Before him stood a most warlike man, fully armed. The man took off his helmet and stepped back – and King Hrolf realized it was Queen Thornbjorg.'

They put out the fires and captured the Irish king, accepting his daughter Ingibjorg and 'much wealth in gold and silver and all kinds of treasure' as the price of his freedom.

And so the 'bridal quests' end with another lesson on the importance of listening to the queen.

The Saga of Hervor and Heidrek

Another one of the Sagas of Ancient Times that contains legendary valkyries is the *Saga of Hervor and Heidrek* or, as Christopher Tolkien translated it in 1960, *The Saga of King Heidrek the Wise*. According to Tolkien, this saga has 'little or no historical authenticity', though he added, somewhat perversely, that he prized it for its historical elements, which 'come down from a very remote antiquity'. Those elements include four poems, around which the anonymous saga-writer constructed a none-too-tidy plot.

The story references the age of the Goths and the Huns (possibly the fifth century). In the Viking Age the story ranges from Norway east through the Baltic to the Black Sea and ends with genealogies of Sweden's kings. The oldest copy of the saga was penned by an Icelandic lawyer named Haukur Erlendsson, as he tells us in letters from 1302 and 1310, though he only copied the parts he liked. A longer (but much later) manuscript suggests that the saga was first composed for Queen Ingigerd of Sweden in the 1120s; Ingigerd's mother was a princess from Kyiv and her husband is the last king listed in the genealogies.

The plot revolves around a flaming sword forged by dwarfs. The first poem, 'The Death Song of Hjalmar', tells how the Viking warrior Angantyr and the Flaming Sword came to be buried on the Danish isle of Samsø at about the time his only child was born.

Hervor, says the prose between the poems, grew up with her grandfather, a chieftain, thinking she was the swineherd's bastard. A difficult child, strong as a boy, she preferred archery and swordplay to sewing and embroidery. As a teen she ran off and lived wild in the woods, robbing and killing passers-by before being hauled back home in disgrace. When she learned that her true father was the famous Viking warrior Angantyr, she resolved to be like him. She dressed as a man, demanding her mother equip her 'as you would your son'. She joined a Viking band and quickly rose to lead it.

She called herself Hervard, the masculine form of the name Hervor. She also changed her pronouns to he/him – at least in the Old Norse original, though not in Tolkien's translation. As Miriam Mayburd notes in the journal *Arkiv för Nordisk Filologi* in 2014, Tolkien simply avoided the 'gender issues'. Such misgendering and deadnaming is considered hate speech today.

'Hervor's Song'

Raiding near Samsø, Hervard proposed they break into the grave mounds to steal the treasure buried there with Angantyr and his companions. The other Vikings feared waking the dead, so Hervard rowed to the island alone, vowing to regain the Flaming Sword, also known as Hjalmar's Bane. It would 'never rust', the saga says, and could 'cut iron and stone as easily as cloth, and bring its bearer victory in all battles'. It was also cursed: each time it was drawn, it must kill. It would destroy her lineage.

Here the saga-writer inserted the second poem, known as 'The Waking of Angantyr'. It is told mostly in dialogue, first between Hervor (who now identifies as a woman) and a shepherd, then between Hervor and her father. In the poem, the mounds are veiled in flame. The graves magically open; the dead rise like smoke. Hervor faces down her ghostly father, forcing him to give up the cursed sword. She begins, in my translation:

Awake, Angantyr!
Hervor wakes you,
your only daughter,
yours and Svafa's.
Hand over the sword,
the sharp-edged blade
the dwarf-smith made
for Sigrlami.

She calls to him for three stanzas, cursing him for keeping silent. When her father finally answers, he first claims the sword was not buried with him. Then he warns her to flee:

Hel's gate is shut.
The grave mounds open.
The island erupts
in eerie fire.
Awful it looks
all around you:
Girl, while you can,
go back to your ships!

But Hervor is not afraid:

No such bonfire
could burn in the night
that I from your flames
would flee in terror.

This maid's heart
won't hammer her chest
if she sees the dead
walk out their door.

The poem is eerie and otherworldly and has been popular, in English, for hundreds of years. Some say it inspired the Gothic novel. Readers of fantasy recognize Hervor as the source of J.R.R. Tolkien's warrior woman in *The Lord of the Rings* (1954), Eowyn of Rohan, who fears nothing but being trapped in a caregiver's role.

Better titled 'Hervor's Song' (as it is in Icelandic), it was the first Old Norse poem to be translated into English, in 1703. As such, it crafted the image we hold today of the fearless Viking warrior who laughs in the face of danger – and that warrior is a woman.

'Not Like Men'

'Hervor's Song' is 'perhaps less esteemed today', notes Jenny Jochens in *Old Norse Images of Women* (1996), than it was in the 1700s – or even when J.R.R. Tolkien and his friend E.V. Gordon were teaching at Leeds University. It was then that Gordon wrote his *Introduction to Old Norse* (1927), the textbook in which I first encountered the poem.

But, as Jochens continues, 'the poem remains a remarkable illustration of the perception of a viking woman in the post-viking age'. It is also a remarkable illustration of the fluidity of gender in these stories and of what it means to be a valkyrie.

In the Gordon edition, Angantyr remarks in a key stanza, *Kveðkat þik, mær ung, mönnum líka* ('It seems to me, young maid, that you are not like men'). To which Hervor answers, *Maðr þóttumk menskr til þessa* ('Men thought me man-like until now'). Both *mönnum* and *maðr* are forms of the Old Norse word for 'man', which, as in English, can mean 'people' (i.e., both men and women). *Menskr* or 'man-like' could mean 'human' or 'normal' or, more tongue-in-cheek, 'manly' or 'mannish'.

Translators trying to present 'Hervor's Song' as poetry – preserving some, at least, of the rhythm, rhyme, alliteration and use of metaphor of the original language – struggle with these lines. Christopher Tolkien (1960) translates Angantyr's 'not like men' as 'unlike mortals'; Patricia Terry (in *Poems of the Vikings*, 1969) as 'not at all like other people'; Paul B. Taylor and W.H. Auden (in the *Elder Edda*, 1970) as 'No mortal maiden to me you seem'; and Sandra Ballif Straubhaar (in *Old Norse Women's Poetry*, 2011) as 'hardly human'.

Some translators apparently assume that a warrior woman who wants a cursed, flaming sword must be a deity (an immortal), while the others merely find her strange.

Between the Worlds

I find her extraordinary. The poem continues, in my translation:

Unlike all others
you are, young maid,
to go out at night
about the grave mounds,

in your Gothic armour
and engraved spear,
your helmet and byrnie,
to our hall's door.

People thought me
man enough,
until I set off
to seek your hall.
Now hand over
the byrnie-hater,
the shield-beater,
Hjalmar's Bane.

Beneath me lies
Hjalmar's Bane;
sheathed in fire
is the sword.
I know no maid
now above ground
who'd dare to hold
it in her hand.

Hervor not only dares, she insists, and finally her dead father walks out of his grave and hands it to her. She says,

Well done, I say,
son of Vikings,

to give me the sword
from your grave mound.
Better, I think,
to own this blade
than have all Norway
under my hand.

The last line assumes, of course, that a woman *could* rule all Norway. Hervor's ambition here seems to have no limits. As Mayburd notes in her 2014 journal article, she has become 'a being not limited by any gender at all'.

When her father reminds her of the sword's curse, and says it will destroy their lineage, she shrugs it off. Her sons' fate – supposing she were to have sons – is their problem. The poem ends with her sending Angantyr back to his grave and reflecting, in my translation:

I seemed to walk
between the worlds,
when all about me
fires burned.

Is she referring only to walking between the worlds of the living and the dead? Or also between the worlds of men and women?

The Curse

My answer to that question might be different from that of the medieval saga-writer. Understanding ancient poetry – even if we can translate it accurately – is tricky. We need to peel back centuries of bias. We also must examine our own.

What I find obvious in a story – that women can be as brave and brutal as men – other readers have seen merely as feminist wish-fulfilment. Like these readers, the medieval author of the *Saga of Hervor and Heidrek*, writing for a Christian audience well after the end of the Viking Age, rejected the idea of real warrior women. Though he or she inserted 'Hervor's Song' into the saga, happily preserving it for us to enjoy, the picture it creates of a courageous, ambitious valkyrie, equal to any man, is quickly undermined.

After winning the Flaming Sword, the saga says, Hervor returned to the shore to find her band of Vikings had deserted her. She made her way alone to a king's court, where she won at board games and befriended the king's son, Hofundur. The sword's curse ended this peaceful interlude: Hervor killed a man who unsheathed the Flaming Sword to take a look at it.

Fearing the king's vengeance, Hervor went raiding again with a Viking band 'for a long time and was very successful at it'. Then she got bored. She decided to go home and take up embroidery – seriously, that's what the saga says. She married Hofundur and had two sons, one of whom (the King Heidrek the Wise whom Christopher Tolkien thought the saga was about) killed the other.

The rest of the saga tells how the curse on the sword destroys everyone in her family, as predicted. As in the Sagas of Ancient Times more generally, Jóhanna Katrín Friðríksdóttir notes in *Women in Old Norse Literature* (2013) that valkyries and other 'unruly women are evoked for the purpose of being stigmatized'. They 'function strictly as a warning': don't let your daughters run wild.

'The Battle of the Goths and the Huns'

The final poem in the *Saga of Hervor and Heidrek* 'is now recognized to be perhaps the oldest of all the heroic lays preserved in the North', wrote Christopher Tolkien in the introduction to his 1960 translation.

'The Battle of the Goths and the Huns' tells of a war fought some 400 years before the Viking Age began. It, too, features a shield-maid named Hervor. It is set beside the forest named Mirkwood, on the border of the kingdom of the Goths, which was ruled by one of Hervor's two brothers, and the land of the Huns, to which her second brother had fled to raise an army to challenge his sibling's rule. Hervor commanded the border fortress, having chosen the life of a warrior over that of a wife and mother. She was 'happier in battle than chatting with suitors', the poem says.

One morning, from the tower above her fortress gate, she watched as a great cloud of dust rolled out from the shadows under the trees. It glittered as it moved. She summoned her army. When the Huns arrived on their fast horses, glittering in ringmail and gilded helmets and wielding their deadly compound bows, Hervor was ready. She rode out of the fortress at the head of her warrior band and 'a most mighty battle arose'.

But Hervor was badly outnumbered, and at last she and her champions were killed by her brother and his Hun allies. One captain survived; he rode night and day to bring news to Hervor's other brother, the king of the Goths. 'In no brotherly fashion have you been treated, my noble sister,' he said. He took no time to mourn, but set forth at once to avenge her.

He met the Huns on the plains of the Danube. There battle raged for days until the Goths, their ranks constantly reinforced as the news spread, finally repelled the Hun invaders, leaving 'such carnage that the rivers were choked and turned from their courses, and the valleys were filled with dead men' – and at least one dead woman.

If 'The Battle of the Goths and the Huns' is truly the oldest epic song of the north, then the idea of the warrior woman or valkyrie was embedded in Norse culture from the very start.

3.
The Icon

'I am a shield-maid. I wear a helmet among the warrior kings, and I wish to remain in their warband. I like to fight. [...] I was in battle with the King of Gardariki and our weapons were red with blood. This is what I desire.'
– Brynhild in *Volsunga Saga*, chapters 25 and 29

THE VALKYRIES IN VISUAL ART

' love being king. I love my people, but it's all meetings and raven-mail and meetings that could have been raven-mail. I miss fighting,' says the Marvel Comics Valkyrie, also known as Brunnhilde or Val or Angry Girl, as played by the Shakespearean actress Tessa Thompson in the 2022 superhero film, *Thor: Love and Thunder*.

Valkyrie was introduced to the Marvel Universe in 1970, the creation of Roy Thomas and John Buscema. She was loosely (very loosely) based on the character of Brynhild, who appears in *Volsunga Saga* (another of the Sagas of Ancient Times) and several poems in the *Poetic Edda*. Unlike Brynhild, Valkyrie does not wear a helmet. In her first appearance, in *The Avengers #83* comic book, her two white-blonde braids are wrapped with blue ribbons to match her cloak. She wears four arm guards, a wide metallic belt and strappy black shoes, and carries a spear. Her armour, worn over what looks like a black one-piece bathing suit, is limited to two metallic cones, accentuating her Barbie-doll figure.

In her extraordinarily complicated comic-book existence, the Marvel Valkyrie is killed off and resurrected several times, before being recreated in the film *Thor: Ragnarok* in 2017 by dark-haired and dark-skinned Thompson. Her armour was also upgraded to smooth curves of metal that cover more of her torso and don't guide an enemy's blade directly to her heart.

Appointed king of New Asgard after Thor joins the Guardians of the Galaxy, the Valkyrie is his equal as a fighter. As a member of the Avengers warband, she has superhuman strength and 'extensive combat prowess learned through centuries of training and battlefield experience', according to the Marvel Fandom Wiki. She rides a flying horse – or pilots a spaceship. She's also an alcoholic who suffers from post-traumatic stress disorder (PTSD), having been the only one of the valkyrie sisterhood to survive a battle with Hel, the Norse goddess of death. She's witty and sharp-tongued and clearly shows her love of fighting in the movies' many battle scenes.

As Thor states in *Love and Thunder*, introducing Valkyrie: 'This is the army right here. It's sleek, it's slender, it's powerful, it's beautiful.'

The Hårby Amulet

Sleek, slender, powerful, and beautiful: these adjectives also aptly describe the little gilt-silver amulet discovered in the Danish village of Hårby in 2012. The Hårby valkyrie is the only three-dimensional image we have of a warrior woman from the Viking Age – if, in fact, it represents a woman.

Like the Tessa Thompson-inspired image in the Marvel Exiles comic-book series, the Hårby valkyrie does not feature pointy, cone-shaped breast armour. In fact, the amulet's lack of any 'obvious breasts' leads Neil Price, in *Children of Ash and Elm* (2020), to wonder about its 'gender ambiguities'. From this time period, he points out, 'We have so few three-dimensional human images that we do not know whether this was artistic convention or even a Viking-Age cultural preference for a flatter chest.'

The figurine also has no hips or buttocks. Its seemingly sleeveless, pleated tunic or robe hangs straight to the broken bottom of the amulet, at about the level of its knees. The figure's long hair is twisted into a ponytail, a hairstyle that, says Price, is 'conventionally taken as a feminine marker', though the sagas often describe male warriors with long, beautiful hair.

The amulet's round face and enormous eyes look feminine to me, but the only thing clearly non-masculine about it is its lack of facial hair.

Could the Hårby valkyrie depict a boy? Yes. Could it depict a superhuman demigoddess? Yes. Could it be showing that carrying a sword and shield was 'a perfectly ordinary aspect of a woman's life' in the Viking Age? Yes – but when Price suggested as much in the catalogue for the 2013 museum exhibition in Copenhagen, where the amulet was displayed, it sparked a storm of protest.

The argument devolved to one point. Judith Jesch, author of *Women in the Viking Age* (1991) in a July 2013 post on her blog,

'Viqueen' said: 'We know that warriors were men.' As she clarified in *Viking Wars* (2021), edited by Frode Iversen and Karoline Kjesrud: 'There is no doubt that human beings are capable of most things, and it cannot be denied that the existence of female warriors or military leaders in the Viking Age remains a possibility. Indeed I have always acknowledged this possibility even though I have also argued that the strongly binary emphasis on gender distinctions in a variety of evidence from the Viking Age itself means that it remains unlikely.'

Valkyrie Icons

Flat metal icons thought to depict (supernatural) valkyries have been found throughout the Viking world, from England to Russia. Less than 4 cm (1.6 in) long and cast of silver, copper or bronze, their design is so similar that – like today's emoji – they must have symbolized something recognized widely at the time, though their exact meaning has been lost.

These valkyries are not pretty in the way the Hårby valkyrie is pretty. They lack her delicate nose and mouth, her enormous doe eyes and, in most cases, her elaborate hairstyle. Shown in profile, some of the warriors in these flat icons have unattractively long, pointy noses. They wear weird hoods or helmets or hairstyles or simply have a Neanderthal-like brow ridge. They stride out forcefully, carrying a shield – sometimes awkwardly gripping it by the shield boss and sometimes with it strangely tucked up into their armpit. Some carry a sword or spear in the other hand; some seem to manage sword and shield in the same hand.

They look more like trolls – or like Price's 'demons of carnage' – than like we imagine Lagertha, Thornbjorg, Hervor and the other potential brides in the Sagas of Ancient Times. You wouldn't be surprised if one of these metal valkyries poured a trough of blood over a battlefield, rode a corpse-eating wolf, or exuded an evil smell.

Sexing the Icons

These icons are thought to depict valkyries because they have long hair, no beards or moustaches and wear long, pleated gowns that seem to trail on the ground. Male warriors, the thinking goes, would show more leg; they'd be wearing short tunics or baggy knee-breeches. Long gowns, everyone agrees, are hard to fight in.

Using hairstyle to determine an icon's sex is chancier. A man's long hair, for example, plays a part in a famous scene in *The Saga of the Jomsvikings*. Seventy Vikings had been captured in battle and lined up to be beheaded. A slave was assigned to each captive to 'twist a stick in his hair', exposing his neck. One young man was vain about his hair, which was 'both long and as gold as silk'. He was ready to die, he said, but he didn't want to be led to his death by a slave. He asked for a warrior to hold his hair 'and pull it away from my head so that it doesn't get all bloody'. A warrior volunteered, wrapping the hair around both hands. As the executioner struck, the young man jerked his head back and both the warrior's hands were cut off at the elbow.

During the time of King Harald Bluetooth, who ruled *c.* 958–86 (and for whom the Bluetooth technology was named), short hair was apparently the fashion for men. A 3 cm (1.2 in) tall, three-dimensional figurine unearthed in 1796 in Norway was rediscovered in the collection of the Danish National Museum, to great hoopla, in late 2025. It is 'as close as we will ever get to a portrait of a Viking', said curator Peter Pentz. Carved out of walrus ivory, it was probably the king piece for the game of *hnefatafl*, sometimes called 'Viking chess'. This king parts his wavy hair in the middle; it is just long enough to tuck behind his ears, while the back is cropped a little shorter. He also sports well-groomed facial hair. His thick moustache curls up at the tips. His cheeks are smooth, but his long chin beard is braided into a single thick point, unlike that of his successor, King Svein Fork-Beard (963–1014) whose beard, apparently, was split and braided into two points.

Good Luck Charms?

Though widespread, valkyrie medallions are not common – nowhere near as common as swords. We have over 3,000 Viking Age swords from Norway alone; valkyrie icons might number in the dozens (though no one has done a scientific count of them). Many are what archaeologists call 'stray finds'. Like the Hårby amulet, they were discovered by chance on the surface of the ground or through the use of a metal detector. Since they were not excavated from a burial or structure, the context in which they were found gives us no hint as to their gender, time period or social role.

The hollow bottom of the Hårby valkyrie makes experts think she was fixed onto the end of a pin – whether a cloak pin or a hair pin is hard to say. A bit of wear under the knot of her ponytail suggests the link of a chain might have rubbed there.

With the flat metal valkyries, it's not clear if they were worn like pendants, sewn onto clothing, affixed to sheaths, mounted on weapons or horse equipment, or carried in a pouch. In addition to the valkyrie figures, museum collections contain similar flat metal badges fashioned as miniature ships, spearheads, hammers, swords, shields, falcons, dragons, wolves, horses, wheels and people, both men and women, who are tearing out their hair or bearing weapons, standing or riding or both.

These little icons might have been good luck charms or religious tokens. Just as a devotee of the Thunder God Thor might wear a small copy of Mjolnir, Thor's magic hammer, this theory goes, a devotee of All-Father Odin might wear a tiny valkyrie to symbolize hopes for an afterlife in Valhalla.

Another suggestion is that they functioned like the challenge coins modern soldiers must produce on demand to prove they belong to a certain unit.

One scholar suggests they were didactic toys, meant to inspire girls to learn the martial arts.

Recent work by archaeologists studying how these icons were manufactured has led to a fourth theory: like medieval pilgrims' badges, they might commemorate participation in a ritual parade or procession.

The Workshop

Excavating the Viking Age market town of Ribe in Denmark, Søren Sindbaek and two colleagues from Aarhus University uncovered layers of workshops that could be scientifically dated, from the early eighth to the early tenth century. Some were the shops of jewellery makers, who created oval brooches and other common Viking Age ornaments by pouring molten metal into ceramic moulds.

The archaeologists did not come upon a treasure trove of jewellery itself. Their finds were the kind only a scientist – or a puzzle enthusiast – could love: they collected more than 7,000 tiny fragments of ceramic casting moulds.

As Sarah Croix, Pieterjan Deckers and Sindbaek wrote in 'Recasting a Viking warrior woman from Ribe: 3D digital image reconstruction compared', published in the *Journal of Archaeological Science* in August 2020, 'The ceramic moulds were formed over models, and were usually crushed after use to retrieve the cast object. The fragmentary state, quantity, and visual complexity of this material call for highly efficient techniques of study.'

As reported by Andrew Curry for *National Geographic* (5 August 2021), the fragments were the size of fingernail clippings. Once they were all photographed, the researchers used a variety of digital image reconstruction techniques to try to reassemble them.

For example, they found that 10 of the 7,000 fragments came from three similar moulds dating to the early ninth century. The researchers wrote in 2020: 'The fragments show the detailed image of a human figure clad in a long dress with a train and carrying weapons, commonly associated to a type of small pendants interpreted as depicting a mythological female figure known as [a] "valkyrie".'

In a follow-up paper published in *Medieval Archaeology* in August 2021, 'Assembling the Full Cast: Ritual Performance,

Gender Transgression, and Iconographic Innovation in Viking-Age Ribe', the same authors 'argue that the common theme of the images is not the portrayal of heroic or mythological beings, but is instead ritual performance, in which women played a central role'.

The Oseberg Tapestry

The key to their interpretation was realizing that the same set of images they found in the Ribe jewellery workshop are depicted on a tapestry found in the Oseberg grave mound.

Uncovered in 1904 in southern Norway, and dated by tree-rings to 834, the Oseberg ship burial is the most lavish Viking grave known. The mound held a beautifully carved, full-sized dragon ship, turned so its high spiral stem faced the fjord. In a log chamber erected on the ship's deck, two women were buried in royal splendour. They had carved wooden beds with feather pillows and eiderdowns. There were iron lamps on long poles, a boxy chair, a stool and a plethora of textile tools. A line of chests along one wall had once held clothing, though only scraps of wool and silk survived. There were shoes and combs and seven glass beads; presumably the women had been buried with more jewellery, but the grave had been robbed long before the archaeologists arrived.

Some objects seemed to have had ritual use: a pouch of cannabis seeds, a long wooden horn, whistles, a bell and iron rattles attached to a snarling animal-headed post. Most important for this discussion, two long, narrow tapestries lined the chamber's walls. One showed a battle scene, the other a parade or ritual procession. On the ship's deck was a richly carved wagon that was a close match to the processional wagon depicted on the tapestry.

Many of the images found in the Ribe jewellery workshop match details from the Oseberg tapestry's parade: wagons, horses, women carrying weapons, people dressed as animals or wearing antiquated horned helmets. 'I'm sure this is what the small amulets are showing,' Sindbaek told *National Geographic*. 'We've got exactly the same range.'

He doubts the women depicted with weapons were warriors in real life. 'It's not showing us combat – you couldn't go into battle in a dress with a long train. Female warriors were a thing, but that's not what they're showing us in these amulets.'

He and his colleagues also doubt, however, that the women with weapons are meant to depict mythological valkyries. Instead, they were real women involved in rituals that show the ambiguity of Viking gender roles. Said Croix, 'It's an important reminder that we can't assume ideas about gender roles are fixed or permanent.'

The Drinking Horn Motif

There is another group of tiny two-dimensional silver icons dating from the eighth to tenth centuries that have been labelled 'valkyries'. These figures do not carry weapons. They also appear in profile and, because of their long hair and robes that trail on the ground, are said to be women.

Yet in addition to the male Vikings who were proud of their long, silky blond hair, as noted above, the Icelandic sagas describe several male Vikings who wore gowns so long they dragged on the ground. A chieftain's gown in *Egil's Saga* was made of silk embroidered with gold and had gold buttons all down the front.

Another, in *Njal's Saga*, aggravated a feud because it wasn't clear if it should be worn by a man or a woman.

Some of these so-called valkyrie icons hold out an object that looks like a cup or a drinking horn. The interpretation of these amulets as valkyries rests entirely on the description by Snorri Sturluson (1179–1241) in the *Prose Edda* of valkyries as goddesses 'who serve in Valhalla, bringing drinks and taking care of the cups and ale casks'.

Most experts commenting on these images say the woman is offering her cup to someone unseen, such as a dead hero arriving at Valhalla. It's not the only possible interpretation. Says Ing-Marie Back Danielsson in her 2007 thesis from Stockholm University, *Masking Moments: The Transitions of Bodies and Beings in Late Iron Age Scandinavia*: 'Interpretations of apparent females just standing there waiting to serve a man's arrival are of course largely androcentric, not at all scientifically neutral and objective.'

Lady with a Mead Cup

Rather than a valkyrie at the gates of Valhalla, an alternative interpretation of these images is that of the Lady with a Mead Cup. As Christopher Abram points out in his 2011 book, *Myths of the Pagan North*, 'High-status women were also expected to honor their guests with drink here on earth. This depiction could, in other words, relate to a perfectly ordinary aspect of a woman's life.'

The Lady with a Mead Cup archetype is based on the character of Queen Wealhtheow in the Old English epic, *Beowulf*. When Beowulf and his men come to the king's hall, Queen Wealhtheow ceremonially presents them with a cup of mead: She 'went on her rounds, / queenly and dignified, decked out in rings', reads Seamus Heaney's translation, published in 2000, 'offering the goblet to all ranks / [...] until it was Beowulf's turn to take it from her hand'. Yet the next lines seem to describe the icon just as well: Beowulf 'accepted the cup' and vowed to kill the monster Grendel. 'And I shall fulfil that purpose, / prove myself with a proud deed / or meet my death.'

Whole books have been written on how and why Queen Wealhtheow served the mead: entering the hall with the intoxicating golden drink, she drew all eyes. By offering the cup first to the king, she enacted 'an archaic ritual of lordship' that underscored his pre-eminence. As she brought the cup to the warriors, each in turn, she fixed their status, their rank in the king's band. By drinking, the warriors accepted their rank and assented to the king's rule. 'So did the queen act to help achieve cohesion and unity of purpose between lord and follower in the royal hall,' writes Michael J. Enright in *Lady with a Mead Cup* (1996).

Yet, as Back Danielsson asks, 'How close must a drinking horn be next to an (alleged) woman, before the idea comes to mind that she actually could have taken a sip herself?' Could not this icon of the valkyrie with cup in outstretched hand be not the queen offering the cup to a male warrior, but a woman warrior lifting her goblet to make a heroic pledge the way Beowulf did?

The Gotland Picture Stones

Images of valkyries have also been identified in stone carvings, most prominently on the picture stones found on the island of

Gotland off the eastern coast of Sweden. These stones marked graves dated from around 800 to 1100.

The famous red-painted stone known as Tjängvide I, now in the Swedish National Museum, for example, has two panels of carvings surrounded by interlaced borders. The bottom panel shows a dragon ship with two spiral stems, like that on the Oseberg ship. It carries nine passengers, most with swords and helmets. The top panel is dominated by a rider on a rather odd horse facing a figure with a drinking horn and something else in her hands. (Back Danielsson suggests no horn, but two 'wriggling snakes'.)

The standing figure is taken to be a woman because her long hair is twisted into a ponytail and she's wearing a long, trailing robe; it also looks like she's wearing a sword. Behind her there's a dog or a wolf, two people fighting (one wearing a long robe, one wearing a short tunic), and another person (very blurred, but possibly wearing a long robe) facing something that might be a fortress or a cave. Above the horse and rider is a figure flying through the air – or is he lying dead in the distance? He (given his short tunic) is holding on to something that's been damaged too badly to make out. The stone's blunt images tantalize: what story do they tell?

Most scholars count the legs on the horse and say it is Sleipnir, Odin's eight-legged steed. The pictures, therefore, tell the story of a valkyrie welcoming the god Odin home to Valhalla.

And yet, Snorri Sturluson, in the *Prose Edda*, is the only source we have for the idea that Odin's horse had eight legs. When art historians interpret the painting of an eight-legged bison at Chauvet Cave in France, dated to about 30,000 BCE, they explain the extra legs as the artist's attempt to show motion or great speed.

Valkyrie-Rider Amulets

A similar scene, of a standing person facing a rider on horseback, was popular as a metal pendant or amulet. For his article 'Myths in Metal: Armed Females in the Art of the Viking Age', published in the magazine *Hugin & Munin* in May 2018, Leszek Gardela examined 20 examples made of copper alloy or silver from Denmark, England and Poland.

Looking at what Gardela calls one of the 'most evocative examples', from Tissø in Denmark, I see a horse with the normal four legs – so it's not Sleipnir. The rider is wearing baggy trousers (a man?), but has long hair knotted in a ponytail (a woman?). Gardela, looking at the original icon, says the rider is carrying a sword; I, looking at a photograph, see something stubbier, maybe even a cup or drinking horn. There's clearly a spear tucked under the rider's leg (Gardela points out that it's of the 'so-called "winged type" typical of Western Europe') and what might be a spur on the rider's heel. A 'round feature with a swirling pattern' on the haunch of the horse, more visible on some of the amulets, looks to Gardela like a shield; I'm inclined to think it's the rider's cloak.

The standing figure looks very much like some of the more troll-like valkyrie icons discussed earlier, with a weird hood or helmet, a pointy nose, a prominent shield and a trailing robe. This figure is clearly holding a cup or drinking horn.

Does this image, again, depict a valkyrie greeting Odin or a dead warrior at the gates of Valhalla? Gardela thinks a different story is being told. Admitting that his interpretation 'requires a stretch of the imagination', he concludes that it refers to an episode in the story of Sigurd the Dragonslayer.

The Legend of Brynhild

The story of Sigurd the Dragonslayer, of course, is also the story of Brynhild the Valkyrie. 'Brynhild is the paramount figure of Germanic legend', writes Theodore M. Andersson in *The Legend of Brynhild* (1980), 'but she has been subordinated more often than not to the male object of her passion. Her story is thus normally referred to as the legend of Sigurd.'

For hundreds of years, Brynhild's story was one of the most popular in the north. Its characters were alluded to in poetry and prose and listed in genealogies. Episodes were woven into tapestries and embroidered on wall hangings; carved in stone on runestones and crosses and baptismal fonts; carved in wood on the doorposts of Norwegian stave churches; and, if Gardela is correct, cast into jewellery.

It is Brynhild on whom the Marvel Valkyrie is (loosely) based, as I mentioned before.

It is Brynhild on whom the German composer Richard Wagner (1813–83) based his beautiful but tragic young woman in horned helmet and metal bustier, with spear and winged stallion, who sings as she fights. Wagner's Brünnhilde is the star of *The Valkyrie*, which is part two of his famous *Ring of the Nibelungs* opera cycle. The stirring prelude to Act III, popularly known as *The Ride of the Valkyries*, depicting the valkyries carrying dead heroes to Valhalla, is one of Wagner's most-beloved works.

Wagner was familiar with the German epic poem *Das Nibelungenlied*, dated to about 1200, which also tells Brynhild's story. But Arni Björnsson, in his book *Wagner and the Volsungs* (2003), finds that 80 per cent of the motifs in Wagner's opera cycle derive from the Icelandic versions. Wagner himself wrote to a friend in 1851 about borrowing a copy of *Volsunga Saga* from the Royal Library in Dresden, as quoted by Jesse Byock in his 1990 translation of the saga. 'This book I now need for repeated perusal,' Wagner wrote. 'I want to have the saga again; not in order to imitate it [...], rather, to recall once again exactly every element that I already previously had conceived from its particular features.' *The Valkyrie* premiered in Munich in 1870.

From Victor to Victim

Volsunga Saga was stitched together in the late thirteenth century by an unknown Icelandic author from a sequence of older poems preserved (more or less) in the *Poetic Edda*. Snorri Sturluson also included a summary of the legend of Brynhild in the *Prose Edda*. Her story is told, as well, in *Thidrek's Saga*, among a number of hero tales from Germany; this saga is thought to have been written in the mid-1200s at the court of King Hakon IV (1204–63). Finally, a number of Faroese ballads, which may have been sung since the Middle Ages, preserve the tale.

Andersson, who has studied the development of the legend, argues that the later the version, the more romanticized it becomes. Brynhild's ambition is turned into passion; her crisis of honour becomes a fit of jealousy. The story's focus shifts away from her internal struggle to keep her oath to marry only a man who knows no fear. Instead, the crisis becomes her inability to fulfil the demands of society by being a good, submissive wife – despite knowing she'd been tricked into marrying the wrong man.

'The story is no longer of Brynhild's thwarted will, but of her blighted love,' writes Andersson. Brynhild is no longer a 'powerful and independent queen' who is 'in control of her destiny and able to punish those who crossed her'. Instead, she is a victim.

Of the oldest version, with a 'victorious' Brynhild, 'grief-stricken but triumphant', only a little bit remains. Our only copy, in the *Codex Regius* manuscript of the *Poetic Edda*, is missing a couple of hundred stanzas – or however many would have fitted on one sheet of parchment which, when folded, would make a gathering of eight finished pages.

J.R.R. Tolkien (1892–1973), who wrote his own version of Brynhild's story in an epic poem (published in 2009 in a volume called *The Legend of Sigurd and Gudrún*), imagined a 'medieval fan' snitching that gathering, says Tom Shippey in a chapter in *Revisiting* the *Poetic Edda* (2013). Shippey refers instead to a 'medieval vandal'.

Like the other Eddic poems, Shippey adds, this *Brot af Sigurðarkviða* ('Fragment of the Song of Sigurd'), is 'all but impossible to understand'. It assumes you already know the story, as most people in the Viking Age did.

Odin and the Volsungs

As it has come down to us in *Volsunga Saga*, the story includes several mentions of valkyries and other powerful women. It begins in a mythic past when King Rerir prayed to the goddess Frigg for a child. Frigg told her husband, the god Odin, to send a 'wish-maiden'– a valkyrie – to bring Rerir a magic apple. Rerir's queen soon bore a child, who became King Volsung.

When he grew up, Volsung married that same valkyrie, who was apparently ageless.

Inside the king's hall stood the trunk of a great tree, called *Barnstokk* ('Child-Trunk'). Its branches pierced the roof and bore beautiful blossoms. During the wedding of Signy, Volsung's only daughter, a stranger entered the hall. In my translation, 'He wore a cape of two colors. He was barefoot and had bound his linen breeches tight about his shins. He had a sword in one hand, and his hood fell low over his face. He was an old man, very tall, with only one eye.' (The 'one eye' is the giveaway: it's Odin.) He thrust the sword into the tree's trunk. Whoever could draw it out, he said, in a sword-in-the-stone moment, could keep it.

Sigmund, Volsung's oldest son, won the magic sword. King Siggeir, who had just married Signy, Sigmund's twin sister, was jealous and began to plot against his new in-laws. When they visited him in Gautland, Siggeir's army attacked, killing King Volsung and taking his ten sons captive. They were set in stocks where, each night, one was killed and eaten by an old she-wolf (said to be King Siggeir's mother) until only Sigmund was left. With his twin sister's help, Sigmund killed the wolf and escaped.

Sigmund and Sinfjotli

We've already met Sigmund. He and his son Sinfjotli are the heroes who greeted King Eirik Blood-Axe at the gates of Valhalla in the poem commemorating Eirik's death in 954.

In the saga, when Sigmund escaped from the evil she-wolf, his sister helped him hide out in the woods for many years. When he complained he was lonely, she sent him her son by King Siggeir as a companion. But the boy turned out to be fearful, so (with Signy's approval) Sigmund killed him.

Then Signy and Sigmund slept together, and Sinfjotli was born. He turned out to be afraid of nothing, so he lived the outlaw life with his father/uncle.

Robbing a house, they came upon two wolfskin cloaks. They put them on and were transformed into wolves. They lived as wolves until they learned to break the spell. Then they attacked King Siggeir, killing his and Signy's other children, before he captured them and buried them alive.

Again with Signy's help, Sigmund and Sinfjotli escaped. They burned down King Siggeir's hall, with him in it. After a powerful speech, in which she revealed that Sinfjotli was her and Sigmund's son by incest, Signy decided the honourable thing to do was to die with her husband (whom she had never liked). 'Everything I have done has been in the cause of vengeance' for King Volsung and her brothers. 'I have no more reason to live,' she said, and walked into the fire.

King Sigmund

Sigmund took charge of his father's kingdom, married and had a son named Helgi. He is the hero we've already met in the series of poems in the *Poetic Edda*, who was named by a valkyrie, reincarnated and married to another valkyrie (the one who rode the corpse-eating wolf).

Here in *Volsunga Saga* the story is a bit tamer. Rather than as a valkyrie dressed for battle, Sigrun is introduced as one of several handsome women riding by in magnificent clothing. Nothing is said about her giving Helgi his name. Instead, she seems fully human.

She had come to ask for Helgi's help in avoiding being married off to a suitor she disliked. He agreed and sailed south, reaching the suitor's kingdom without any magical help. The focus of the episode is on the shouting match between Sinfjotli and the suitor's father, King Granmer, who insulted Sinfjotli by calling him (accurately) a corpse-eating wolf. Sinfjotli parried by calling Granmer a witch, a valkyrie, a female wolf on whom he himself had sired nine wolf cubs, a mare and a goatherd.

Then the battle began and, as Helgi's side faltered, Sigrun's true nature was revealed. On the battlefield, Helgi's men 'saw a large troop of shield-maids. It was like staring into flames': Sigrun had come. The battle won, Helgi married her and their part of the saga is ended.

Instead the story follows Sinfjotli until he was poisoned by his father/uncle's queen. He was put into a boat to be ferried to his burial, but the boat, the boatman and the body all disappeared before King Sigmund's eyes – perhaps another way of getting to Valhalla?

King Sigmund killed his treacherous queen and remarried, but he soon lost his luck. 'A man came onto the battlefield wearing a black cloak with a hood that fell over his face. He had one eye and carried a spear in his hand.' It was Odin again. Sigmund's magic sword broke against Odin's spear. When his young queen found him, barely still alive, he told her to save the broken pieces of the sword for their son.

The Dragonslayer

That son is Sigurd the Dragonslayer. He was raised by a foster-father, Regin the Smith: 'He taught him many skills, games and lore, and to speak many languages, as was usual for a king's son.'

Sigurd was given Grani, a horse chosen by Odin himself. He learned of the dragon Fafnir and the hoard of gold he guarded, and had Regin forge him a sword out of the pieces of his father's magic one. 'When he pulled it from the forge, the other smiths thought its edges flickered with flame.'

Regin told him that Fafnir used to be human – Regin's own brother – and that the gold was the compensation the gods had paid when Loki the Trickster killed their third brother, who had taken on the shape of an otter. Regin instructed Sigurd in how to kill the dragon: 'Dig a deep hole and sit in it. And when the worm crawls to the water, strike him in the heart and so cause his death.'

Sigurd did so, engaging in a riddling conversation with the dying dragon that was the inspiration for a similar conversation between Bilbo Baggins and the dragon Smaug in J.R.R. Tolkien's *The Hobbit* (1937).

Sigurd then roasted the dragon's heart for Regin to eat, but when the hot drippings burned his finger, and he put it in his mouth, he suddenly understood the language of birds. Some nuthatches in the bushes warned him that Regin planned to betray him. Sigurd should kill his foster-father and keep the dragon's gold all for himself. They also told him to ride to Hindarfjall and find Brynhild, who would share her 'great wisdom'.

Sigurd followed their advice, killing Regin and loading the hoard – including the dragon's 'helm of awe', a ringmail byrnie made all of gold, and a magic ring – onto his sturdy horse. Grani refused to move until Sigurd mounted as well.

These are the episodes most frequently depicted in the visual arts: Regin reforging the magic sword, Sigurd stabbing the dragon from below, roasting the dragon's heart (with the detail of his finger in his mouth) and listening to the birds, and Grani overloaded with both rider and gold.

Sigurd Meets Brynhild

Sigurd rode Grani a long way from Fafnir's lair. He thought he had crossed into France, the saga says, when he saw before him a great light, like a fire burning. It lit up the heavens. When he came to the place, he saw before him a fortress with a banner flying above it.

Or, as *Fafnismál*, the 'Song of Fafnir' in the *Poetic Edda*, puts it, in my translation:

High on Hindarfell sits a hall,
wrapped around in flame.
Magicians lit those fires
of blazing river-light.
There on the mountain
sleeps a battle-wise warrior.

Crossing the ramparts Sigurd saw an armed warrior lying on the ground. He rushed to see if the warrior was alive and, unlacing the helmet, sat back in surprise. The warrior was a woman. She barely breathed. Drawing his sword, Sigurd sliced through her ringmail byrnie and slipped it off her. She awoke as if from a deep sleep.

Rising, she recognized the sword, which she called Fafnir's Bane, and the helmet of awe. She introduced herself as a valkyrie who had been punished by Odin for killing the wrong king in a battle. She explained, 'Odin pricked me with a sleeping thorn and said that I should never again have the victory. He said I must marry. And I swore this oath in return that I would marry no one who knew fear.'

Sigurd asked her to teach him wisdom, and she agreed. Rising, she found a cup and a cask of liquor. They shared the drink and talked of many things: how to carve victory runes on a sword, how to protect a ship from storms, how to heal wounds. 'I've never met anyone as wise as you,' Sigurd said. 'What other advice can you give me?'

Support your kinsmen, she said. Be patient with their failings. Don't be a flirt or quarrel with drunks. Never swear a false oath. Control your temper – but don't let anyone call you a coward. And if you're caught travelling after nightfall, don't make your camp beside the road. You never know what might come by.

The Banner

The poem *Sigrdrifumál* ('The Song of Sigrdrifu') in the *Poetic Edda* tells the same story, adding more advice, including, in my translation:

I advise you as well
to swear no oath
that you won't hold to.

The faithless have a horrible
fate: Forever cast out,
cut off like wolves.

By the end of the episode, they have vowed to marry each other.

This first meeting between Sigurd the Dragonslayer and the valkyrie (in the poem she is called Sigrdrifa, but in the saga she is Brynhild) is what is depicted on the amulets that show a rider being greeted by a standing person bearing a cup or drinking horn, according to Leszek Gardela. In his article 'Myths in Metal' (*Hugin & Munin*, May 2018), he says he bases this interpretation 'on a careful reading of the iconographic features of the miniature figurines'. *Volsunga Saga*, he points out, specifically mentions Sigurd's long hair, the sword he carried, his golden spurs and the drink Brynhild offered him. The saga does not, however, say that Sigurd was riding Grani when Brynhild handed him the cup, weakening Gardela's interpretation.

Many experts have puzzled over the strange object lying under the horse in these amulets. In the clearest examples, it is shaped as a square, divided into nine blocks. This, says Gardela, is the banner that Sigurd saw flying over the valkyrie's ramparts. 'It lies on the ground signalling that the challenge has been overcome and that Sigurd has already won the hand of the valkyrie.'

The Second Meeting

Brynhild next appears in a domestic setting, sewing alongside her sister Bekkhild, who is the model noblewoman, admired not only for her skill at 'stitching fine clothes with gold thread', but also for her intelligence and social graces. Brynhild, too, says *Volsunga Saga*, was 'more skillful with her hands than other women'. While visiting her sister, she spent her time embroidering a tapestry depicting the great deeds of Sigurd the Dragonslayer.

Leaving Hindarfell, Sigurd too eventually arrived at the estate run by Bekkhild and her husband, not knowing Brynhild was staying there. One day when he was out hunting, Sigurd's hawk landed on a tower near Brynhild's window. Climbing up to catch the bird, Sigurd peeked in the window and realized she was sewing his life story.

Surprisingly, though, he failed at first to recognize her as the warrior woman he had met on the mountaintop – and whom he had pledged to marry. He asked Bekkhild's son, Alsvid, who she was, for 'both her beauty and her work seemed of great worth'.

Alsvid replied that she was the daughter of King Budli and the sister of Atli (the historical Attila the Hun). There was no use pining for her, he added. 'There's never been a man before that she's let sit beside her or to whom she's served a drink of ale. She would rather be on the battlefield, winning all kinds of fame.'

Brynhild, however, did allow Sigurd to sit next to her. But when he kissed her and said they should marry at once, she replied, 'We're not meant to live together. I am a shield-maid. I wear a helmet among the warrior kings, and I wish to remain in their warband. I like to fight.' She said she must soon leave to review the troops.

He wasn't easily put off, and finally they vowed again to marry no one but each other.

The Ring of Fire

Sigurd rode away, with all his gold, on Grani. Crossing the Rhine, he came to the castle of Gjuki, king of the Burgundians. Queen Grimhild, seeing his worth (and wealth!), decided he would be a good match for their daughter, Gudrun. She served Sigurd a magic potion, 'and with that drink he forgot all about Brynhild'.

Sigurd married Gudrun and became blood brothers with her brothers Gunnar and Hogni. When Gunnar decided to ask for Brynhild's hand in marriage, Sigurd agreed to accompany him. Brynhild's father, King Budli, did not refuse, provided Brynhild herself agreed. She was so proud, he said, she would only marry a man of her own choosing.

They rode on to her sister Bekkhild's estate; her husband directed them to Brynhild's own hall nearby. The only one she will marry, he warned, is the man who rides through her wall of flickering flames.

'They found the hall and saw the flames: They saw a fortress roofed with gold, and fire burned all around it.' But Gunnar could not make his horse leap the flames. Sigurd offered him the great-hearted Grani, but Grani would not leap for him either. Then Sigurd took on Gunnar's likeness, using magic Queen Grimhild had taught him; he also attached his golden spurs to his boots. When he felt the spurs, Grani surged forward. 'Now there came a great roar. The fire flared up and the earth quaked. The flames leaped high into the sky. No one had ever dared such a ride before. It was as if he rode into darkness.'

Passing safely through the wall of fire, Sigurd dismounted and went into Brynhild's hall. He introduced himself as Gunnar, King

Gjuki's son. He announced to Brynhild that 'you are to become my wife, since I've ridden through your flickering flames, with your father's approval and your foster-father's, and if you agree'.

Brynhild sat on her throne, as regal as 'a swan on a wave', wearing her helmet and ringmail byrnie, with her sword in her hand. 'Do not talk like that,' she said. 'I was in battle with the King of Gardariki and our weapons were red with blood. This is what I desire.'

The false Gunnar replied: 'You have accomplished many great deeds, but now you must remember your oath: you swore to marry the man who rode through your flickering flames.'

Brynhild Betrayed

According to *Volsunga Saga*, Brynhild 'realized the truth of his answer'. Her own oath had trapped her. It was binding and irrevocable. By riding through the wall of fire, this man had proved himself without fear. They exchanged rings and slept together for three nights, and though he lay his sword between them on the bed, she considered herself married.

As Karl Siegfried points out in a post on 'The Norse Mythology Blog' (6 March 2013), 'the German *Nibelungenlied* portrays Brynhild (as Brünhilde) in a very different light'. Both women are 'tricked into marrying unworthy men by the deceit of the hero (Sigurd in Iceland, Siegfried in Germany). However, the Christianized German version adds a disturbing extra scene in which Siegfried violently rapes the shield-maiden in her own bedroom to teach her the virtue of wifely obedience.' As translated by Margaret Armour in 1999, the passage reads in part:

Then Siegfried got hold of Brünhilde. Albeit she fought valiantly, her defence was grown weak. […] She squeezed his hands till, by her strength, the blood spurted out from his nails. Then he brake the strong will that she had shown at the first. […] Siegfried pressed her down till she cried aloud, for his might hurt her greatly. She clutched at her side, where she found her girdle, and sought to tie his hands. But he gripped her till the joints of her body cracked. So the strife was ended.

As Karl Siegfried commented in his blog post: 'You may choose to read this as a wrestling match rather than a rape, but the sexual element really is clear in the text. The "strife" occurs in bed […] and begins with Siegfried tearing Brünhilde's nightgown.' *Volsunga Saga* 'presents us with a hero who begs a wise Valkyrie to share her knowledge', Siegfried concludes, whereas the Christianized *Nibelungenlied* 'gives us a rapist who violently puts a headstrong shield-maiden in her (domestic) place'.

Brynhild's Revenge

Returning to the version in *Volsunga Saga*, after Brynhild's father held the marriage feast, she and Gunnar went to live with Gudrun and Sigurd in King Gjuki's castle. One day while the two women were bathing in the river Rhine, they got into an argument about whose husband was best, and Gudrun revealed that it was actually Sigurd, disguised as Gunnar, who had ridden through the wall of flame on Grani. Sigurd was the only man without fear.

Brynhild went home and took to her bed. When Gunnar came to ask her if she was ill, she said, 'Don't concern yourself with that, for you will never again see me gracing your hall, neither drinking nor playing games nor holding friendly conversations nor stitching fine clothes with gold thread nor giving you good advice.' [...] She bid her chamber door be opened, so that her lamentations could be heard far away. She cried, 'I swore an oath to marry the man who rode through my flickering flames, and that oath I will keep or else die.'

The importance of her oath is even clearer in the poetic versions of the tale. Writes Jóhanna Katrín Friðriksdóttir in a chapter in *Revisiting the Poetic Edda* (2013), 'What marks Brynhildr as subversive is her deliberate and (self)-conscious use of language.' Like a man, 'she takes oaths that she makes every effort to fulfill, as well as holding others to their word.' Oaths, in the Norse world, were 'inextricably bound up with honor', Friðriksdóttir adds. 'Oaths are not to be undertaken lightly, for they imply a sacred and solemn duty to oneself and one's honor, the community, and, in cases where they invoke a bond with the recipient, another person.'

To assuage her honour, Brynhild demanded that Sigurd be killed for deceiving her. Gunnar and Hogni argued that, as Sigurd's blood brothers, they were powerless to act. So they recruited their third brother, Guttorm, who was young, reckless and had never sworn any oaths to Sigurd. Strengthened by his mother's witchcraft, Guttorm snuck into Sigurd's room and stabbed him as he slept. He died in Gudrun's arms.

When she learned of Sigurd's death, Brynhild first laughed, then cried, then stabbed herself. She lived long enough – at least in *Volsunga Saga* – to walk onto Sigurd's funeral pyre and be burned with him.

Sister of Attila the Hun

Though Sigurd deals with dragons and dwarfs, has a magic helmet and sword, understands the speech of birds and can take on the likeness of another man, no one doubts Sigurd is human, not a god.

Yet Brynhild, said to be a supernatural valkyrie, does little that a real woman couldn't do. The magic surrounding her is, I think, a matter of interpretation. Is the ring of fire around her fortress magic, or a moat filled with firewood? Is her deep sleep due to Odin's spell, or to smoke inhalation? If you read her story with an eye towards history, it's possible to see her as an ordinary woman. Unless you assume it's unnatural for a woman to be both a source of wisdom and a renowned warrior. Or unless you assume that women don't mean to keep their word when they swear an oath.

The focus on Brynhild as one of Odin's mythical valkyries has eclipsed what is, to me, her more intriguing connection: she is the sister of Attila the Hun. That name places the action of her tale in the far-distant past even for the Viking poets who wrote about it: Attila died in 453, in what is now France. His empire extended east as far as China, though his supply lines by then were fraying, and a hundred years later the Huns would be gone.

But not forgotten. As in the saga, the Huns intermarried with the Burgundians and Goths. Poems and songs kept Attila and his heroes alive in legend. Their customs became legendary too – particularly, perhaps, their acceptance of warrior women.

For the Huns originated in the Altai Mountains of Mongolia and Kazakhstan. They bred fast horses, rode like centaurs and fought with small but powerful compound bows. Speed, accuracy and surprise were their battle tactics. Unlike their European enemies, who depended on shields and spears, nothing about Hunnish warfare favoured men over women. And while new to the West, it was an ancient form of battle in the Huns' homelands. Archaeologists in the steppes have unearthed an unbroken string of burials of warrior women from Attila's time back two thousand years. These women were the original Amazons, and the inspiration for the Vikings' valkyries.

4.
The Grave

The fight was not gentle where she set her hand.
Gjuki's daughter felled two warriors.
She struck Atli's brother, he was carried away.
She'd struck such a blow, his leg was cut off.
She struck another; he never got up:
she'd sent him to Hel and her hands never shook.
– from 'The Greenland Lay of Atli', in the *Poetic Edda*

REAL WOMEN WARRIORS IN THE VIKING AGE

After the funeral of Sigurd the Dragonslayer and the valkyrie Brynhild, her rival Gudrun was given in marriage to Brynhild's brother Atli (Attila the Hun). He was not content. He believed he should also have received, as compensation for his sister's death, some of the gold Sigurd took from the dragon's hoard. Concealing his motives, he invited Gudrun's brothers Gunnar and Hogni to visit; when they refused to hand over the gold, he and his warriors attacked.

This is the fight described in 'The Greenland Lay of Atli'. (Why the compiler of the *Poetic Edda* thought the poem was composed in Greenland we don't know). The fight also appears in *Volsunga Saga*, where it is said of Gudrun, in my translation: 'When she saw that the battle was going against her brothers, she called up her courage, put on a ringmail byrnie, took up her sword and fought beside her brothers, where she did as well as the boldest man. Everyone said the same, that there could hardly have been a better defence than they saw there.'

Gudrun had not been introduced as a valkyrie. She was a wife and a mother. Yet both the poet and the saga-writer had no difficulty imagining her as a well-trained warrior. She did not merely wave an axe about or slap her breasts with a sword, as did other saga women. She incapacitated two men, without being injured herself. To cut off a man's leg requires a substantial, well-directed blow. It's not just a lucky shot.

For over a hundred years, though, readers of these and other Old Norse texts have considered Gudrun and the other women warriors they describe to be mythical – as fabulous as the dragons.

'Proper' Vikings

Along with literature, history and art, our view of the valkyries has been shaped by archaeology. But archaeologists – like all of us – have their biases. An important one in this context is what Neil Price in the catalogue for the 2013 exhibition at the National Museum of Denmark called 'the idea that "proper" Vikings were necessarily male'.

This prejudice has led archaeologists to explain away the weapons they sometimes find in women's graves. They must be gifts, or else symbols of power and status. When those same weapons are found in a man's grave, though, they are assumed to have belonged to the man when he was alive and to mark him as a warrior.

To unpack this prejudice, we have to understand how archaeologists work, both in the past and today. When I first began writing books about the Viking Age 20-some years ago, one archaeologist I interviewed described the development of excavation techniques over the last 100 years as 'increasingly comprehensive destruction'.

A second expert I consulted pointed out that at some universities, archaeology is classified as one of the humanities: it's more like history or literature than chemistry or physics. For a scientific experiment to be valid, any scientist, following the published methods of the original experimenter, should be able to reproduce the original results. In archaeology, that's simply not possible. When they excavate a gravesite, archaeologists destroy it. They dig up the ground, sift it, sort it, save certain things and dump what's left. What they leave for posterity are their notes, maps, sketches, published reports and collections, all of which are forms of interpretation, and so susceptible to bias.

Sexing by Metal

The sorting step is crucial to our understanding of valkyries and other women warriors in the Viking Age. In her influential 2007 PhD dissertation from Stockholm University, *Masking Moments: The Transitions of Bodies and Beings in Late Iron Age Scandinavia*, Ing-Marie Back Danielsson traces today's biases to an archaeological 'manifesto' written in 1837, before archaeology was even a profession.

People interested in past cultures were then known as antiquarians; their collections, or 'cabinets of curiosities' were the forerunners of our museums. There were no standard procedures then, as there are now, for how to dig up, sort through and save things they might find buried in the ground. Some antiquarians numbered, boxed and stored the human and animal bones they recovered from burials; others reburied the human bones and dumped the rest. Many of the things that modern archaeologists prize, such as rusty boat nails and broken bits of pottery, were routinely discarded. What the antiquarians generally kept were shiny things that looked good displayed on a shelf. This focus on museum pieces continued in Viking studies into the 1980s.

The antiquarians in 1837, says Back Danielsson, 'stated, as a matter of fact, that swords belonged to men and needles to women.' Their decision was based on no evidence beyond their own opinions of what were appropriate occupations for men (warfare) and women (embroidery) – and it is true, as we've seen, that Viking women in sagas and poems are often praised for their embroidery.

That rule for sorting graves was updated slightly in 1876. Graves with swords were still categorized as male, while those with jewellery, not just needles, qualified as female. The practice continues – if sometimes subconsciously. Writes Back Danielsson, 'Since we today seem to "know" that you bury either a) a woman or b) a man with corresponding materials, then that is what you look for.' Based on her work, the technique has come to be known, somewhat snidely, as 'sexing by metal'.

Sexing by Bones

The other way to determine the sex of a burial is to examine the bones. Osteologists are taught that a woman's skull is smoother, and her brow ridge more rounded, than a man's. Her long bones are more slender and less robust. Her pelvis is shaped differently.

But there's no absolute scientific scale for this smoothness, roundedness or robustness – it's all relative. Men of some cultures might be smaller and slenderer, their features smoother and more rounded, than women of other cultures. Age also plays a part: people's bones change during their lifetime. As women age, their skulls get craggier – more man-like – while years of hard manual labour can make a woman's bones look as robust as a man's.

Even distinguishing a female pelvis (presumably designed for childbearing) from a male one isn't easy. Back Danielsson refers to a diagram, in a 2006 textbook, in which 'the ischium-pubis index is plotted against the angle of the greater sciatic notch'. This diagram derives from research done in the 1950s measuring a series of skeletons from a single population (defined as 'Eskimo'). It is presented as a teaching tool. But, rather than sorting obviously into two groups, the pelvic measurements lie on a spectrum, with 'immense differences' within each sex, Back Danielsson notes. 'Equally, there is no certainty in deciding where the border lies between the sexes in the diagram – where the dots/squares cease to be "male" and the "female" start.' Sexing by bones, too, is an interpretation.

Viking Burials

Being able to take such precise measurements on a series of Viking Age pelvises, and to compare one to another, is usually not possible. Few Viking skeletons are in good enough shape. After 1,000 years in the soil, the bones are degraded, or missing. To increase the level of difficulty, the most common Viking Age funeral – like that of Sigurd and Brynhild – involved fire. In these cremation burials, the bodies were first burned on a pyre, then the bones were retrieved and crushed before being buried.

How have archaeologists sexed these graves? Some used bits of bone, assessing the smoothness of a skull, for example, based on a small piece of uncrushed brow ridge. But the usual way was sexing by metal. When a sword was found in a grave, the grave was classified as male.

Discussing the 'foundational' work of Haakon Shetelig, published in 1912, Leszek Gardela notes in *Women & Weapons in the Viking World* (2021), for example: 'The absence or poor preservation of osteological material from Norwegian Viking Age graves created serious problems in establishing the biological sex of the deceased. Following traditional research paradigms, Shetelig was therefore compelled to consider weapons (swords, shields, axes, spears and arrowheads) as diagnostically "male" goods, whereas objects of domestic use (e.g., spinning and weaving tools as well as other utensils) he considered as items characteristic of women.'

This 'traditional' connection between artefacts and sex doesn't hold up to scrutiny. The first osteological evaluation of a Viking Age burial ground was performed in 1948 by a physical anthropologist in Sweden. Of the 224 graves excavated, only 56 could be sexed by their bones: 34 were labelled male and 18 female. Of these 56 graves, just 13 contained artefacts. Even accepting that the bones were sexed accurately, writes Back Danielsson, "we are left with some 13 of 224, or 5%, that convincingly supports the "knowledge" of male attributes (such as a sword) to certain fragmented bones ("men") and female attributes (such as needles/jewellery) to somewhat different fragmented pieces of skeletons ("women").'

The vast majority of Viking burials, in this and other graveyards, cannot be sexed by either method.

Bones versus Metal

The question of which is more accurate, sexing by bones or by metal, achieved some notoriety a few years ago.

In 'Warriors and Women,' a 2011 paper in the journal *Medieval Europe*, Shane McLeod reported on his work to determine the ratio of Norse women to men in England in the late ninth century. This was the age of the Great Heathen Army, which legend says was led by sons of the Viking hero Ragnar Lothbrok. (The valkyrie Lagertha was not their mother.) The era has been brought to life in the 13-book 'Saxon Stories' historical novels by Bernard Cornwell, published between 2004 and 2020. These books and the related Netflix series, *The Last Kingdom* (which premiered in 2015) focus, in large part, on the hero Uhtred of Bebbanburg and his love-hate relationship with the warrior woman Brida.

McLeod re-examined two sets of Viking burials linked to the Great Heathen Army: seven graves in which scholars sexed the dead based on what had been buried with them, another 14 in which the dead were sexed by their bones. In the first group, only one body was considered female; in the second, six were. McLeod concluded that sexing by metal was 'highly problematic'.

His work went mostly unnoticed until September 2014, when a blog post on the science fiction and fantasy website Tor.com went viral. 'Better Identification of Viking Corpses Reveals: Half of the Warriors Were Female' misinterpreted McLeod's results. The pseudonymous blogger 'Stubby the Rocket' concluded, incorrectly, that valkyries made up half of the Great Heathen Army.

Not half. Not even close to half. Women accompanying an army are not necessarily fighters themselves. (Neither are all the men.)

But two of the six graves classified by their bones as female did contain weapons: axes, seaxes, parts of swords and pieces of shields and one knife.

This is 'a discovery of undeniable importance', Marianne Moen points out, revisiting the controversy in her 2019 PhD dissertation from the University of Oslo, *Challenging Gender: A reconsideration of gender in the Viking Age using the mortuary landscape*. 'The presence of even a few female warriors has implications,' she argues. 'A society which allowed female warriors is not one where women were locked into social expectations of passivity.'

The Valkyrie of Nordre Kjølen

Our current social expectations have allowed us to forget that archaeological proof of valkyries or shield-maids is well over 100 years old.

In August 1900, a young man began digging into a mound on his family farm at Nordre Kjølen in the village of Åsnes, Norway. He was not an archaeologist. He'd never excavated a burial before. The pieces he collected included bones of a human and a horse and the metal remains of several weapons: sword, shield, axe and arrows. He did not make any sketches or take any notes, but when an archaeologist later came to look at his collection, both he and his father described what they remembered about the discovery process. After the shield boss was destroyed in a fire, they donated the rest of the items from the grave to a museum.

Both the human and the animal bones were 'exceptionally well preserved by Norwegian standards', notes Gardela in *Women & Weapons in the Viking World* (2021). Gustav Guldberg (1854–1908), a professor of medicine at the University of Oslo's Institute of Anatomy (and an expert on whales) was called in to look at them. 'To everyone's surprise,' writes Gardela, Guldberg concluded 'that the deceased person was not a man – as one would normally expect at that time, based on the "martial nature" of the grave contents.'

In his published report on the grave in 1901, Guldberg's colleague Gustav Mørck (1848–1919) wrote, in Gardela's translation: 'The discovery from Åsnes appears to testify to the idea that shield-maidens really existed in history.'

Osteologists studying the skeleton in 1984 and 2019 agreed that it was female. For the 2019 *National Geographic* documentary, *Viking Warrior Women*, Caroline Erolin of the University of Dundee's Centre for Anatomy and Human Identification reconstructed her face, revealing what seems to be a battle injury: a sword wound to the woman's forehead. As it showed signs of healing, it may or may not have led to her death.

In January 2025, Marianne Moen, now head of the archaeological section of the Museum of Cultural History at the University of

Oslo, and her colleagues received permission to try to sequence the DNA of a bone sample taken from the skull. Their results, expected in the spring of 2026, will 'open up broader discussions about gender identity in the past and how contemporary researchers relate to this', Moen writes.

Amazons of the North

Gardela has been publishing academic papers on Viking warrior women since 2013. He collects much of his previous work in *Women & Weapons in the Viking World: Amazons of the North* (2021).

While he 'did not undertake any new osteological analyses of Viking Age skeletal materials', but 'decided to trust the published reports as regards the sex of the deceased', as he explains in a blog post on Medievalists.net, he designed an otherwise rigorous protocol: 'I decided to personally examine the relevant finds in Scandinavian museum collections and, through visits to various archaeological sites, to immerse myself in the dramatic landscape in which they were originally discovered. In the course of the "Amazons of the North" project all these first-hand experiences, together with a thorough literature review, involving reading hundreds of pages of nineteenth- and twentieth-century journals and site reports, have enabled me to identify around 30 potential graves of Viking Age women buried with military equipment.'

Of these 30, he concludes, 'around 10 can – with some caution – be regarded as the graves of women buried with actual weapons or objects that could be used in armed conflict'. In the others, the 'military equipment', such as a small axe, was more likely a household tool.

Gardela found two graves with battle axes, two with shields, three with swords, four with spears and seven with arrowheads – though whether the arrows had been in the woman (killing her) or beside her (as possessions) was impossible for him to tell. The other weapons, he says, might have played roles in pagan rituals and processions. They could be 'symbols of status' or 'an expression of some form of literal or metaphorical empowerment of the dead'.

Or they could be proof of real valkyries. 'Biological sex is not at all a barrier to perform well on the ancient, medieval or modern battlefield,' he writes. 'The only barriers that exist are in the human mind and in the form of social conventions.'

The Birka Warrior

One of Gardela's 10 'graves of women buried with actual weapons' is the Nordre Kjølen grave, discussed above; another is the warrior burial known as Bj.581 from Birka, Sweden.

Bj.581 'had long been held up as an "archetypal" warrior grave of the mid-tenth century', writes Neil Price in *The Viking Way* (2019). It was 'always assumed to be male'. In 2017, Price was one of 10 authors of a DNA study that 'showed conclusively that the person was female', he writes.

The paper, 'A Female Viking Warrior Confirmed by Genomics' (2017), published in the *American Journal of Physical Anthropology*, was highly technical. It met all the standards of modern peer-reviewed science; unlike the excavation of a grave, DNA analysis of bones is highly reproducible. The study's lead author, Charlotte Hedenstierna-Jonson of the Historical Museum in Stockholm and the University of Uppsala, Price and their co-authors from Stockholm University, Uppsala University and the Evolutionary Biology Centre in Uppsala were not prepared for the backlash that followed.

Price, in *The Viking Way*, says that 'a lively international discussion ensued'. Eventually, however, the team of researchers had received so many negative comments that they felt it necessary to publish an expanded paper: 'Viking Warrior Women? Reassessing Birka chamber grave Bj.581' appeared in the journal *Antiquity* in 2019 with Price listed as the lead author (i.e., target of criticism).

In his later book, *Children of Ash and Elm* (2020), he revises his earlier description of the discussion about Bj.581 as 'lively': 'The ensuing debate on the apparent "female warrior" of Birka went viral and now convulses Viking studies, in an at-times vituperative discussion that has little to do with women and war but more concerns underlying fault lines of gendered assumption in the discipline and beyond.'

The Real Valkyrie

Bj.581 is the burial at the heart of my book *The Real Valkyrie: The Hidden History of Viking Warrior Women* (2021). Bj.581 was dug up near the Viking town of Birka, on an island in Sweden's Lake Mälaren, in 1878.

Unlike the Nordre Kjølen shield-maid, the Bj.581 valkyrie was not excavated by an amateur. By the time he began working on this grave, Hjalmar Stolpe (1841–1905) – an entomologist with the Swedish Academy of Sciences who had originally come to Birka looking for insects preserved in amber – had excavated over

500 burials on the island. Trained in stratigraphy, he produced 'meticulous' scientific reports, according to Hedenstierna-Jonsson. She calls his field drawings on graph paper – a technique he introduced to archaeology – 'exceptional'.

He carefully labelled every bone and artefact he retrieved from each of the 1,100 Birka graves he excavated; these are now stored in the Historical Museum in Stockholm. 'To this day', Hedenstierna-Jonsson writes in *The Birka Warrior*, her 2006 PhD dissertation from Stockholm University, 'the material constitutes an essential reference material for study of the Viking Age'.

Bj.581 was, Stolpe wrote, 'perhaps the most remarkable of all the graves in this field'. It was a chamber grave, built like an underground room 3.45 by 1.75 m (11.3 x 5.7 ft) in size. It was prominently sited, on the end of the headland near the Warrior's Hall, and marked by a great standing stone. It was as visible from the town below as from the waters of Lake Mälaren.

By the time Stolpe arrived, though, the roof beams and ceiling of the chamber had caved in and the stone had toppled over and sunk into the grave. The stone was too large for Stolpe and his team of seven labourers to move by hand. So, using a then-brand-new technology, Stolpe broke it apart with dynamite. He then carefully sketched and retrieved the contents of the grave.

The Warrior's Bones

Bone preservation at Birka is generally poor; the soil is too acidic. In many of Birka's graves all that remained by the time they were opened were a few loose teeth.

By comparison, Bj.581 is remarkably well preserved. She is one of few Birka skeletons to have a complete backbone. She has two ribs, bones from each arm and leg, part of her pelvis and her lower jaw. When she was dug up, her skull was also recovered, but it has since gone missing. Anatomical collections were in fashion in the late 1800s, and archaeologists often lent or traded bones with their friends. Skulls were particularly popular.

Unlike the Nordre Kjølen skeleton, that of Bj.581 is too degraded for the bones to show any signs of action, illness or battle trauma. The mature appearance of certain bones and the level of wear on her molars, however, tell us she was at least 30 when she died, maybe as old as 40. Her bones tell us, too, that she ate well all her life. At over 170 cm (67 in) tall, she was taller than most people around her: the average height of a Viking man at the time was 165 cm (65 in). The chemistry of her teeth tells us she was not a native of Birka, but was born somewhere in what is now southern Sweden or Norway and moved, as a child, farther west, possibly to Great Britain.

Her skeleton is also characteristically female, as osteologists had pointed out at least twice before 2017. The genomic tests that confirmed this involved extracting DNA from one tooth and one arm bone. The scientists sequenced the DNA and searched for Y chromosomes, the genetic signal of maleness. Their results fell far to the female end of the spectrum. There was no question about it: the skeleton buried in Bj.581 was female.

In their published papers, Hedenstierna-Jonsson and her colleagues list a dozen scholars since 1966 who have labelled Bj.581 a warrior's grave. 'As far as we are aware, this warrior interpretation has never been challenged,' they state, adding, 'We strongly followed the same military reading [...] for the same sensible reasons [...] In doing so, we find no problem in adjusting for the new sex determination.'

The Ultimate Viking Warrior?

Some of their critics do have a problem with it. They suggest that originally there must have been two people in the grave, a male warrior and his female wife or slave – and that the man has disappeared without a trace, leaving behind only his weapons.

For the woman buried in grave Bj.581 was surrounded by weapons. None of them are fancy. None are simply for show. Her two-edged sword is a type rare in Norway and Sweden, but more often found along the Vikings' East Way, the trade route through what is now Russia and Ukraine to Byzantium and the Silk Road.

Her long, thin-bladed scramasax, in its elaborate bronze-and-silver ornamented sheath, is also Eastern, inspired by the equipment of the Magyar horse archers who harassed the Vikings along the East Way.

She was an archer too: by her side was a cluster of 25 armour-piercing arrows. Between the arrows and the scramasax was a bare spot the right shape for a bow, which may have disintegrated. It may have been a Magyar bow – the distinctive metal rings and fittings of Magyar bow cases and quivers were recovered from other Birka graves, though not this one. Magyar bows were composites of wood, sinew and horn, bent into a reflex shape. Small and handy on horseback, they shot twice as far as an ordinary wooden bow.

But Bj.581 was not solely a mounted archer. She was buried with almost every Viking weapon known: sword, scramasax, arrows and bow, axe, two spears and two shields. She was buried with more weapons than any other warrior in Birka – more than almost every Viking in the world. Of those Vikings found buried with any weapons at all, 61 per cent have one weapon; only 15 per cent have three or more.

Or War Leader?

Bj.581 is remarkable not only for its complete weapon set and its impressive location. It is also one of only 18 of the 1,100 graves excavated at Birka to contain a horse – and it contains two, a stallion and a mare. Both are clearly riding horses. One of them was bridled with an iron bit; a second bit was found nearby. A pair of iron stirrups are all that remain of her wood-and-leather saddle. By their placement, it looks as if she was buried seated on her saddle.

A final touch elevates her rank from warrior to war leader: a full set of pieces for the board game *hnefatafl*, or Viking chess, was placed in her lap. From the Roman Iron Age through the high medieval era, from Iceland to Japan, the combination of game pieces, weapons and horses in a grave has indicated a war leader. Game pieces symbolize authority and a flair for strategic thinking. They express the idea that success in warfare does not depend on strength alone, but also on tactical skill and good luck.

Despite the clear results from the DNA study, the sex of the warrior in Birka grave Bj.581 remains one of the biggest controversies in Viking studies. Were the valkyries and shield-maids whose stories we've enjoyed in this essay merely myths? Or were they – like Sigurd the Dragonslayer and the male heroes of Norse legend – more like exaggerations?

Defending their findings in 2019, the team that tested her DNA said that Bj.581 'suggests to us that at least one Viking Age woman adopted a professional warrior lifestyle'. They added, 'We would be very surprised if she was alone in the Viking world.'

We can't go back in time to see who was actually fighting on the battlefields and sailing the dragon ships of the Viking Age. The only way to find more real valkyries is to DNA test more of the skeletons buried in warrior graves that have been, as Bj.581 was, always assumed to be male.

In the meantime, evidence from the ancient sagas, songs and histories, the visual arts and archaeological digs give the creative writers of today ample licence to imagine whichever kind of valkyrie they care to. In the stories that follow, you might meet valkyries who are demigoddesses of fate descending like lightning bolts on their flying horses, transforming into swans and living forever. Or you might meet ordinary Viking women who train hard, fight with bitter courage and die heroically alongside their men. Or, like the legendary male heroes of the Viking Age, the valkyries of these modern tales might be a little bit of both: human and supernatural, sex-kitten and kick-ass fighter. Above all, valkyries then and now are always memorable. They combine what we desire with what we most fear.

Modern Short Stories of Valkyries

Light As Air, Light As Dawn

Ryaan Akmal

The frenzied pulse of battle thrumming through Svipul's wounds finally stilled. The last of her focus narrowed to a single point – to those eyes. They glittered with pity and another, unplaceable sentiment. "*You fought well. Let Valhalla's gates open and bring you peace.*" Then, embracing, lifting, flying, light as air, light as dawn.

* * *

For how cavernous the great hall yawned, the air swelled full to bursting with the cacophony of merriment. Even before Svipul's eyes adjusted to the blinding glare, the clinking of horns and the stomping of boots was instantly recognizable: a rabble of warriors returned from battle. Bowered by a vaulted wooden ceiling, endless throngs of men huddled around masterful oak furnishings, a powerful golden light suffusing the scene. The scale of abundance Svipul beheld left her slack-jawed and stunned. Her first thought was of where such vast quantities of wood were gathered; what bounty such a forest might offer her village.

"You must be new, are you not?" Svipul turned to follow the graceful, echoing voice, and beheld a woman clad in gleaming gold vestments of war. Behind that gilded helm, intensely inquisitive eyes roamed Svipul's body. "There is much for you to see."

After a moment of wordless gawping, Svipul mustered, "Is-is this—"

"*Valhalla.*" The warrior woman's words dripped with reverence. "The domain of the Allfather, the bastion of the Einherjar, the home of the Valkyries," her gaze settled on Svipul's face, "and the newest of their rank."

"I don't understand, how did I come to be here?" Svipul looked upon her own sturdy, but unblemished hands. "I am hardly a warrior befitting the Einherjar, much less the Valkyrie."

"I have my guesses, but on that—" the Valkyrie's head suddenly jerked downward. Following her gaze, Svipul peered past the ground of the hall and observed the distant forms of warriors clashing on a stark, barren plain. "Another battle of mortals has started, come." The golden Valkyrie took Svipul's hand in her own and the two of them plunged through the space between realms, alighting in the Midgard sky above the conflict. "We must attend to our work." The warrior woman let go of Svipul's hand and glided to where the fight rampaged thickest.

Shocked to find herself still floating, Svipul called after the golden shape in the distance, "But what do I do?"

A great shout echoed back, "Choose a soul from the dead and take them to Valhalla!" Through the hail of arrows and the vanguard of shields, Svipul scarcely discerned the Valkyrie's figure embracing a fallen warrior, then shooting cloudward in a blazing ray of light.

Surveying the rest of the clamoring scene, Svipul made out the figures of other flying warrior women, each selecting their slain and carrying them up to Asgard's highest reaches. Now bereft of those dazzling beams, the sky of the mortal realm hung sallow and sickly. Svipul hovered low over the clashing axes and spilling blood, scanning the faces of fighters for anyone she recognized. Had her father or brothers been forced on to the battlefield? She had joined the counter-offensive despite her life as a farmer, in the hope that war would not reach the meager homesteads of her village. Comforted by the absence of any familiar faces, Svipul turned to her task as a Valkyrie.

Everywhere she looked there was death. Each confrontation of wills left more deceased and injured strewn across the battlefield. In the short time she had spent examining the two armies, the slaughtered had outnumbered the living. With every rent wound and corpulent stare, Svipul felt the hole in her chest widening, a strange amalgam of horror and shame torn open in her mortal life when the first of her comrades was struck low. She had difficulty remembering the moments before her own death; had she taken the lives of someone else's comrades? Is that why she had ascended to Valhalla? Her eyes caught on a warrior grimly engaged in his task, muttering something under his breath with every foe he felled. An uncanny recognition flagged in Svipul's mind, when suddenly, she felt countless eyes upon her – the glares of the living and the dead alike, judging, questioning, why she was levitating up there while they were stuck in the blood and filth.

Svipul could not bear to witness any more, taking her face in her hands and floating upwards, higher and higher, away from the cries of pain and the labored, final breaths. To select one of the dead to take to Valhalla was an impossible task. Among this legion of the fallen, how could she know who was worthy and who was not? Now far below her, the squall of battle quieted to a whisper, but still, Svipul could hear it. Nascent tears formed a film over her sheltered vision, a single droplet left to fall on the battlefield below. When next her eyes opened, she found herself back in the great hall, bathed in Valhalla's resplendent glow.

That echoing voice called out to Svipul, "I was wondering when you would be back, the battle is nigh over." The golden Valkyrie's brow furrowed. "You did not bring a warrior to be Einherjar?"

Svipul's fingers twitched, hands resisting the urge to curl into fists. "Not a moment ago I fought in my first battle, and now I am dead, roaming the hall of Odin. I am to be a Valkyrie when the most wicked weapon I am accustomed to wielding is a hoe. I am told that I must save the souls of the dead, and yet I do not know why *my* soul was saved!" Her breath ran fast and shallow. "I am Svipul," she thrust a finger at the golden Valkyrie, "what do I call you?"

A smile tugged at the corner of the Valkyrie's mouth. "Svipul, I apologize. I am Brynhildr. As you have no doubt gleaned, one among us easily swept up in the task at hand."

Svipul's cheeks bloomed scarlet and her hand dropped to her side. "I am sorry, there was no need for such an outburst."

Brynhildr responded gently, "As new as this is for you, it is the same for us. One has not been added to our number since our kind existed."

"Then why me, why now?"

"It is the work of our Lady Freyja, no doubt." Brynhildr's gaze grew distant, staring past Svipul, through the Einherjar and the walls of the great hall. "Her actions are rarely transparent, and her gracing Valhalla is even rarer."

Svipul exhaled deeply. "I simply need someone to tell me what to do and I can do it."

Brynhildr's gaze lost its distant focus. "As Valkyrie, we serve drink to the Einherjar and pull the glorious from battle to join their ranks in Valhalla."

"But how do I know?" The words were quiet, questioning themselves. "How do I know who is deserving of Valhalla?"

Brynhildr's helmet cocked to one side. "I suspect it is different for every one of us." She looked across the sea of Einherjar. "I take the warriors who lead the charge into battle. Their bravery shows their passion for the fight and their willingness to draw their blades, come Ragnarök."

Svipul turned the words over in her mind. Is passion what makes a warrior? She recalled her own position in the center of the formation, crudely exposed after the enemy pierced through the front guard. "I don't know that—"

"Hah!" Giant hands clapped the shoulders of Svipul and Brynhildr, a towering Valkyrie adorned in rusted, well-worn armor looming over them. "Brynhildr, you truly take the first to die?" Dark eyes peered down at Svipul. "You want to know who to really take from the fields of battle?

Shrugging the hand off her shoulder, Brynhildr retorted, "Hjalmþrimul, should she really be heeding the advice of one who has never taken any?"

Disregarding Brynhildr, the massive Valkyrie continued, "It is an easy choice. Take the strongest."

Svipul responded seriously, "And what makes someone the strongest?"

"This new one thinks too much." Hjalmþrimul gestured widely. "Ours is a work in service. Simple, but important. Fill horns with mead. Pull warriors from battle. Stock the Allfather's army for Ragnarök." She regarded Svipul squarely. "You seek advice? Take the warriors who kill the most."

Before Svipul had time to consider Hjalmþrimul's words, a slight figure draped in an elegant weave of mail interposed herself between the two of them. "That is enough, I believe she understands your position."

Hjalmþrimul put her hands up and stepped slowly backwards. "Well, then I am glad to have solved her problem."

The silver Valkyrie turned to Svipul. "I am sorry for Hjalmþrimul's…frank speech. While brash, she is an excellent Valkyrie, and a warrior I would gladly ride through the twilight of Ragnarök with." She presented a set of intricately interlaced mail armor. "I am Eir, and this is for you."

Svipul hesitantly took the gleaming byrnie in her hands. "Thank you, I am Svipul." She hefted the linked chains. "I must admit, I do not know that I am worthy of such a gift."

Eir's cool eyes radiated warmth, and a patient smile subtly curled on her lips. "Then I suppose it is a gift you must become worthy of. Having already met Brynhildr," she gave the golden Valkyrie a nod, "I am sure that you are well on your way to becoming the Valkyrie you are meant to be."

Svipul's heart swelled at the Valkyrie's words, but the gnawing hole remained. "Eir, what makes a warrior worthy of Valhalla?"

"I do not know that you will find any more wisdom in my words than from the other Valkyries of our realm," Svipul's eyes pleaded, and Eir continued, "but I ascend with the fallen who most deftly defended their comrades. If we are to stave off the specter of Ragnarök, we require a shield."

"Thank you Eir, for your guidance," Svipul lifted her new hauberk in the direction of Hjalmþrimul, "and your protection." Eir's smile returned and she took her leave, tending to a company of Einherjar. Brynhildr stepped away as well, arms filled with horns of mead.

As alone as one could be in Odin's hall, Svipul finally had a moment to think. As much as Hjalmþrimul's bluntness nettled her, she could not easily reject the counsel offered. In cultivating the Einherjar, the value of battle prowess was self-evident. Svipul's thoughts drifted back to her combat troop, to the few veterans of war in her company. They all seemed broken in some way, somber and haunted or glib and volatile. Some did not recognize themselves without an axe in hand and others cursed the armaments they owed their lives to. The mighty may be an asset to the Einherjar, but were they the ones deserving of Valhalla? Her judgement meant not only the salvation of the chosen, but the condemnation of the souls left to the battlefield. It was not a decision to be made lightly.

In considering the souls that may be worthy of Valhalla, Svipul found herself contemplating Eir's ascendance of the warriors that safeguarded their allies. For a peaceful instant, she could imagine her father and brothers embraced in Eir's arms, destined for Asgard. Indeed, these were men deserving of Valhalla, but were they fit to be Einherjar? Freshly killed on the field of battle, Svipul understood how necessary strength and offense were to victory. Disarmed and mortally wounded, she recalled her own helplessness – until those eyes, those words. Svipul longed to return to that blessed moment, to leave behind her tangled ruminations; being lifted up from the mortal realm, she had felt weightless, perfect. It was a sensation she wished all that died in battle could experience. And yet they could not.

Out of the corner of Svipul's eye, she caught the movement of a shadow shouldering its way past the masses of Einherjar. She turned and beheld a Valkyrie wrapped in dark, padded furs with various knives strapped across their body. The Valkyrie's voice rang deeply, "Svipul, I am Hervör alvitr. I was told of your quandary by Brynhildr."

Svipul mustered a tired smile. "It is good to meet you Hervör alvitr, but I fear that my issues may not easily be resolved with more of the Valkyries' wisdom."

"That is what I have come to discuss. While we have experience as Valkyries, the truth is that your plight differs greatly from our own." Svipul's brow furrowed. "We have simply always…been. To us, the saving of souls has long been a function of our identities, not a choice to be consciously made."

"Then who could help me make that choice?"

Hervör alvitr, lips pursed, paused to weigh options. "While you may wish to speak to our queen, Lady Freyja, few have the power to travel to her realm. You would have better hope of obtaining an audience with Odin."

Impulsively, Svipul blurted, "The Allfather would receive me?"

"Receive? Yes. Regard? That is more difficult to answer."

"Then, where do I find him?"

"Ascend to the height of Asgard. There, you will find Odin's quarters. And remember to temper your expectations, my kin. Your answers may not lie beyond yourself." After a moment's hesitation, Hervör alvitr finished, "However, I hope you find what you journey for." Svipul nodded solemnly to the Valkyrie in black, and Hervör alvitr melted back into the crowd of Einherjar.

Svipul donned Eir's armor; the chains of mail weighed heavy on her shoulders. Feet rising from the ground, her flight felt more controlled, more within her power. She soared from the grand gates of Valhalla and made her way skyward. As Svipul ascended, the realm of Asgard spread open before her, golden light illuminating the deeply lush green of forests and the unthinkably vast towers of the Aesir city, all somehow dwarfed by a lone, jagged peak, thrust cruelly through the sky of the heavens. Her destination clear, Svipul willed herself ever upward, cresting braids of flaxen clouds as the summit of that grim slate mountain fast approached.

Emerging from the increasingly ashen and blustering haze accompanying Asgard's upper reaches, Svipul beheld a humble oak chamber hall built atop the plateau marking the pinnacle of the realm. Alighting near the entryway, the building was not unlike the communal hall Svipul was accustomed to visiting in the neighboring settlement to her village. Meekly, she knocked on the door and it swung open. At the head of the hall, a figure wizened with age sat on a wooden throne, leaning forward on one hand, already gazing towards his guest. The man was wrapped in a loose, ancient cloak, making it impossible to know the bulk of his body. One eye was the turbulent gray of the storm, the other, a yawning, murky void.

Svipul took to one knee and turned her gaze downward. She pronounced, "Allfather, I am a new Valkyrie brought from the mortal realm. I request your insight." Desperation tinged her words. "Why am I here? What do you seek in the Einherjar? How am I to serve you?"

The silhouette of the figure remained motionless, but a voice, at once hollow and choral, resounded, "You are new, you say?" Odin's gaze was steely. "When burdened with knowledge, nothing is ever new. Simply sooner than desired." He sighed deeply, wind whistling over the desolate peak. "Always sooner."

"Allfather, if you know of me, then—"

"I need no knowledge of you." His response was flat, uninterested. "The Valkyries do my bidding, but they are not my responsibility."

Svipul's left eye twitched. "I only wish to—"

"Yes, you only wish to serve. Very well. You asked me what I seek in the Einherjar?" The gale whirling about the mountaintop abated for a brief moment. "I seek more of them."

In spite of herself, Svipul's head snapped up to look at Odin. "Allfather, I simply—"

"Passion, strength, protection, cleverness, they mean little to me. Irrespective of design, the mightiest shields are the thickest." A cutting edge accompanied his words. "And a mighty shield is what I require for the coming of Ragnarök."

Svipul found herself studying the floor once again. Her hands shook. Every word from Odin pulled that cavernous hole buried in her heart farther open, a confirmation of her weakness and ineptitude as a Valkyrie. That battlefield loomed in her mind, the blank gawping of the countless corpses she had left behind, unable to fulfill her responsibility. "Then, Allfather, I would ask that I be returned to the mortal realm. I am not fit to be a Valkyrie as you require."

The sound of faraway thunder, the layered voices rumbled darkly. "I grant you an audience and share my wisdom, yet you would ask me for a boon and abandon your duties?" The slumped form shifted, sitting straighter. "What *is* your name? The impudence of my vassals will not go unanswered."

Whatever fate the Allfather decreed would surely be a just and proper punishment; indeed, to think she could be a Valkyrie was the greatest impertinence Svipul could imagine. She felt a strange relief as her responsibility began to lift. "I am Svipul, my lord."

Suddenly, the Allfather's voice fractured into individual, frenzied, chiming components.

"The seeress did not mention the name Svipul in enumerating the legion of Valkyrie."

"Somehow, this Valkyrie exists apart from the prophecy of Ragnarök."

"What does it mean?"

"Has fate turned?"

"We know too little, always too little."

"We know much, but we did not know this."

"Can destiny be guided?"

"What is to be done about her?"

The clamoring voices ceased. No longer stupefied into inaction, Svipul turned her gaze glacially upward to find Odin standing at his throne, eye wide and tempestuous. Now whole again, the Allfather's chorus resounded. "Svipul, you truly are new. I regret my callous regard of your earlier requests. However, I cannot honor your final demand." Svipul's eyes narrowed. "You must stay and attend to your duties as a Valkyrie, although you have my blessing to pursue that obligation as you find best. To that end, I offer you a boon within my power to provide."

Svipul rose slowly from the ground, that familiar weight returned to her shoulders. Beyond the depression in her core yawning ever larger, nothing had truly changed from her exchange with Odin; her duty and the internal strife it brought remained. She could only think of one other being who might hold the answers she sought. "If it is within your power to grant, I would have an audience with Lady Freyja." In the king of Asgard's generally impassive countenance, Svipul caught a flicker of discomfort.

Nevertheless, Odin lifted a palm to the air. "Very well." Calling upon an ancient magic, a pulsing, violent rift opened at the Allfather's fingertips and he motioned towards the portal. "Freyja awaits." Svipul cautiously approached. As she crossed the threshold, Odin's voice called after her. "My favor is yours from this point on, I will be following your journey with interest." Within the gateway, the world hummed with a rattling, pounding energy, and when the chaos grew to its zenith, all fell silent.

A floral scent washed over Svipul, her mail gently clinking in the breeze. She found herself on a verdant meadow spilling vivaciously into the distance. The scene was engulfed in the pure light of dawn, making the splendorous gold of Valhalla feel hollow and lacking by comparison. A voice, warm as Svipul's surroundings, rang out: "Welcome to Fólkvangr. It must have taken some effort to find your way here."

Consumed with the landscape in front of her, Svipul could not bring herself to turn towards the speaker. She called back, awe coating her words, "What is this place?"

"This is my domain. The battle-slain not taken to Valhalla join me here."

Tears spilled from Svipul's eyes even before her knees hit the ground. She pictured that desolate battlefield blessedly empty of the dead, free of those accusing stares. Between heaving gasps and choking sobs, Svipul blubbered, "So they all found rest?"

Soft hands were placed on her shoulders. "They always do."

Pushing aside tears with her palms, then her wrists, Svipul weakly mustered, "Thank you. This alone has been worth the journey." The void shrank, but did not dissipate.

"I am glad to have been of some comfort."

With a final exhale, Svipul composed herself and knelt before the goddess. "Lady Freyja, I must know, why was I made a Valkyrie? Who am I to make Einherjar?"

"Svipul," Freyja's tone was patient, but hesitant, "you must know, I had no grand plans for you as a Valkyrie. I was simply answering a prayer." Svipul looked up at the goddess in confusion, then recoiled in shock. Freyja's eyes glittered with understanding and care, but they were altogether unfamiliar. "The warrior who mortally wounded you in battle desired for

Valhalla to be your fate." Standing over Svipul at her dying breath, those eyes glittered with pity and…guilt. *Let Valhalla's gates open and bring you peace*. Those words were a wish, not a decree. "That decision made you a Valkyrie, but the path you choose now is your own."

Svipul looked at her hands. She was destined for the field of Fólkvangr, but became a Valkyrie by the words of the very warrior that killed her. Shakily, she rose to her feet. She spotted two tiny figures waving at her in the distance. The choice remained; what kind of Valkyrie would she be? Svipul waved back to the distant outlines. The purpose of the Einherjar was to avert the destruction of the nine realms. Who would make that possible? The two figures dropped out of view, finding a peaceful spot to rest in the grass. Perhaps the prevention of Ragnarök required a new type of warrior: a kind not simply devoted to destruction. To save every realm, perhaps the Einherjar were in need of soldiers who sought to save every soul. Svipul felt the chasm in her chest finally begin to close. "Thank you Lady Freyja, I believe I am ready to serve my purpose as a Valkyrie." Scarcely feeling the weight of her chains, Svipul took to the sky.

* * *

Dagný's increasingly shallow breaths stuttered as he choked on his own oozing blood. At long last, death would come for him. How many had he made experience this same moment: the desperation of clinging to life already gone? How many had suffered by his hands? The last of his focus narrowed to a single point – to those familiar eyes. They radiated warmth and hope. "*Those you killed have found peace. Let Valhalla's gates open, that you may find yours.*" Then, embracing, lifting, flying, light as air, light as dawn.

The Battle of Weaver's Field

Don Bisdorf

Two shots cracked across the darkness of the hay field, and two men fell.

Mick Weaver had shot first. His brother had the barn insured, thc *family* barn, and Mick figured half of that insurance money was his by right. But he knew Josh would complain, and Josh would whine, and Mick was *done* with that. He'd brought his automatic, a weapon he liked to pose with in front of the mirror. He liked to watch himself casually tuck it into the back of his pants, and draw it with the same "I kill men with this every day" ease. He liked to practice racking the slide, ejecting a round and catching it in the air. And he liked to aim it on its side, held flat, palm down, like the tough guys on Netflix did. That was how he'd shot Josh: a lazy draw from the back of his pants, aim flat and squeeze the trigger. The *pop* had lit up Josh like a camera flash, snapping a freeze-frame of Josh's surprise, his baseball cap, his denim overalls, his old shotgun, and the bullet hole, dead center in the chest. Pride had leapt in Mick's throat – *damn*, no one had been around to see it – in the split-second before Josh's shotgun tore off the right side of his face.

Josh had hesitated on the trigger for two reasons. First, he suspected that this whole thing was another of his brother's tricks.

Maybe Mick had staged the whole argument, with a bulletproof vest under his shirt, and cops hiding behind the hay bales, waiting to arrest Josh for attempted murder. Second, he wasn't even sure the shotgun would fire. His grandfather had killed a bear with it; his father had blasted dozens of squirrels and Uncle Art's rear windshield; Josh himself hadn't touched it in the ten years since his father died. It had slept in a closet with a box of shells, and he'd brought it out to the hay field in the middle of the night to prove to Mick that he was serious this time. After the hammer blow of Mick's shot had startled him into pulling the trigger, he'd hung onto consciousness just long enough to see what the shotgun blast did to his brother, and he figured that Mick knew, at the end, that Josh had indeed been serious.

Both men lay in the moonlit hay field for a few long minutes before they were prepared to admit that they weren't dead.

Gingerly, Josh felt his chest, searching for a bullet hole, or even blood, and finding nothing but denim. There had been pain when the bullet hit – oh yes, absolutely – but now he felt only a chill from the grassy earth beneath him. He found it easy to sit up, to breathe, to listen to the peep of the distant tree frogs, to look over and see his brother also sitting in the newly sheared grass, staring back at him.

"What," Mick said, "the *fuck.*"

Josh struggled with a reply until he noticed they weren't alone. Someone else stood nearby, leaning back against the big ragged wheel of a hay bale. She had fair skin and pale blonde hair in a braid down her back. Her black t-shirt bore the logo of some heavy metal band, all scratchy lines and umlauts. She wore dark jeans with ripped knees and sturdy boots, and an unlabeled bottle dangled from her hand.

Shaking her head, she gave an amused little huff and raised the bottle to her lips, tipping it back for a deep pull.

Mick's usual instincts towards a pretty blond sputtered out in the face of the fact that *he'd shot his brother in the chest* and now, there Josh sat, blinking and breathing. (Something wanted to remind him that half of his own head should be missing, but he pushed that thought as far away as he could.) "Who the hell are you?" he snarled.

She wiped her mouth on the back of her wrist. "Herja," she said, an unfamiliar accent bending her vowels. "And it's not a pleasure to meet you. This is not the *worst* duel I've ever seen, but it's in my top ten."

"It wasn't a duel," Josh said.

"Shut the fuck up," Mick told him, because as usual, Josh wasn't paying attention to the important thing. "Are you supposed to be an angel?"

"Valkyrie," Herja said. "But don't get your hopes up. Mead-halls in Valhalla have been packed full for a thousand years. Not that you two would qualify."

Josh's voice came out weak and pleading. "Can you maybe call us an ambulance? Because…I mean, we shot each other. Didn't we, Mick?"

"Shut the fuck *up*, Josh."

"You two *tried* to kill each other," the woman with the braid said. "That makes this a field of battle, so here I am. I get to decide who lives and who dies. But the two of you are so pathetic that I say *neither* of you wins. Go home and we can all forget about it. The sooner, the better."

Mick hauled himself upright. "Did you call me *pathetic?*"

Herja, in mid-drink, nodded before swallowing. "Look, why are the two of you here, now, tonight, with weapons? Love? Power? Revenge?"

"My barn," Josh said. "He burned it down."

He threw a wave toward a huddle of dark shapes at the far south end of the field. Daylight would have revealed them to be a white two-story farmhouse, four pickup trucks in various states of disassembly, two rusting tractors, and the blackened walls of a half-collapsed barn.

"I did *not,*" Mick snapped. "You didn't wire it up right when you set up all that hydroponics gear. All those power strips and extension cords. Just a matter of time before the whole thing went up in flames."

Now Josh crawled to his feet. "You think I don't know you've been sleeping in there, hiding out from your girlfriend, stealing my weed? You must have tripped over a wire, or passed out with a lit joint."

Mick turned to the strange woman, gesturing at his brother. "You hear this? He can't own up to his own mistakes. He's been whining his whole life, thirty-five fucking years, whining in my ear. I can't *take* it any more."

"*I'm* the one who has to clean up your mess all the time," Josh said. "I have to lie for you to the cops, cover your rent when you go bust at the casino. For two months now, Cherise has been banging on my door looking for you, yelling about the three thousand dollars you stole from her. Every time I start getting ahead, you screw up and drag me down with you."

"Like I said," Herja put in. "Pathetic."

Mick took an angry step toward her.

Suddenly her free hand gripped a spear, taller than she was, its blade a foot long and aimed at Mick. Until now he'd only seen spears in martial arts movies, and Herja's wasn't as pretty or elegant as those. It looked *used*, its shaft ragged, its edge chipped. This was a spear that had killed.

Not to mention that she'd pulled it out of the air, like a damn magic trick.

He stumbled back. "You really are," he breathed. "You're a motherfucking *Valkyrie.*"

"A what?" Josh asked.

"You know. Like from that song."

"What song?"

"The *song*, from *Apocalypse Now*, where all the helicopters come in. Da dahh da da *dahhh* da..."

Herja grounded the butt of the spear and leaned on it. "I should have slept through this century."

"No, wait." Mick knew that there was always an angle, and the important thing was to keep talking until you found it. "If you're a Valkyrie...then you don't get to...you're just supposed to carry us off to..."

The woman shook her head. "First of all, like I said, Valhalla's full up. Second of all, yes, I *do* get to. Odin made us the choosers of the slain, so here I am, choosing to tell you that this didn't happen."

"That's not how it works! I read it in...in..."

"If you say the Thor comics, I really will stab you."

Josh got louder, more confident. "If you're supposed to choose who wins, you should choose *me. He's* been cheating and stealing and lying all his life." He scowled at his brother. "Ever since eighth grade, when you were stealing beer from the gas station. And Darla caught you at it, but you said she had to keep quiet or you'd tell her folks she'd been screwing Randy."

Mick barked a laugh. "Like you're some model citizen. After screwing up and getting nowhere your whole life, Dad leaves you the farm, leaves it to *you*, for God's sake, not me, and what do you do with it? You're sure as hell not farming."

"What do you call this?" Josh pointed at the hay bales.

"This wasn't you. Jamie McGinnis gave you a hundred bucks so he could cut grass for his cows."

"How about my hydroponics tanks in the barn? The barn you *burned down.*"

"You were just growing weed in those tanks, Josh, and you were losing money on *that*. No one wants to buy from you when they can pick up a bag of Emerald Dreams and a bottle of gummies from the dispensary. You're just selling what you can to the high school kids."

"Says Mister High Finance. You're the one who stole money from his girlfriend so you could make good on the money you lost in that, what was it, that NFT scam? And the NFTs were supposed to pay back…"

"You two don't need me for this." Herja picked up her spear, strode over to Josh and thrust her bottle into his hands. "Get drunk. Call each other names until you pass out. I have better places to be."

With that, she started to walk away.

Mick stared after her. Then he stomped over to his brother, who flinched, but Mick only snatched the bottle away. He took a sip, choked, spat it out. "What the hell is this?"

"Mead," the Valkyrie called back. "Keep it. Consolation prize."

For a brief moment, Mick was ready to leave well enough alone. Of all the lucky breaks that had saved him from a sorry end, time after time, this was on a whole different level. His brother had shot him dead – the closed-coffin kind of dead – and an honest-to-Jesus Valkyrie had swooped down and put him right again.

But she had been kind of an asshole about it.

And, as always, the feeble ember that was Mick's sense of self-preservation died under his certainty that he was *owed* something.

He shoved the bottle back at Josh. "If you really are a Valkyrie," he told Herja, "then you *don't* have better places to be."

Herja paused.

"You know what war is like now. It's all drones and IEDs and missiles exploding other missiles. It's not…it's not war like *you* used to see, where men stood toe to toe with the enemy, close enough to see them die. They weren't fighting so some military contractor could get rich, or some politician could make the newspapers forget about their sex scandal. They fought for themselves. They were *warriors*."

Mick pointed to his brother. "That's *us*. We chose this, eyes open, guns out. We deserve you better than *anyone* in this fucked-up world."

Herja half-turned to face him. "You *want* me to let you die?"

"I want you to admit that this was a…you know. An *honorable battle.* Then you can go off and snatch some suicide bomber for all I care."

At first she didn't reply. Then she turned around and marched back toward him, and something in the way she carried her spear told him she wasn't bringing an apology. He scrambled in the grass for his pistol, but by the time he had it in his hands, right side around, Herja had already stopped in front of him, with something fierce in her eyes.

Her words hissed out through clenched teeth. "You don't know a damned thing. War has *always* been like this. It's always been about vanity and greed and stupid arguments that could have been settled a hundred other ways. It doesn't matter whether it's a knife or a nuke. You people just like to slaughter each other and you dress it up like some kind of profound human experience."

"But…"

"I know, this is my *job*. My sisters and I, we're supposed to choose who stands and who falls. We are the referees of the worst possible game. So trust my professional opinion when I tell you that there's no *honor* in war. It's just blood and pain."

Josh knew he should keep quiet, but the words jumped out. "You choose wrong, though."

She turned that awful gaze on him. "What?"

"You choose *wrong*, sometimes. The people who die in war. Innocent people. Kids."

"You think you could make better choices," she declared. "You don't like who we take from the battlefield."

"Uh..."

"*Good.*"

Distantly, thunder rumbled in the dark.

"If you want everything fair and just," Herja told them, "do it *yourself*. If you have a problem, figure it out. If you have an argument, settle it. Because when you start a war, you don't get to decide who dies, who suffers, who bleeds. *We* do. If you don't like it, then make it right before you bring us down.

"Or we will make it *hurt*."

The second stroke of thunder went off right on top of them, with a blaze that lit up the sky from horizon to horizon. The flare revealed a ring of colossal shapes surrounding the field, tall as skyscrapers, as mountains – silhouettes of titanic figures with cloaks and spears. One blink of white fire, and then the terrible shapes vanished into darkness.

Josh rubbed the memory of lightning from his eyes. When he could see again, Herja was gone. Only he and his brother stood amid the rolled-up hay.

Mick looked at him, and he looked back, and tried to think of what to say. Josh didn't know what to do with...had it been a religious experience? Some kind of Viking miracle?

A miracle who no longer stood between Josh and Mick. And Mick had his pistol in his hand, and Josh only had a mostly empty bottle.

Josh tried not to look too hard at the pistol. "Mick..."

"The mead," Mick grunted, hoarse.

"The...what?"

"The *mead*. Don't you get it? She gave us a...a *sign*. We don't need the hydroponics." Mick pointed at Josh, at the bottle. "We can brew *that* stuff."

Much as Josh was relieved that his brother hadn't decided to find out whether Josh would stay dead this time, he didn't like how the weed tanks had retroactively become a "we" thing. "Mick..."

"Listen to me. We take the insurance money from the barn, buy some distilling gear. We can sell to the rich tourists up at the lake. Tell them it's artisanal and traditionally brewed and all that bullshit."

"I'm not going to..."

"Josh, a Valkyrie came down from heaven – or Valhalla or wherever – and *spoke* to us. It's *divine fucking intervention*. You'd have to be a goddamn idiot..."

"Mick!"

Josh pointed toward the road. When Mick turned, he saw a familiar pair of headlights approaching the farmhouse. He recognized the bass grumble of a well-cared-for '69 Jeep Gladiator.

"Isn't that Cherise?" Josh asked, but Mick had already turned his back to the road and started running, through the bales of hay, toward the high grass and the trees beyond.

Much as Josh enjoyed getting the last word, for once, he knew Mick would be back. Sooner or later his brother would turn up with a scheme or an excuse, or just to crow at Josh's latest screw-up. Sooner or later they'd be yelling at each other again, throwing beer cans and digging up all the old grudges. And sooner or later...

His toe bumped the shotgun.

He crouched in the grass, set down the bottle, and picked up the weapon. When he broke open the barrel, a whiff of gunpowder stung his nose. And when he plucked out the shell, there was no denying that it had been fired.

Mick had been right. It had been a sign.

He couldn't do anything about world peace. But he figured that between the barn insurance and whatever the farm was worth, he could put together enough money to get far away from Mick Weaver.

Strike of the Valkyries

Kay Hanifen

"Another!" a warrior called, throwing his tankard of ale on the ground. He was a long-dead fighter who died heroically in a war no one is alive now to remember, his name and face forgotten to history, but rewarded in the halls of Valhalla. With a sigh, I picked up the tankard and filled it with more of our finest mead. As thanks, he cupped my ass and tried to pull me into his lap. I jerked from his grip. The gall of some warriors.

"Alvitr, give me a hand?" Eir called as she carried out the prize from today's hunt. The wild boar was a favorite of the dead men, but the size and the toughness of the meat made it a pain to carve and serve. Even better, ravens swooped down, swarming us and sometimes tangling in our hair as they attempted to steal bits and pieces from dinner and with our hands full, the men took every advantage to grope us as we brought it in. I hurried over to her, nearly tripping over a broken spear (why did Odin include those in the interior design again?) and taking on some of the burden of the boar while the pigs all around me tried to grab my ass.

I was a goddess, a divinity, but as warriors stopped praying to us in favor of other, newer gods, our sacred duties had been reduced to becoming glorified barmaids. The occupants of Valhalla had forgotten that they were only here because we allowed them to come. They had forgotten to give us the respect we were owed.

"We are nothing but glorified servants to them," I said to my fellow Valkyrie, Hildr, as we cleaned up the remnants of today's meal while the warriors were off testing one another in combat for the day, entertaining themselves like little boys playing swordfight with wooden sticks. The halls were a mess after every meal, chunks of flesh and vegetables on the ground and dried mead making the tables sticky. "Are you not sick of this?"

Hildr laughed. "I thought I was the only one."

"I doubt that," I replied, wiping down a table. "I'm sure we've all grown weary of these pigs."

"What do you recommend we do?" she asked, glancing around mischievously.

Admittedly, I hadn't gotten that far yet. "How has the human world handled this kind of thing?"

She shrugged. "I suppose we can look in on them. It's been a while since we've gone to Midgard. It was peasant uprisings mostly – killing the jarls who failed to properly care for their people – but that won't work for the dead."

I hummed thoughtfully. "It's been so long since we've been called upon that I have no idea what humanity has been up to. Perhaps they found a more relevant strategy since then."

It didn't take long to convince the rest of the Valkyries that something needed to be done. We were all tired of these drunken men, their wandering hands, and this utterly thankless job. Once everyone was agreed, we decided that a journey to Midgard was in order to explore how the humans had handled situations such as this.

Times certainly had changed. When we left Valhalla, we were drawn to a continent we only knew from the slurred accounts by Leif Erikson as he muttered into his ale about being one of the greatest explorers in history. There was a battle waging there, one that felt familiar to us.

Since Erikson's time, the strange continent had transformed. The world was full of strange machinery and weapons far deadlier than any of our people's wildest dreams. The year was now 1921, and the site of a future battle was in a place called Blair Mountain. Thousands of armed villagers stood against an army of soldiers, all over something called unions and strikebreakers.

"What are strikebreakers?" I asked an old woman dressed in black. Some of the men around her had referred to her as Mother Jones.

She reminded me of the Norns, making her presence oddly comforting. Though there was worry in her eyes, she smiled when she replied, "Where have you been, child? Is today your first day on earth?" Her accent was different than the others there, lighter and lilting.

"First in a long time," I replied.

She gave me an odd look at that but seemed uninterested in pursuing it further. "Well, the short version of it is that my boys are on strike, so the coal companies brought in soldiers and strikebreakers to work in the mines instead."

"Strike?" I repeated.

Her brows furrowed in confusion. "You truly have been living under a rock, haven't you?"

"What is a strike?" I repeated, growing impatient.

"They refuse to work until their demands for better pay and treatment are met. Honestly, my dear, how have you not heard about this?"

I felt the words like a seed germinating within me, an idea growing and preparing to bloom. "And striking works?"

"Sometimes. Sometimes it ends in disaster, but it's still the best tool of the working class. You are the ones doing the labor, and therefore the ones with the power. The greatest trick they ever pulled was getting people to forget this fact. Those fat cats cannot get fatter if the mice refuse to work."

A grin spread across my face. "We may not meet in Valhalla, but you, Mother Jones, are a true warrior."

She raised her brows at that, but before she could respond, I was gone, the rest of the Valkyries joining me in Valhalla to devise our strategy and list of demands.

For days, we planned and debated as the men left for their daily battles and hunts. In short order, we had a letter to submit to Odin:

Dear Odin All-Father, Lord of the Aesir, Raven God, etc.,

We of the Valkyries have grown tired of our treatment at the grabbing hands of the dead in feasting in Valhalla. We were once sacred and holy, and now are treated as common barmaids. This ends now. These are our demands. If they are ignored, we will cease all work.

No more unsolicited groping in the halls of Valhalla.

You will give us permission to amputate the digits of anyone who touches us without permission. We know that our weapons will leave permanent wounds on the dead, but we do not care. This will be an effective deterrent.

The men must clean up after themselves to the best of their ability.

The men must express proper gratitude to us as goddesses in our own right.

The ground will be cleared of tripping hazards such as broken spears, axes, and shields. We don't care if you want the aesthetic to hearken back to the aftermath of battle. We have spilled mead and food, leading to irate warrior spirits.

You will control your ravens and ban them from swooping at us as we set out the dishes.

We will be allowed two days off a week for our own revels, preferably Frigg's Day and Laugardagr.

We thank you for your cooperation in this matter.

The Valkyries

Once the letter was completed, we tied it to one of Odin's ravens and sent it to him. The tension among us was thick and electric as Thor's lightning as we awaited his response.

After a full day of getting groped by ungrateful men, we finally received a reply. One of his ravens landed before me with a letter tied to his leg. As soon as the men were off for their daily play fights, I gathered the rest of the Valkyries and stood before them.

"We have received the All-Father's response," I announced, and then began to read.

Valkyries

What in the Nine Realms are you on about? Do your duties. The All-Father commands it.

"Well," I said when I had finished reading, "I suppose that is that. It seems that Odin too has forgotten that we are goddesses deserving of respect. So, let us teach him along with the other denizens of Valhalla. Are we all in agreement?"

I scanned the crowd of women. We had little to lose and much to gain from temporarily forsaking our duties. Just long enough for the men to get hungry and tired of doing everything for themselves.

"We are," Eir said, a mischievous smile growing on her lovely face. "We should ask Heidrun if she would like to join us in the strike. The old goat must be growing tired of being thanklessly milked for her mead every day."

We found her in her usual spot munching on the leaves of Yggdrasil, her udders heavy with mead and waiting to be milked. Eir was the one to explain our plans to her.

"Hmm," the goat hummed, still masticating on some leaves. "I must eat, and I must be milked, but perhaps a compromise can be reached. You will continue to milk me, and I will refuse to give

Odin or any other inhabitant of Valhalla my ale. You Valkyries, of course, may drink however much you like."

We exchanged glances and nods. No one seemed opposed, so Eir said, "We accept your proposal and look forward to partaking in your mead. If I am being honest, I have not partaken in so long that I rather have forgotten what it tastes like."

Heidrun gave a bleating chuckle. "Well, milk me now and enjoy your strike. May you emerge victorious."

"Well, you heard the goat," I said. "Find us a bucket. It's time to party."

Hildr milked her as Sveidr, our resident musician, pulled out her fiddle and began to play a lively tune. Soon, we were all drinking and dancing, having more fun that we'd had in centuries. The mead filled our hearts and bellies with warmth, and one of us went to the kitchen and brought back the wild boar we'd put on a spit for dinner.

We tore into the creature's flesh without utensils, eating with our fingers in primal ecstasy. When was the last time I had eaten for pleasure or danced or sang? The revel was a welcome break from servitude, so naturally, it did not last nearly long enough.

"There they are!" one of the hallowed dead exclaimed, pointing a finger. A mob of men formed behind him, all looking hungry and irritable. "Where is our dinner?"

"We won't be serving it tonight," I said. "We will not be serving the halls of Valhalla until our demands are met. You may take up your complaints with the All-Father."

"You cannot abandon your duties like that!" another man whined.

Hildr grinned and rested her elbow on my shoulder. "Watch us."

"We will force you to submit to us," the first man said.

We all exchanged glances at that and then burst out laughing. Did these men truly believe that they could take a Valkyrie in a fight? The gall of some mortals never ceased to amaze me.

"You can certainly try," I said, nodding to our archers. Their eyes lit up with my meaning as they drew their bows and arrows. "But it would be far more pleasant for you if you simply took your complaints to the All-Father. We do not ask for much."

"You will be punished for this!" another voice yelled out.

"And you forget that you're only here because we bore you here." With a gesture, our archers unleashed a volley of arrows, drawing and loosing them so quickly that the sky above us briefly went black with their shadows.

And, chastened like the dogs they are, the souls of Valhalla turned and ran with their tails between their legs. In our drunken state, it was one of the funniest things we'd ever seen, and we spent the night imitating them and breaking down in fits of laughter.

The next several days were spent in this drunken revelry. We ate the food and drank the mead intended for the warriors who grew more and more irritated with our antics by the day. But what could they do? We were goddesses and warriors. Any who tried to challenge us wound up having to stitch themselves back together.

Odin found us during one of our rest periods, his single eye twitching. Hugin and Munin shifted on his shoulders in obvious agitation. "Valkyries, what do you think you're doing?"

"Exactly as we warned you we would, All-Father," I replied, tipping my glass of mead at him. "Our demands were reasonable.

Agree to them and get the rest of the dead in these halls to do the same, and we will return to our sacred duties."

"Alvitr," he growled. "If I did not know better, I'd believe that Loki had escaped his bonds below the mountain to sow chaos."

"No, you're merely reaping the fruits of your own disrespect." I finished off my mead and grabbed an apple from the fruit basket, taking a loud bite. "We will not work unless you change things around here."

"You lazy, spoiled children!" The light around us dimmed in the darkness of Odin's fury. Some shifted anxiously, unnerved by his wrath. Admittedly, my heart too pounded in my chest, but we could not afford to back down. We were warriors. Yielding was not in our vocabulary. "I am your king, the Lord of the Aesir!" he shouted. "You will not defy me."

"Try us. We are as much warriors as your army of the dead. You know that better than anyone else."

A hand brushed my arm, and I glanced over to find Eir beside me. Her eyes were wide, warning me to tread carefully. I nodded my understanding.

"We do not intend to disrespect you, All-Father. We simply wish to be afforded the same reverence as the rest of the Aesir. Is that truly so burdensome a request?"

He crossed his arms, his birds puffing up as though attempting to do the same. "And how do you expect me to convince the drunken souls of Valhalla to change their ways after millennia? What do you expect me to do for the two days a week you are given your break?"

"You're the All-Father," I snapped. "Do not act so helpless. They love and fear you in equal measure. All you have to do is raise your voice at them and they will cease their behavior. And as for the two days off, I am sure you can figure something out. Send them on a hunt for a Blahaj or a Djungelskog."

"What are those?" he asked, furrowing his grey brows.

"Entirely made-up creatures. You're as much a trickster as Loki. Send them on wild goose chases on those days."

"And you have the same regard for duty as he. I grow tired of this conversation. You will end this foolish tantrum at once or you will face consequences." With that, he vanished in a puff of smoke and raven's feathers.

We were all silent for a moment, utterly stunned. Then Hildr began to giggle. The rest joined in one by one until we were all doubled over with laughter.

The All-Father did seem to take one thing I said to heart. He was as much a trickster as Loki, so it should have come as no surprise when our drunken revels became more akin to drunken brawls, women fighting over who might have cheated on whom and whether or not that spilled drink was intentional. It was all over petty concerns, but the sudden discord was suspicious.

I forced myself to sober up, willing the alcohol from my system and watching the revels with fresh eyes. Valkyries drank, danced, and brawled while Heidrun ate, flicking her ear at a fly buzzing around it. At first, it barely registered, but as the night wore on, the little insect nagged at me. It struck me when I spotted it buzzing between Hrist and Brunnhilde just before they broke into a fight.

When had there ever been a fly in the halls of Valhalla?

In all my time here, I couldn't remember when I had ever seen an insect buzzing about. Finishing my tankard, I watched it, stalking it with my gaze as it flitted around us. It was keeping its distance from me in a way that felt almost conscientious. Taking my tankard and my shield, I moved carefully between the dancers and the fighters, keeping the insect in my sight. Once I was close enough, my arms shot out, and I trapped it in the cup with my shield, nearly hitting Hrist in the process.

"What was that for?" my sister Valkyrie demanded, her voice high at the surprise.

"Loki," I said, "I know it's you in there. Reveal yourself and I will not squish you."

Suddenly, there was a weight in my arms as Loki transformed back to his preferred form. I dropped him with a disgusted sneer. "Odin put you up to this, no doubt."

Loki rubbed his back where he had landed on the floor before getting to his feet. "Believe me when I say I like this as much as you do. But better to be causing mischief with some Valkyries than chained with your own child's intestines below a mountain."

"You like this as much as we do?" I repeated.

He grinned wolfishly. "You've caused more chaos in the halls of Valhalla than I could have ever dreamt of. I'm impressed. Unfortunately, my freedom is dependent on sowing discord among you lot. So how about you go back to neglecting your duties so that I can go back to fulfilling mine?"

I bit my lip thoughtfully. "Or, have you considered getting a bit of revenge on the All-Father for your predicament?"

He arched a fiery red eyebrow. "I'm listening."

"Continue causing minor mischief here, and whenever we pretend to break out into a fight, you go and agitate the other souls in Valhalla. Sabotage their armor, put caltrops in chairs, and do everything you can to make them put pressure on the All-Father to give in to our demands."

"And what do I get in return?" he asked.

"We will add your conditional freedom to our list of demands," Eir said, making everyone look at her in surprise.

"Are you sure that is wise?" Hildr hissed.

Eir nodded. "The world has stopped believing in us. We all can feel it. Loki is no longer as powerful as he once was. None of the Aesir are. Besides, I believe he has learned his lesson."

"Oh certainly," Loki replied, just a little too eagerly for my taste. "I will gladly help you ladies out."

Eir looked to me. "Well, shall we send the All-Father an update to our list of demands?"

I grinned. "Certainly, my lady." After a short hunt for a pen and some paper, I wrote this:

> *Dear Odin All-Father, Lord of the Aesir, Raven God, etc.,*
>
> *We of the Valkyries have added to our list of demands. We now require that Loki's freedom be permanent. He must no longer be bound below the mountain and Sigyn must no longer be bound beside him.*
>
> *With Respect,*
The Valkyries

Loki himself transformed into a raven to drop off the letter, much to our collective amusement. Odin's response came a few hours later.

> *Valkyries,*
>
> *Surely you cannot be serious. Why would you concern yourself with a traitor imprisoned under a faraway mountain? Return to your duties or face the consequences of your actions.*

Playing dumb was not a good look on the wise All-Father, especially when Loki escalated his tricks and pranks among the human souls in Valhalla. Between the maggots in the food, the crumbling tables, and the weapons breaking at inopportune moments during combat and hunts, the dead warriors seemed to be on the verge of a riot. Odin seemed to be feeling the pressure, cajoling and threatening us almost daily.

It all came to a head when the great human hero Sigurd approached with the men of Valhalla. He bowed before us. "My ladies, we have done you wrong, and we recognize this. How might we put this to right so that we can return to normal?

"Normal," I repeated. "What does normal look like to you?"

He blinked, a flush rising on his cheeks. "My ladies?"

"Tell me what you consider to be normal?"

"You serving us food and drink," he replied uncertainly, like a child knowing they were giving a teacher an incorrect answer to a question but unable to think of anything else.

"And cleaning up after you, and being groped, and tripping over discarded weapons, and working day in and day out without so much as a thank you," I retorted. "We have grown tired of your disrespect, and we will not resume work until changes are made."

"What changes, my ladies?" a voice called out from within the crowd.

"It is all rather reasonable. You will clean up after yourselves, show proper gratitude, not touch us without permission," Eir said. "We will receive two days off to enjoy as we please and can punish you for groping us with the permanent removal of a finger. The rest can only be granted by the All-Father."

"We accept these terms," Sigurd said. "And we will attempt to persuade the All-Father to do the same. After all, he needs his army for Ragnarok. Perhaps we will borrow your strategy and refuse to fight if he will not agree to your demands."

This sent the nearby ravens into a tizzy. They swooped and circled, flying in the shape of a ball before dissipating, revealing Odin. "Traitors! Disobedient curs! You dare undermine my authority?"

The army of souls immediately fell to their knees, earning a scoff from me. So much for standing up to the All-Father. "We beg your pardon," Sigurd said, the picture of deference. "But we are in agreement that this work-stop must cease. And the Valkyries have a point. We have failed to give them the proper respect they are owed, so we humbly ask that you accept their demands." There was a moment of awkward silence. Then he looked up sheepishly. "...Please? We're hungry and thirsty, with nothing to eat or drink in weeks."

Odin pinched the bridge of his nose. "And if I agree to your demands, will you resume your duties?"

"With haste, my lord," I replied, exchanging stunned glances with my fellow Valkyries.

"Fine." He threw up his hands in frustration. "Fine, we accept your terms. Now get back to work."

A collective cheer rose from both us and the spirits of Valhalla. We resumed work, and the men and crows remained on their best behavior. After about a week, one man forgot himself and reached his hand up my skirt. I grabbed it around the wrist, slammed it onto the table, and drew my sword, neatly chopping off the first knuckle of his pinkie finger.

"Consider that a warning," I growled, letting go of him.

He screamed and held his hand to his chest. The finger's blood was already slowing as the wound scabbed over. Instead of growing back like the limbs lost during their daily battles, this remained a stump after the bleeding stopped.

"Anyone else?" I asked the horrified crowd. They instantly became much more polite and have stayed that way ever since.

I'm not sure what Loki had been up to after he left the halls of Valhalla. Judging by his dress the last time he visited, some decades seemed to have passed on Earth, and he mentioned becoming a patron of the arts. Something about inspiring a comic book writer to immortalize him in fiction, whatever that meant. "Trust me," he'd said with a wink, "it will pay back in dividends."

Time passed, and the new status quo soon replaced the old. We fell into our routine, but now, they knew and respected the true power we held.

Fólkvangr

Ikechukwu Henry

The rain had not stopped since dawn, yet the battlefield still breathed heat like the inside of a dying forge. A pale mist clung low to the ground, twisting in slow coils above sprawled bodies, as if reluctant to leave them. The mud was not the clean brown of farmland after rain but a black, glistening sludge that clutched at boots and pulled at the dead with the same blind insistence.

Lyra's horse moved with the cautious precision of a creature that had seen too much of this world. The animal's flanks quivered with each step, not from exertion but from the smell. It was not simply blood. Blood she had known in life – copper and iron in the air, the sourness of sweat beneath it. This was the thick, cloying stench of flesh cooling in the open, of bowels loosed in death, of rainwater sinking into wounds and carrying whatever had once been warm into the soil.

She did not look away from the corpses. Her eyes moved slowly, scanning. She had been trained never to blink too long in a place like this. Sometimes the souls lingered near the bodies, hesitant, shivering in confusion. Sometimes they wandered, unaware they had crossed the threshold. Valkyries had to see them before the mists took them.

Above her, the clouds were a heavy, seamless gray. She could feel the gaze from beyond them, a weight on the crown of her head. Skuld was watching. She always watched the first collection after a battle.

Her orders had been specific. A single name had been given, spoken in the clipped, quiet tone Skuld used when she wanted no hesitation: *Jarl Eirik Haaldren.*

She found him quickly. Even in death, the man's presence was a hard thing to miss. He lay on his back, one arm thrown out as if warding off an enemy, the other curled tight to his chest where an axe had split him. His face was fixed in a snarl, teeth bared, as though he still fought whoever had felled him. The Echo hovered over him like a shimmer in the air, invisible to mortal eyes but to her as clear as a torch flame in the dark. She could taste it already: iron determination, a hunger for conquest, the high-pitched thrill of a man who believed his name would be carved into sagas.

It was clean. Predictable.

She dismounted, boots sinking a hand's breadth into the muck. The cold was everywhere – wet in her hair, beneath her armor, against her teeth when she breathed. She knelt by the Jarl and placed her fingers against his brow. His skin was still warm. The Echo flinched at her touch but had no strength to resist. She drew it in.

It entered her like a draught of burning liquor – hot, bright, and almost tasteless in its simplicity. Pride. Rage. A flash of his wife's face, not in tenderness but in the way she had urged him to bring home more land. Then it was gone, stripped of all its edges, leaving behind only a pale, obedient spirit ready for the endless drills of Valhalla.

She rose, but before she could turn back to her horse, something brushed against her awareness. It was faint at first, like the low note of a distant horn. She turned her head slowly.

Not far away, near the remains of a trampled campfire, a young man sat propped against a broken wagon wheel. His chest rose and fell in shallow, irregular movements. He was alive, though barely. A harp lay across his lap, one string snapped, the others sagging like exhausted sinews. His fingers rested on it but did not move. His eyes were half-closed, turned towards the sky.

She should have looked away. He was not on the list. He was no hero, no wielder of great death. But his Echo…

It pulsed, not in the rigid beat of ambition or rage, but in a strange, layered rhythm that wrapped around her senses. She could hear it before she touched it: notes of laughter, of sea wind across a quiet harbor, of words unspoken between lovers in the warmth of a winter fire. Beneath it all lay a steady acceptance, not defeat, but a stillness she had never tasted in any other soul.

She walked toward him. The mud tried to pull her down as if to remind her of her orders, but her steps did not slow. His gaze shifted to her when she drew close. There was no fear in it, only recognition – as though he had been expecting her.

"You are the chooser," he said, his voice barely more than a breath.

"I am," she answered, though the words felt heavy.

"I have no place in your halls," he murmured. "But if you will, take this with you." His fingers lifted slightly, touching the harp.

She knew Skuld could see her from the clouds. Every heartbeat here was watched. She should have turned away, let his soul dissolve into the mist when his breath stopped. That was the way for the unchosen.

But the Echo called to her in a way she had no language for. It was not brighter than the Jarl's, nor larger, but it was alive in a way that made her chest ache. Consuming it would be an act of vandalism, the destruction of something that deserved to outlast stone.

Her hand rose, trembling. She placed her fingertips on his brow, not with the grip of a collector but with the care one might use to close a child's eyes. She did not take it all. She pulled free a single thread – a memory.

It struck her like a shaft of sunlight piercing ice. A woman's face, framed by dark hair, her mouth curved into a smile so sudden and genuine that it startled even in recollection. The sound of her laugh was clear as bells. She could smell the faintest trace of baked bread, could feel the warmth of a hand in hers.

Lyra pulled back sharply, afraid Skuld would sense the exchange. The young man's breathing had stilled. His Echo still shimmered around him, whole, untouched but for the one stolen fragment. Without a chooser's claim, it would dissolve soon.

She stood and forced herself to walk away. Every step felt like it cracked something inside her. When she mounted her horse again, she did not look back.

Above, the clouds shifted slightly, but the weight of Skuld's gaze did not lessen.

* * *

The stables of Valhalla smelled of warm hide and clean hay, yet even that comfort felt hollow to Lyra tonight. The wide hall was dim, lit only by a row of torches that burned in steady orange lines down the length of the stalls. Their light caught in the glossy feathers of the winged horses and in the curve of polished tack, throwing shadows that clung to the beams above.

Her mare shifted inside her stall as Lyra loosened the saddle straps. The sound of leather sliding free was slow and deliberate, but her hands did not match the calm of the motion. Her fingers curled too tightly around the buckles, tugging them harder than they required.

She had not spoken since returning from the field. The other Valkyries were absent, either feasting in the great hall or reporting directly to Skuld. That left her alone with the quiet creak of wooden stalls and the soft rustle of horses breathing in unison.

The stolen memory had not faded. It had not dulled into the indistinct haze that most Echoes became after she took them. It lived in her as if it had always been there. The woman's laugh was still in her ears, each note bright and unbroken. When she closed her eyes, she could see the glint of light in the strands of her hair, could feel the heat of a hand clasped in farewell. It was as if the skald had hidden this memory deep inside her ribs, where even Skuld's gaze could not pry.

That frightened her more than she wished to admit.

She removed the bridle, careful not to let the bit clang against the mare's teeth. The animal nickered softly, leaning its head toward her shoulder. Lyra rested a hand against its neck, feeling the strong pulse beneath the skin.

The pulse brought something else with it – another Echo, one she had not thought about in years. The feel of her own brother's wrist when she had gripped it as a child, dragging him away from the burning outer wall of their farm. His skin had been hot, slick with sweat, his breath ragged in her ear. She remembered the smell of rain on dirt, the flash of fear when an arrow passed so close she felt the wind of it.

The memory should not have been there. She had been chosen after death; her own Echo should have been erased before she ever donned the armor of a Valkyrie. Yet here it was, sharp and solid as the skald's.

She pulled her hand back from the horse, unsettled. When she turned toward the far end of the stable, she froze. Skuld stood in the open doorway.

She had not heard her arrive. The Norn's presence was like the sudden onset of winter: the air heavier, the light thinner. Her armor was darker than any Lyra had seen on another Valkyrie, each plate carved with runes so fine they seemed almost to writhe when the torchlight touched them. Her eyes held no warmth. They fixed on Lyra without moving, as if the younger Valkyrie were already pinned in place.

"You were slow returning," Skuld said. Her voice was level, with no hint of accusation, but the absence of tone made it more dangerous.

"The mud was deep," Lyra answered.

"And yet the Jarl's spirit was delivered promptly," Skuld continued. She stepped into the stable, her boots leaving no sound on the stone floor. "No delay there."

Lyra kept her gaze steady. "I did my duty."

Skuld stopped a few paces away. Her eyes searched Lyra's face for something. Lyra could feel it – the strange, pressing sensation of Skuld's attention reaching deeper than sight, probing for any flicker of doubt.

"The Echoes," Skuld said at last, "are a disease, Lyra. You know this."

Lyra's stomach tightened. "A disease?"

"They spread inside you, slow at first, until they root themselves in your will. Memories breed hesitation. Attachments. They weaken the soul. Our task is to make the Einherjar ready for the final war. Soldiers cannot carry such weight."

The words were meant to be truth. Yet in Lyra's mind, the skald's laugh rose again, unbroken by death.

"Is hesitation always a weakness?" Lyra asked.

Skuld's eyes narrowed. "Always. Do not let sentiment blind you. I have consumed more Echoes than any Valkyrie alive. I have tasted the last breath of kings and the cries of children. I know the cost of letting such things live."

Lyra's fingers curled against her palm. "And what is that cost?"

"Disobedience," Skuld said. "Defiance. A soldier who remembers why he fought in life may question the orders of the gods in death. Such a warrior could refuse to stand when Ragnarök comes. One act of hesitation can unravel the line."

Lyra felt her heartbeat quicken, but it was not fear. It was something sharper, something that burned in the space between her ribs. She thought of the skald again, the quiet steadiness in his eyes, the certainty that his death was not a defeat. That was not disease. That was strength of a kind she had never seen in Valhalla's halls.

She took a step forward, closing the space between them by half. "What if such a warrior would fight for reasons the gods cannot command? What if that makes them stronger?"

Skuld's gaze darkened.

The words had escaped before Lyra could weigh them, yet there was no pulling them back now. The air between them felt denser, as if the walls themselves had shifted closer.

Skuld reached out, her gloved hand coming to rest against the side of Lyra's head. Her touch was cool but not cruel. Then, without warning, a flood of sensation crashed through Lyra's mind.

It was not her own.

She stood on a cliff edge, the world below awash in fire. A great serpent coiled through the burning seas, its scales flashing like molten iron. Above, the sky split as a wolf's jaws closed over the sun. The ground trembled under the march of an army that stretched beyond sight. At the head of it stood Odin, his single eye locked on something in the distance – something Lyra could not see.

The vision tore free as quickly as it had come, leaving her breathless. Skuld's hand withdrew.

"This is what is at stake," Skuld said softly. "When that day comes, every soul in Valhalla must move as one. Anything less will be the end of all things."

Lyra's vision swam. But the skald's laugh still sounded in her mind.

She steadied herself and, without warning, let one of her own Echoes rise. It was the image of a father she had once taken from a dying field – a man stepping between his son and a spear, taking the blow without hesitation. She forced the memory into Skuld's mind with the same piercing clarity Skuld had used on her.

For the briefest instant, Skuld's jaw tightened. Her eyes shifted, almost imperceptibly, toward the floor.

It was enough.

In that crack, Lyra felt something. Not just resistance but a wall built over centuries, and behind it, a memory Skuld guarded with a ferocity that was almost pain. Lyra glimpsed only a fragment: Skuld on her knees beside a man's body, her hands bloodied, her face empty of expression while something deep within her screamed. Then it was gone, the wall slamming shut.

Skuld's voice was sharper now. "Be careful what you touch, Lyra. You are not ready to see the whole truth."

But Lyra had seen enough to understand. The most powerful Echoes – those tied to love, to sacrifice – were not weakness at all. They were dangerous to the gods because they gave a soul the will to resist. The Valkyries' work was not about preparing the army. It was about removing the only part of a soul that might question orders.

Skuld stepped back. "You will report for the next collection at dawn. And you will remember what I have said."

Lyra nodded once. She kept her eyes down until Skuld's footsteps faded and the stable door closed.

Only then did she look toward her mare. The horse's dark eyes met hers, unblinking. She wondered, for the first time, whether the skald's memory had been more than a theft. Whether it had been a key.

* * *

The Bifrost was not the rainbow bridge mortals spoke of in their sagas. To mortal eyes, it might have looked like a ribbon of light stretching between realms, but here, standing upon it, the truth was stranger. The bridge was made of translucent stone that pulsed with shifting color, not in clean bands but in deep, slow ripples like light moving under water. Every step sent faint vibrations up through the soles of Lyra's boots, as if the bridge itself were aware of her passing.

Below, there was no sea or earth. Only darkness, vast and soundless, stretched out in all directions. The bridge seemed to float over an absence so complete it had weight.

The air was still. Her mare's wings were folded tight, the great muscles beneath their feathers tense. The souls she carried walked behind her in silence, their armor gleaming without a single dent or stain. Their faces were blank. Every memory, every attachment, every pain or joy that had once shaped them was gone. They moved because she moved. They would fight because someone told them to fight.

She had delivered such warriors countless times before without hesitation. But not now. Not after the skald's laugh, the father's sacrifice, her own memory of her brother's escape. Those threads were tied so tightly in her mind that she could no longer pretend their absence made the warriors stronger.

The other end of the bridge glowed with the cold light of Valhalla's gates. They were open, the spears of the honor guard crossed in silent readiness. Beyond them lay Odin's army and the endless training grounds. She did not slow her pace until the faint warmth of another light touched her from the left.

It was not the hard, metallic gleam of Asgard's halls. This light was softer, golden, and it came from a path that curved away from the main bridge, a span she had been taught to ignore.

Fólkvangr.

Every Valkyrie knew of it, but the stories had been told with faint condescension – Freyja's meadow-hall, the place where half the slain went when they were not worthy of Valhalla. It was a consolation prize for warriors of lesser renown, a place without the glory of Odin's host. She had never been told what those halls were truly like.

She stopped.

The souls behind her stopped too, their eyes still empty. The bridge beneath her boots gave a low hum, as if aware she had broken the rhythm of her duty.

She turned her mare toward the side path.

The moment she did, the light around her shifted. The golden glow grew warmer, washing over her like the first sunlight after a long winter. Somewhere ahead, she could hear the faint murmur of voices – not the hollow chants of drilled warriors, but the rise and fall of people speaking to one another as if they knew each other's names.

Her horse moved forward without needing the reins. The souls followed.

She had not taken more than ten steps before the air changed again. A chill, sharp and sudden, cut through the warmth. It came from ahead, not behind.

Skuld stood on the path. She wore no helm, her pale hair falling loose over her shoulders. Her eyes were fixed on Lyra, but there was no surprise in them. She had been waiting.

"You cannot take them there," Skuld said. Her voice was soft, almost patient, and all the more dangerous for it.

Lyra tightened her grip on the reins. "Why not?"

"Because they are needed." Skuld took one step closer. "You think you do this for their sake, but it is vanity. When the serpent rises and the sky burns, every sword will matter. Do not rob the world of its defense for the sake of your sentiment."

"They are not swords," Lyra said. The words came out low, steady. "They are people."

"They were people," Skuld corrected. "Now they are weapons. That is the mercy we give them."

Lyra felt the pressure in her skull a moment before it struck. Skuld was not moving, but the vision came all the same – fire curling through the air like smoke given weight, the roar of Fenrir's jaws, the earth breaking apart under the feet of giants. She saw Valkyries falling from the sky, their wings burning, Odin standing knee-deep in the dead. The sense of it was overwhelming: not just death, but the inevitability of it, the pull toward an ending no will could resist.

The vision shattered, leaving her breathless. Skuld's eyes had not moved from hers.

"This is what will come," Skuld said. "This is why they must forget."

Lyra's pulse thundered in her ears. She could feel the memories inside her pressing upward, not in chaos but in a steady, relentless tide. The skald's laugh. The father's sacrifice. Her brother's escape. And others – faces, voices, sensations she had carried without realizing. Every Echo she had failed to strip entirely now rose, crowding against her mind.

She let them come. She let them spill outward, not as an attack but as a flood.

The bridge trembled beneath her feet as the memories poured into the air, each one sharp, clear, and whole. A woman standing in a doorway waiting for her husband's return. A boy carving a wooden toy for his sister. A mother holding her child for the first time. The souls behind her stopped, their blank eyes flickering as something passed through them.

One by one, they began to remember.

A man at her left gasped, pressing a hand to his chest as if feeling a heartbeat for the first time in years. Another turned his head slowly toward her, his face twisting in recognition of a life he had thought gone.

The golden light ahead grew brighter. It was then that she saw her. Freyja walked toward them, her feet silent on the bridge. She did not wear a crown or armor. Her hair was the color of ripe wheat, her face unguarded, her eyes deep with something Lyra could not name. She said nothing to Skuld, nothing to Lyra. She simply opened her arms.

The newly awakened souls began to move toward her. They did not march. They walked, some halting, some with sudden, urgent steps, each drawn by the warmth in her gaze.

Skuld's expression did not change, but her hands clenched at her sides.

"You will be cast out for this," she said quietly.

Lyra met her eyes. "Then I will have no master."

She did not follow the souls into the golden light. She stood where she was until the last one had passed Freyja's side and disappeared into the glow.

When it was done, the warmth faded from the bridge, replaced once more by the cold of the void below. Skuld turned away without another word.

Lyra mounted her mare. She looked once toward the gates of Valhalla, their light distant and cold, then toward the place where Freyja had stood.

The path was empty now, but she knew it was there. She would find it again. And when she did, she would bring more.

She rode into the dark, not toward Asgard, but away from it, her armor heavy with the weight she had chosen to carry.

The Swan-Helm Thief

E.K. Larson-Burnett

Whenever there was a task no Swan Maiden wished to touch, it found its way to the youngest of them.

Patrol the fields after battle, counting the corpses so the Allfather's tally would be exact? Send the Untried *Valkyrja*. Retrieve the broken banners mired in mud? A duty for the Untried *Valkyrja*. Keep watch over the wounded lingering between life and death, ensuring none slipped away unnoticed? The Untried *Valkyrja*'s burden, naturally. She had not yet been trusted as an escort, that great honor in which she imagined her spear catching the light as she chose the best of the fallen. No – her lot was the errands between glory.

The elder Swan Maidens said she had a good bearing with her flight cloak, a strong throwing arm, no tendency towards hesitation. But for so long, they seemed to agree she lacked something harder to name – the gravity of a chooser, the weight in the gaze that made warriors still their breathing when they saw her shadow.

So for centuries, while others swooped down over red fields to claim heroes, she was resigned to watch from afar.

Until now, her first true flight.

The morning dawned cold and bright with the promise of battle. By the toll signaling war's end, however, it had grown murky and wet. It hardly mattered. Today, the Untried *Valkyrja* swept alongside – at last not trailing behind! – her elder sisters. *At last*.

The wind tore through her wheat silk hair as the current bowed under her swan-feather cloak, its magic bearing the long, corded strength of one who could lift shield and fallen warrior alike, draping over limbs lithe yet resilient. Her gaze, sharp but tempered by youth and newness to the task, cut through the rising powder that curled like smoke beneath her.

The great Swan Maidens – at last she among them! – lifted their spears and scanned the field of broken men and shattered shields, the blood-matted snow melting away in the rain. This was the moment she had dreamed of. She would be allowed to choose a fallen worthy to ascend to Valhalla, to claim her place as a chooser of souls.

The Untried *Valkyrja* tightened her grip on her spear as they slowed beside a cluster of bodies that had been dragged out of the thick of the killing. The air purred with ancient power, the quiet pulse of death waiting to be called.

Her elder sisters glanced at her knowingly before moving on to their own silent tasks. No words were needed. This was her first rite, her moment to prove herself.

She alighted, breath shallow with anticipation, and knelt beside a young warrior with a fragmented breastplate. Planting her spear alongside his bent form, she reached out gently, proud to see the steadiness of her hand.

Almost against reason, and not knowing what moved her to do so, she lifted her helm and set it upon the crimson frostmelt.

She had never seen her sisters do this, never heard it spoken of. The helms – those sacred swan-feathered crowns – were the Allfather-given source of the *Valkyrjar*'s immortality, the force which bound their souls beyond mortal frailty.

To remove her helm, even for a moment, was to risk everything.

She felt, though, that it was right to shed the immortal weight, if only for a moment. To stand among the dying as one who might soon join them. Perhaps it was the first true heft of her calling settling on her shoulders, the somber understanding that to choose the worthy was not simply to wield power, but to witness mortality in its rawest, most unforgiving form.

To be mortal – vulnerable, finite – meant seeing beyond the gleam of spear and shield, to the fragile breath beneath the armor, beneath the flesh. It was a feeling the Untried *Valkyrja* did not yet understand, but one she could not shake.

For a moment, the world was still.

The fallen warrior lay stretched upon the frost-hardened earth of the open plain, rain tracing dark rivulets across the cracked and battered cuirass. His ribs rose no more, ice gnawing inward, whitening the skin beneath plate and leather, his face drawn and windbitten, eyes half-lidded as if reluctant to surrender to the cold embrace of death.

Around him, the empty echo: the silence of endings and beginnings. The sky was low and heavy, the distant thunder a muted drumbeat.

Beneath the hush, the Untried *Valkyrja* probed. She sought more than flesh and armor. This was no mere counting of bodies, but a reckoning of spirit, and she would make her assessment properly.

She studied the fallen warrior's frozen form, tracing with eyes intense and unyielding the faintest motes of resistance. The way his fingers curled as though still gripping a weapon, the rigid set of his jaw speaking of a will that had resisted the Norns' weft longer than most…

She searched for the subtle gravity of courage borne through endless pain, the stubborn echo of honor refusing to fade. Not the outward marks of battle, but the stone-solid resilience shaping the soul's architecture – the refusal to yield in the face of fear, the steady resolve to stand when all else faltered, the unbroken thread of loyalty woven through suffering.

Yes, she determined. *He is worthy.*

With careful reverence, the Untried *Valkyrja* lowered herself until her brow pressed to the icy ground beside him, a gesture of solemn submission to the sacred duty. She intended to call the warrior's spirit forth, to bind it gently and bear it to the halls of the honored dead.

As she lifted herself, sharp realization jarred like a hot quake in her core.

Her helm was gone.

She spun, heart pounding, but it was not where she had left it, nor anywhere else. The *shhh-shhh* rustle of her sisters' cloaks marked their departures one by one.

She was alone. And her helm – the very essence of her power – was gone. All that remained was a sodden scrap of paper fluttering at her feet.

Hands now shamefully shaking, she snatched up the parchment before it could flee in the wind and unfolded it.

If you would have your helm again, guard me
until sundown.
No tricks.
Meet me in the city's lower quarter.

The Untried *Valkyrja* should have been escorting her chosen to Valhalla, embarking on that first flight of glory she'd long anticipated and for which she'd been so patient.

Instead, she stood on the now-empty battlefield, helmless and powerless, the weight of her failure pressing outward from within her, a storm cloud fit to burst.

Of course it would happen to her. Such bad luck was the only card available to her, and she would be castigated for it severely, she knew.

But there was no choice. She tucked her spear under one arm and set her jaw.

She would follow the thief's terms. She would protect him until sundown, retrieve her helm, and then return to the battlefield and hope it was not too late to claim the fallen warrior's soul for the Allfather.

* * *

It did not take long for the Untried *Valkyrja* to find the thief in the city's lower wards; luckily, she still had her swan-feather cloak, and her flight was swift. She followed the helm's resonance and discovered him in a dirty, low-ceilinged dwelling, squatted over a body wrapped in undyed linen. He did not startle at her sudden presence – of course, because he had orchestrated it – but neither did any flicker of awe touch his eyes.

She, half of heaven's fire, and he, but a common wretch. He ought to have trembled.

Yet it is you who is under his thumb, she reminded herself, finding the telltale hump of her helm protruding from the body's wrappings.

"We owe our patron great debts," the thief said, his voice thin and young. "He promised retribution, and this—" he gestured at the body, "—is half of his reckoning. I don't fear for myself. But my brother deserves to rest, no matter what debts we carry. The burial hill is on the other side of the city."

The Untried *Valkyrja* regarded him: the gaunt hands clutching the coarse linen, the hollow set of his jaw, the cold defiance in his eyes. No trace of honor, no hint of heroism. Just a common criminal.

The body beneath the cloth was no better – another wretch fallen far from any battlefield worthy of Valhalla's halls.

Neither of these brothers deserved her sacred attention. She had been moments from choosing a valiant soul, a name to be sung for ages… Instead, she was tethered to this petty mess.

Yet there the thief sat, mocking in his audacity.

The sting of frustration curled in her chest. She forced herself to bite back the sharper words that swelled on her tongue. Pride be damned – her helm was stolen, and without it, she was nothing more than a mortal shadow. She needed it back.

"Protection, then," the Untried *Valkyrja* said, her voice steady though her insides churned. "Until sundown."

His dark eyes flickered with relief. "That's all I ask." He stood and gestured to the body. "You may carry him."

Ha! A bitter jest. As if it were some honor to bear the corpse of a criminal through the filth and shadows of this city.

Her jaw tightened, a flare of anger rising inside her chest, but she forced her hands to close around the body, trembling from the prick of indignity. To think that she, semi-divine and favored by the Allfather himself, was reduced to hauling this wretched load through the grime of earthly streets.

She glanced at the thief, whose expression held neither shame nor gratitude – only the weary weight, it seemed, of a man who had long since abandoned hope for anything better.

Resentment smoldered hot in her gut, but she swallowed it down. For all her fury, she needed her helm. And so, with a steadying breath, she lifted the burden, bracing against the chill that seeped from the corpse.

She was not pleased. She had failed today, greatly, and every movement nettled. This was no ride of splendor, no honored escort of a fallen hero. It was a trek through the muck and shadows, guarding a criminal who dared to claim love as his final act.

This was her path now.

"You'll follow?" the thief questioned. When she nodded, he ducked outside.

The Untried *Valkyrja* shifted the weight of the body awkwardly, muscles straining, back stiffening. She was mortal. She followed the thief.

Immediately, the rot of the street clung to her, mud sucking at her steps, but her cloak would not carry the weight of the dead man; it was meant for her alone, her and the souls of the worthy.

Narrow alleys twisted like a serpent's coil, but the thief navigated them with quickness, a sure-footed ease indisputably born of years skulking through the city. Meanwhile, the Untried *Valkyrja*'s steps grew heavier under the weight of the body – and her growing doubt.

She had dreamed of the sky's great charge, of flying alongside her sisters to claim the valorous dead and escort them to Odin's golden halls, where heroes feasted and tales were sung. That was the honor she hungered for – the honor every untried Swan Maiden coveted.

This was far less radiant: escorting a dead criminal through unsewered streets to what would fast become a forgotten grave. Not even a proper choosing, not even to Freyja's fields of Fólkvangr – the gentle resting place for those fallen in battle but deemed unworthy of Valhalla's feast.

This was just another mortal errand, dull and unbecoming.

This is not the duty I was meant for, she seethed, biting the inside of her cheek to quell the bitter spark of resentment.

"You seem annoyed," the thief said, breaking the silence.

She scoffed and met his eyes, unwilling to soften. "I imagined glory. Names remembered long after the blood has dried."

He shrugged. "Not all worth is sung in halls or carved on stone."

The muscles in her jaw feathered. She wanted to argue, to reject this sour truth. But the ache in her limbs and the hard cold worming beneath her skin whispered otherwise. Her worth certainly would not be sung, nor carved, anytime soon.

Suddenly, the sound of harsh voices and heavy footsteps.

Figures rounded the corner – rough men moving fast.

The thief cursed under his breath. "Patron's dogs."

The Untried *Valkyrja*'s breath hitched, arms straining under the bulk of the body. She dropped it to the grimy stones with a careless thud, ignoring the thief's sharp protest.

"Keep behind me," she instructed, voice tight as the Norns' knots.

She paid no heed to whether he obeyed; as the first of the pursuers closed in, she squared her shoulders, wheeled her spear around, and readied herself – not for the glory she craved, but for this gritty, unyielding task thrust upon her.

Without her helm, her strength was mortal and her reflexes slowed, but fury surged through her veins, lighting within her a desperate flame.

Steel flashed.

The battle was sudden, raw – a flurry of fists, the scrape of blade against stone. She fought with clumsy determination, each weak thrust of her spear reminding her of what she had lost.

The Untried *Valkyrja* parried a wild strike, stumbled on blood-slicked cobblestones, and barely twisted away from a blow meant to cleave bone. Her breath came sharp, chest burning with human strain and grit.

Out of the corner of her eye, she saw the thief standing over the shrouded bundle, brandishing a flimsy dagger. Protecting his dead brother.

The last two pursuers closed in fast, snarling as they swung crude blades. The Untried *Valkyrja* met the first with a violent thrust of her spear, catching his wrist and sending the weapon clattering to the ground. He stumbled, clutching his injured arm, then fled.

The second lunged, wild and furious, but she sidestepped, slamming the butt of her spear into his ribs with bone-crushing force. He gasped, doubled over, and crumpled to the cobbles.

Silence settled like cold ash, broken only by the drip of snowmelt from a nearby eave and the thief's quickened breathing.

The Untried *Valkyrja* composed herself. She wasn't proud, exactly, of the way the fight had gone, but it was over, and her ward was unscathed.

She looked at the thief, now crouched and fussing over the body. When she'd dropped it in her haste to fight, the wrappings had come partly undone. The thief seemed frantic to smooth the shroud, tucking the folds under the dead man's shoulders as though to ensure his comfort.

"You treat him like a king," she remarked flatly.

He shrugged and sniffled, and when he spoke, his voice was low and rough. "He's my brother. Every choice he made... He did his best. Every risk he took was for my sake. To take care of me." A pause. Then, again, softer: "He's my brother."

She grunted, shifting her spear. "Odin doesn't fill his hall with thieves and criminals."

"Then Odin's missing some of the best of us," the thief replied.

His care of the body gave her pause. Words caught in her throat.

Half the slain to the Allfather's hall, half to Freyja's fields. She had always thought the latter a consolation prize, Fólkvangr a meadow for those who had fought without shining, whose courage had failed to meet the Allfather's measure – a place for the not-bright, the not-bold.

But as she looked at the shrouded man and the brother kneeling beside him, a tug of doubt pulled sickeningly at her lungs.

Before the thief tucked it back into the linen, the Untried *Valkyrja* saw the brother's hand – limp and fish-belly pale, but callused and strong.

The image lingered: not the hand of a warrior, yet still marked by the small, relentless work of keeping another alive.

If every act had been for the sake of another…was that not its own form of heroism?

She set her jaw and looked away. "We should move," she said, wishing to scatter the thought.

* * *

"My brother wasn't a hero," the thief began as he walked alongside the Untried *Valkyrja*. He glanced over constantly – not at her, but at the body, to make sure she was carrying it properly. "Not by any of your songs or stories. He was a thief, yes – had to be. We were orphans, left to rot in the gutters. We were both just kids when he started taking, but he only took what we needed to live."

She glanced at him, skeptical but listening, annoyed by the rain in her eyes and the stiff, wet cold of mortality.

"He didn't steal to get rich or brag. He just took whatever would keep us from going hungry or freezing." He paused, touched a hand to the wrapped body, voice roughening. "Once – more than once – someone caught him and beat him near to death. Even then, he made sure I had something to eat the next day. Told me not to waste myself worrying about him."

The Untried *Valkyrja*'s mind stirred restlessly.

Watching her Swan Maiden sisters tend to the fallen, she had always believed worthiness meant grandeur – glory in battle, names carved in stone, songs that echoed through Valhalla. But here, carrying this broken man, she realized her understanding had been too small. There were different kinds of bravery.

And this one, the one of the man on her back, was born not from the clangor of war, but from the quiet, desperate need to protect another. From love.

She frowned, that reluctant knot tightening in her chest.

Is it enough? she wondered. Could such hidden courage carry its own weight in the balance of the slain?

She had no answer – only the thief's steady words, and the slow thaw of something unfamiliar going cold, hot, cold, hot within her.

"I never asked him to be brave," the thief continued, words muddied by what she knew was a too-tight throat. "But he was brave all the same. Not for glory or songs, like your warriors, but because he wanted to keep me alive. That was his fight. Every night, every risk he took…it was for me."

A question began to take shape, one the Untried *Valkyrja* had never heard her sisters ask:

Might worthiness be more than the bright blaze of glory?

Could love, fierce and shadowed, hold its own place among the honored dead?

The thief looked up, catching her gaze. A slow, sad smile softened his dirt-smudged face. "There's valor no one sees. But it's the kind that keeps the world turning."

The Untried *Valkyrja* swallowed hard, the weight of the body suddenly lighter – or perhaps it was the weight of her own judgement, beginning to shift.

* * *

The rain eased to a stubborn drizzle. More of the patron's men appeared, but the Untried *Valkyrja* met them head-on, dispatched them with maddening difficulty. Her spear found its mark enough times to keep the thief and his brother's body safe, though each blow reminded her sharply of her mortal limits. She yearned for her helm.

They moved on.

Soon, the burial hill rose before them, shadowed by gnarled trees and wild nettles.

The Untried *Valkyrja* followed the thief to an empty space upon the rise, both of them slipping in the mud. *Not ideal conditions for digging a grave*, she thought bitterly. Then she frowned, hesitating.

What did this man deserve? The thief's fierce devotion had made her question everything.

She watched as he began scraping at the earth with a worn blade, undaunted by the slow progress, the wet slide of mud, the stink of nearby bodies yet unburied.

"Is this what you want?" she asked, voice low. "For him to lie forgotten?"

He kept at his work, scalp gleaming through the soaked-stringy strands of his hair. "Better forgotten than left to rot in the canals, or dragged through the courts for sins he committed only because no one else would care for us – for me."

She nodded and lowered herself carefully to her knees. Knowing the thief was watching, she slowly, reverently, laid the body of his brother nearby. Then she began to help him dig – her fingers cold, the muck colder still.

It took hours. The icy glare of the clouds dulled into dusk.

Together, they lowered the brother's body into the shallow grave.

The thief breathed hard and ragged as he reached down and touched his brother's linen-wrapped head. He seemed unashamed of his tears, and that, too, the Untried *Valkyrja* mused, was a form of courage.

"He never dreamed of glory," the thief rasped. "Just wanted to keep me alive. I owe him this much."

All the world narrowed to the two of them – the thief-brothers – and she remained still and silent. She shivered, sensing this was a different kind of battlefield: less stained with blood, yet no less fierce.

For isn't a true battle measured not only in steel and fire, but in the quiet bravery of love? Yet here, no triumphant cheers rang out – only the soft, relentless hush of parting.

Since her earliest days, the Untried *Valkyrja* had yearned for this day – her first true flight, soaring through storm and shadow, choosing the brave and the bold to ascend to Valhalla's golden halls. This was the honor she had craved.

Yet now, as the thief's weeping devotion settled like a balm, she saw the gleaming spread of the Allfather's design not as the sole measure of worth, but as only one part of a larger tapestry.

This – this humble burial on a forgotten hill, with no songs or feasts awaiting the fallen – felt, somehow, just as sacred.

She traced the arc of her hope and purpose, bending it toward a truth she had not fully known: that worthiness was not measured solely by deeds shouted from the mountaintops, but by the quiet courage to love and protect, to endure hardship not for fame, but for those who could not fight for themselves.

The dead man before her would not claim a place at Odin's table. His story would not be carved in runes or praised by skalds.

But he would find rest.

The Untried *Valkyrja* rose, the spear once heavy now light in her hand. With a gentle prod, she eased the thief away from the grave.

"May I?" she asked, gesturing toward the shape lumped against the body.

The thief nodded mutely, and she shifted the linen aside to retrieve her helm. When she settled it upon her head and felt the soft sigh of warmth spread through her, she began to speak, beckoning forth the brother's soul.

Her voice, steady and clear, wove the ancient words – not a call to Odin's golden halls, but a summons to the softer embrace of Fólkvangr.

A subtle shimmer stirred in the linen folds. The brother's pale hand twitched, then lifted, fragile as frost yet full of lingering life.

The Untried *Valkyrja* reached down and took the soul's hand gently in her own, the weight of death giving way to something tender, alive.

The thief's breath caught, his expression cracked open wide and searching.

"He'll rest with Freyja," she told him. "Her fields…aren't for those who seek glory. They're for those who fight quieter battles. Love, sacrifice, survival."

His eyes glassed with tears. Finally, there was awe in his gaze, and it was not for her, but for the soul of his brother, his hero – and that, she knew, was right.

She reached out and squeezed the thief's shoulder, a quick promise. "This is honor, just the same."

The thief nodded.

Holding the soul's hand, her swan-feather cloak *shhh-shhh*ing with the lift of the wind, the *Valkyrja* rose slowly, a calm settling over her as she embarked on her first true flight.

This wasn't the grand choosing she had dreamed of, but perhaps it was something truer.

Worth: it was not found only in the loud blaze of battle.

It was found in the steady flame of love, burning on untended. The fiercest courage of them all.

Flight School

J.B. Riley

June 20th

Why did Mom let Dennis do camp sign-ups this year? This cheap-ass camp sucks, just like him. Instead of *finally* being a senior junior counselor at Whispering Meadows after whole eons of waiting I'm stuck here for the *entire* summer? Jesus. It's not like Dennis has to pay for it, Daddy always does, but now Mom decides to listen to gross Dennis and his stupid combover and now my life *totally* sucks!

Plus I have to write in this stupid journal. "It's part of the agreement" Dr. Dietrick says. "No one else will read it. Your private thoughts alone, to help you work through your anger."

"Work through your anger" my ass. That's what horse camp is for, Dr. DickTrick. No skanks to come at me. Well, okay, some of the girls are total bitches but as a senior junior counselor? This is the year they would all finally have to be nice to me.

But now instead? I'm here. Thanks for nothing, Dennis. I hope you choke on it. I hate you. I hate Mom, and that lame new school even though it's supposed to be "safer" and all those stupid skanks at my old school and I *hate*, *hate*, *hate* this place.

I even sort of hate Daddy. Six weeks putting up with his new girlfriend would suck but at least there'd be decent WiFi.

Literally dying here.

June 21st

No, seriously this sucks!!!!! There aren't even any horses yet. I guess they're bringing them in from somewhere. I should have been on middle jumps by now and instead I'm stuck doing nothing. Plus some really disgusting old hairy dude who must be the janitor drank my pineapple-coconut conditioner and my Hair. Is. Wrecked. That's the last time I leave stuff in the shower building. This would never happen at Whispering Meadows. Well okay it would but only because some of those bitches always thought it was funny to steal my stuff. But as a senior junior counselor I could make them give it back.

You know what's even worse? There's no one here I can talk to. Like, literally. All the other girls are from some sort of weird foreign exchange program and none of them seem to understand me, no matter how loud I talk. Plus they're all tall and blond and compared to them I look like a twelve-year-old boy. I am totally asking for a boob job for graduation.

Also I didn't think to pack the Keurig and I'm *dying* for a latte. All there is to drink is water and some sort of odd-smelling fermenty stuff they call mead. It tastes like it has alcohol in it, which between that and all the busty foreign chicks is why I think this camp must be run by Europeans. Or it's a cult.

June 22nd

OMG I'm exhausted.

These loud horns blew this morning and I ran out of the cabin thinking it was the horses finally coming in and instead there's some old busty blonde foreign chick with a whistle and a clipboard standing in the middle of the paddock. I guess she's the program director? Anyway, she yells something that sounds Swedish and suddenly everyone else is doing jumping jacks and swinging their arms and then they start running stupid laps. They all have long legs and move like frickin' gazelles and meanwhile I'm trying to explain that I have asthma it's, like, a *condition*? and I could totally have an attack and die if I have to run laps and she Totally. Ignores. Me.

So I ran. Seriously I thought I was going to really-actually-not-just-to-get-out-of-gym-but-really-truly die.

Finally she blows her whistle and the blondes stop running and I sort of manage not to fall over and she blows her whistle again and suddenly there's a blonde next to me and I'm grabbed by the wrist and the world spins and I land ass-first on the ground.

Next thing I know I'm on top of this girl punching on her and the whistle is blowing and everyone is yelling and I get grabbed and yanked upright and I think "Oh, shit I'm getting expelled again" but then?

They start cheering. The blonde I was punching sits up and wipes blood off her mouth and, like, grins and says something and everyone laughs but it doesn't feel like they're laughing at me and the program director smiles and nods.

Then another blonde comes over and takes my wrist and, like, slowly turns it and shows me how she slips her foot behind my ankle so I can feel when I unbalance. She doesn't let me fall, she just does it again. Then she lets go and has me grab her wrist and eventually I figure it out and when I do it faster and she falls everyone cheers again. The program director comes over and gives me this little silver charm shaped like a fist and I guess it's like a scout badge? She shakes my hand and everyone cheers again.

At dinner some of the blondes waved me over to their table to sit with them and I don't care but it is nice to not sit alone even if they still won't speak English.

June 27th

I know I'm supposed to write every day in this dumb journal but – seriously – I've been sooooooo tired. Every day at totally the crack of dawn it's the horn and exercising, then running, then throwing each other around the paddock and now we are also running an obstacle course and picking up and carrying these stupid heavy logs, all before lunch.

Plus after lunch we have been spending hours using these wooden sticks to whack at each other. It hurts a ton even with the padded jacket they gave us to wear so I have been trying *really* hard to not get whacked and I guess I'm fast with my stick because I don't get hit very often even though they're all taller than me with longer arms.

This is still the weirdest horse camp I've ever been to but it doesn't totally suck and the girls are actually decent when you get to know them. Inga braided my hair the other night and that was nice, and Astrid has this hand cream that really helps with the blisters.

Also no matter how much I eat I think I'm losing weight anyway. Now if only my boobs would grow!

July 3rd

We are working with these big padded dummies to learn where to hit opponents. Where has this been all my life? At first it really hurt my hands but now I know how to wrap my wrists, plus do palm strikes and elbow strikes which don't hurt at all. I'm too short to hit the dummy in the head very hard but Freya (the program director, she's actually pretty cool) painted marks on the dummy where no human wants to get hit at and I can reach a whole lot of those.

July 10th

I don't know how far we are running now– there are bridle trails we run in a big loop and it's hard because it's up and down hills but it's not too bad even carrying logs on our shoulders.

Freya keeps watching me fight with my pole and it's a little creepy but she keeps smiling and nodding so maybe not. Then this morning some big bearded dude showed up and he's totally old but still totally hot in a Hemsworth sort of way. He must be the camp director because he spent a lot of time talking with Freya and watching us but that isn't creepy at all except he wears an eye patch which, look, I know this is weird but it makes him even hotter.

You're just a journal. Don't judge me. (Dr. DickTrick if you are reading this? Gross, you perv.)

July 25th

They gave me a real sword! I'm paired up with Brigitta and I have this metal ring shirt now and these armbands and a real helmet and it's like literally *Game of Thrones*. The first time Brigitta got her sword through my guard and hit me it hurt way worse than the pole ever did but my new shirt protected me and I didn't get cut. She froze when I yelped and I lunged and hit her back and she yelped and then we both burst out laughing.

It was awesome.

August 1st

After our run this morning we prepped the stables. The horses must be coming! I can't wait.

August 2nd

I can't. I just – I can't. You'll never believe in a million billion years.

OMG I can't even barely write.

They can fly.

The horses.

They have wings.

I've named mine Peaches.

August 3rd

Hi Journal! It's me again. I might be the shortest, darkest and flattest-chested camper here but even Hildy (who's scary good in everything) has to admit I'm the best rider. Squee!

They're all stuck on a lead rope to keep them only five feet off the ground but Freya watched me for, oh, like 30 seconds and removed my leader. She smiled, nodded and waved an arm and Peaches and I were off. It was glorious. I didn't want to land but when she blew her whistle Peaches turned all on his own and we landed smooth and soft as silk. The silver charm I got already for riding has wings and it's the coolest one yet!

More later – I have an apple from dinner I want to feed Peaches before lights out.

August 4th

Okay there is one downside to flying horses? All the flying horse shit. It's not like they wait until they're on the ground. They shit anywhere and everywhere like 1,200-pound pigeons and we get stuck cleaning it up. I had to climb up on a ladder and scrape shit off the roof of my cabin this morning.

Still worth it.

Peaches already knows me – he sticks his nose over his stall door and whinnies when he hears me coming. Sure, I've been bringing him apples and carrots but I think he just likes me.

It's really nice.

August 10th

Peaches is the best! It's like he can read my mind and do what I want him to do before I ask him to do it. We are practicing swooping down at a human-sized post set up in the middle of the paddock. Odie (Mr. Hottie Camp Director, I don't care he's named like that dog in *Garfield*, he's *still* smokin') nailed a big wooden bowl to the top to hold cantaloupes and I have been practicing slice them in half with my sword *exactly* when Peaches snaps out of his dive to fly up again. Freya is also making me practice with a long sharpened wooden pole. She told me if I can stab the melon without the pole hitting the ground again (which popped me out of the saddle like a penny being flipped and I'm glad I learned how to tuck and roll in hand-to-hand drills), I can try it with a real spear. I can't wait – axes come next and Odie says they haven't had a camper master the axe since the Dark Ages (I think that means the 80s).

August 17th

OMG – I can't believe there's only one more week. I need to spend as much time as I can with Peaches so I'm not going to write in this journal for a while (I bet you'll miss me)

Hildie and I also have a shot at the camp record for doubles Obstacle Course on the last night and we're going to practice hard. I want that record – fingers crossed!

August 23rd

We did it! We busted that record up! We beat it by almost a minute and the other girls picked us up and carried us all the way to the cafeteria where Freya and Odie had a cake ready and everything. Margritte brought out her harp and we sang camp songs and danced around the campfire in a circle. It was awesome and I can't believe it's my last night! Olette gave me a friendship necklace and Sigrid made a woven leather bracelet with a little carved charm on it that looks just like Peaches. I was so embarrassed I didn't have anything to give them, but they just laughed and hugged me and I might have cried a little. We all put our charms on our bracelets and you know what?

I'm going to miss my friends.

OMG – I still have to pack, and say goodbye to Peaches, and Freya said she needs me to stop by her office right before lights out.

* * *

Carol eyed her daughter as she slouched into the passenger seat.

"Feet off the dash," Carol said automatically, then braced herself for the coming explosion. "Honey, listen. I know you were probably disappointed you didn't go to Whispering Meadows this year—"

"Are you kidding? Camp was awesome, Mom, and you know what's so cool? They want me to come back next summer as a counselor. Like, a job where I get paid and everything. Can I do it?"

Was that – was her daughter smiling? Something was different. Instead of pallid skin and a sneer, Molly was tanned, lean and possibly taller. Her sun-streaked hair was gathered in a neat braid that highlighted bright green eyes ordinarily half-hidden under unkempt bangs. She wore old jeans, a new "Camp Valkyrie" t-shirt, and a braided leather bracelet around her left wrist from which dangled an assortment of silver charms.

"Well, honey, we'll see—"

"Thanks, Mom! Hey, can we swing through Starbucks on our way home? I'd slaughter hordes for a latte."

Carol nearly drove over the curb. Molly, thanking her? She eyed her passenger. Despite the changes it looked like her daughter. It sounded like her daughter. Time for a test.

"Sure, honey. Before I forget, do you want to go shopping for back-to-school this weekend?"

"That would be great. I brought some things home with me, but I could definitely use new clothes." Molly turned toward her mother and grinned. "I'm going to need larger bras."

Whatever alien had taken over her only child, Carol fervently hoped it would stay a while. They rode in silence for a bit, then Carol cleared her throat. "Did you keep your journal up, like Dr. Dietrick asked?"

Molly shrugged a shoulder, looking out the front window with a light smile. "As best I could. We were really busy and you would not believe the things I learned."

"Well, if you need to backfill any entries maybe you can work on that this weekend. You know it's required to keep you in the new school."

Molly's smile got bigger. "I don't think I need that anymore, Mom. Regular school will be just fine."

"But honey—"

"As a matter of fact," Molly's grin was wolfish as she fingered the tiny battle-axe charm on her bracelet. "Regular school will be just awesome. I can't wait for it to start."

The Confessions of Valdis the Forgotten

(Or: How I Became the Most Hated Valkyrie in All Nine Realms)

Laura Shenton

Listen, I know what you're thinking. Another sob story from some washed-up warrior maiden who couldn't hack it in the big leagues. "Oh, woe is me, I'm forgotten to history, nobody remembers my great deeds." Well, buckle up, buttercup, because that's not what this is. This is the unvarnished truth about why I, Valdis Ironwing, am not remembered in your precious sagas, why my name doesn't trip off the tongues of skalds, and why even the other Valkyries cross themselves when they hear it whispered on the wind.

The truth is, I was forgotten on purpose. And honestly? Good riddance.

You see, everyone loves to romanticise us Valkyries. Oh, we're so noble, so fierce, so devoted to duty. We ride our magnificent steeds across battlefields, our armour gleaming, our hair flowing like spun gold in the wind, selecting the worthy dead with the solemn grace of divine judgement. We're the ultimate warrior goddesses, right? The perfect blend of beauty and battle-fury, carrying fallen heroes to eternal glory in Valhalla's golden halls.

What absolute horse muck.

Let me tell you what it's really like being a Valkyrie, at least what it was like for me. First off, the job description is criminally misleading. "Choose the slain," they said. "Escort souls to glory," they said. What they didn't mention was that you're essentially providing cosmic transportation with a side of supernatural waitressing. Half the dead warriors go to Odin's hall, half to Freyja's Sessrúmnir – which sounds prestigious until you realise you're basically running a divine taxi service between battlefield and banquet hall.

And the dead? Oh, don't get me started on the dead. Everyone assumes warriors who die gloriously in battle are automatically noble, honourable souls worthy of eternal feasting. Ha! I've collected murderers, oath-breakers, and cowards who got lucky with a posthumous sword through the chest. But apparently, dying with a weapon in your hand automatically qualifies you for the VIP afterlife experience. The bureaucracy of it all made my teeth ache.

But I'm getting ahead of myself. Let me start from the beginning, when I was young and stupid and actually believed in the mission.

My sisters – and I use that term loosely, considering what backstabbing harpies most of them turned out to be – were always the golden girls. Brunhild with her dramatic tragic romance stuff, always mooning over some mortal hero and making grand speeches about fate and duty. Gunnr, who couldn't shut up about courage this and honour that, like she'd swallowed a scroll of military ethics. And don't even get me started on Skuld, playing both sides as a Norn and a Valkyrie – talk about a conflict of interest. These were my role models, the shining examples I was supposed to emulate.

Well, I tried. Odin knows I tried.

For my first few centuries, I played the part perfectly. I swooped down onto battlefields with all the dramatic flair you could want, my midnight-black wings (not white – I was never one for the angelic aesthetic) spread wide against storm clouds I'd personally arranged for maximum atmospheric effect. I wore my battle-scarred armour with pride, my hair braided with silver wire and raven feathers. I looked the part, I sounded the part when I delivered my pronouncements of who would feast in Valhalla and who would rot in the mud.

The problem was, I was good at it. Too good.

See, most Valkyries develop a kind of professional detachment. You swoop in, you point at the worthy dead, you escort them to their eternal reward, you serve them mead, you fly off to the next battlefield. Rinse, repeat, collect your cosmic pay cheque. But I? I started paying attention. Really paying attention.

I noticed that the "glorious death in battle" requirement was being interpreted pretty loosely. A farmer who grabbed a pitchfork and got trampled by cavalry? Warrior. A merchant who swung a hammer once before getting his throat cut? Warrior. A frail elderly man who happened to be holding a kitchen knife when he died? Congratulations, welcome to Valhalla, here's your eternal drinking horn.

Meanwhile, the women who fought just as fiercely – the shield-maidens, the berserker wives, the mothers who died defending their children with improvised weapons – they didn't count unless they'd specifically trained as warriors and died in what the All-Father deemed "proper" combat. The double standard made my blood boil.

But the real breaking point came during what mortals call the Battle of Stamford Bridge – 25 September 1066. I remember it like it was yesterday because it was the day I finally snapped.

I was assigned to collect a Norwegian king named Harald Hardrada, who'd been cut down by an English arrow after spending the entire battle making catastrophically bad tactical decisions. This was supposed to be one of the last great Viking invasions, a clash of heroes worthy of song and saga. Instead, I found a stubborn old fool who'd led thousands of men to pointless deaths because he was too proud to negotiate and too greedy to stay home.

But according to my orders, Harald was a "great warrior king" who deserved a place of honour in Valhalla. The English farmers and fishermen who died defending their homes from his raiders? Not warriors. Not worthy. Left to rot.

I'd had enough.

Instead of delivering Harald to Odin's hall, I dropped him off at Hel's domain with a cheerful, "Enjoy eternity, you warmonger!" Then I went back to the battlefield and started collecting every single defender I could find – including a miller's wife who'd hit a Viking with a rolling pin, a child who'd thrown stones at raiders, and an elderly priest who'd died trying to protect his church's gold from being stolen.

I escorted them all to Sessrúmnir, figuring Freyja might be more reasonable about the whole "worthy of paradise" thing. She was, actually. Took one look at my collection of supposedly unworthy dead and nodded approvingly. "Finally," she said, "someone with some sense."

That should have been the end of it. But no, I had to keep pushing.

Word got back to Odin about my little stunt, and he was not pleased. I was summoned to Gladsheim for what I assumed would be a dressing-down and reassignment to some less prestigious battlefield. Instead, I found myself facing the entire court of Asgard – gods, goddesses, my sister Valkyries, the whole celestial peanut gallery.

"Valdis Ironwing," intoned the All-Father from his high throne, his ravens perched smugly on either side of him, "you have violated the sacred laws governing the selection of the slain."

"I improved them," I shot back, because I've never been able to keep my mouth shut when it would be wise to do so. "Your "sacred laws" are arbitrary nonsense that elevate murderers and ignore heroes."

The gasps from the assembled crowd were audible. You could have heard a pin drop in the hall of the gods. My sister Valkyries were staring at me like I'd grown a second head, probably already calculating how to distance themselves from the coming fallout.

Odin's single eye fixed on me with the intensity of a collapsing star. "You dare question the wisdom of the gods?"

"I dare question the wisdom of sending pillagers to paradise while leaving actual heroes to rot in common graves," I replied, because apparently I had decided that day was a good day to commit career suicide. "Your system is broken, old man."

The silence that followed was the kind of silence that precedes very bad things happening to very stupid people. Even Loki, who was usually good for some supportive snark during these kinds of divine tribunals, was studiously examining his fingernails.

"Very well," Odin said finally, his voice carrying authority and barely contained rage. "If you find our methods so distasteful, perhaps you would prefer not to participate in them at all."

And that's how I became the first Valkyrie to be fired.

Not killed, mind you – that would have made me a martyr, someone future generations might remember with sympathy. Not imprisoned, which might have suggested I was dangerous enough to be worth containing. No, I was simply…dismissed. Stripped of my official duties, my divine authority, my access to the rainbow bridge, and most importantly, my place in the records.

They erased me. Not just from their books, but from history itself. Every saga I should have appeared in, every battle where I'd collected the dead, every interaction with mortals or gods – all of it wiped clean as though it had never happened. The cosmic equivalent of deleting someone's social media accounts and pretending they never existed.

My sisters didn't speak up for me. Not one. Brunhild gave me a pitying look and muttered something about "choosing battles wisely". Gunnr actually had the audacity to tell me this was all for the best, that I'd "lost perspective" and needed time to "reflect on proper conduct". The rest just avoided eye contact entirely.

Cowards, every last one of them.

So there I was, an unemployed Valkyrie with nowhere to go and no one to complain to. I couldn't return to Midgard permanently – I was still technically divine, just unemployed divine. I couldn't stay in Asgard – I'd been made persona non grata in the most public way possible. And I sure as Hel wasn't going to crawl back to Odin begging for forgiveness.

Instead, I became a freelancer.

Turns out there's a surprising amount of work for an experienced psychopomp with flexible ethics and a grudge against the establishment. Dead souls who got overlooked by the official collection system, ghosts with unfinished business, spirits who wanted to file complaints about their afterlife accommodations – suddenly I was busier than ever.

I set up shop (metaphorically speaking) in the spaces between worlds, the forgotten corners and abandoned battlefields where the official Valkyries never bothered to look. I collected the souls everyone else ignored: the peasants who died of disease, the children who starved during sieges, the slaves who perished building their masters' war machines. I gave them choices about where they wanted to spend eternity, something the official system never bothered with.

And you know what? I was happy. For the first time in my immortal existence, I was actually helping people instead of just shuffling paperwork for the cosmic bureaucracy.

But apparently, even that was too much for my former employers to tolerate.

See, my freelance operation was making the official Valkyries look bad. Word was getting around the nine realms that there was someone willing to collect the souls everyone else deemed "unworthy", someone who actually listened to the dead instead of just sorting them into predetermined categories. Suddenly, people were asking uncomfortable questions about why the gods only cared about certain kinds of death, certain kinds of sacrifice.

The All-Father sent Brunhild to "reason" with me.

"Sister," Brunhild said, landing her white-winged horse nearby with typical dramatic flair, "you have to stop this."

"Stop helping people?" I asked. "Stop doing the job we were supposed to be doing all along?"

"You're disrupting the natural order."

"The natural order is rubbish, and you know it."

Brunhild sighed, the kind of long-suffering sigh people use when they think you're being unreasonable. "The All-Father is willing to forgive your past transgressions if you cease this… unauthorised activity…and formally request reinstatement."

I looked at her for a long moment, this sister who'd once stood with me in the storm-winds above a hundred battlefields, who'd shared the burden of impossible choices and the challenge of divine duty. Now she was just another corporate enforcer, delivering ultimatums from management.

"Tell the All-Father," I said carefully, "that he can take his forgiveness and shove it."

Brunhild's face went white, then red, then settled into the kind of cold fury that only comes from realising someone you care about has chosen to be your enemy. "You're making a mistake, Valdis."

"No," I replied, "I made a mistake when I spent centuries pretending your system was just or fair or worth preserving. This is me fixing it."

She left without another word, and I haven't seen any of my sisters since.

That was the end of my brief career as a reformed Valkyrie. Within a week, I found myself cut off from the streams of power that let me travel between worlds, stripped of my ability to open passages to the various afterlives, effectively neutered as a psychopomp. They didn't just fire me – they made sure I couldn't keep doing the job even as a freelancer.

So here I am, stuck in the spaces between spaces, able to observe but not interfere, watching as the same broken system grinds on century after century. The Valkyries still swoop down on battlefields, still apply their arbitrary standards to determine who deserves eternal reward. Wars change, weapons change, but the fundamental injustice remains the same.

And I'm still forgotten. Erased so thoroughly from history that even when mortals try to research Valkyrie lore, my name never comes up. No sagas, no eddas, no folk tales. It's like I never existed.

Which brings me to why I'm telling you this story now.

See, I've had a lot of time to think – and I mean a *lot* of time, because immortality is a real tedium when you're unemployed – and I've come to some conclusions about my situation.

First: I was right. The system is corrupt, unjust, and serves the powerful at the expense of everyone else. My getting fired doesn't change that; it just proves that even the gods would rather silence critics than address legitimate complaints.

Second: I was also kind of a pain about it. Not about the principles – I stand by those. But my execution was…let's call it suboptimal. Dropping Harald Hardrada off in Hel's domain was emotionally satisfying but strategically stupid. Insulting Odin to his face in front of the entire court might have felt good in the moment, but it guaranteed that any chance of reform would die with my dismissal.

Third: Being forgotten to history isn't actually the worst fate that could have befallen me. It's freed me from the burden of reputation, from worrying about how future generations will judge my actions. I can be as petty, vindictive, and righteously angry as I want without concern for my legacy.

And finally: I don't regret any of it.

Not one single moment of defiance, not one challenged authority, not one soul I rescued from cosmic injustice. Even knowing how it would end, I'd do it all again. Because at the end of the day, being a forgotten rebel who stood up for what was right beats being a remembered hero who perpetuated an evil system.

But here's the thing that really gets me, the final insult that makes me want to scream loud enough to shatter the walls of Valhalla: they didn't need to erase me so completely. They could have just let me fade into obscurity naturally, the way most people do when their time passes. Instead, they made sure I was actively forgotten, systematically removed from every record and memory.

Why? Because they knew I was right.

If they'd been confident in their system, in the justice of their methods, they would have been content to let history judge between us. The fact that they felt the need to erase me entirely proves they knew their position was indefensible. They couldn't refute my arguments, so they made sure no one would ever hear them.

And that, more than anything else, is what makes me the way I am. Not the righteous anger, not the defiance of authority, not even the spectacular way I flamed out of my celestial career.

It's the fact that I was right, and they knew it, and they erased me anyway.

So here I sit in my self-imposed exile, watching the world burn through the same cycles of violence and injustice, knowing that somewhere out there, my sisters are still playing divine taxi service for unworthy dead while actual heroes rot forgotten in unmarked graves. And every time I see it happen, every time I witness another example of cosmic unfairness, I feel that familiar surge of rage that got me into this mess in the first place.

You want to know what it's like being a forgotten Valkyrie? It's like being the only person in a room who can see that the emperor has no clothes, screaming the truth at the top of your lungs while everyone else pretends not to hear you. It's watching the people you once called sisters perpetuate a system they know is broken because changing it would require admitting they were wrong. It's being vindicated by history while simultaneously being erased from it.

It's knowing that somewhere in Valhalla, Harald Hardrada is probably still holding court, regaling other dead kings with tales of his glorious battles while the farmers and fishermen who died stopping his invasion are nowhere to be found. It's realising that the cosmic order values the wrong things for the wrong reasons and will continue to do so long after everyone currently involved is dust.

It's being absolutely, completely, unapologetically right about everything and having precisely zero power to do anything about it.

And you know what? I'm okay with that. Because at least I'm not serving mead to murderers and calling it justice. At least I'm not pretending that dying with a sword in your hand automatically makes you a hero worthy of eternal reward. At least I'm not perpetuating a system I know is fundamentally evil just because it's traditional.

I may be forgotten, I may be powerless, I may be stuck in cosmic purgatory for the rest of eternity. But I'm not complicit. I chose principle over position, truth over comfort, righteous anger over willful blindness.

Does that make me problematic? Absolutely.

Am I proud of it? Oh yes.

So the next time you hear some saga about the noble Valkyries and their sacred duty to choose the slain, remember that there was once one among them who looked at that duty and said, "This is unfair, and I won't be part of it." Remember that not all of us were content to be divine waitresses serving unworthy dead in cosmic restaurants that cater to the powerful.

Remember that some of us cared more about justice than job security.

And if that makes me the biggest problem in all nine realms? Well, I'll wear that title like a badge of honour.

After all, someone has to.

* * *

Valdis Ironwing, the Forgotten Valkyrie, last seen arguing with a flock of ravens about proper combat ethics somewhere between Midgard and everywhere else. Still unemployed, still angry, still absolutely right about everything.

Saving Souls

Nina Shepardson

Hilda soared over the ford, unseen by the warriors battling to control it. One army wore green tabards with a lion rampant stitched in gold over their mail. They were hard-pressed by a force bearing round shields painted pitch-black, so the phoenix rising from orange flames stood out more boldly.

Both sides claimed to have the favor of Hilda and her sisters, but the truth was, they didn't care what heraldry mortals wore or who had the better claim to any given stretch of land. Hilda's eyes passed over men and women who fought competently, going where their commanders bid and standing their ground in a fight they might win or lose. Her heart throbbed with fury when soldiers fled or cut down enemies who had surrendered, but she knew punishing them wasn't her job.

Drifting above the ford, Hilda felt pulled towards one young man as if he were a magnet attracting iron filings. He bent to lift a comrade who groaned and clutched his midsection, blood seeping from a wound and reddening the shallow water.

"Leave me, Egil," the injured man said as the phoenix warriors advanced, but Egil ignored him. Slinging his friend's arm over his shoulder, he staggered back toward shore, where a line of pikemen waited.

One of the phoenixes charged into the ford and swung a mace at Egil. Burdened with his comrade's weight, he couldn't get his shield up in time, and the weapon clanged against his helmet. His eyes unfocused, and for a moment his uneven pupils fixed on Hilda.

Egil's opponent pressed the advantage, driving him to his knees with another strike of his mace. His comrades caught up with him, and one drove a sword into Egil's chest.

The body that fell face-down in the water was dull and grey, but the spirit rising from it shone like the sun.

Hilda couldn't have resisted the urge to sing if she'd wanted to. She sang the praises of the young man's valor and stretched out a hand to him. Just as she hadn't cared which side he fought for, she didn't care that he'd failed to save his comrade. All that mattered was that, in the face of danger, he had tried.

Egil turned his radiant face up to her. "I *did* see you before," he whispered.

He reached out to take Hilda's hand, but before he could, something threw its arms around him from behind.

"Sindre?" he asked, but it wasn't the soul of his friend – now also dead – that clung to him. Sindre's spirit would go to some other destination; Hilda didn't much care where. Hilda and her sisters were charged with selecting the brave, and Egil certainly qualified. Who else could make a greater claim on him?

The water of the ford bubbled and turned into thick, oozy tar. The thing that pulled Egil away from Hilda's outstretched hand seemed made of the same stuff.

Hilda pushed her voice higher, into a shriek that could shatter glass. She pulled her wings in tight to her body and dove. She grabbed the arms wrapped around Egil's chest and tried to wrench them apart. They flowed around her intervening hands, molasses-sticky, and reformed. Three more pairs emerged from the gooey mass of the thing and latched onto the soldier.

Even after death, Egil showed his courage, struggling against the entity that held him. He thrashed and bellowed a war cry. He braced ghostly feet against the ground and drove his elbows back into what would have been the thing's gut if it were human.

"He is ours!" Hilda shouted. "See how he fights? He is ours!"

The creature gave no sign that it had heard her, much less that it cared. In the end, it yanked the warrior away from her, drowned him in itself, and slurped back into the waters of the ford.

Hilda wailed, and all the fighters around her shivered as something deeper than their ears heard her cry.

* * *

Hilda's sisters gathered in the courtyard. They sat on benches under trellises festooned with wisteria, perched on the edges of cool fountains, leaned against statues of white marble. The blessed dead had been shooed away from this space for a time, although the sounds of their laughter and music could be heard from within the halls that bordered the courtyard. If they thought this gathering of the sisters was strange, it would slip from their minds soon enough, as all worries did in this place.

One by one, they told stories of disasters like the one Hilda had endured. Dagrun raged about losing a nurse who had treated the plague-stricken and contracted their ailment herself. Guðlaug's crimson hair writhed in an absent wind as she told of feeling a man ripped from her arms after he had been trampled standing alone against an oppressive emperor's cavalry. Hilda related her own story, and her sisters bared their teeth in sympathy.

It was rare for one of the sisters to see or interact with their cousins, who scooped up the souls defined by some trait other than courage. While in the mortal world, they were as invisible to each other as they were to humans, unless they happened to lay claim to the same soul. Yet such things had happened, so they knew the tar-like beings were none of their kindred.

Hilda's sisters went silent. They'd reached the end of their knowledge. A cheer went up from inside the nearest hall as the blessed dead started some sort of game or contest. A part of Hilda felt pulled to go inside, to cheer with them. She forced herself to stay out here, thinking about the problem, even as a few of her sisters drifted back towards the doors.

None of them knew what the tar-things were or where they'd come from. Maybe…maybe someone else knew?

The sisters usually didn't give any thought to their cousins or to mortals who weren't near death. Even the gods were distant. They were too busy keeping the world running to visit the sisters. But their cousins and the mortals and the gods all existed, and they certainly knew things the sisters didn't.

One order of cousins gathered the wise, didn't they? Yes, Hilda thought they did. They chose the greatest thinkers, philosophers, and scholars for their halls. Hilda and her sisters knew how to wield every weapon humans had devised and some they hadn't. They knew how to lay siege to a castle and how to break a siege.

Yet unlike their scholar-cousins, there were vast swathes of knowledge they ignored.

"What if…" The sisters who'd been heading for the doors turned back at the sound of her voice. "What if we asked our cousins who choose the wise? Maybe they know what these things are and how they have the power to steal souls." The words felt strange, like she had to push them through a hole that was too small for them.

Her sisters looked confused at first, as if they were trying to remember who she was talking about. "They might," Dagrun said. She scrunched up her face, visibly struggling to remember something. "I saw one of them once. There was a man who took up arms to keep a mob from burning his library. He'd never so much as raised a hand against another human before, but he loved knowledge and couldn't let it be destroyed. Oh, he was glorious!" Her voice lost its hesitance for a moment, and Hilda couldn't help beaming at her. "One of our cousins came," Dagrun said. "We struggled for the soul. He was…" She shrugged. "Like us, but not like us," was the best she could muster. "I don't think they usually fight. But if these soul-thieves try to take someone they've claimed, I think they will be fierce."

"Then we must go to them and ask for their help." Hilda's sisters nodded, but none of them moved. Instead, they cast bewildered looks at each other.

Hilda tried to remember where the choosers of the wise gathered. What did their halls look like? Surely, she had seen them from above while bringing in a soul. Clockwise…she thought if she walked clockwise from her sisters' halls around the abode of the gods, she'd come to the halls of the wise.

"I know how to get there," she said, surprised at her own understanding.

The others perked up. "Then…you'll go?" Guðlaug asked.

"I'll go," Hilda affirmed.

* * *

As far as Hilda knew, there had never been any travel between the halls of the brave and the wise and the kind. Despite that, not a single weed or crack marred the ring road that connected them.

When the top of a great dome poked over the horizon ahead of her, Hilda looked back. The halls of the brave were just visible. Hearth-smoke floated up from the chimneys, and the peaked roofs shone in the afternoon sunlight.

She approached the dome, thinking this must surely be the central structure. There was some kind of sliding panel in the roof but no door. Instead, a silver door shone in a much shorter wall beside it. When Hilda pressed a hand against it, it opened easily, presenting her with a view of an elegant foyer.

Hilda stepped inside, unnerved by the quiet of the place. The denizens of these halls were among the blessed dead, so where was the singing, the laughter, the stomping of feet?

"Oh, hello there."

The door at the other end of the foyer – this one made of dark wood – opened, and a face peered around it. The door opened wider to reveal the whole person. His build was much more slender than Hilda's, and he wore a tunic and trousers of linen instead of armor. But magnificent wings, not so different from Hilda's own, sprang from his back.

"Have you been sent here with some message from the gods?" the man asked.

"No," Hilda said. "I'm here for help. I need to know things."

The man blinked several times in quick succession. Apparently, a message from the gods was the only reason he could conceive for a cousin to visit, and it was taking some time for him to adjust to the truth. "Things about what?"

"Some kind of strange beings are stealing the souls of the brave—"

That was as far as Hilda got before the man's wings snapped outward. At their full spread, they stretched across the foyer. His wispy black hair lifted as if in a breeze, and his gentle face hardened. "It's not only the souls of the brave they've taken. We've lost some of our dead to them, too."

The man's wings settled back into their folded position as he whirled around. "The greatest minds in human history have been working to understand what's happening. Come, I'll take you to them."

The chooser of the wise, whose name was Fannar, led Hilda through a gallery where vast maps stretched across the walls, past the great dome she'd seen earlier ("I wish there was time to show you the planetarium"), and through a maze of bookshelves. Finally, they arrived at what Hilda first thought was a feast hall. A long table dominated the room, and more than a dozen people sat around it. But instead of being piled high with platters of food and flagons of mead, the table was covered with books and scrolls.

People – mortal people – scribbled notes, passed the books back and forth, and called out questions to each other.

Fannar introduced Hilda to the wise dead, their names and professions flowing over her like a river. They stared at her in fascination. Fannar had to stop one of them from running out of the room to see if he could find any historical records of such an "inter-institutional colloquy."

When Fannar explained why Hilda had come, they all started talking at once. Fannar waved and shouted until they quieted, then designated a woman with a long silver braid to speak for the group.

"We believe," she said, "that a god is behind this."

"Which one?"

"Not one of our own gods."

Hilda tried to process this and failed. "What other gods are there?"

"In this world? None. But ours is not the only world."

The woman accepted a brass device from another wise one and began shifting parts of it around. It was apparently a model of the universe, with components representing a plethora of worlds. She pointed at one, then another, theorizing about which plane of existence the interloper god might have originated in.

Hilda's head spun. She held up a hand, and the woman with the braid stopped speaking. "Why would some god from another world want to steal our souls in the first place?"

"To gain a foothold here," the woman said. "Having souls under their dominion would allow them a sort of cosmic legitimacy…"

She launched into another long explanation that went over Hilda's head.

Hilda's fury over the pilfered souls now had a target. She wanted to race out of the halls of the wise, find this invader god, and pummel them until they released the spirits that rightfully belonged among the brave. Her feet refused to carry her, though. A voice in the back of her mind whispered that surely it couldn't be so easy to defeat a god.

She tried to quash that traitorous voice. Cowardice had no place among her kind.

Was it cowardice, though?

Hilda had flown over a thousand battlefields. She'd seen people fighting each other on foot, on horseback, on ships. With her experience of warfare, she knew it wasn't all about stabbing or shooting. Someone had to direct the troops. Some soldiers devised clever traps or worked out ways to undermine enemy fortifications. Generals spent as much time poring over maps as they did swinging swords or firing bows.

Courage was laudable whether the cause was won or lost, but strategy increased the chances that the cause would be won.

It wouldn't be easy to defeat a god, even one who was still weak and vulnerable in this world. Her cause was more likely to be won if she had wisdom on her side.

"Will you come with me?" she asked.

"What?" The braided wise one had still been talking and seemed to think Hilda's question was directed at her.

Hilda pointed at Fannar. "If your mortals can figure out where this god is and how I might be able to hurt them, will you come with me? As...an advisor?"

Fannar's lips twisted, and the corner of his right eye twitched. "I've never…I've never been in a battle before." His obvious struggle to think about something so far outside his experience reminded Hilda of Dagrun. "But this must stop!" Power seeped into his quavering voice, and several wise ones ducked as Hilda instinctively spread her wings. "We cannot keep losing the best among mortals, those who have plumbed the deepest secrets of the universe!" The eyes of the knowledgeable dead widened as Fannar's hands clenched into fists. "Yes. I will go with you, my cousin who chooses the brave, and I will help you avenge our lost souls."

* * *

Hilda and Fannar set out from the halls of the wise with the gods' abode at their backs. It felt strange to be walking for an outward journey. Usually, the choosers of the slain flew. They passed over a featureless plain, into a rolling fog that grew denser and denser. As it began to thin out again, they found themselves soaring over the mortal world.

The wise had explained why walking in the same direction would bring them to a different destination, but all the jargon and diagrams had made Hilda's eyes glaze over. Eventually, she decided to just accept that it was so.

As they walked, Fannar talked about his area of expertise, which turned out to be music. Hilda was interested at first. She rejoiced in all the activities of the blessed dead, but there was nothing she loved more than belting out a boisterous drinking song or rousing anthem. Unfortunately, Fannar didn't want to actually sing. Instead, he expounded at great length on musical theory, the lives of famous mortal musicians, and the alterations made to folk songs as they were passed down from one generation to the next.

Then he mentioned a song that had been written to commemorate a great battle.

"That's not how it went at all," Hilda said.

"What?"

"The defenders weren't outnumbered ten to one. They were at a disadvantage for numbers, but their positioning more than made up for it."

"You were there," Fannar said wonderingly.

"Of course," Hilda answered. "Just because the defenders' situation wasn't as hopeless as your song says doesn't mean none of them were brave. And there was courage on the other side, too."

"Yes, yes, but what I mean is, you're an unbiased primary source for that battle! All the historical accounts we have are either non-contemporaneous or were written by people with a vested interest in portraying one side or the other favorably. I don't suppose you'd be willing to speak with—"

He broke off as Hilda raised her hand. "Do you see that?"

Fannar squinted. The mists had thinned, but what lay before them wasn't any scene of the mortal world. Instead, a lake of black tar bubbled and sloshed. Despite the apparent thickness of the liquid, they could see through it as if it were clear water. Below the surface lay a landscape of ash, studded with obsidian trees. Here and there, tar-things like the one that had ripped Egil from Hilda's grasp oozed along on unknown errands.

"Are you clear on how to lay out the runes?" Fannar asked. From anyone else, the question might have sounded condescending, but Fannar spoke like he'd consider it a failure on his part, not hers, if she didn't understand.

When Hilda had asked him to join her as an advisor, she'd expected him to uncover the location of a god-killing weapon in a hidden vault somewhere. Or maybe he'd devise a mighty spell to rend the deity limb from limb.

What he'd done instead was ask whether they even needed to kill the god in the first place. Apparently, a very specific confluence of circumstances was required for an incursion like this. If they could seal the rupture this god had made in what Fannar called "the wall of the world," they could stop the loss of souls. And truthfully, he *had* devised a mighty spell, just not the one Hilda had thought he would.

"I can do it," she told him, and withdrew a vial of silvery liquid from the satchel she carried. The greatest spells, Fannar had told her, were worked in blood. Several of the wise ones had given their own blood for this endeavor.

Hilda uncorked the vial, but then she hesitated. Fannar had assured her that the invader would have consumed the souls it had claimed to increase its power. The thought made Hilda seethe with rage, but under that, there was...doubt? To vanquish a single spirit was one thing, but how many of the brave had this thing stolen? How many of the wise and the kind? She couldn't quite shake an instinctive feeling that so many souls together wouldn't be so easily conquered.

Still, she began painting the runes on the ground at the edge of the grotesque lake. Fannar did the same, the two moving away from each other around the circle.

Then Hilda stopped. "Something's happening."

Down in the god's realm, the tar-things had paused in their wanderings. They didn't really have faces, but they seemed to be orienting themselves in the same direction. A direction from which something huge approached.

"Quickly!" Fannar called. Like Hilda, he feared the approaching thing was the god itself.

Hilda wanted to punch that god. She wanted to stab it, burn it, punish it for having deprived brave souls of the eternal joy they'd earned. It didn't matter that it was a god, that it could probably kill even a higher being like herself. All that mattered was to throw herself at this vile enemy.

Except she didn't think it was the god. The closer it got, the less it looked like a single shape. Instead, it was a mass of smaller shapes moving as one.

"People," Hilda breathed. "Fannar, those are people."

A crowd hurried across the blighted landscape of the intruder god's home. They carried clubs and staves fashioned from the trees of this bleak realm and shook them menacingly at the tar-things. And right at the front was…

…a young man whose green tabard bore a golden lion rampant.

"They're not gone! Fannar, look, they're still whole! We can save them!"

Fannar broke into a grin. "You were right," he told her, inclining his head. She hadn't spoken of her belief that the lost souls weren't unrecoverable, but he must have sensed it. "But they need our help. Look." He pointed to where several of the tar-things were moving to intercept the blessed dead.

Hilda prepared to launch herself into the other world, but then she stopped. Was it her time with Fannar that was making her pause to consider? "How? When one of those things claimed a soul, I wasn't able to stop it."

"Those souls are in the process of escaping. They must have fought some of those servitors before and won, or they'd never have gotten this far. They're carrying weapons made from the material of that world. Perhaps the denizens of this other dimension can be harmed by—"

Hilda hadn't been so influenced by Fannar that she was going to stand still and listen to that whole lecture. She dove into the lake of tar. It felt as sticky as she expected, but only for a moment. Her body cleaved through some kind of membrane, and then she was plummeting through the air. She snapped her wings open and glided to the ground near an ebon tree. Fannar landed behind her with a thump.

The souls pointed and shouted. "The gods are with us still!" someone cried.

Hilda wrenched a large branch free from the tree. Fannar chose one that was smaller but ended in a wicked point.

The lost souls had reached the line of tar-things, but they were undaunted. Egil swung a stout branch at one of the servitors, and just as Fannar had deduced, it slumped to the ground.

As she had on the battlefield where she'd lost him, Hilda sang. She sang as she charged and attacked with her own branch. Another of the tar-things fell before her.

Even in the midst of battle, it struck her that there were more people in the crowd than just those souls who'd been lost among the brave. Behind Egil, a woman with hair like a cumulus cloud drew and fired a bow crafted from the strange materials of this place. She wore a soft tunic instead of armor, but who said the wise couldn't also be brave? Fannar must have felt the same, for his voice joined hers.

Behind the souls who fought stood an inner ring. These gathered around a few children and old people. In the mortal world, Hilda was nearly blind to any she wasn't called to choose, but she recognized these as the healers and nurturers, following their nature even in this accursed place.

An old man among the company limped. No doubt Fannar had some theory as to how one of the blessed dead could be injured. The tar-things didn't care. One lunged for the man, but a woman interposed herself, slashing at it with a sharpened rock tied to a branch. "Leave my patient alone!" she bellowed, and Hilda knew her for Dagrun's nurse.

Fannar speared another tar-thing right through its middle, and their line broke. "Go, go!" Hilda urged the souls, and they sprinted up the slope leading to the surface of the lake.

A few tar-things that had come from farther away surged after the retreating souls, but one man stood in their way, holding a bow like the one the wise woman had fired. He was unarmored and wasn't built like most of the fighters Hilda had carried, but he looked as immovable as a boulder.

Hilda cast down her branch, grabbed a bow and arrows from a passing wise one, and ran to his side just as he loosed an arrow of his own. They fired together, arrow after arrow, until no more tar-things stood.

Most of the others had made it back into the proper gods' realm by now. Fannar stood by the exit, waving frantically to them.

"With apologies to Guðlaug," Hilda said, grabbed the stalwart soul under his arms, and flew.

Hilda and Fannar broke the surface, side by side.

"We can't rest yet!" Fannar said. "Hilda and I must finish painting the runes to close off this portal, but more of the false god's minions may come."

Brave ones and wise ones, even a few kind ones, ringed the lake, bows aimed downward as Hilda and Fannar completed the runic circle. Slowly, green grass and healthy brown earth covered the lake of tar, like new skin closing over a wound. The mist filtered in afterwards, reclaiming this space as part of the in-between.

"Where do we go now?" Egil asked.

"Follow us," Fannar said, "We'll take you where you need to be." He'd come far out of his comfort zone, but now he was back on familiar ground: leading the souls of the recently deceased to their new homes.

Their first stop was the halls of the kind, where Hilda met more of her cousins. Then they brought the wise back to the great conglomeration of libraries and lecture halls.

Hilda and Fannar stood just outside the great silver doors. The brave waited a short distance away for Hilda to take them home.

"Well," Fannar said. "It was an honor to fight alongside you."

To fight alongside you. Not words she would ever have expected one of her cousins to say.

"We wouldn't have succeeded without your expertise." Not words she'd ever expected to say to a cousin, either. "The blessed dead would have been lost forever. All are in your debt."

"And in yours."

There was a long pause, during which none of the brave expressed impatience. On the contrary, they had drawn away and seemed to be studiously not paying attention to the two higher spirits.

"You would be…welcome…here, if you ever wished to visit." Fannar's voice was halting, his eyes downcast.

Hilda's voice was equally hesitant as she said, "I think I would like that."

They exchanged small smiles, and then Hilda departed to shepherd the courageous dead to where they belonged.

The Brightest Star

Zac Sherman

The world ended in a maelstrom of fire and blood. The sky was split in two, riders of woe circled the earth, causing floods and rending winds. It was an axe age, sundering the bones of humanity and the world alike.

Then, it was over. And I still had to go to work.

I float through the halls of the hospital. Float is a bit of a misnomer. I exist on two planes of reality, one of which is Earth. On the other plane, my composition and form of locomotion is so different as to be entirely incomprehensible to humans.

Sometimes, it's even incomprehensible to me.

I don't know how long it's been since Ragnarök – centuries, at least. Though time is difficult for me. On Earth, it moves straight, but slowly. When I fully inhabit the other place, it moves sideways, skipping like a stylus trying to find the grooves of a record. My sisters and I are given times of rest between our bouts of work on Earth. When I return to the planet, it has sometimes been a day or a lifetime that has passed.

I enter the room of the Girl. I have other charges, but I spend most of my time with her. She's been in and out of St. Anne's Hospital for three years. She is small. Smaller than when I first met her. Her therapies make it hard for her to eat, and harder to keep what is eaten down. I have held her hair on more than one occasion as she vomited. I do so subtly, of course. She isn't supposed to know I'm here. Technically, I'm not supposed to materialize any portion of myself while on Earth, but the occasional interaction is harmless enough.

Besides, just watching is boring.

It was more exciting during the age of the gods. My sisters and I would ride into battle as axes splintered shields and life-drinkers pierced the hearts of combatants on the battlefield. That was a glorious time. We Valkyrie took flight, bearing those worthy few who died in battle to Valhalla, where they waited for the greater glory of Ragnarök.

At the conclusion of Ragnarök, the gods and giants fought and died. But we did not. The Earth was born anew, and we shield-maidens were left to sort out what our place in this new world was. There was debate, of course, but in the end, we decided to just keep doing what we had always done: escorting souls to the next phase.

In this way, we are similar to humans. We are all creatures of habit. And when faced with uncertainty, it is the habits we have established that guide our actions like drums driving the march of soldiers. What else could we do, but follow the beat of that eternal drum?

In this new age, we have had to expand our search for worthy souls beyond the battlefield. War is not conducted the way it used to be. It is done with drones and missiles and computer screens. It is… difficult for us to fathom this. Instead, we choose to escort those who are enmeshed in different battles.

Mine battle cancer.

I stand beside the Girl's bed. She's sleeping. Her hair was auburn, usually in a pixie cut, but it is gone now. Her cheeks are sunken. When we first met, they were round and full. Healthy. Tubes twine in and around her body like so many serpents. The breathing tubes in her nostril slip out and she starts to wheeze. This is something that happens every so often. Gently, I push the tubes back in. At this point, it's reflexive enough that I hardly think about it anymore. I don't do this because I care about the Girl. It is just something to keep me busy – after all, if I have to watch over her, I might as well be useful.

Herja would be upset by my interactions with the Girl, such as they are. Herja is my superior, a Valkyrie of no small renown. But she is also mired in the old ways. The gods are dead. We may still have to do our jobs, but surely, we can be a bit more relaxed about how we do them.

Besides, I'm still pissed at Herja for assigning me to this plague-house. She said it was because I'm uniquely suited to deal with sick children – whatever *that* means. After three years of it, I think Herja is full of shit – that's a word I learned from the TV in the Girl's room. The new age has many words that I fancy. Boondoggle is among them.

The Girl shudders. She's dreaming, but beset by a nightmare of some sort – I can see the vague shadow of the dream-terror. It is a creature, much like me, though not from the same plane of reality. I give slight substance to my voice and speak to the girl.

"You are a warrior," I murmur, soft as the morning tide. "You stand with an axe in hand before a great dragon. Its fire slams against your shield; the shield has taken so many blows that its oaken frame is now blistered and blackened. But it still holds."

I place a hand on her forehead, but I don't materialize it. That would be too much contact. "You have battled this monster for years. Still, you stand. There are heroes I have known who despaired after one day of hard battle. You are beyond them."

The Girl's whimpers fade. Her face relaxes. I can only influence her dreams so much, and have a fairly limited frame of reference for what to impart. I wish I could give her something better – perhaps a calming moment on a beach, lounging in the sun, with a coconut drink of some sort in hand. But all I know is the battlefield. And here, amidst the beeping of machines and the scent of industrial cleaner that permeates St. Anne's Hospital, a battle *is* being waged.

A battle that soon, the Girl will lose.

* * *

I exist only in dreams now. It is a strange place to be, almost like another plane of reality. In dreams, time is fluid. I'm almost always younger in my dreams, a bright-faced child, and dressed accordingly. I had an obsession with patches back then. I think it started with Girl Scouts, then just kind of spilled over into the rest of my life. I had this khaki jacket that I just plastered with patches. Some were fandom patches, with the appropriate cartoony characters and silly catchphrases to go with them. Others were from places I'd been. I bought a whole collection of National Parks patches, but my rule was I couldn't sew them into the jacket until I'd actually been to the specific park each one represented (a girl can't attach a patch she hasn't earned, after all).

The first National Park that got the needle and thread treatment was Arches Park in Utah. It's gorgeous. Hundreds upon hundreds of sandstone arches that stretch beyond sight, flushed red against the heat of the desert. They stand like passages to another world. Antediluvian doorways, waiting for someone to step through – and no, I did not know the word antediluvian when I first went to Arches Park. But when you're bedbound, you have plenty of time to read.

We had to stay on specific paths, because if we stepped in the wrong place, we could disturb the ecosystem. Our guide, this scruffy man with a voice that sounded like a human Brillo pad, pointed out potholes in the basin of the area. Pools of water collected in them, some only as deep as my thumb; others deep enough that I couldn't see through to the bottom.

"Those are ephemeral pools," the tour guide rasped out. "That means they don't last long. Some of the shallower ones might only make it a day before they evaporate. But each one is home to an entire ecosystem. Hundreds of creatures live in these tiny potholes of water, if you can believe it."

If you can believe it was one of the tour guide's favorite conversational tags.

Someone asked what happened to the insects, shrimps, and tadpoles when a pool dries up. The tour guide shrugged. Sometimes they survive by transitioning to another pool. Sometimes they don't.

If you can believe it.

It is strange that such an impressive-looking place could be so fragile. Pools teeming with life that could disappear at a moment's notice. Lichen-covered ground that could be ravaged by human footfall.

As soon as we got back to the hotel, I sewed my Arches patch onto my khaki jacket. It was really too hot to wear the stupid thing – we were in the desert after all – but I insisted on donning my freshly emblemed jacket. I was just so excited to have my first National Park patch.

It was also my last National Park patch.

A few months after we got home, I got sick. I had become an ecosystem out of balance, something living and reproducing inside me at a prolific rate. All of my plans and the patches that would testify to where I'd gone and what I loved disintegrated before my eyes before they ever had a chance to exist.

* * *

Most people know that the Valkyrie escort the worthy slain to Valhalla. Our stories have permeated the culture, which does please me some. But that wasn't our only function. Sometimes, we also decided which combatants survived a battle. If a warrior was particularly bold or cunning or honorable, we could decide to spare their life.

We don't do that anymore.

Herja is waiting for me. She is more beautiful than I, resplendent in form and impeccable in her poise. She lounges on a chair of light, her wings pulled in tight against her body, their golden light shining like a beacon. I feel self-conscious of my own dross-like wings. Some shield-maidens shine more brightly than others. I'm not sure why. I am only sure that my light is inferior; it always has been. It is a selfish desire of mine to have a greater light, one to rival even Herja's, perhaps. But by either my action or intent, I have never proven worthy of that honor.

I escort the worthy, but am not worthy myself. The old bards would make a poem of that.

"You requested an audience, Svav?" Herja says. Her voice is a song that could drive sailors to dive overboard to reach it or lull warring factions to peace. I have seen great power in the point of a spear; greater power in the voice of the mighty.

I give a short bow. "My assignment is almost over. I request that my next assignment be…different."

Herja cocks her head to the side. Coupled with the wings, it makes her resemble a giant bird. "What is the reason for this request?"

I hesitate. Obedience is life to Valkyrie. But in the old days we could see the fruits of our obedience: the worthy in Valhalla, the gods boasting of our victories. Now, we don't even get to enter the Beyond that we guide souls to. It's an impermeable barrier to us. A frustration.

"I think I would be better suited to escorting different souls to the Beyond," I say. "I have great interest in drug addicts. Theirs is a long-term battle, similar to the patients I observe at St. Anne's. There are those in that population who engage the battle worthily." Even if they are destined to lose it.

"And they are almost always adults," Herja says, her voice clipped. I can tell she isn't pleased. She glides down from her chair, her motions fluid. "What is the reason for this request?"

I hesitate. What *is* my rationale? Working at St. Anne's has drained me. After my sessions observing the Girl, I feel unsettled, like there is a swill of stormwater in my belly, churning relentlessly. I don't like it.

But I can't say any of that to Herja.

"I simply think I would be better suited to different work," I say.

"But I have assigned you to *this* work. It is an honor."

I bow my head. "I am aware. But I wonder if your assessment of my abilities was incorrect."

A thunderstorm crosses Herja's face. She doesn't like being told she's wrong. It's gotten worse in recent years. I suppose that when one is filling in for a god, one can't help but start behaving like a god.

"If there is an issue, it is not because of my assignment, but because of your comportment." Comportment? What does she mean by that?

"You are the one I need at St. Anne's. There are many children there who will be worthy, and you have the privilege of escorting them." Herja brightens and places a hand on my shoulder. Her touch is fire. "The first one is the hardest. Your current assignment will expire soon. Once she is escorted to the Beyond, you will find it easier to collect the others." Collect. Expire. Such whitewashed terms for the reality of death.

I consider pushing further, but decide against it. Herja isn't in the mood. If I give her time, she might change her mind, especially if I can make it seem like her idea.

"As you say." I nod and turn to leave.

Herja tightens her grip on my shoulder, stopping me. "Sister, you have broken one of the essential rules of our company."

I turn back, carefully keeping my face from betraying the fear that feasts within me.

"You have interacted with the child. A sister saw you in her dreamscape yesterday."

If I had a heart, it would have skipped a beat. Thankfully, I have none. "The interactions were limited. Watching for three years has been tedious," I blurt out. "In the old times, we only watched a combatant for one or two days. We were even permitted to bless them."

"I am aware. But these are not the old times. We don't interfere; we just observe." Herja leans in close, a look of concern plastered on her face like an ill-fitting mask. "If you materialize for the sake of the child again, I will have to discipline you. Neither of us wants that."

Discipline is another of those whitewashed words. Essentially, it means 'rip your essence apart and scatter it through the cosmos'. This is how some stars are made. Though my luminosity is slight enough that I imagine I would only make a single, lusterless sky-candle, if that.

Not worthy enough to even make a star in death.

I shudder at the thought of *discipline*. To tell the truth, I'm surprised it took Herja this long to notice and bring it up. "I'll correct my behavior from now on."

"See that you do." Herja lets me go. Her face lights up with a smile, so beautiful that it can't be anything but sincere – can it?

"And remember, Svav, we are doing a good work. It is a privilege to be part of that."

I nod and back out of the room. With a flash, I am back at St. Anne's, surrounded by the beeping of devices and the low growl of a dozen machines that are breathing, expelling, expunging, moving relentlessly. They are not monsters. Many of them are helpful, in fact. But they *sound* like monsters.

I look at the Girl, shivering beneath three blankets. No matter how many covers I put on her, the warmth can't reach her anymore. She has lived among the monsters for far too long. Perhaps it is a mercy that we are at the end. She is so tired. I can tell that she is having nightmares. I reflexively reach towards her, then stop myself. Herja is watching. I can't interfere.

It is not my place to interfere.

* * *

I exist only in dreams now. My body is too emaciated for me to exist much in the real world; it's been that way for a while.

I think I am cleverer in my dreams, able to express myself in ways I couldn't through waking speech. When I'm awake, I can describe one arch at a time: its weathered serpentine lines, glowing rusted red in the sun. But in my dreams, I can see the *entire* park at once – thousands of arches, clear in my mind. Maybe that's the way all language is: just a pale shadow of the intent and imagination it is trying to represent. It is the single arch that leads to a greater reality beyond itself.

The flipside is that in my dreams, the bad things take on fuller form as well.

The dragon comes for me. It's bigger than it's ever been before, so colossal that it blots out the sun. It crashes through Arches Park. Sandstone arches crumble against its motion. Stones that took eons to form pulverized to chalk in seconds. Its feet stamp on the potholes that make up the ephemeral pools of the basin, killing the simple creatures that live in each of those cells. Its destruction is so wanton, and made worse by its indifference. It seems as if it doesn't even realize what it's doing: that it's destroying something beautiful.

I hide beneath the shadow of an arch, my knees pulled close to my chest, shuddering. Sometimes I have a shield and a sword, but not today. I have nothing and the bad thing is so big and I am so small.

And tired.

That is something they don't tell you when you first get sick, that at some point, you'll still be afraid, but it will be nothing compared to how exhausted you are. I have existed in nightmares and dreamscapes for so long now that my terror is a grain of sand compared to the boulder of weariness.

I would like to rest.

As the monster crashes closer to me, certainty settles in my soul. This is the end.

I run a hand over my khaki jacket. The back is bereft of patches, and the front panels have only a smattering of adornments. I haven't gone where I want to go. I haven't done the things I want to do. Even in my weariness, I still want to experience life. I want to audition for a school play, my nervous knees knocking together as I read for a part; I want to learn to put makeup on, pump my own gas, fall in love. I want to blanch in bio and get all fussy because dissecting frogs is gross, but I have to do it anyway because, goddamn it, that's part of growing up!

And I want to see my fucking National Parks.

I step out of the arch, picking up the only weapon I can see, a single stone. There, dwarfed by the behemoth before me, I stand with a desire to live and a stone that might as well be a pebble for all the good it will do.

The Good Voice tells me I'm brave. That I'm a warrior. I would like to be brave, at the end.

* * *

Facing an enemy you can defeat is a form of bravery I am familiar with. Facing an enemy greater than yourself – one that will almost assuredly defeat you in the end – is something else entirely.

I can see into the Girl's dreamscape. She manifests realities she does not fully understand – by Hel and her father, Loki, even I don't fully understand this reality. Three years of suffering, and she still clings to life's bizarre wonders. That is exactly the sort of person who deserves an escort from the Valkyrie.

That is exactly the sort of person who deserves far, far more.

I reach towards her, Herja be damned. I don't just manifest partially, as I have up to this point. I manifest fully.

I stream into the Girl's body, imbuing her with my essence. I breakdown, becoming smaller than the human eye can see, splintering into hundreds, thousands, millions of discreet pieces. I swarm the cancer cells in the Girl's body, waging war against them at the subatomic level. It is a fiercer battle than sword and shield, axe and bow – it is my personal Ragnarök.

It is over in less than a second.

I leave the Girl, something of her clinging to me as I go. Before I have even fully rematerialized in the hospital room, I see Herja standing by the door, shaking with fury. She is clad in armor; its auric glow like a consuming star.

"I told you what would happen if you interfered," Herja growls. "I warned you, sister."

I don't have anything to say in my defense. There are rules that govern the interactions of spiritual beings with the material world. For centuries, those rules dictated my life. But after three years with the Girl...they just don't seem to matter anymore.

"Say something," Herja snaps, unnerved by my silence.

"I saw her," I say, my voice soft.

"What?" Herja blinks in confusion.

"I had to help because I saw her." I can tell that Herja doesn't understand. But that's fine. She doesn't need to.

I wonder what it will be like to die. For someone who has spent their entire life escorting the dead, my own expiration is something I've never really considered. Strangely, I'm not afraid or regretful.

I start to glow. Light stretches out from my body and wings like hands reaching out. Herja's eyes widen as my light grows brighter and brighter.

* * *

I clutch the stone in my hand so hard that blood trickles down my palm. I hurl the rock at the monster that looms above me, for all the good it will do. Then, the monster vanishes, dissipating like smoke before a fan. The flying rock sails through open air and clatters to the ground. It vanishes and so do the ruins of Arch Park.

I wake up.

I'm in pain, but it's a better pain then I have been in. It's the discomfort of a body that can heal, rather than the agony of one that has become defunct. Breathing is easier, and, for the first time in months, I'm *hungry*.

My khaki jacket is draped over me. Where did that come from? I clutch it in my hand. There's a new patch sewed on it, one that resembles an armor-clad angel, of all things. Weird.

Something flashes before my eyes. I'm not sure how to describe it: all brilliant light and warmth so complete that it's more comforting than being wrapped in a blanket and huddled next to a blazing hearth. In a way, the light is like a star.

It's the brightest star I've ever seen.

The Wyrd Sister

D.L. Stille

Every time a child is born, Skuld must go.

It is not pleasant.

It used to be. There was a time when the screaming, too-small tangle of flesh and bone would become a great hero. It would enter the world with a golden thread glimmering in its tightly clenched fist.

Skuld herself had been a great hero once – she still remembers those glorious flights, the azure glow of endless sky, the cheers of the worthy who followed...

But much had changed since then. The old gods were gone. Skuld's sisters had called her home, and now, instead of leading lionhearted warriors to Odin's sprawling hall, she must visit simple huts to see the newly born.

And Skuld must go to them all. Even the ones born with dull, unremarkable threads. Even the ones who do not cry at all.

It is a job her sisters cannot do, for they cannot cut across skies and worlds as Skuld can: not anymore, for even the immortal grow old and weak.

When Skuld returns from her latest outing, she can see the signs of her sisters' age: Verthandi's ghost-white hands tremble as she clutches a tablet of bone, and Urd struggles to thread the thin, taupe twine through the tablets' holes. But still, they sit under the ash tree, Yggdrasil, endlessly weaving. The tapestry of life is never finished.

The twins look up at Skuld with heavy, vacant eyes, and give her no more than what they always do:

Wordless acknowledgment in a cold, dark world.

* * *

Months pass like minutes under the ancient tree; years buzz and gather like flies over a rotting corpse.

Overhead, the sky is a silent ocean of endless grey, punctuated by clouds that inch along like glaciers.

Skuld lies flat on her back. The grass beneath is frozen and hard, poking her flesh like needles.

Her eyes wander to Yggdrasil, to its bare bones and withered heart. When was the last time its trunk was full and plump? When was the last time verdant leaves enveloped its branches?

When was the last time a hero was born?

Thousands of bands dangle from the ash tree's boughs. They were once artful, tightly woven and adorned with rosettes, diamonds, and chevrons. Now they are haphazard, monotone, fraying, and flat. Skuld has not brought back anything worth weaving in a long time.

Still, her sisters add to the bands, eternal and indifferent.

A raindrop lands on the bridge of Skuld's nose. It trickles down to her cheek, then to her lips, and she lets it linger there, savoring its vague sweetness, a vaguely pleasant taste that cuts through the otherwise sour air.

A child is born. Skuld stands.

She does not say goodbye. The immortal rarely find meaning in such a transient phrase.

* * *

The flight across worlds is always too short. Skuld wants to linger up here, but even her mount knows the truth: there is no time to taste the silver of the clouds, to savor the scent of cool, crisp air. Her steed, Elvindr, does not dawdle: when they see the land of mortals, he dives towards the field below.

When they land, Elvindr fades into wind and mist; he will return when needed, but he is not needed for this.

Skuld climbs the yellow hill to the small thatched-roof home. The windows are open, curtains flapping in tempest-tossed gusts. Thunder crashes, but it does not drown out the mother's screams.

She slips through the door, the lock clicking to greet her. One midwife reaches between the mother's legs; a shaking, green apprentice wraps her arms around a pail of water.

A single candle flickers on the windowsill. Crimson stains the blanket thrown over the dirt floor.

Skuld crouches beside the mother, whose head is thrown back, whose lips quiver as she pleads toward the heavens.

Skuld prays too, even though she knows most of the gods have turned into stories and stone after years of standing too still.

The midwife cradles a small, noiseless thing. Skuld's shoulders fall. She digs her fingers into the dirt. It is a feeling she has known before; a feeling she will know again.

Skuld can sense her sisters' empty gaze slither across time and space. Their apathy wraps itself around her neck and tightens.

Something burns inside Skuld, crackles and hisses like a growing flame. She snatches the child from the midwife, and she takes it into her arms, breathing hot air onto its frozen face.

Its eyes flutter open.

The midwife looks up at Skuld, her eyes wide with horror.

"You're not supposed to do that," the midwife says, with the wisdom of the thousand women that have come before her.

Skuld clutches the infant close to her chest.

The candle goes out. The winds halt. The storm dies.

"Goodbye," Skuld says, and she slips out the front door.

* * *

She does not know if the child can survive the flight between worlds, so Skuld travels only across this one. She searches for warmth, for sunlight, for white-sand beaches and sun-dappled meadows.

She finds a hollow and hides there, in a wild paradise cradled by the towering strength of ancient blue mountains.

Tall grass tickles the child and it giggles; the birds chirp in reply. Skuld has never seen anything more beautiful than this plump bundle of skin and dreams. She has never seen anything so bright and full of promise. The child's bright eyes glitter and shine like flecks of gold in a riverbed.

For a moment, Skuld forgets herself. She smiles back. She sips this moment slowly, the nectar sweeter than any she has ever tasted.

Skuld wonders who this child will be. She pictures a seasoned warrior, broad-chested and proud. War-drums beat steadily across victories and triumphs until the child, now a man, is the last one standing on a smoking battlefield.

Skuld pulls a blade of grass from the earth, twisting it like twine.

The sharp edge cuts her finger, and her blood stains the green grass red. Skuld frowns.

It doesn't matter: that fate seems too bloody for this little lamb, anyway. She imagines, instead, a warrior of words, a conqueror of the quill, whose voice carries across nations and centuries.

She plucks another strand of grass. She twists again; it is too dry. It cracks and splinters.

Skuld's fingers tense. Possibility splits and diverges from the child like Yggdrasil's branches. A thousand futures, and none of them seem right, feel right. They all feel like a dream, some even a nightmare.

The child croons.

Skuld wonders if this child isn't meant to change the world. She wonders if it is not meant to climb mountains or traverse tumultuous seas. Maybe it is meant to make flower-crowns out of dandelions and to sing solstice-songs by a crackling hearth.

But as she reaches for another blade of grass, a breeze tunnels through the valley. The grass shudders.

The wind whispers the truth. There is no place in this world for a child that belongs to Death.

The wind stops. A shadow creeps over the sun.

Hel is murky. "Fie," she snarls. "Fie."

* * *

Skuld wants to ask Hel about the others – about Odin, and Freyja, and even Tyr, and why Hel still wanders the worlds while her brethren hide away...

But Hel does not seem like the type who answers questions. Before Skuld can begin, Hel simply shakes her head, her dark eyes wide with warning.

Hel escorts Skuld back to the thatched-roof hut. She lets Skuld carry the child.

"The mother must see the child," Hel says. "She must see he is gone."

Skuld does not understand why Death demands such cruelty. Why must this mother look upon a child that does not breathe, that does not cry? Why must that image be carved into the folds of the mother's fragile mind? Why must it destroy her, its aftershocks shaking her every time she sees a crib, hears a nursery rhyme? Why must it haunt her as long as she breathes?

But Hel glares at her again, and Skuld knows she cannot ask.

Skuld halts at the base of the hill. The hut waits silently.

This cannot be it. Heat builds in Skuld's eyes. She squints, her eyelids like dams, but the tears burst through. Their salt burns her cheeks.

Skuld must be more than this. She must be more than the harbinger of death. She must be more than the one who returns to distant stares, grey skies, and a dying tree.

Hel places a hand on Skuld's shoulder. But there is no comfort in the gesture. Only a light push. "She must see the child," Hel repeats.

Skuld does not move. It cannot be the same. It cannot be over and over again, over millennia and eras, until finally she looks the blazing Sun in the eyes and explains that her child, the Earth, is gone.

She presses the child against her chest. Already the child grows cold, grows quiet.

Its life slips through her fingers, and holding the child is like holding water. So she steps forward, up the hill, to bring the child home one last time.

The hill is steeper than she remembers. The ground is softer. Her feet sink into crumbling earth. But Hel breathes down her neck. Her breath is frigid and biting, as sharp as her ancient teeth.

She repeats herself with each of Skuld's steps. "She must see. She must see."

Skuld slides into the door again. The mother's eyes are red and dark like cherry pits; the midwife whispers softly in her ear. The apprentice cleans her bare legs. Still, the mother does not move from the floor; she only gasps and sobs and stares upward at straw and reeds as though she is trying to bore through them, to appeal to the dispassionate stars.

Hel waits on the other side of the door. There is an order to these things. Skuld must go first; she always goes first.

Skuld kneels beside the mother. The mother does not look at her; she does not dare look at fate, so unjust, so cruel.

The child is quiet and cold. The midwife takes it from Skuld's hands, and passes it to the mother.

The mother finally looks away from the ceiling. She sobs into her child's hair, as thin and soft as peach fuzz.

Hel steps into the room. Skuld knows it is time to go.

Hel places her hand on Skuld's shoulder. It is kind this time. "She must see," Hel said, "so she can become."

Skuld stares at Hel as she reaches for the child. For a moment, the mother tightens her grip. But the midwife whispers again, and the mother relinquishes him. Hel cradles the never-born in her arms, and she leaves.

Skuld wonders if Hel has sisters. If they will regard her and what she brings.

Skuld has never stayed this long. She wonders what will become of this mother.

No – she wonders what the mother will *become*.

And then Hel's words propagate, their roots winding their way through Skuld's body, through her throat, surfacing at her lips.

Skuld speaks to the woman.

"This is an end," Skuld says. The mother does not move. The midwife narrows her eyes. Skuld is not supposed to speak.

Or maybe she is.

She's never tried.

"This is an end. But it is not yours."

The midwife's furrowed brow softens. She cups her hand over her mouth, leaning into the mother's ear. Skuld can hear her own words, repeated, but better, softer in the sage's soothing voice.

"There is more, after the end."

Skuld knows the world is hard. She knows how quickly the world can change. She knows you can be a warrior of legend, a favorite of the gods, guiding fearless *einherjar* with song and mead to Valhalla – and she knows that the gods who loved you can leave you, close the doors of their great halls and swath themselves in apathy.

She knows that the world can be cold and unfeeling.

But there is more.

Hel's words echo again. *She must see.*

"He is gone. And he will be with you always. But you are more. You can be more." Skuld reaches for the mother's hand, but the midwife shakes her head. She steps in between, taking the mother's hand in her mortal one.

Again, the midwife repeats Skuld's words, but with a humanity Skuld can't quite grasp, a tactfulness that remains just beyond her immortal reach.

"You can make flower crowns and sing solstice-songs. You can watch the sun rise and set. You will have victories to celebrate and stories to spin," Skuld says. "This is not your end."

This is not Skuld's end.

There are more mothers than this one. More who need these words, who need to know that they are not broken, that they can fight great battles and write great poems:

There are more women who need to know that they can become Valkyries.

"You can still become," Skuld says.

The mother shifts. Her head turns, and she looks at Skuld. The mother's gaze is not empty. It is not indifferent.

It is impossible. It is full. It is breaking. It is sad and enraged and hopeful, all at once, a tangled meadow of wildflowers and weeds, overgrown and overrun.

The mother clenches her fists, and releases an agonized cry, one that shakes the earth and rattles the bones buried beneath.

When the mother unfurls her fingers, something new is there. Something Skuld has not seen.

Skuld takes it.

"You're not supposed to do that," the midwife says, but this time, her voice quavers. She does not sound sure.

"Actually – I think that I am," Skuld replies.

She leaves, and she does not say goodbye.

Because this is not the end.

* * *

The thread is cobalt blue. But in the light it is emerald green. And if she holds it close to her face, Skuld can see fibers of pearl and violet.

It is complicated, but new. Muddied, but iridescent.

It is beautiful.

When Skuld brings it to her sisters, Urd stands on wobbly legs, and plucks an old band from the tree, one that had been long forgotten. Beneath it, Skuld sees a bud has sprouted, small and fledgling, but brimming with promise.

The twins hold the new thread in their hands. Verthandi smiles; Urd laughs.

There is brightness in their eyes; a new warmth overcomes the pallor in their faces.

The twins begin to weave – and this time, their hands do not tremble.

Her Terrible Swift Sword

Susanna Fraser Stone

Gettysburg, Pennsylvania
July 2, 1863

The songs and poems of martial glory somehow failed to mention that battlefields *stank.* They reeked with the summer stench of unwashed men in unwashed clothing, of new sweat layered over old, of the piss and shit and blood that came with terror and death, all of it stewed together in the sulfur-smoke of gunpowder.

Surely this sweltering Pennsylvania hilltop was a foretaste of the hell her mama swore she was bound for, but Vinnie stood strong upon it. She reckoned she'd have the chance to compare war to hell soon enough, since her regiment had run out of ammunition.

Then through the din of the fight she heard her colonel's commands – *Fix bayonets* and *right wheel forward.* She grinned fiercely. Once you had no more bullets to fire, you could run away – or charge straight at the enemy, armed with steel and daring. As their left flank swung into line with the rest, Vinnie nudged her twin brother, who stood beside her, frowning as he slotted his bayonet into place.

"Mad Vinnie," he mouthed. He alone of all the men in the 20th Maine Infantry knew that Vinnie stood for Lavinia rather than Vincent.

"Steady Gus," she countered.

Such they had been to one another for over eighteen years now, from their shared cradle to this desperate battle. Her wildness and his calm had always made them pull together all the better in twin-harness. He'd stood beside her when everyone else had forsaken her, and she vowed to do no less for him.

Now with the rest of their regiment they plunged down the slope of Little Round Top, shouting their defiance of the enemy's rebel yell. Vinnie laughed aloud, giddy with battle madness, mighty and invincible.

But as she stabbed downward, a wild-eyed, wild-bearded rebel soldier thrust his bayonet straight up into her chest – and around it blossomed a pain sharper and just *more* than any she'd known before. As she fell backwards, Gus's wail of "Vinnie!" rang in her ears above the shouts and clash of steel on steel.

Her back slammed into the rocky, blood-spattered ground, and she stared up into a sky turned dazzling sharp, with no smoke and dust to obscure the blue sky and golden sunlight. The stench too had fled, replaced by the pinewood and sea salt aroma of her home village on summer days when the wind blew in from the shore. She still heard the battle, but as dim and distant as a nightmare fading with the sunrise.

And then, seeming to come down straight from the sun, appeared the most beautiful woman Vinnie had ever seen, with red-gold hair in thick braids down to her waist, bright blue eyes, and full red lips made for cursing and kissing. Or maybe for cursed kisses – Vinnie knew all about *those*. The heavenly vision wore armor like something out of Sir Walter Scott's novels or *Sintram and His Companions,* looking mighty and majestic in it. And to cap it all, she flew upon great wings thick with silver-gilt feathers.

"So I'm dead, then," Vinnie said.

The battlefield angel smiled, with a playful twinkle in those so-bright eyes that made Vinnie think of Gus when they'd joined in mischief as little children. Or of Lottie, when they'd sneaked off into the barn together or fallen behind the others skating, seven short months ago. "What gave it away?"

"I never saw any angels when I was alive."

The beauty laughed. It was a beautiful laugh, light and rolling like waves crashing ashore, but – Vinnie was a bad girl and a disappointment to her family. And weren't devils just fallen angels? "Unless you're a devil, but I never saw any of those, either."

"Angel is closer." She stooped and held out a strong, long-fingered hand for Vinnie to grasp. "My name is Olrun. Have you ever heard of the Valkyries? We aren't as well-known as we were in former times."

Vinnie considered this, while dimly aware that on the living ground of the battlefield, her comrades were cheering. Good, the charge must have worked, and – she somehow knew – Gus still lived, unwounded. "A little," she said at last. "From fairy stories. They're *real?*"

"As real as Valhalla, where you are now bound." She beckoned with her outstretched hand.

"Valhalla?" That too sounded familiar from some of those childhood tales of knights and battles she'd always loved so much.

"Valhalla the hall of Odin, where the bravest and most worthy warriors train every day and feast and sing every night as they prepare for the Battle of Ragnarök at the end of days."

"Wait...Odin and Valhalla are real? But not Jesus and heaven?"

The Valkyrie's smile grew gentle. "Say rather that mortal minds cannot comprehend all that lies beyond them in eternity. It encompasses Odin and Jesus and a great many more aspects besides. But I serve the divine in the form of Odin Allfather, who calls the worthiest warriors to his hall...and it is ever a privilege and a joy to claim a woman for that number. So come with me now, Lavinia Merrill, warrior of the Army of the Potomac. Valhalla welcomes you. And I see you, all that you are and yet will become. You belong with us." She stooped lower and kissed Vinnie, a gentle yet wildly sensual benediction.

Welcomed, seen, and wanted for who she truly was. With no further hesitation, Vinnie reached for Olrun's hand and rose up out of her body. She stared down dispassionately at her mortal self, dirty, sunburned and bloodstained. Such a soft, young face. They'd been fools not to know her for a girl. Though truly a great many of her brother soldiers looked just as pretty and beardless. Among them Gus, who had run back to kneel at her side now that the fighting had paused for moment. He shook the limp corpse. "No, Vinnie, please, no! Wake up, wake up."

She couldn't leave Gus here. He'd never manage without her. But nor could she break free of Olrun's grip as together they rose away from the hot and bloody Pennsylvania hillside into a swirl of many-colored light.

* * *

Gus had only enlisted to watch over her, and now he was left with no one to watch over *him.* Oh, he'd talked of going for a soldier ever since the war began, more than two years ago now. But he hadn't hungered for the excitement of battle or dreamed of glory as many boys had, especially in those early days when everyone thought the fighting would be over by Christmas. No, for Gus it had been a matter of duty and principle. He believed the Union should be preserved and slavery abolished, and therefore he must be willing to lay his life on the line just as other men and boys did.

Their mother, though also hating slavery and loving the Union, had prayed fervently and daily for the war to end before her only son turned eighteen. And on the twins' eighteenth birthday in November 1862, when Gus spoke of joining up, both their parents had pleaded against it. He was their only son! Who would look after dear Lavinia and their four younger sisters after their father was gone, if he got himself killed?

Gus had found himself suspended between two competing duties. Since he was the calm and steady twin, Vinnie expected he'd likely stay at home. Everyone knew how their parents felt about his threat of enlistment. No one would think him a coward for choosing the quieter duty to his home and his womenfolk.

Just a few weeks later, before the second wartime Christmas but after the creek in the Gilbert farm woods had frozen solid, all the youth of their village had gone on a skating frolic. Vinnie had fallen behind everyone else with Lottie Shaw. This had become their habit in recent months, so they could kiss and fondle and talk of how someday they'd get a cottage somewhere and be happy spinsters together for the rest of their lives. It wasn't impossible. Lottie's family was the richest in their village, and she had a little inheritance from her grandmother that would be hers to spend as she liked on her twenty-first birthday.

And maybe Vinnie would still be alive and well, sneaking away to kiss Lottie in the hayloft or behind the schoolhouse, if they hadn't been so caught up in each other that icy afternoon that they hadn't heard the young Methodist minister and his wife coming down the creek on their own skates. But instead there had been shame and scandal, with Lottie packed off to her relatives in Boston.

Since the Merrills lacked convenient distant relations, Vinnie had been left to bear her share of the shame at home. Two days of her mother's tearful remonstrations and her father's silent disapproval had been too much for her. On the second night, Gus found her out in the barn, dressed in his outgrown winter clothes and cutting off her hair.

"You can't run away!" he exclaimed.

"No, I can't stay here. Surely you can see that."

"Mama will come around," he pleaded. "Give her time."

"She says I've disgraced the whole family, I'm sure to burn in hell, and it's even worse than if I'd been caught in *bed* with a boy because then I could just marry him. Would *you* stay for more of that?"

"I wouldn't," he allowed after a moment. "But I'll miss you terribly."

"I know. So will I." They'd never been separated for a whole day in their lives, and the thought of abandoning Gus was even worse than being torn away from Lottie. "But I can't stay."

"Where do you mean to go?" he asked.

"I'm going to enlist, of course." Off his stunned look, she added, "I can pass for a boy!"

"As long as you keep your clothes on."

"That's the idea. And if everyone thinks I'm a boy, no one can fault me for liking to kiss girls."

"You're not going to have much opportunity for that in the army."

Vinnie waved this objection aside. "Please don't try to stop me."

He stood silent for a long moment, and Vinnie held her breath, waiting for him to shout for their parents. But instead he said, "I'm going with you."

"What?"

"I'm going *with* you. Now I know what I'm supposed to do. Before, I didn't know whether my duty was with the army or at home, and I couldn't imagine leaving you behind. But if you're going, then I belong with you. It's all simple, now."

* * *

And that was why it was Vinnie's fault that Gus was all alone on the Gettysburg battlefield. Yet she forgot her brother and her heartbreak in sheer wonder as the rainbow light surrounding her and Olrun coalesced into a feasting hall far bigger than anything she'd ever seen on Earth, roofed with golden shields supported by beams of silver spears.

Olrun set Vinnie on her feet and spread her arms out in a grand, sweeping gesture. "Welcome to Valhalla."

At table after long table feasted countless men and not a few women from what must be every race of humanity ever to walk the earth, clad in everything from leather loincloths to blue paint on bare chests to tunics like something out of Bible story illustrations to knights' armor to modern uniforms very like her own.

Wait, wasn't that…a blue-coated figure sprang up from a nearby table and ran to greet her. Little Silas Favreau from her very own company in the 20th Maine. He'd fallen at Chancellorsville, two months before.

"Vinnie, you're here!" He caught her by the shoulders and pulled her into a backslapping masculine embrace. "Wait, you're a *girl.*" He blinked surprise. "Did Gus know?"

She laughed. Apparently death hadn't made sweet, brave Silas any cleverer. "Of course he knew. He's my twin."

Her twin, left behind on that stinking field of blood.

"Oh yes, how stupid of me. But come, have a seat, fill your plate. There's no hardtack or salt beef *here.*"

Indeed, the succulence of roast pork and beef filled the air, and Vinnie's stomach rumbled. She glanced back at Olrun, who smiled at their reunion and waved her forward. "I've other soldiers to meet. Your armies are swelling our numbers today."

She took a step towards the feast, where other Union soldiers had broken out into the chorus of the *Battle Hymn of the Republic*. But she couldn't forget Gus. "No," she insisted. "I must go back. I can't leave Gus. He wouldn't even be there if it wasn't for me."

Olrun laid a gentle hand on Vinnie's shoulder and gave her a push. "It is right that you should remember and miss your brother. You can sing of his deeds with your comrades. But you cannot return to the land of the living once you are dead."

"But there must be a way! *You* go between there and here."

"I'm a Valkyrie. It isn't the same."

Inspiration flashed like lightning. "Could *I* become a Valkyrie?"

Olrun's lovely lips shaped themselves for a quick *no,* but then she paused. "It isn't usual, for one born a mortal."

Vinnie crossed her arms. "Not usual isn't the same thing as not possible."

"You may petition the Allfather, but he may say no. In fact, he almost certainly will."

"Then at least I'll know I tried."

Olrun considered her for a moment, then laughed. "I like you, Lavinia of the Army of the Potomac. Very well, I'll present you to Odin." She glanced at Silas. "Save her place, in case he refuses her."

"Yes, ma'am. Good luck, Vinnie." He grinned at her as he turned to join the chorus singing *Glory, glory, hallelujah!*

At the distant far end of the long hall, Vinnie saw what must be Odin – a giant, magnificent figure in armor like Olrun's, enthroned on a dais overlooking the feasting warriors. His silver beard flowed down over his chest, one eye was covered with a patch, and a raven perched on each mighty shoulder. She gulped in sudden fear of petitioning someone so august and mighty – truly a god – face to face. But Gus needed her. The same duty that had made him go to war at her side called upon her to see him through to its end.

As they passed between the tables, soldier after soldier cheered and raised a glass to them. Vinnie took special note of a man in the gray uniform of a Confederate officer who gave her a respectful nod.

"*They're* here too?" she whispered.

"You'll meet warriors from both sides of every war," Olrun said with a little smile. "And if you join us Valkyries, you'll claim from them all for Valhalla."

"But...how can you be an honorable warrior for a dishonorable cause? And there are black men here. *He* probably owned slaves."

"Even the worst of causes generally have some good men fighting for them. If you'd been born in your South, *you* might have been a Confederate rebel yourself. Any who come *here* must have enough wisdom, once the scales of mortality have fallen from their eyes, to see all the warriors they feast and fight alongside as brothers and equals. Many cannot. That man could and did."

"Do the others go to hell?" Vinnie asked. Such a hell seemed far more just than the one her mother had threatened for her.

"That, I do not know, only that the gods show both justice and mercy. But they are not welcome in Valhalla."

At that, Vinnie cast the rebel officer a nod to show her own cautious respect. "Not all of our men would pass that test, either," she admitted.

Both Olrun and Vinnie fell silent as they approached the god. Olrun knelt in graceful obeisance. Vinnie tried to copy her, but knew herself as clumsy as a newborn foal.

"You may stand, Lavinia Merrill. I find your nation has no great knack for kneeling." Odin's voice was deep, kind...and *American.*

When Vinnie stood and met his twinkling eye, she saw not a knight or a Viking of olden times, but a Union general in a blue coat with gold braid and buttons. The beard, eyepatch, and avian companions remained unchanged. One of the ravens tugged at the fringe of his epaulet and croaked at Vinnie.

"Yes, sir," she said simply. "You…changed."

He chuckled. "I can appear in any number of forms without changing my nature." Before her eyes, he shifted through three more guises – what she thought must be a Roman centurion, then an African chieftain, and lastly an Indian chief with a splendid eagle-feather headdress, before settling into his Union uniform again. "This one best suits *your* eyes. I believe you have a petition to make of me."

"Yes, sir." Was it wrong to call a god nothing grander than *sir?* He did not seem offended, and she supposed he was her commanding officer now. If *sir* was good enough for Colonel Chamberlain or General Meade, maybe it was fitting for the commander of the army of the dead.

"Speak it, daughter."

"I went to war alongside my twin brother. He only came because of me, because I was running away from home and he felt responsible for protecting me."

He raised the eyebrow over his good eye. "*Only* because of you?"

Had she been so caught up in herself and her reasons for running away that she hadn't seen all of Gus? "Maybe not only," she admitted. "He believed in our cause, he wanted to do his part, but my parents wanted him to stay home because he was their only boy. He was a dutiful son, more than I was ever a dutiful daughter. And when we got to the army, when we saw our first battle...you must understand that he's never a coward, he never holds back, but he doesn't glory in it. He's not caught up in that sort of wild rapture, like being drunk but without the stumbling."

"So he's no berserker, as my Vikings would say, while you are a splendid one, my daughter."

She glowed under the divine praise, but she had to speak for Gus. "He's splendid in other ways." It was important that Odin understand that. "He's splendidly kind and loyal. He was willing to sacrifice himself for me. I want to go back so I can protect him. Olrun says you can make me a Valkyrie."

"Are you certain that is what you want? It is an eternal service."

"Isn't all of Valhalla?"

"Yes, but you must understand that you cannot aid only your brother, and you will not be the sister he had before. Unless he falls as you did, he will never even know you are there. You will be a guide to many soldiers, choosing and serving those bound for Valhalla from this day until Ragnarök and the end and renewal of all things. Will you accept this service?"

She could bear all that, as long as she could help Gus. She hesitated for just an instant, then looked to the still kneeling Olrun. "Is it a good life? Er, a good eternity?"

Olrun smiled her beautiful smile. "I love it. And I'd love to share it with you." One bright eye shivered in a wink.

Vinnie turned back to the god. *Her* god, now. "Yes. I accept."

"Very well." He stretched out his hand and spoke words in a language Vinnie couldn't comprehend. She felt herself change, a dislocation even greater than death. Light flowed through her, she stretched and grew, fell on her knees…then rose to her feet, a Valkyrie. Like Olrun.

Yet not exactly like. Her hair was her own chestnut brown, only brighter and grown back to its woman's length. In place of armor, she wore a rippling tunic in Union blue, and her wings and her boots shone gold. "Thank you," she breathed.

"Are you satisfied?"

She smiled, blinking back tears. "Mine eyes have seen the glory."

"Ah, yes. That's a grand song, and a true one, that your army marches to. But now you need a terrible swift sword." He snapped his fingers and conjured it, a beautiful thing, slim and graceful, with an eagle at its hilt. He passed it to her, and she found she had a belt and scabbard waiting to hold it. "Now go. Weigh souls on the battlefield. And watch over your brother, as long as his war lasts."

Olrun held out her hand. Vinnie took it, and together they flew.

* * *

For two more years, Vinnie served Odin on the battlefields of her own nation, her own war. She visited Gus for a time each evening and on every day that his duty called him to march into combat. Though he did not see her, she thought he sensed her presence and took comfort from it. Just after Gettysburg, she watched over his shoulder as he wrote two letters – a grieved and angry one to their parents, and a wistful and kind one to Lottie. And as the months dragged on, she watched him stay the same steady

Gus she'd known while she lived, but also grow into a brotherly guardian to new recruits.

"This war can't last much longer," Olrun commented to her on the last day of March 1865, after they'd escorted souls to Valhalla who'd fallen during a skirmish in the Virginia countryside.

"I know." And it would be a victory for Union and for liberty, the very causes she'd fought for while she lived. But now she wept for all that had been lost, and all she was about to lose forever.

Olrun kissed a tear from her cheek. "You're grieving it?"

"Only because of Gus." The longer the war had gone on, the more she had grown into the role of a Valkyrie, the more she had understood that by accepting Odin's offer she had only delayed her parting from her twin.

"It's not too late," Olrun pointed out.

While the Valkyries did not themselves kill, they could influence the fates of soldiers. Vinnie had been doing all she could to guard and shield her brother. If she withdrew that protection, he might well fall, and she could personally escort him to Valhalla. She'd realized that within days of receiving her terrible, beautiful swift sword, and realized just as soon that she would never do it. "No," she said.

"He has become a valiant warrior. He'd be welcome, and happy, in Valhalla. Especially once he sees *you.*"

"He would. But he'll be happier if he goes home to Maine, lives a long life on our farm, has any number of children and grandchildren, and when he dies goes to whatever paradise waits for the peacemakers and life-givers."

Olrun kissed her. "You've become a good Valkyrie."

"I learned from the best."

* * *

She wept again nine days later as she waited invisible by Gus's side at Appomattox Court House as General Lee surrendered to General Grant.

"If only Vinnie were here to see this day," he murmured to the soldier who'd become his best comrade in two years of war.

"You'll go home and name your firstborn son for him."

Gus smiled a private smile, and Vinnie knew with a touch of god-sight that he would father his own set of boy-girl twins and name them Vincent and Lavinia. It wasn't everything. She would miss him down through eternity. But it was enough.

Stone Heart

Deborah Tapper

They were stealing Asta's eyes.

Her sword-hand was already gone and Signy could see a gaping hole in her ribs where her heart had been. She screamed a furious challenge, sword rattling from its scabbard as her huge mount swept down from the clouds.

The thieves abandoned the corpse, but they didn't stay to fight. A hole opened at their feet and they dived in, the ground closing again just as Hemingr landed. Signy vaulted off his back and slammed her blade into the earth, but it stayed shut.

And Asta stayed dead.

Everything was churned to bloody mud and bodies were strewn around like fallen leaves, the groans and pleas of the dying echoing across the battlefield. Ignoring their cries for help, Signy sheathed her sword then retrieved two short daggers from a nearby corpse, binding them to Asta's oozing wrist with strips torn from a dead man's cloak.

"Too late." Hemingr was always more feral once he'd shed his wolf-shape. Huge and scarred, with wild grey hair and corded muscles.

"Not too late." Signy didn't look up. "I can still bring her back."

"Not her body," Hemingr rumbled. "We can only take her soul to Freyja."

"Lend me an eye, Hemingr."

"You think she'll see with a wolf's eye?" The big man snorted. "Besides, I need them both. If I can't see, how can I fly? Give her your own eye, Signy. Or get hers back from those sorcerers."

"We don't know if they were sorcerers."

"They vanished into the ground." Hemingr stamped his foot over the place where the hole had appeared. "And they smelled of sorcery."

Cursing all sorcerers, Signy found a pebble and pressed it into Asta's empty socket. A bigger stone filled the hole in her chest.

"A stone for a heart?" Hemingr's shaggy brows drew together.

"It's all I've got."

"I see dead men everywhere." Hemingr gestured to the battlefield around them. "And dead women. They all have hearts. And eyes."

"And I can't use them."

"Why not?"

"Because they *are* dead. Or so close to death that it makes no difference."

"She's dead, Signy." Hemingr looked increasingly uneasy. "I don't know why you're doing this, but you should stop now. It can only lead to trouble."

"I thought you liked trouble." Asta's leather jerkin lay discarded on the ground where the thieves had tossed it away. Signy folded it back around the limp figure, buckling it firmly in place. "Asta Haraldsdottir," she said. "Wake up."

The dead woman didn't stir.

Signy drew a knife, but Hemingr's powerful fingers snapped around her wrist before she could cut herself. "There must be another way."

Signy met his gaze. "I'm open to suggestions."

"Leave her body where she lies and take her soul to Freyja." His lips lifted, revealing sharp teeth. "That's why you're here. But don't risk a blood calling."

"I *can't* leave her." Signy jerked free. "She mustn't die, Hemingr."

"Everyone dies eventually," Hemingr said, his lips thinning. "Even the gods."

"Asta Haraldsdottir doesn't, not for another twenty years." Signy faced him, fingers folding around the blade so it pressed into her palm. "Not until her daughter's grown."

Hemingr's amber gaze flicked to the motionless woman. She looked very young, no more than seventeen at most. "She has a daughter?"

"Not yet. But she will."

"And this daughter will be a great warrior, worthy of Freyja's Hall…?" He arched an eyebrow.

"She will. But there's far more at stake." She took a step towards him, grip tightening on the blade until the razor edge broke through her skin. "It's about a foretelling."

"What foretelling?" His nostrils quivered, catching the scent of her blood.

"One that says two humans will survive Ragnarok: a man – and a woman." She was so close now, they were almost touching. "If Asta dies here, that woman will never be born."

"Who said this?" The big man's eyes narrowed. "Skuld?"

Signy nodded. "She came to me last night, at Sessrumnir. I couldn't tell if she was a dream or reality, but she said Asta Haraldsdottir has to live."

"And she expects us to make sure this foretelling comes true?"

"Not us," Signy said. "Me."

"Then use my blood." Hemingr put his hands on her shoulders, tilting his face down to hers. "Not yours."

He was ready to die for her. Signy tensed, wanting to hit him. Or hug him. She settled for a wry smile instead. "A wolf's blood?" she said, keeping her voice deliberately light and mocking.

He wasn't fooled. "Better a wolf's than a Valkyrie's if the calling goes wrong."

That was true. But she wasn't going to back down now. "It won't."

She dipped a fingertip in her blood and drew three summoning runes on Asta's face. A fourth on her throat and a fifth above the stone heart. Two on her arms and two more on her legs. Then she sang the calling chant. "Asta," she said as she finished. "Asta Haraldsdottir – come back."

The body shivered.

Signy sang the chant again. And a third time.

Asta sat up.

"Asta Haraldsdottir…" Signy examined the motionless face, looking for any flicker of life. "Can you hear me?"

Hemingr growled under his breath. "Her soul's gone."

It should have been waiting with her body, but perhaps the sorcerers had taken it, too. Signy pushed that possibility aside. "Then I'll go after it."

"I knew you'd say that." Although the big man sounded resigned, the ghost of a smile flickered along his lips. "Think she can ride? If we go now, we should catch her soul before it gets too far along the road."

His uncomplicated loyalty touched her, but she didn't let it show. "I'm not asking you to come with me, Hemingr. It could be dangerous."

"Now you're being deliberately insulting." The smile became a snarl, a flash of sharp teeth. "You're slow, Signy. And you won't catch anything stumbling along on your own two feet."

He rolled his shoulders, leaned forward – and was a wolf before his palms touched the ground.

Signy got the dead woman onto his back and climbed up behind her. Then Hemingr leapt into the air again, racing north towards frozen Niflheim – and Helvegr, the long, dark road that led to Hel.

* * *

Other souls were trudging north, heading for that lightless realm of ice and fog. Young and old. Rich and poor. Fair and ugly. Those who'd died warm and peaceful in their beds marched beside victims of murder and accident, rubbing shoulders with the souls of warriors who hadn't been chosen to sit in either Valhalla or Sessrumnir.

Signy saw them all.

And then she saw Asta's soul.

Hemingr was already diving down, landing in front of her. The shades fell to their knees as Signy sprang off his back. And Asta's spirit knelt with them on the icy ground, bowing her head.

Before Signy could say a word, a warrior jostled through the kneeling souls, kicking them aside. A formidable man, tall and proud, his soul still bearing the wounds he'd received in battle. "So you've finally come for me, Valkyrie," he said. "I fought bravely. And with honour."

"As did I." A second warrior shoved his way after him. "I deserve Valhalla and glory, not an afterlife in Hel!"

"I serve Freyja." Signy stood very straight and stern. "Not Odin."

"So you shepherd dead women to Sessrumnir, rather than escorting actual warriors to Valhalla…!" The first man sneered, lip curling. "Don't you want to serve mead to real heroes, girl, and be loved by them? Or perhaps you're lying and you're not a Valkyrie at all." His hand went to his sword hilt. "I heard they ride magnificent horses, not filthy vargr."

Hemingr growled, baring his teeth.

"And you're keeping company with a revenant," the warrior continued. "So are you witch or monster, girl?"

"You died a coward," Signy said calmly. "Your wounds are all in your back, not your chest."

The warrior sprang at her with a curse – and Asta's soul was on her feet in an instant. Leaping to defend her. Drawing the shade of a sword from its scabbard. Deflecting the blade the dead warrior aimed at her head. There was a brief, furious flurry of wraithlike steel – then the man was flat on his back, sword gone and the point of Asta's weapon at his throat.

"Say the word, Lady," she said. "And I'll see he dies a second death."

Signy shook her head. "Let him go, Asta Haraldsdottir," she said. "He's not worthy of your blade."

Asta sheathed her sword and the disgraced warrior scrambled away. "I curse you!" he snarled, jabbing a finger at them. "Both of you – and the vargr with you!"

"Run away," Asta said. "Before I defy my Lady and take your head."

The warrior hesitated, his face twisting with rage and fear. Then he spat, spun around and barged through the astonished shades, stomping away.

The second warrior followed him.

Once they'd gone, Asta knelt again and laid her shade-sword at Signy's feet. "I serve you, Lady," she said. "And I'm yours to command."

Signy gestured to Asta's body, sitting stiff and oblivious on Hemingr's back. "Then I order you to live, Asta Haraldsdottir."

* * *

"It's no good." Asta pulled a frustrated hand over her face, glowering at her corpse. It lay passively on the ground, real eye shut and the stone eye staring up at nothing. "I can't get in…!"

"Try again." Signy's voice was tight with tension.

"It's not whole," Hemingr rumbled, watching as the shade struggled to force her arms and legs into the awkward flesh. "She needs the missing parts, Signy."

"A warrior can live without a hand," Signy said. "Or an eye."

"But not without their heart."

"Can you remember what happened?" Signy asked Asta. "On the battlefield?"

The shade sat back on her heels. "Four of them," she said. "They seemed to spring up from the ground right beneath my feet. I was fighting – and then I was here, walking with the other dead."

"You don't remember your death? Or starting out to Hel?"

Asta shook her head.

"They hurled your soul out with their evil sorcery." Hemingr showed his teeth. "They must've meant to destroy you, but you were too strong."

"Not strong enough." Asta scowled at her unco-operative body. "I'm dead. And I died by sorcery. There's no place for me in Sessrumnir. And no place among the living, either."

"Unless we find your heart," Signy said.

Asta was frowning. "Why me?" she asked. "I'm no one special. Why would sorcerers come for me – and why have *you* followed me here with this revenant thing that used to be my body, Lady?"

Hemingr raised an eyebrow. "Perhaps we should tell her."

Signy sighed. "Skuld made a prophecy," she said. "And you have to live."

"*Me*...?" Asta's eyes opened wide in shock.

"You." Signy put a hand on Hemingr's shoulder. "You'll win your seat in Sessrumnir, but not for another twenty years – when you fall fighting alongside your daughter."

"My daughter...!"

"She avenges your death." Signy knew she shouldn't be telling Asta so much, but she needed to convince her. "And she earns her own place in Freyja's Hall, as do so many of your descendants."

"But I'm only a humble shield-maiden, Lady." Asta looked dazed. "There are others far braver and nobler than me. Why should my line be singled out for such honour?"

"Because a distant daughter of yours will live through Ragnarok." Signy held Asta's gaze, trusting the prophecy wouldn't be affected if she knew. "And that distant daughter will be mother to a new race of humans."

"We don't have much time." Hemingr raised his shaggy head and sniffed the air. "The blood calling won't last long, Signy. If we don't retrieve her heart soon, your runes will fail and her flesh will die."

"How long?"

He sniffed again. "A day at most."

Signy's hands clenched. "So where did they take her heart?"

"There." Asta pointed northwards. "I can still feel it beating."

Hemingr nodded. "Hel," he said.

"Only one day…" Asta gazed at the dark horizon. "We'll never get there in time."

"Of course we will." Hemingr grinned suddenly, flashing his long teeth. "And you shouldn't give up so easily, Asta Haraldsdottir."

* * *

They took Asta's body with them.

Signy was tempted to leave it hidden under a pile of rocks, but there was no way of telling how much time they'd have left after they found the missing heart.

Hemingr hurtled north.

He flew faster than thought, crossing from Midgard into Niflheim, where darkness and icy mists rose to engulf them. A great chasm opened in the ice ahead and he plunged in, racing through the lightless cold like the swiftest arrow.

Once they drew close to Hel, he stopped and they concealed Asta's body. Then they moved more carefully, avoiding the watchful guardian and stealing up to the towering fence that surrounded the dead's realm.

A fence made entirely of corpses and bones.

Asta nodded when they asked if she could still feel her heart beating. "I can feel my fingers, too," she said. "And I can see. Only shadows, but I think they must be the sorcerers."

"Can you see where they are?" Signy asked.

"It's too dark." Asta sounded frustrated. "But I can find them. Once we're inside."

"I'll distract Hel and her underlings." Hemingr stretched, flexing the long run out of his muscles. "You find Asta's heart."

"Be careful, Hemingr." Signy frowned at her huge wolf-warrior. "Don't do anything reckless."

"You know me." A quick wink and he was striding boldly away.

Climbing the corpse fence was harder than Signy expected. The bones were slippery, shifting under their hands while the bodies groaned and muttered. Some clutched with rotting fingers or snapped broken teeth, trying to bite. Others wailed or screamed so loudly, Signy was afraid they'd be discovered long before they'd reached the top.

The thunderous knocking startled her, and she almost fell. Hemingr had reached the gates and was pounding on them with both fists, yelling for someone to hurry up and let him in. "I'm Hemingr the Berserker!" he bellowed. "Come to offer my services to the Queen of Hel!"

There was a moment's stunned silence.

Then chaos broke out.

Signy swung over the top of the fence, landing surefooted in the darkness. "Let's go," she whispered as Asta dropped down beside her. "He'll keep them busy."

They left the uproar behind them and ventured further into Hel.

* * *

The closer they got to Asta's heart, the stronger it beat. She could see more through her missing eye, too. "There's a house, Lady," she said to Signy. "Made of skulls. They're inside, all four of them."

The house was surrounded by bones, which began to stir and mutter the instant Signy and Asta got close. Signy drew her sword. "Be careful," she said to Asta. "If they kill you a second time, they'll kill your soul."

The shade-sword glittered in Asta's hand. "I'm not afraid."

The bones shrieked and shattered under their swords as they stormed the skull house. Smashing through the doors. Bursting in. Screaming their war cries.

The sorcerers scattered.

Two women and two men, all shades. They howled frenzied chants, calling on the crow magic, the wolf magic, the dead magic...

And the dead answered.

The walls heaved and shook as the skulls became skeletons draped in decaying flesh, shade-swords appearing in their hands.

"Get your heart!" Signy swung her sword and scythed into the shrieking dead, beginning to cut her way through. "I'll hold them off."

"My place is by your side, Lady!" Asta was fighting just as furiously.

"You don't have to prove your courage to me, Asta Haraldsdottir." Signy leapt and parried, sword flashing, moving like a whirlwind through the dead. "Just do what I *say*!"

It was hard to leave the fight. But Asta obeyed. Her sword swept shades aside as she darted across the floor, following the pull of her heart.

Signy concentrated on the dead. Slicing and slashing. Hacking and hewing. Fighting her way slowly through towards the sorcerers, who flinched and shuddered with every blow. Their wild screeching grew even shriller, feverish spells splitting the air.

Signy reached the first one.

And sliced him in half.

The other sorcerers cried out in unison as she came for them, her blade crusted with dead flesh. The blood pounded in her veins, muscles singing as she swung the sword again and again, oblivious to everything except the shrieking sorcerers and the endless dead, who wailed and crumpled as the sword tore into rotting flesh and bone.

She cut down another sorcerer – a woman this time – then Asta was beside her again, sword flying. They waded through the dead together. Shoulder to shoulder, fighting their way to the last two sorcerers, who broke and ran.

Asta sprang on the woman, cutting her down as she fled. Signy went after the man, pinning him to the ground and pressing her sword against his throat. "Who sent you to that battlefield?" she demanded. "Who told you to go there and kill Asta Haraldsdottir? Tell me now – and I might spare you."

The sorcerer hurled spell after spell at her, but his magic needed his companions and she deflected all his attempts effortlessly. "Just kill me, Valkyrie," he growled. "I'd rather die forever than face their fury."

"Whose fury?" Signy leaned closer. But the shade only set his teeth and wrenched his throat along her blade, the sharp edge slicing through his flesh.

Signy cursed and dropped the sword, pressing her fingers over the wound, trying to staunch the bleeding. "Who sent you?" she hissed. "*Who*?"

She was holding shadows.

Then nothing.

* * *

Asta's body was still where they'd left it, but there was no sign of Hemingr.

The runes had faded to the silver of old scars, blending back into Asta's skin until they were almost invisible. "We're just in time," Signy said, hoping it wasn't too late. She pulled the leather jerkin open, exposing the stone in Asta's chest. "Give me your heart."

"Promise me, Lady," Asta said as she handed it over. "If my body dies and traps my soul inside, you'll cut off my head and burn my corpse to ashes so I won't come back as a revenant."

"I promise." Signy replaced the stone with Asta's beating heart. She returned the eye to its socket and bound the hand to the stump. Then she drew new runes, chanted the spells of healing – and the shattered ribs reformed, growing back across the hole. Veins and muscle snaked along them, vanishing under a covering of new flesh. The eye blinked and the hand reattached, fingers twitching.

And Asta climbed back inside.

She sat up slowly. Flexing her sword hand, laying her fingers over her heart, her face breaking into a delighted smile. "It worked..." she said. "I'm alive!"

"Then let's go." Hemingr emerged from the darkness behind them, transforming into his wolf-shape before they could ask any questions.

* * *

Asta was asleep by the time they reached the battlefield.

"She'll wake again as soon as we're gone," Signy said as Hemingr laid the sleeping woman carefully onto the ground.

"Will she remember anything?" He straightened, looking down at her peaceful face.

"Only that she fought bravely, and that's all that matters. Anything else will seem like a fading dream."

"And if someone else tries to kill her?"

A raven arrowed down like a shadow, landing lightly on Signy's wrist. "She'll watch over her," she said. "She's under our protection now."

"And her daughter, when she's born?"

Signy lifted her arm and the raven spread powerful wings, launching back into the sky. "That's for the future to know." She slapped Hemingr's shoulder. "So did you spend the entire time shouting and bragging outside the gates – or did Hel let you in?"

"She let me in, of course."

"And?"

"I offered my services as her champion, so she had me fight her best warriors." The huge man looked smug. "She was very impressed."

"I expect she was." Signy raised an eyebrow. "Was she beautiful?"

"The living half of her was."

"And did you do anything else except fight…?"

"We should leave." Hemingr nodded to Asta. "So she can wake and go back to her life. She's got twenty years, Signy – let her enjoy them."

"You mean you're not going to tell me."

Hemingr grinned, shook himself – and was a wolf again.

As they swept into the sky, Asta sat up on the battlefield, gazing at the bodies strewn around her. Her sword hand went to her heart, then her eye – touching uninjured flesh with wondering fingers.

She glanced up. Still half caught in a dream, almost believing she glimpsed a young woman astride a flying wolf.

Almost believing the woman waved before they both vanished.

Shaking her head to clear it of such strange fancies, Asta retrieved her sword and left the battlefield, beginning the long journey home.

Valhalla is a Lie

Benjamin Thomas

We lit a fire in the dead woman's chest because we needed heat, and the aroma would keep unwanted animals away. We found her body in a greenhouse, clutching a triangular shard of broken glass. The blood on her wrist was coagulated into a syrupy, purplish gel, and her torso had been split open and picked clean.

"Reminds me of a turkey," Cat said and screwed a silencer onto her sidearm.

"Oh man." Egan dropped his pack against a raised garden bed filled with weeds. He rubbed his thinning stomach. "Remember Thanksgiving? Family and food? God, what I wouldn't give for a bowl of stuffing."

"I never liked stuffing," I said. They both stared at me. "What?"

The setting sun burned red ribbons across a clouded evening sky. We could taste a coming storm in the air. Feel it in the amplified ache pulsating through our joints.

"How much farther we got?" Egan asked. He unzipped the top part of his pack and started fishing through the contents like a claw arm in one of those vending machine games.

Cat threw a fistful of dead plants on the fire. Sparks cascaded upward like inverted snow. The glow illuminated her face, her buzzed hair, the scar running along the ridge of her left cheek.

"About a hundred miles, give or take. Figure fifteen or so a day puts us about a week out."

Egan tossed a bag of rice from hand to hand and smirked. He was missing two top teeth but somehow managed to keep the hiss at bay. "What pioneers we are. You know, if covered wagons forded the River Styx and not some brook out west."

"Please," I tossed a stone at the flames. "The west is nothing but charred land at this point. Would probably be easy to walk across if it weren't for, you know, falling spears and all."

Cat stopped cleaning her pistol and unsheathed her knife. "You don't really think it's all burned, do you, Gray?"

My full name was Grayson. Everyone always dropped the second syllable, as if it was too much of a chore for anyone to say. I could have insisted on it, that or sir, given my rank in this ragtag delivery mission, but I never did. When you watched your friends, your mates, your fellow rogues, and survivors – whatever we were going by at that point – be hunted, claimed, and skinned alive… titles just didn't seem to matter that much.

Cat scooped a fistful of semi-solid blood from the dead woman's arm and slathered it atop her head.

"Jesus, Cat," Egan said, his lip curled.

She took the knife and dragged it across her scalp, peeling away the crimson cream and what hair that had managed to grow in the last few days. "Do you know the last time I was able to shave with *anything*?" She scraped the side of the blade against a nearby block of wood. "I might be used to it, but razor burn is still a bitch."

Cat started shaving her head nine months ago, the same time she got the scar on the side of her face. Four of us were on a recon run when cloud cover swept overhead and, in a violent flash of lightning, a battalion of them dropped from the sky, spears raised from the backs of winged horses and war cries screaming from their blood-starved mouths.

Their red eyes burned beneath sleek battle helms.

We fought. Shot one in the shoulder and the torso. Watched her drop and writhe on the ground while her fellow riders raged on, hungry for us. For our souls. Cat screamed as she was lifted off the ground by a fistful of her own hair. She swung and clawed and spasmed like a feral animal pressed into a corner. The winged warrior thrust her spear at Cat's neck, missed, sliced open the side of her face, and dropped her to the ground ten feet below. She scrambled away on a broken ankle and sprained wrist.

The greenhouse glass – what was still intact – reflected our firelight like funhouse mirrors. Cat insisted on first watch. For the second time in our month-long endeavor, I pulled rank and ordered her to close her eyes. She was asleep in minutes, hand resting on the hilt of her knife.

I started to zone out and was drawn back by the sound of a stick scraping in the dirt. I looked up to see Egan sketching stars in the ground at his side. He saw me watching and flicked his makeshift pencil into the fire, absentmindedly staring at the container strapped to the bottom of my pack. "What do you suppose is in it?"

The container, the size of a shoebox and wrapped in a gun-metal grey casing, was the reason we left Buffalo and headed east with strict instructions and the GPS coordinates for our drop point. If I imagined hard enough, I could still taste Niagara Falls.

"I've told you before." I leaned back, using my pack as a cushion. "It's not our job to know. Just pretend it isn't there and close your eyes."

"That an order, sir?"

"Depends on whether you need it to be or not."

It should have been. Maybe if I directed him to sleep then and there, Cat and I wouldn't have found him later that night, thirty yards away and face down in the dirt as blood seeped from holes in his back the size of arrowhead stones. Cat ran a hand over her head and cursed. "At least when one of *them* dies, they don't leave a corpse."

I took a sharp breath and nodded at the ground. "That's most of our food."

Scattered near Egan's body and the spot where he went to take a piss was the rice. Little grains of edible confetti. The packaging was shredded, and we picked as many grains from the dirt and muck as we could, but we only salvaged a couple of ounces. More unnerving than the loss of our rations was the fact that the Valkyries were coming in quietly, no longer riding on battle cries and thunderstorms.

The moon danced behind fast-moving clouds, covering the ground in shadow puppets. Had we seen lightning? I couldn't remember. Exhaustion started to fog my brain, strain the muscles I needed most.

Cat checked and rechecked her pistol, ensuring each time that it was loaded. "I can't. I just – what the actual fuck, Gray? It's been three years of this shit. *Three years.* They were supposed to take us to the afterlife, prep us for the end, not hunt us down like rabid dogs."

"Maybe that's what they're doing," I said quietly. "Maybe this is how they choose who goes with them."

"They haven't been choosing...they've been *killing.*" She dropped her hands against her sides. "They aren't even bringing us into battle anymore. Now they're taking us out in our sleep. How does that make sense? How are they supposed to select warriors when we aren't *actually* fighting?"

"We have been fighting," I said. "For decades, Cat. Whether physically or ideologically, the world's been a battleground since before we were born. The books just said they'd pick who does and doesn't go with them, not when or why. Worthiness is at their discretion."

"I don't care what the books say," she snapped. "Valhalla is a goddamn lie. Being chosen to fight at the end isn't worth this. I don't care if it's some kind of test or just the way the world is actually ending. *Nothing* is worth this."

"We have a hundred miles," I said.

She laughed. "Yeah? And do you remember the first hundred? We lost four that week alone."

Caleb. Jim. Shay. Vikki. Three of them died together. "Everyone knew the risks, Cat."

She palm-slammed the magazine of her gun. "Doesn't make it right."

* * *

We were up, right as dawn started to break. I can't say for sure how long either of us slept. It's an elusive state of mind that tends to play with your perception of reality. As Cat walked the perimeter, I split open the last can of beans we had, label long gone. They simmered over the embers in the dead woman's rib cage, her flesh sizzled away and her bones stained from smoke and ash. I tried to think of how they found Egan and not us. Maybe it boiled down to it just not being our time. That was part of the fear: we just never knew when.

While we were eating, Cat looked up from her makeshift bowl. "We can't raid a town just the two of us. Abandoned or not, that's where they'll get us."

"It's either that or we starve."

"We'll hunt game."

"Cat." I scraped the bottom of a collapsible bowl. "We haven't seen so much as a single deer in days."

"Then we hunt rabbit," she snipped, then pointed her spoon at the case strapped to my bag. "Maybe there's food in that."

"If there is, it's not for us."

"Even if it means we die getting it to the coast?"

"Arriving without it is the same as being dead. And I'd take my chances with the ravens and their goddesses given the choice."

Before leaving, we paid our final respects to Egan. Cat rested two small stones over his eyes, pennies long since run out.

"He had two kids," she said when we were a few miles away, cutting through a dense wood to try and avoid the open road.

"Back in Buffalo?" I asked. Before all of this, I would have been ashamed not to know this basic level of information about someone on my team. Now? Now, not knowing made it easier.

"No," Cat said and paused against a massive oak. She rested her foot on a moss-covered rock and took a swig from her canteen. "They died when everything first happened."

"Fuck."

We were shouldering our packs when she asked if I thought they were better off that way. Sometimes, in rare moments of introspection, I caught myself wondering.

"No," I said. "If we died then, we would lose the opportunity to fix now."

* * *

Cat was right, based on training: towns weren't doable with only two. Our survival was based on area surveillance and avoiding predictable places. It wasn't feasible for one person to watch all the headings simultaneously. Storm clouds could roll through in seconds.

We ducked behind a burned-out car in the corner of a trash-strewn parking lot. Cat rested her rifle on the trunk while I used the hood. My crosshairs rested on the shattered front door of a mom-and-pop grocery store. Two buildings down was a bank, and across the street from that a gas station with only one pump still standing.

"I'll go," Cat said and slung her weapon over her shoulder. I put my hand out. "No. I will."

"Don't be stupid," she said. "I hate towns, which means I'll be more on edge and more aware of what's going on around me."

"All the more reason for you to keep an eye on my ass. Circle around that hill, and get a vantage point looking down. Put yourself as close to the bank as you can – if a hurricane comes, try for the vault. Probably be safe there."

She nodded, looked me in the eye for half a second, and then ran in a crouch toward the woods.

Cat radioed from her perch a few minutes later, and I gave the skyline a final scan. Clouds like snowbanks rose on the western horizon, but aside from those the sky was clear. I was fooling myself, trusting the horizon, especially after last night…Egan.

I rushed from the burned-out car to the side of a bus terminal. Counted to ten, listened for wings, hooves, and the quick, sleek sound of unsheathing metal.

"Go," Cat's voice crackled.

My pack jostled as I bolted for the store. I scanned the alley next to the building as I rushed by. Caught a glimpse of three bodies, a flash of scarlet robes. My chest seized, and I dropped, sliding until the momentum stopped. I quickly rose to one knee with my rifle raised and pressed against my shoulder. The tatters of an American flag curled in the breeze. Snapped the side of the grocery store. I relaxed and radioed the false alarm to Cat.

The grocery store doors were chained and locked from the inside, but the glass on the bottom right panel had been smashed in. It crunched under my feet as I crouched through the opening. There were three cash registers at the front of the store, one of which was toppled upside down on the floor. Ceiling lights hung from single chords, and the aisles were littered with crumpled newspapers, empty boxes, and streaks of blood.

I pressed the button on my radio. "How's it looking, Cat?"

"Still clear. Hey, while you're in there, I'd kill for some peanut butter."

"From the looks of it, we'll be lucky if I find an empty jar."

Before the reaping or the rapture or whatever you wanted to call it (maybe the great culling of all humankind), wise people grocery shopped around the perimeter of the store and avoided the aisles. Fresh food and produce were always on the outside looking in. Now? It wasn't worth the time to look and try to find a half-rotten vegetable or plastic container full of browning fruit.

Surprisingly, on the bottom shelf in aisle three, I scored a box of pasta. Somehow it was missed when the store was raided the first time, and then the second, third, and so on. I shoved the blue box into my bag and froze at the suction sound of a cooler door shutting. I turned my radio to near-silent and held my sidearm out as I walked around the end of the aisle.

The smell of spoiled dairy and mold drifted towards me. I gagged, bit my tongue to keep from making noise. Sunlight beamed through a jagged hole in the roof. Dust motes swirled in the makeshift spotlight.

Sweat beaded on the back of my neck. Each step forward caused my heart rate to jump ten beats. A breeze blew through the hole and scattered papers across the floor with soft, scraping sounds. A cooler door opened and shut quickly; I spun, fired two shots…and gawked at my reflection in the spider-webbed glass.

An involuntary breath left me, and I relaxed. Cat's voice was in my radio speaker. I turned it up to hear the end of her question. The word *happened.* I pressed the button, started to respond, and the Valkyrie dropped through the ceiling, her booted heel colliding with my chest.

I stumbled backwards, collided with the floor, and rolled. My sidearm went one way, the radio another. My bag's strap caught on the edge of an overturned shopping cart. The Valkyrie swung, I rolled but was snagged by my bag and the cart. Her spear drove into the top of my shoulder. The joint exploded in searing pain. I kicked at the weapon's staff, shed my pack, and rolled. Cat was screaming through the speaker while thunder exploded overhead. I scrambled to my hands and knees, then to my feet, and stumbled across the dirty floor.

The Valkyrie swung her arm in violent strikes and shattered the cooler doors with the end of her spear. She was tall and dressed in scarlet robes with shining armor across her chest, wrists, and thighs. Her helm was narrow and angled straight, while her wings – my God, her wings – were curved behind her and pressed together to stay out of the way as she navigated the confined space of the grocery store with divine grace.

The Valkyrie shrieked and the entire store shook. Her piercing outcry slashed at my ears like knives. A light snapped free from its precarious cord and ricocheted off the top of an end display. Cans of stale food rolled from the shelves and across the floor. Her eyes burned red like blood-soaked flames. I could see the hunger in them, and it made my stomach drop. I was going to die.

The ringing subsided, and I could hear pops of not-so-distant gunfire. I screamed Cat's name. Pressed against the toppled end of an aisle, I tried to gauge the run to the door. A crash erupted in the back of the store and I jumped up to run, surprised by the sudden maneuverability I felt. It took a second to remember my pack was gone – there was nothing on my shoulders, not even my rifle.

At the other end of the aisle, I could see my pack's strap wrapped across the shopping cart, the container clipped to the bottom of the bag. Goddamn it. Cat was right: towns aren't doable with two people. How stupid had we been? Was she still out there? Had she shot straight and made a run for the bank like I told her – ordered her – to do?

I pulled my knife from the back of my belt, its blade the length of my forearm, and took three deep breaths. "One. Two."

I jumped around the endcap and sprinted for the back of the store. I was halfway down the aisle when the Valkyrie jumped on top of the shelf, knees bent and arm raised. She thrust her spear forward with the look of death in her eyes. I deflected, felt the collision reverberate through my knife and into my wrist and elbow.

The block bought me time but not enough. The Valkyrie was on me, jumping from the shelves and slamming her boot into the top of my shoulders. She thrust her spear into my back three inches from my spine. We both howled as she ripped her bloody weapon out and drove it home. My chest exploded in pain as the air was forced from my lungs. I gasped, wheezed, and couldn't get air.

The Valkyrie rolled me over with the toe of her boot. Coppery warmth washed over my tongue. She reared back, mouth open, and the air chilled as it mixed with her frozen breath. My vision blurred. Pain vibrated through my chest, and as she brought her spear down toward my throat, the minor god's body lurched forward, spraying red from a sudden spat of holes.

She exploded into mist before she hit the ground, her presence in this world gone. Cat was in her place, holstering her sidearm and limping on one side.

"Get up," she urged and tried to help me stand. "Grayson, please. Please get up. Come on."

I put both my palms up and motioned for her to stop. She didn't, just shifted her attention to assessing the damage. Her fingers came off my chest; blood dripped from their tips. I pointed toward my bag, toward the container. Cat understood and went to retrieve it. I struggled to sit against the shelf, still amazed at what I had seen in the Valkyrie's eyes – the hunger, the want.

I coughed and drooled blood.

Cat crouched in front of me, my bag on top of her own. She held out my pistol, but I didn't take it.

"I'm not shooting you," she said. "So, either take it and do it yourself or take it in case another one comes back."

I laughed, and the pain made me wince. When I breathed, my chest hissed. "Take it; you'll need the bullets."

I could see the muscles in her jaw tense. "I'm leaving you one." She started unloading the weapon, but I put my hand on top of hers and shook my head.

"I won't use it. You know where to go?"

Cat gritted her teeth and nodded.

"Get on with it."

She looked to the door and bit her bottom lip, nodding in quiet agreement. She made a fist and slowly tapped it against my knee.

"I had a daughter," I said. She stopped moving and looked at me.

"What was her name?"

"Ashley. She died when they first came. Was out with friends and didn't have a chance."

"Maybe," Cat said quietly. "Maybe that was better."

I shook my head. "If you die at sunset, you'll never get to see the dawn again."

"And if you die in the middle of the night?"

"At least you got to see the stars. Get that where it needs to go, Cat."

She nodded, raised her hand in a wary salute and left. I rested my head back against the barren shelf and stared at the ceiling. The air started to chill, and around my body, the pool of red grew larger. Like small, rapid firecrackers, I heard the sounds of hooves in the distance. Thunder rumbled overhead. I closed my eyes, ready for the ride.

A Scream to Split Stone

M.M. Williams

All that remains of my father is an arm.

I notice this fact only briefly as we run out and form a protective ring around the approaching supply cart. Our pitiful old defenses of wooden pikes wobble and fall under the onslaught of the once-men. Death-blue limbs paw against the back of the cart, and maws of rotted teeth clack in anticipation.

My breath is cold against the morning air. Just as we have done every time, I run to the west side of the road, bracing my hayfork against the ground as if waiting for a charging boar. The creature impales itself, pushing forward without pause until it reaches the end of the spikes.

I know her face. This body was once my friend. Now she reaches for my flesh, pushing hard, with more once-dead behind her. The underfed muscles in my arms shake as I try to drive my knees and toes into the softened ground, to keep them back long enough for the cart to pass.

But more are coming, and my hayfork is slipping against my wet palms.

"Help!" I cry.

The warriors are too busy. Other women are trapped. One screams as they surround her. I hear her kick, claw, curse before being ripped apart They descend upon me, and I am ashamedly frightened stiff at the knowledge of my death, the first press of my feet to the thorny paths between worlds.

A mighty swoop cuts the air as someone bats the creatures across the face.

"Up!" shouts Drifa, one of the weavers, holding a spear.

I crawl fast, trying to rise. My heart forces me to grab my pitchfork again, as an honorable warrior would, but my legs root themselves at the sight in front of me. Shadows among the trees. Hundreds.

"Go back, my girl," she orders. I obey, running with coward's haste towards the mighty gate of Geirheim.

"Get everyone in!" Rota thunders as I blow past her. She is yanking the cart faster than its wheels can turn through the mud. "Get them IN!"

The other women cry with exertion at the effort of pulling the gate closed far faster than its heavy hinges wish to go. Drifa is running toward the closing opening. She darts in without a moment to spare. Pale hands and drooling faces appear in the gap right after. It closes with a boom and a spray of thick, black blood.

Finally, I'm able to kneel and pull the arm from its spot, wedged in the spokes of the cart's wheel. He must have reached to the cart for help in his last moments. I know these fingers, this coarse hair, the ink-marks from his youth, faded with age.

The limb is heavier than I thought it would be.

The sole remaining cartman – young, fair-haired, familiar, but nameless to me – collapses upon the road. His left leg is bent. "I did all that I could."

"How could this happen?" Old Gudrun asks, her wrinkles creasing impossibly deeper. "The road was clear. We drew them away to the east…"

We had, at the cost of four lives and two strong horses.

"More from the south," is all the explanation he can summon.

The grief and torment begin immediately, everyone tumbling toward despair. For my part, I am too small to think beyond this moment. Among the supplies within the cart is a blood-soaked sword I recognize. Its owner is nowhere to be seen.

Guthr Swanwhite steps forward, lays a hand upon my shoulder. "Take it to him, Eir. He should not happen upon this by himself."

I don't complain about the chore, or the opportunity for privacy. I grab both the arm and the sword and flee toward the houses, my dirt-caked skirts heavy with each step.

There is no smoke in the air. Most homes are dark, saving precious wood for moments of utmost need. Already, there are arguments and weeping throughout the small city, curses thrown toward the gods and each other. I hear the sounds of angry men slapping their women, children crying in fear.

Among the bloody remnants of our supply runners, there are provisions enough for a week, I think – if we ration more strictly than we have already. The loss of fine men and warriors helps us in that way, I suppose. Fewer mouths.

I duck my head. My insides burn at what I have become.

In the woods, more carts are overturned. Precious cabbages and apples and furs are spilled around them, surrounded by creatures who see no difference between such things and the leaves – whose tongues water only at the thought of living flesh.

How long behind the walls of this forsaken port city can we last before our desperation drives us to become as they are?

I scurry to the shore, trying to ignore the scratch in my throat, the dead weight in my arms. No matter how I try not to, I can't avoid looking at the old burial mound, its former entrance sealed with boulders. They are inside, the once-dead, scratching at the stone, mewling and croaking into the damp shadow. Olrun Moonmad sits atop the mound in naught but an underdress, one horn of drink cradled against her breast, many others scattered about her muddied feet.

The docks are empty. The fisherwomen have ventured further out today, to chase the fish that have fled the harbor. I rest Father's arm out of sight, behind the old millstone. A dark-haired bundle is crouched by the shallows, all pointed elbows and knees as he watches the mud for eels, a pronged spear in his hand. Barely thirteen, with only the first hints of hair upon his chin and bony chest.

He is, as of the closing of the gates, the last of his line.

This he realizes as he sees the blade in my hand.

The blood is dry, the metal flat and cold in my palms. "Your brother's sword," I say gently. "Yours now, Sigurd."

I see it, his desperate reach for masculine pride, but no matter how he tries to turn to stone, still his lip shakes and his eyes brim with salt.

"My stomach is sour," I say. "Will you take my place upon the boat tonight and watch over the children there?"

There is little power in the lad's muscles – I know that well enough – but he needs to see himself as grown if he is to survive this darkness. And though I sense he bristles, scrutinizing my eyes to find any hint of condescension, I also sense in him relief at my offer. Relief at the prospect of not standing atop the walls tonight, watching for the stumbling shells of his kinsmen.

Relief at the prospect of a quick escape.

"They will need capable guards," I say, and it is not a lie. "Strong men and women who can fend off the enemy if the gate is breached, long enough to cast off."

"But there is no way to fight," he whimpers. "You cannot kill what's already dead."

"Then you shall help to sail. Sail far away, to a new home. It will be an honorable voyage. You will be protecting them just the same as your father and mother did, and your brothers."

"I'll go on the boat," says Sigurd a minute later.

I offer him one last nod and walk back to the millstone. When he thinks I can no longer see, he curls into a shaking ball.

I gather the dead arm once more. The urge to fetch Rota pokes me gently, but I am too numb to rise or walk. We were not always cordial in our dealings, my father and I, but for all his faults, his care was true. My youth was not plagued by bruising hands or biting words.

With cracked fingernails, I dig a grave and lay the arm inside. I have heard the voices of poets with unstained boots and unbattered shields, speaking of battle and how love cannot exist near rivers of blood. Here have I learned to see the lie of those poems.

There would be no pain behind my chest bone, no burning blade sawing through my throat, were it not for love. There would be no fear had we no hope or dreams.

No, here at the last edge of the world, behind the walls of teeth-scratched stone, love remains.

And that is why we weep.

* * *

My meal today was a leaf of cabbage rolled tightly around old greens and scraps of fish skin. I now sip at weak broth, taking my watch atop the wall. More of the once-dead have gathered. What draws them hither, we do not know, but the woods are now closed off to us entirely. We are at the mercy of what little food we have left behind the walls.

I can scarcely remember anything besides hunger. When I have a rare moment to reach for the past, only one memory remains unblurred in the haze. As first blossoms of spring arose some months ago, I discovered stolen kisses behind haystacks, love atop the root-wrinkled skirts of the trees.

One night, a full moon, I stole from my bedroll and slipped toward the door, though my escape was not unnoticed. My father's new wife, Rota Redhair, sat by the hearth with legs propped high, as she often did when the children in her belly grew large.

"What is that horrid yowling?" I asked.

"One of the field cats, I think, asking for a spot by the fire. Perhaps in her heat. In any case, it ought to head back to its work."

I continued to the door. Of all the members of the household, she would surely not judge my brief escapes, and I doubted she would pass the news to Father, either.

"Eir," she called before the door could close, one brow quirked into an arch. "You know you should not waste your favors or your time on beardless, penniless men."

I knew, now that I was in new possession of a woman's body, that my father was in search of a wealthy man to take me to wife. Still, I could not bear the thought of simply waiting for my chains. Nor did I believe that Rota, despite the duty placed upon her to scold me, truly disagreed with my choices.

I rolled my eyes. "We are careful."

I walked through the night into the old apple grove, to the base of our tree. Ten minutes passed. The first whispers of foot-crunched leaves set my heart to flight, but my excitement withered when I saw only a hunched woman, shuffling on, hair a graying cloud – an oddly familiar cloud, though I knew it was only a trick of the darkness. With a sigh, I sat until I heard another approach. The next time, when I saw who was walking, my heartbeat sped and did not slow.

I would have known the shape of his shadow anywhere.

The dark outline grew larger. He rubbed at his neck, as if sheepish for meeting me too late.

"It is the strangest thing," I said upon a laugh. "In the trees, I saw someone who looked like your mother."

No response, only a gurgle, as he came into the moonbeams, his legs melting under his weight. As he tumbled to the ground, his palm peeled away to reveal bloody pits near his throat, blackened by the moonlight. My scream shook the leaves. He crawled toward me, a plea in his eyes. From the shadows, a second cloud-haired creature stumbled.

And my love was torn from Midgard by the same one who brought him into it.

* * *

Fifteen days after my father's burial, good news comes. A family of gulls came to roost upon the cliffs, to the delight of our remaining archers. For the first time in two weeks, we taste something besides muddy eel flesh.

The news, however, is but a candle in the abyss. The villages in the east have now all fallen, we believe, driving the dead to our stronghold. The crowd outside has grown too heavy, and the timbers and stones of the walls are beginning to lean. The gate has been piled high with a waterfall of rocks. We will only leave Geirheim by boat or death.

The chieftain has called a Thing.

I shuffle slowly – my speed of body and mind decrease more each day. By the docks, I hear raised voices.

"Curses, Olrun!" Regin Longarm, our most skilled fisherwoman, huffs. "You shall rust the metal!"

Olrun continues with her task. She is dumping her strange mead all over the spears.

Madness seized her months ago, at the first breach of her own village walls and the loss of all her kin and children. How she managed to run here alone and unarmed, we do not know. What acuity she must have once had is gone now. Her days are spent half-undressed among barrels of drink, creating foul concoctions as she mumbles about moonlight and herbs. The beauty of the heavens has sucked her away from the mortal realm. A strange woman, perhaps, but harmless enough to not deserve my fear or judgement.

Months ago, before stepping through these gates, I might have snickered behind my hands or, worse, thrown harsh words at her. Now I have only compassion.

I press a hand upon her skeletal back, my other palm against my nose to guard from the fierce reek of her mead-coated skin. "How fare your girls today, Olrun?"

Her four daughters lay in pieces in whichever place she comes from, but she doesn't seem to know that. Her dark eyes gleam with affection as she pours drink after drink over the fishing spears.

"Their favorite," she says with cheer. "Yes, yes, their favorite. They are finally ready. Ready to wash away…"

"What do you mean?"

"Is it not a beautiful place, Eir? The hearth is so warm, the tables so full. I've seen it. She found me. She told me this will close the door for the restless spirits. This will wash them away."

"Who found you?"

"Lady Freyja. She speaks to me. Visions in the night. Visions among the stars, bouncing like rabbits in the meadows."

The mere allusion to seiðr makes me wary. Not long after my arrival, four men and women were cut at the throat for suspicion of bringing forth these foul creatures. The chieftain does not trust magic.

"Do not speak of this to the men," I whisper to her before shuffling away fast.

I walk quietly into the longhouse and sit at my stepmother's side. Rota pats my knee, a grand show of affection from one who dislikes touch as much as she does. She has not shown much happiness since the little ones succumbed to fever on the long journey to Geirheim.

At the front of the hall is the mountainous chieftain. He had many wives once, as powerful men often do. Only one, Skogul, remains alive, sitting to his left.

Nestled in the corner, Guthr Swanwhite sits upon the lap of her husband Agi. He plays with her hair, so blonde it's nearly white. Though I have not known them long – they arrived here in Geirheim only days after us – I know they share the sort of love where two blend into one, twined together like rope. It makes me ache.

It is not long before the room is filled with the adults who remain, nearly all women. Women holding babes with one arm, corralling toddlers with the other. Women with hair uncombed and unbraided. Women who have seen their lovers and children fall, and then watched their lifeless bodies flood with ravenous murk and stumble toward them, hands outstretched as if begging for a final embrace.

Women who have nearly been driven to step into those embraces.

For most of the Thing, I do not listen. It is hard now to listen to anything save the howling of my empty insides. Though from what I can hear, it seems little more than an argument between the leading couple.

"Barnstock still stands," the chieftain says at one point. "How long it will hold, I do not know. We have one sailboat left.

The strongest of us could make the journey and return with more boats."

"The land is lost," Skogul insists. "We must away to the islands while we can, back and forth until we are all safe. We've delayed too long already. The younger women and the children must go, at the least."

"There is no safety in the islands," he says simply. "Some of the dead, I hear, are spat out by the sea. This is a trick of Loki, of that I am certain."

"But—"

"Silence, woman!"

My stomach is growing nauseated, my eyes heavy with illness and fatigue, but even then, I feel doubt. Though the great trickster is no stranger to misdeeds, I do not feel his touch here. There is no benefit or amusement for him in such relentless death or hunger. Whatever mysterious evil is at work in this world, I do not believe he or any of the gods are responsible

Perhaps it is foolish, but still I hope that they will save us.

* * *

I do not know at what point I fall asleep in the longhouse, but no dreams can come before Sigurd rustles me awake.

"I tried to fight them," he says shakily. "I swear it, Eir."

Black ice shoots through my blood. "The once-dead?"

"No. The men."

I shoot to my feet, not bothering to put on my boots before running to the harbor to a sight that nearly kills me. Most of our bearded men have taken the last sailboat, thrown out all the children who slumbered there for safety. Those tasked with guarding the boat and the young float face-down in the water of the harbor, unmoving.

"Rota!" I shout through a parched throat. "Drifa! Anybody!"

I cry for help until the beach is filled with twenty women and our handful of remaining men – the wounded and Agi. No one cries. Shock has seized us all, rendered us more helpless than before.

Bad fortune, however, rarely appears as a lone traveler. This we remember as the west wall suddenly begins to fall. Great blocks of stone crash slowly against the grasses, and the creatures begin to force themselves inside.

Geirheim has met its end.

Skogul does not hesitate to take the reins of the runaway horse. "Carry the children and the wounded to the longhouse," she says in a hushed voice. "Barricade the doors!"

I run without a destination, grabbing whoever is small and carrying them to the longhouse. Far down the road, I see Agi running to warn and save the people in the homes close to the walls. I watch as the once-dead who have already entered the city chase after him, throwing arms toward his stomach. Women run to and fro as quietly as possible to avoid the notice of the once-dead. They travel slow and do not seem to see well, but still, we must hurry. Poor Sigurd is carrying three little ones, shuffling with all the speed he can manage. I help him inside the longhouse and order him to block the doors behind me. If I die today, I shall do so on the field of battle.

Then I see Agi walking down the road in silence, clutching at his stomach. A red stain races down his hips, his legs.

How Guthr holds back her scream, I do not know, but I feel as if I see her die. As quietly as they can manage, she and some others carry him to the end of the dock. The ends of her swan-white hair pinken with each brush over the lifeblood of her beloved. In spite of the creatures starting to mill about the city, all of us women who remain outside drift toward the beaches and the dock.

Drawn like moths by the last spark of love we shall ever see.

"We shall save you," Guthr breathes as her hands slide over him with no particular destination. "There is yet air in your lungs and a beat in your chest."

"A chest you must pierce," Agi says, calm as fresh snow. "Do me the honor of a swift death. Spare me the feeling of their teeth."

All has gone silent now, save for the growing noise of the dead.

"No," she sobs. "No, no, no—"

"Do not cry for me, sun-eyes," he says with a smile. "When next we meet, by the hearth of Valhalla, I will have saved you the ripest strawberries."

Their lips meet, and during their kiss, he fades, the last of his air gifted to her. At least, it seems this way by the way she ceases to breathe, as if to hold his soul inside her own chest.

Regin holds out a fishing spear. Guthr, blue at this point, finally releases the last bit of him into the wind. She places the spear tip against his breast, her tears dripping from her chin. It takes effort to break through his chest bone. She whines.

And then he is gone.

Silence. Nothingness.

We are empty now.

All at once, Guthr's face pulls into a growl, her teeth bared, her jaw dropping wide. She screams. The once-dead turn and begin to hobble in our direction, and still she screams.

Skogul stares at the diminishing outline of the sailboat, and she screams, too. Regin, with a kick at the empty fish barrels, joins the chorus. A scream to rattle the soil, to part the clouds, to call down lightning to crack the oaks and scorch the soil.

It shakes within me, too, this scream of thundering horses and beating hooves, of torn earth and quaking stone. I grab hands with Rota and we scream.

So long have we prayed to and heard nothing from the gods. Only now do we know the full wrath of Lady Freyja, of shattered love and forgotten vows, of cages and the rusted chains which stain our necks. We have carried this wrath from our births, hardened blood passed from womb to womb, from our mothers and our foremothers. It breaks the bonds of reason and consumes our flesh.

We scream and the cliffs begin to crack.

Guthr grabs a fishing spear, bolting for the once-dead. We follow, each woman taking a spear of her own. The dock rumbles with our charge, rippling the water of the harbor.

Our screams and our spears do not falter. Our courage does not break. The noise within us shakes the very earth, wobbling the once-dead, forcing them to the ground, where with thrown spears and thrust spears and filleting knives, we break their blackened hearts.

For our children, and our brothers and sisters. For our forebearers and the men and women with whom we found love and safe harbor.

For us, and the life and wishes and dreams that still burn within our chests.

It is only after fifty have fallen that we cease our scream and come out of our trance to see that the corpses now lay still as corpses should.

"Olrun's mead!" Skogul cries. "They are weak against it!"

No, not only weak. It is their bane, the whip that drives them permanently from this realm. The corpses now lay still as corpses should. Olrun Moonmad has seen what we could not.

She stands atop the remaining walls of Geirheim now, holding a bowl and a horn, bidding us to the gate. Already Guthr Swanwhite is sprinting, hair flying in ropes thick with blood, ribs expanding with summer air.

For the first time since a moonlit spring night so long ago, a smile breaks across my lips.

It is we who bring souls into this world. It is we who shall force the unwanted back out, over the gap between realms, into the darkness from which they sprouted. We, the last warriors of Geirheim, will carry this mead over land, over sea, and skewer all that dares to stir in the darkness of burial mounds.

From this day on, the dead shall stay dead.

The Death of a Valkyrja

Mae Wilmarth

Three *Konungr* came to their reckoning in one of the last battles for Old *Norðr Vegr*. At the end of the battle, they faced the *Valkyrjur*. The *Nornir* had woven into the threads of fate that these *Konungr* would die – that was no surprise. However, these *Konungr* had not known of their fate after death, which would be exacted by the *Valkyrjur*.

The war did not commence suddenly. In fact, the catalyst was disputed. Some said it was the arrival of the priest Poppo and his influence in the conversion of Harald Bluetooth to Christianity. Some said it was the abandonment of the Gods that drove the most devoted Norse-persons to madness and anarchy against their kin. Had anyone consulted the Gods, though, they might have suggested that it was nothing more conspicuous than the birth of three *småbarn* in the far north of the Norwegian Sea.

* * *

On the black sand beach, waves and wind crashing in united havoc, Ødger peered out at the dark sea under a roiling canopy of thunder and rain. The storm had not yet reached land, but it would soon. Ødger could not help but feel that this was an omen, a sign from the Gods.

But no, he had forsaken those Gods, and he could not think that way anymore. He had sworn his oath to a new God and would have to learn to pray to this one. Letting go was difficult, to pray to the *Aesir* was like breathing – a reflex. Even so, they had not answered those prayers in years. If they had, his wife may still be alive instead of slain in battle. His son may still be alive and could have grown to see manhood.

Perhaps, if his wife and son were still alive, they would see this abandonment as a betrayal of their souls, but he had only made the oath when he learned that he could spend eternity with them in the realm of this new God, a place called *Caelum*. That was what this missionary had told him, anyway. The missionary spoke of many things in the wake of this catastrophe, and Ødger could not help but wonder, as he watched the storm, if his act of desperation had been a mistake.

As if perceiving his thoughts, the missionary, Grimbald, appeared at his side and said, "God is here with us now. Do you sense that? In the storm, in the waves, He is showing you His strength."

Ødger said nothing. He did not want the monk to think him a heretic, but he knew so little about this new God that he feared he would mistakenly cause offense. There seemed to be many rules to this new God, but Grimbald had been very patient in his teachings.

"God has great plans for you," Grimbald continued.

Ødger's curiosity overcame him. "What plans are those?"

"Well, God ordains His strongest and most loyal servants to become divine representations of His greatness here on earth and thus live forever by His side in *Caelum*. You will have salvation through faith and by leading your kin to God."

Ødger smirked. "Not all of my kin will abandon their Gods."

"God is a ruthless and wrathful king. If you undertake the just cause of converting these northerners, you may need to use ruthlessness and evoke fear yourself. While I do not condone war, ruling with a firm fist is not an unjust thing, especially if you mean to save the souls of thousands of men. That righteous work would earn your place next to God, with your wife and child standing behind you. You can redeem their souls, too."

Ødger thought this over, unmoving, well into the night. He thought for so long that Grimbald left to retrieve some seal meat and ale. Grimbald did not stay long on his second visit, because the storm had come in, and there was no light with which to see except when lightning flashed.

Grimbald and the other missionaries had told him many tales of other kings who served this Christ God. The missionaries had painted an agreeable picture for Ødger and his men, who would be the heads of their houses over wives, children, and handmaids.

Another aspect of this religion that Ødger preferred – perhaps more than the idea of the God itself – was the idea of a single divine ruler of one people and the advantages to be gained should he become united with the kings of other peoples. Grimbald had explained this to him but made him swear not to enquire further, claiming this was a secret among the missionaries he believed Ødger was worthy of knowing. Under his surrogate father's rule and long after, Ødger had become ruthless, certainly. He had raided and enslaved most of the west and south coasts, controlling the goods and trade for each clan in his clutches.

Some of his clan left soon after he swore his oath, but that was of no matter. The deserters would only become enslaved by one of the neighboring clans still controlled by Ødger. His stomach grew hot and twisted at the thought. If he could not have his wife and child, then he would have the rest of the world, and once he found the men who had done this, he would make them suffer.

When he returned to the camp they had made in the scorched ruins of their home, he went straight to his *skipstjórnarmaðr* to ask of the captives.

"They came from no clan. They are a new clan, they say, from the north islands. They have come to kill the missionaries in the name of *Óðinn*. Some come from Håkon's clan, some come from Ivar's. Others joined from all around the north."

"Then all around the north we shall fight and show them who their true king is and what a ruthless and fearful God can do."

* * *

Under midday sleet and serrated wind, *Konungr* Håkon stood on the porch of his longhouse and watched the *seiðr,* Agnarr, hasten up the hill.

"Håkon, *Konungr*," Agnarr shouted between heavy breaths. "I have seen… I…"

The old man stopped just several strides from Håkon and leaned over, hands on knees, to catch his breath. Pursuing him up the hill from the stables was another *seiðr*, Hrafn, who reached Håkon breathlessly and returned to the *Konungr* the brooch upon which they had cast their sorcery.

"Well, did it work?" Håkon asked impatiently, tucking his mother's brooch safely within his *feldr*.

Agnarr suffered the last few steps up to the porch and collapsed at Håkon's feet. He sputtered, chest heaving, "The *Nornir* have spoken, but their intent is rather unclear—"

"Your sword will be the downfall of your brother – it must be, if you are to keep the favor of *Óðinn*," Hrafn interrupted.

Håkon narrowed his eyes at Hrafn. He did not quite trust this fellow who had betrayed his brother, Ødger, in favor of Håkon's campaign to rule the coast and cast out these Christian missionaries who would depose the Norse Gods for their one imposing god. Agnarr seemed to trust this man, though, so Håkon tolerated his presence.

"Come inside, tell me all, and do not withhold any seemingly small detail," Håkon instructed, leading the men inside. He poured some ale and stoked the fire.

After they had warmed their hands and thanked their *Konungr*, Agnarr found his strength to speak and told all. "The sorcery worked well. I saw that Ødger will burn the houses of many along the seacoast. He will force all those he enslaves to practice the ways of this Christ God he now worships. He will come to take your life. This is where the fates became unclear: you may die in this battle, but your sword will be the downfall of Ødger. I also believe that, should you remain loyal to the *Aesir*, you will become *einheri*. Lastly, at least one of the *Valkyrjur* will come in disguise."

Håkon said nothing for some time, only watched the flickering flames and sipped his spiced ale. The others did not provoke him, though Hrafn opened his mouth once before Agnarr silenced him with a steady hand on the shoulder. Only when the fire had grown dim, and the creeping draft caused them to tremble, did Agnarr interrupt his master's thoughts.

"The fire grows dim, and the sorcery has exhausted my bones. With your leave, *Konungr*, I might retire to bed."

Håkon blinked at the old man as if he had forgotten he was there. "Yes, of course," he grumbled distractedly, "thank you for all you have done today, both of you."

With the blatant dismissal, Hrafn also retired for the night. Both men looked back only once, watching Håkon stoke the fire. The orange glow only exacerbated the deep lines in his angular face. They could not help but wonder at the fate of their clan and kin in the coming weeks. What they did not hear, and what Håkon did not intend them to hear, was the oath he swore to himself and the Gods: "I will not defy *Óðinn.* I will not abandon the *Aesir*."

* * *

Veborg watched her house burn from Knifehilt Fell. She let the tears run freely from her eyes, giving no care to onlookers. The *níðingr* that dared come to pillage and destroy her home was dead, though not before he and his men had caused irreparable damage. Her father, brothers, and lover had been killed by Rollo, the *níðingr*, and his men. Rollo had used a nasty trick of disguise and entered the home of Veborg's father, *Konungr*

Ivar, under the guise of trade. Until she saw her father's severed head, Veborg had not known the treachery of her shield brother, Ødger, against the Gods and *Norðr Vegr*.

"Veborg?"

"Hmm?"

"I was tasked by your father to give you this letter upon his death." Leif trotted his horse up next to hers and handed her the parchment. He was a gentle man, her uncle. He patted her hand upon her taking hold of the letter, and whispered, "In your own time, but I feel we must speak once you have read it. Also, I believe your words may help our people, if you can find it in you to speak with them."

Veborg nodded her appreciation but did not quite meet his eye. He backed his horse away and gave her quite a bit of space. She did not want it – her father had toughened her beyond the hardness of stone – but she needed it. Removing the wax seal stamped with her father's ring and needing whatever guidance he provided, she read:

> *My dearest daughter,*
>
> *If you are receiving this letter, it is because I have perished and because you are, and always have been, my only hope to keep our legacy alive. Within, I will explain my desires for your path forward and make confessions that, I fear, are long overdue.*
>
> *First, I must ask that you care for your brothers. They are not yet men, and not yet capable of*

defending themselves or ruling with a clear head. I fear they will be obstinate, like my younger self. They adore you, and then they will hate you for a time, as is the way of boys becoming men, but then they will come to love you again and heed your wisdom.

At these words, Veborg sobbed loudly into her hand, and her eyes blurred with renewed tears. Her brothers had not even lived to see ten and five.

Now, before I make my next demand, I must make my confession: I am not your blood father. Your mother was my Queen Wife, and she was your blood mother. However, she made me swear to her, before our marriage, that I would treat you as my own blood kin. I hope I have done that, but it is not my place to make that determination – that is between you and Freyja. What she told me is what I must now tell you in order to fulfill my promise to my beloved Queen Wife.

You have two other blood brothers; they were your shield brothers: Håkon and Ødger. Another thing I must tell you is that your mother was seiðr, and she foresaw that the three of you would engage in a holy war. The Nornir told her directly that the firstborn Konungr of Björn the Worthy would gain the favor of the Gods and maintain an honorable place in Valhöll. Björn, your mother confessed, is your blood father. She would tell me no more but said that you must know your destiny. I believe she saw your choices and the outcome, but she would not divulge that to me and swore that it would stay between her and the Nornir. You know how devoted she was to them.

Now that we have, hopefully, an equitable understanding of your identity, I hope you may sympathize with my next and final earthly request. I believe you are a powerful berserkr who is meant to rule in my stead. You must become Konungr. Perhaps this is not a typical title for a woman, perhaps some will oppose you for appropriating the word, but my belief is not that this is a title for a man or woman or neuter but for anyone able to fill that role – and that is you, Veborg. While your mother did not say, I believe she saw you as her firstborn Konungr. Perhaps I am dishonoring the Fates with this request and declaration, but I have not watched you grow all these years to doubt your worthiness. I say this because I believe that you, with all your conviction and ironclad belief in the Gods, are more capable than any person I have met to be their champion in such a paramount war.

Please, Veborg, I ask you these things, but I trust your judgement. Whatever you believe is your path forward, choose that, and know that I will love you no matter what you do or where I go in the afterlife.

Carry me in your heart always,

Your father, Ivar

The letter ended with his signature and a small emblem of their house that only she and her brothers had known. Now, she would be the only one in all the world to know it.

Turning her horse, Veborg trotted to her uncle, who saw her approach and met her some distance from the surviving clan to gain privacy.

"Did he disclose to you the contents of the letter?"

Leif nodded and explained, "Yes, he told me that he is not your blood father and that he would bestow upon you the title of *Konungr*. I told him that I believed this a wise decision."

Veborg observed Leif, sharply staring into his eyes. The man did not flinch, but she could see water glistening on his lashes after a time. For a moment, she said nothing, then she asked him, "Do you trust me to make declarations, henceforth? Will you stay by my side as kin, mentor, and warrior?"

Without hesitation, Leif slammed his fist to his chest and bowed his head, his proclamation of fealty.

"I will speak to them now," Veborg stated and rode forward to meet her clan. She announced: "This day is one of grave tragedy and treachery, and our hearts shall never forget it. It is with unending sorrow that I mourn those we have lost, but still, my heart is glad that you all – my kin, my clan – are here with me. This act of treachery must not go unanswered, but I will not move against this enemy until I know that my people are safe and the warriors among us willing to fight. Should you have me, I would name myself *Konungr*, as this was my father's dying will, and I believe it is my living duty. I know I am an unconventional choice, and there are many among us who would be worthy of the title. However, as one who is both man and woman, and simultaneously neither, my path forward is as berserker, son and daughter, neither mother nor father but guardian of my kin and clan and any who would worship the *Aesir*."

The clan, thin and battle weary, found it within them to cheer. Some departed but this did not rankle Veborg.

"Shall we call you man, now?" Leif asked, leaning over to whisper.

"Perhaps," Veborg considered, "but woman is acceptable. Perhaps neither, though, for I believe androgyny suits me, as it has suited many warriors in the past."

Leif nodded in understanding. When the cheering died down, Veborg said, "Let us salvage what is left, and once we have tended to our wounded and counted our stores, we will discuss our fate."

With that, above the dissipating black smoke that concealed their home, Veborg and their clan turned back to the only place they had called home.

* * *

Ødger, Håkon, and Veborg flung their banners skyward and converged on the icy shores of Old *Norðr Vegr*. First, ships clashed, then swords, then hearts of conviction and allegiance.

Three siblings bonded by blood and soul came together after years of separation.

Over the hills came bands of men and women bearing arms and throwing themselves into the fray. Word soon spread throughout the encampments that some of the *Valkyrjur* had come with these bands of wayward warriors who claimed no clan or *Konungr* but who declared allegiance to the Gods.

The battle began in a frenzy and was fought only over the course of one day. In the twilight hours, the lines of allegiance and opposition blurred, and Veborg came to Håkon unarmed, as a show of respect, and with a peace offering. Some of his men had attacked theirs, despite the fact that Veborg had declared opposition only against those loyal to Ødger.

"Brother," Veborg said, "I would entreat you to join our people and use our combined strength to end Ødger's false reign."

Håkon considered them and eventually said, "You come to my lands, and you eat my crops and game animals. You call yourself *Konungr* when the lands you pretend to rule were my birthright. Who are you to take these things from me like a coward? Are you no different?"

"It was not you who came to our aid when we were attacked. It was not you who fought for our home all these years, ensured our people were safe, housed, and fed. I have taken nothing from you that you did not already abandon. Father—"

"That bastard was not our father," Håkon spat.

"You know?"

"Of course I know. I know that Björn the Worthy is believed to be our true father. Though, I learned that you were a bastard child born even before they wed. Upon his death, she wed that bastard Ivar and sent me and Ødger away. She told my caretakers that it was for my safety – that my father's enemies might still be hunting his little princelings. Many believe Ivar was one of the architects in the assassination."

"From whom did you hear this? I cannot believe that he would assassinate Björn just to name me *Konungr* and guardian of his children."

Håkon clutched a fistful of Veborg's hair and pulled them close, spittle flying from his bleeding and peeling lips. "I will not be mocked by some swineherd's bastard! I know these things to be true!"

Veborg pushed him away and regained their balance, but they were immediately knocked to the ground by Håkon rushing them suddenly. Veborg landed in the half-frozen mud but braced their legs. When Håkon fell on top of them, Veborg used Håkon's momentum to roll to one side. Veborg pinned Håkon and held a dagger to his throat but was met with the same dilemma.

"We must join arms, brother!" Veborg pleaded.

Håkon slashed his knife, and Veborg could only dive to the side to avoid the blade. Håkon overcame them in turn, baring his teeth, which went from a yellowed ivory to deep red. The blade of Veborg's knife was embedded in Håkon's skull. They had not wanted to kill him, but the *berserkr* in Veborg had only meant to survive what was sure to be a deadly blow.

Veborg gently pushed Håkon off and posed their brother for a warrior's eternal slumber. They could not pull away for some time despite the ongoing sounds of battle beyond.

Suddenly, a dark figure appeared on the crest of a nearby dune and called, "You must fight!"

Veborg started and peered up at the speaker, who was clad in black armor and had painted her eyes black to match. Her long black hair whipped in the wind. She repeated herself, adding, "The tyrant advances. He is slaughtering your people."

Unarmed and unable to retrieve their weapon, Veborg asked Håkon for forgiveness as they pulled his sword from his body. They ran into the fray.

* * *

At the top of the dune, Veborg saw Ødger just paces away. For a moment, their heart ached at the thought of killing their only remaining sibling, but even greater than that was knowing the pain their people would feel should *Norðr Vegr* be lost. There was no time to dwell in these wild emotions, though, for Ødger saw Veborg and advanced.

Iron and steel, sword and axe, clashed louder than any other weapons on the battlefield. The second of silence that followed was said to be a moment of silence by all of *Norðr Vegr*, for this would be the moment their fate would be determined. Veborg and Ødger fought relentlessly as *Sól* drove her chariot over the horizon and *Máni* reigned in the sky. Veborg struggled to handle Håkon's lighter sword at first, but they became accustomed to it swiftly. Ødger fought with a rage that reddened his skin and eyes.

When Veborg grew too tired to continue, and felt that they may not win this fight after all, they sent up a silent prayer to the *Aesir* and especially to *Þórr*. "Give me strength, imbue my sword with your wisdom, your thunder. Give me this in the name of, for the sake of, *Norðr Vegr*."

A great bolt of lightning struck Veborg's blade as sword and axe collided one last time.

* * *

All was dark, and then it was calm but for gentle waves against sand. Veborg was standing beside Håkon and Ødger. Before them stood three tall figures clad in beautiful armor. Behind stood the fallen.

"You, the *Konungr* who have fallen in this holy war, do you know who we are?" asked the woman in the center, tall with red hair and broad shoulders.

"*Valkyrjur*," the three siblings said in unison – one in fear and two in awe.

"Yes, and we have come to claim your souls."

"I must go to *Valhöll*," Ødger said at once.

The woman to the right, clad in black armor with black painted eyes, stepped forward. "We have a special place for your soul, *Konungr* Ødger. Would you come with me?"

Ødger, eager and presumptuous, stepped forward. The raven-haired woman gestured to his men, and all disappeared into the water.

"Where did she take him?" Håkon asked, curiosity and surprise deepening the lines in his face.

The broad-shouldered *Valkyrja* answered, "To *Hel's* realm, *Helheim*."

Veborg stifled a gasp. Håkon shuddered, whispered cruelly, "Damned to eat from plates called Hunger."

"*Konungr* Veborg," the broad-shouldered *Valkyrja* said, "You will come with me, but you may choose where your soul, and those of your people, are bound. Would you become *einheri* and dine in *Óðinn's* hall, or would you join *Freyja*?"

Veborg peered back at their people, who pounded their fists to their hearts and bowed their heads, and then at Håkon, for whom they felt nothing but fondness despite their final encounter in the world of the living. He appeared crestfallen, and Veborg's heart filled with sympathy. Although their mind had been made up long ago.

"We will go to *Freyja*."

Håkon's brow furrowed. "Are you certain?"

"Yes, brother, I feel this is my destiny. And you have earned your place at *Óðinn's* side as *einheri*."

The *Valkyrja* smiled warmly and crossed to Veborg as the other crossed to Håkon. One last time, the siblings embraced, Håkon whispering apologies, Veborg ensuring forgiveness.

"This is a wise choice, *Konungr* Veborg," said the *Valkyrja* called *Brynhildr*, "Freyja had hoped you would decide this, for she will make you *Valkyrja*."

To Please the Gods

Johanna Wittenberg

The midsummer sun was setting as Helga and her four sisters arrived at the All-Ting, the great assembly of free folk east of the mountains.

Helga was the eldest at fifteen. Next came Unn, then Ursa, Tova, and finally little Ylva, barely eleven winters old. There were too many mouths to feed at home and their parents had sent the five sisters away to seek their fortunes at the Ting.

"Find a rich farmer to work for," their mother advised.

Helga dreamed of a more exciting life. "We'll find Queen Åsa at the All-Ting, and she'll make us shield-maidens."

Their brothers had laughed, but Helga ignored them. "They're jealous," she told her sisters. "No lord would have them. But Åsa will take us on."

Five days the sisters followed the timeworn trail. They had no shoes, but their feet were tough from years of going barefoot. Without blankets or tents, they slept rough under the stars. The sisters huddled together against the mountain cold while Helga spoke of the glorious future that awaited them. "We'll fight many battles, win fame and fortune, and please the gods."

One night, Helga dreamed of a mighty woman armed with a spear. Her hair shone silver and swan's wings sprouted from her shoulders. The lady turned her gaze on Helga, sending a shiver down her spine. A Valkyrie.

Their mother had spared them what little bread she could, and slipped them each a withered apple from last year's crop. The sisters knew how to find wild roots and berries. Once they speared a fish in a brook, and another day caught a skinny rabbit in the snares they set at night. But by the time they crested the last mountain and campfire smoke tinged the air, the girls were hungry.

The Ting site lay on the shores of a broad lake, fed by a waterfall tumbling down the rock face of the sacred hill. The plain thronged with warlords' encampments, their banners streaming over a sea of tents. Helga and her sisters gawked as they passed by the camps of chieftains, kings, and jarls.

Helga stopped a boy close to her age who did not look too fierce. "Can you tell us where the camp of Åsa of Agder lies?"

The boy's face broke into a scornful grin. "The girl-queen?"

"Yes," Helga snapped.

The boy waved in a general direction.

They arrived at a sparse collection of ragged tents surrounding a campfire. A tantalizing odor of stew rose from the cauldron simmering over the fire, but the young queen's camp did not look very impressive. A few warriors polished weapons or mended sheaths and harnesses. At their head sat an elderly warlord, gaunt and gray, who wore an air of authority like a cloak. Beside him a young woman presided on a richly carved chair. A beautiful sword shone by her side.

Åsa.

Helga forgot her hunger.

The sisters huddled together outside the ring of firelight, tittering nervously. "Stop giggling!" Helga hissed.

The young queen's head went up expectantly at the sound. "Come forth," she commanded.

Helga squared her shoulders and stepped into the firelight. She glimpsed the look of disappointment that flitted across the queen's face, before the woman transformed her expression into an encouraging smile.

"I am Åsa, queen of Agder. Who are you, and what do you seek?"

Helga prayed her voice would not break. "Lady, I am called Helga Hrolfsdottir." She gestured to the girls who clustered behind her. "These are my sisters. We wish to serve you."

"I already have enough serving women," Åsa said.

Helga swallowed hard. "We wish to fight."

"But you are just young girls."

"We have heard that you train shield-maidens. That is what we wish to become."

Åsa's mouth twitched before she assumed a stone face. "It is not as easy as just wishing for it. It's dangerous, hard work."

Helga bristled at that. "On the farm my sisters and I work hard from sunrise until after dark. We're as strong as our brothers, accustomed to blood and slaughter. If we can butcher livestock, we can kill men. We fear nothing but death without honor. Our wish is to die in battle and earn our place in Freyja's hall." Helga could not stop the passion that poured into her voice until it rang throughout the campsite. The húskarlars' heads snapped up from their work and they stared.

Helga tried to maintain a fierce demeanor under Åsa's scrutiny. "Lady, we already have the strength and endurance of shield-maidens. We need only to trade the pitchfork for a spear and cultivate the battle skills."

"Aren't you needed at home?"

Helga tried to hide her shame. "We are too many. Our family cannot feed all of us over the winter."

After an interminable pause, the queen spoke. "You and your sisters are welcome in my hird." Åsa hauled up her sword and laid it across her knees. "Come forward, Helga Hrolfsdottir, and swear to me."

Helga had imagined this moment a thousand times. Heart racing, she knelt before Åsa and laid her hand on the shining blade. Willing her voice not to quaver, she made her oath. "I, Helga Hrolfsdottir, swear to serve you, Åsa queen, until death releases me from this oath."

Åsa placed a hand on Helga's bowed head. "I accept your oath, Helga Hrolfsdottir. I promise to protect you and your family, to provide for you, to share with you all spoils of war. Rise, and take your place in my hird."

Helga stood on trembling legs. The queen rose and pinned a brooch to Helga's tunic. Fashioned of bronze and shaped like a leaf, it glittered in the firelight.

One by one her sisters knelt and made their oaths, and Åsa pinned brooches to their tunics.

When she'd finished, the young queen said, "Bring your belongings and join my camp."

"Yes, Lady," said Helga. She did not say they had no belongings other than the tunics they wore. Instead, she herded her sisters out of the firelight, where they made themselves comfortable in the shadows.

Åsa called after them, "Be sure to get something to eat. There's plenty in the cookpot."

* * *

The next day, the sisters strode through the Ting site, proudly sporting their bronze pins. Helga made sure they passed by the scornful boy.

"I see you've joined the girl-queen," he sneered. Helga had opened her mouth to retort when Unn charged him. The boy turned and ran. Unn chased him through the camp, shrieking, eyes bright with laughter.

With a squeal, Unn launched into a flying tackle. She landed on the boy's back, bringing him down. They rolled through the crowd, knocking over kettles and buckets, sending the camp into fits of laughter. Unn ended up on top, straddling her opponent.

"Yield!" Unn shouted.

The boy bucked like a wild horse but couldn't shake her off.

She grabbed his arm and wrenched it behind his back.

"I yield!" the boy shouted.

Triumphant, Unn got off him. She reached out a hand to help him up. He grabbed it and yanked her off her feet. In an instant, the two were tussling on the ground again to shouts from onlookers.

Theirs was not the only family with too many children. Over the next days, more young people straggled in. Åsa took them all. Laughter and shouts rang from her camp.

The Ting ended, and Åsa led her ragtag hird back across the mountains. Twenty-four were girls, including Helga and her sisters. They trooped over the steep mountain trails, voices raised in song.

Åsa's party reached the ferry to her island fortress, Tromøy, in the late afternoon of the third day, hot and tired from the journey. The youngsters shed their clothes and splashed, shrieking, into the narrow channel that separated the island from the mainland. Even the horses waded in and swam across. The wagons and gear were loaded onto the flat-bottomed raft, accompanied by an aging sorceress, the cook, and the elderly warlord, Jarl Borg. Two warriors poled the raft across while everyone else swam.

Even Åsa stripped down to her linen shift and dove into the frigid water. On the other side, she pulled herself up on the bank to dry off in the late afternoon sun as if she were one of her boisterous crew. Helga realized the queen was not much older than she.

The sun descended in the sky, lending a chill to the air. They put their damp clothes back on and hitched the horses to the carts, then followed a forest trail across the island to Åsa's steading.

As they emerged from the woods into the yard, a woman appeared in the bower door, a baby in her arms. Åsa hurried to take the child, who squealed in delight and threw his chubby arms around her.

A brown-haired shield-maiden threw down her arms and raced up to the group. "You have brought us…" she trailed off, gawking at the crowd of farm girls and boys.

"New recruits, Ragnhild," Åsa finished with a meaningful look.

Helga gawked at Ragnhild. The shield-maiden stood tall, dressed in trousers and a leather jerkin. In her right hand she held a sword. A seax was sheathed at her waist.

One day, Helga vowed, she would look like that.

The farmstead rang with chatter as they assembled for the homecoming feast. Servers lugged buckets of ale, and wooden cups were shared around. Laughter and song mingled with the woodsmoke. Åsa's high seat was set up in the yard, and she presided over the festivities with her son on her lap.

When the food arrived, silence reigned until the travelers had eaten their fill. Then the ale made the rounds again. The celebration continued late into the night.

In the wee hours, the sisters followed the other women to the bower. There was not enough room on the broad sleeping benches, but Helga and her sisters were more comfortable with makeshift pallets on the floor than they had been in the hayloft at home.

Åsa let them rest and get acquainted for two days. Shy of strangers, Helga and her sisters kept to themselves.

On the third morning Åsa mustered them in the yard. The queen was splendid in a green linen tunic and trews. From her belt hung two swords, scabbarded in tooled leather. Jarl Borg stood on her right, the shield-maiden Ragnhild on the left.

"The Danish king, Rorik, could attack any time," Åsa said, striding from one end of their ranks to the other. Helga poked Unn, who straightened up under the queen's scrutiny. "Your training begins today." Åsa assigned her húskarlar to whip the new boys into shape. "The girls will come with the lady Ragnhild and me."

The shield-maiden led them to a corner of the practice yard, and bade each of them take a long wooden spear shaft from a barrel. Ragnhild lined them up. "Show me what you can do."

The farm girls went after each other with more enthusiasm than skill, swinging their poles like scythes or hoes.

Ragnhild watched them for a few minutes, then called a halt. "Danes are not just thick barley or tall goats. They fight back, and their blades are sharp. They won't hesitate to gut you, and if you want to live, you will get them first." The shield-maiden nodded to a burly húskarlar who took his place across from her. Ragnhild swung her pole at his legs. He stepped away from her blow and retaliated with a sweep of his own weapon, which Ragnhild dodged neatly, countering with a jab.

"Now you try," she ordered.

Helga did her best to emulate Ragnhild's example. Step and swing low. Step and swing high. Step and block. They drilled for what seemed like hours, until Helga longed to hoe a field or shear a sheep.

Late in the afternoon, Ragnhild finally called a halt. "That's enough for today. We'll do more tomorrow."

That night, muscles ached that Helga didn't know she had. She slept well anyway, tired from a day's training.

Ragnhild kept them drilling for the better part of a week, adding more moves but never allowing them to engage with each other. Helga did her best to keep up. Gradually her aches subsided, and the moves became second nature.

After a week, Ragnhild paired them off and let them try their skills on each other. Helga had hoped to be with Unn or Ursa, but Ragnhild split the siblings up. Helga faced a girl about her own age and size. The feral glint in her eye said, *This is not a game.*

The girl swung her spear shaft and Helga brought hers up to block it. Poles met with a satisfying crack, the blow jolting up her arm. Helga recovered instantly and slashed her stick at her opponent, who bared her teeth as she blocked Helga's blow.

All around the practice yard, sticks thwacked. The recruits hurtled into the fray with swinging spear shafts and howls of fury, awarding each other cuts and bruises. They kept the völva and her apprentices busy with bandages and splints.

As they gained skill, Ragnhild tested them each against herself, her flashing pole sending them all to the ground. She drove her farm girls harder than ever, and Helga trained hardest of all, absorbing everything Ragnhild told her, striving to excel. She felt the swan woman watching her.

The day came when Helga's spear shaft swept Ragnhild's legs out from under her. The shield-maiden landed hard on her backside, shock jolting across her features. The girls gasped in unison, and lowered their weapons. Helga froze.

Ragnhild threw back her head and laughed. Åsa strode forward to haul her to her feet.

"I think they're ready to fight the men," Ragnhild said, brushing herself off.

Helga flushed with pride.

The next day the women met the men in the practice yard. They minced across the field toward each other, practice weapons outstretched. When they got within reach, they waved their spear shafts tentatively, pole ends clacking faintly.

"Fight, you cowards," Ragnhild bellowed, striding onto the field and knocking a husky boy down with her spear shaft. Her second whack bloodied his nose. "Come on!"

First blood seemed to break the spell. Roaring, Helga joined the other girls as they charged down on their opponents. Poles smacked into flesh.

"That's more like it!" Ragnhild shouted, banging her sword on her shield and grinning.

After a few whacks, the beleaguered boys shook off their reluctance and fought back. The air resounded with thuds and curses, resulting in blood and bruises on both sides. Ragnhild called an end early before bones were broken.

Jarl Borg nodded approvingly. "Another week of this and I'll begin drilling them in formation."

The farm work could not be neglected, with all these warriors to feed and clothe. The sisters took their turns tending the livestock and the fields, pulling weeds and scaring off the birds. Others added to the food supply by hunting, fishing, and foraging for wild vegetables.

In the long summer evenings, Helga and her sisters worked with the other recruits on their battle gear. The húskarlar showed them how to pad their jackets with layers of wool and coat them with hard pine resin varnish to deflect a glancing blow from an arrow or sword. More evenings were spent fletching arrows.

Ragnhild and Åsa taught the shield-maidens to draw the longbows along with the boys. Helga and her sisters already had the strength to fire arrow after arrow without pause.

They drilled and drilled under the hot summer sun. Jarl Borg taught them formations – first the basic shield wall, then the more complex swine horn. The squads took turns attacking each other, probing for weaknesses.

Åsa had a log boom deployed across the entrance to Tromøy's harbor. "It won't stop them," said Jarl Borg, "but it will slow them down."

The barley turned golden. Every able person turned out to the fields, scything the barley close to the ground, then gathering the stalks and tying them in bundles, leaning them in stooks of a dozen bundles to dry.

Everyone returned to training, for the Danes would have gotten their crops in too.

* * *

Two weeks after the barley harvest was in, Åsa burst into the bower where everyone was deep in sleep.

"The Dane fleet is coming," she cried. "They'll be here by dawn."

Helga and the other women tumbled from their sleeping benches and lunged for their war gear. No one wondered how Åsa knew an enemy fleet was coming. They all knew the queen had her ways.

Helga and her sisters joined the other archers, donning battle jackets. Helga proudly strapped on her short sword, while her sisters tucked axes into their belts. They slung shields over one shoulder and hung their bows over the other.

They mustered with the others beneath the giant ash tree beside the hall while the völva and her women sacrificed a goat for victory. The sorceress carried a bowl of sacred blood through the ranks, sprinkling each warrior for protection. Helga prayed to the swan woman. *Please, Lady, help me fight well. Let me please the gods.*

Near dawn Åsa sent the archers to the log boom. Helga and her sisters ran with the others along the shoreline and took cover in the foliage beside the boom's end. They strung their bows, planted their arrows point down in the earth, and waited.

A horn sounded from the shore. As the sun rose, the first dragon ships surged into the bay. Helga watched them drop sail and sprout oars like spider legs. Soon the water teemed with them, swarming down on the beach.

The warships shuddered to a halt as they struck the submerged log boom.

Helga joined the others, nocking and firing as fast as she could. Arrows whickered from the trees and screams rose from the enemy ships. Unn and Ursa cheered as their volley took its toll. Even little Ylva shouted in triumph.

Bodies splashed into the water as the Danes heaved their dead overboard. Tromøy's archers kept up heavy fire while the enemy struggled to free themselves. Arrows flew from the Danish ships towards shore, but they were firing blind. Helga dodged a few arrows, but most flew wild into the trees.

Despite the archers' continuous fire, the Danish ships broke through the barrier and resumed their approach. Helga shouldered her bow and ran with the others back to the hall, where they mustered in the yard.

Åsa stalked toward them, the sun glinting off her polished brynja. Jarl Borg strode on her right side, her standard-bearer on the left.

"Today, we face our enemy." Åsa's voice rang clear and strong, sending chills down Ursa's back. "The Nornir measured out the thread of our lives on the day we were born. These Danes cannot cut it shorter. Let us fight with honor and die with courage if that is our fate. I fought this same enemy on the shores of Borre and won. With your help, we will win again."

Blood surged into Helga's face. The troops cheered and clashed weapons on shields.

"Archers, take cover," Åsa ordered. Helga and her sisters sprinted for the trees with the other archers.

The first enemy longships grated onto the beach. Danes swarmed over their sides, thick as bees in a hive, lining up in a shield wall. When the first row stretched the length of the beach, a second row crowded in behind, then a third.

The Danish king's war banner streamed over the triple ranks. The early sun glinted on the crested battle helm of Rorik, king of the Danes. Huge men in full war gear surrounded him.

The triple shield wall began to move up the hill.

"Archers!" Jarl Borg shouted. Helga nocked an arrow. Beside her, Ursa and Unn did the same, Tova and Ylva close behind.

From the trees around the hall, unseen bows creaked as strings were drawn. Helga's eyes trained on Jarl Borg. He raised his hand high as he gauged the range. His long fingers dropped and Helga loosed. The arrows whirred into the air, arcing up and lashing down on the invaders like deadly rain.

Danes flung their shields up, but many screamed and fell. The defenders cheered, but still the enemy came on, trampling over their dead. Jarl Borg kept the archers firing, thinning the Danish ranks.

A shout from the enemy, and the Danish horde halted. Bowstrings creaked as their archers nocked. Their commander roared his order and arrows darkened the sky.

"Shields up," barked Jarl Borg. Wood clacked as Tromøy's line of troops racked shield to shield and jerked the solid wall overhead to weather the arrows that hailed down.

An arrow split Ylva's shield. Her eyes grew wide, staring at the arrowhead lodged in the wood so close to her eye.

No death cries came from Tromøy's ranks.

The Danish king stepped out of the line. "I dedicate you all to Odin!" He hurled a spear directly at Åsa.

Åsa swayed out of the spear's path, reached up, and grabbed the shaft as it passed inches from her face.

A gasp rose up from every throat.

"I mark you all for Freyja!" Åsa hurled the spear back into the Danish horde. The unexpected missile struck the bannerman's helmet, knocking him off his feet and sending the Danish banner to the ground.

Tromøy's troops roared at the omen. Helga screamed until her throat was raw.

The Danes paused in their onslaught, momentarily shaken, but the bannerman regained his feet and their commanders rallied them with curses and blows. They resumed their march up the hill.

Åsa pounded the butt of her spear on the ground. "This is our chance!" she cried. "Our chance for peace and plenty. These Danes would take our land, our freedom, our lives. They will keep coming until we stop them. Let's drive them back into the sea. We can do it. The gods are on our side. Tromøy will triumph!"

Their cheers swelled in a deafening wave. Helga was mad with battle-joy, desperate to fight. Ursa's eyes were shining and Tova grinned from ear to ear.

The sisters joined the mad dash as the archers broke cover to join the ranks. They grabbed spears and lined up with their shield-mates, breathless and eager.

"Swine horn!" shouted Jarl Borg.

The ranks brought their shields down, locked together. Helga hefted her spear.

They tightened into a cohesive rectangle of steel and linden. Helga jabbed her spear between the shields in front of her.

"Charge!" shouted Jarl Borg.

For a fraction of a second, Helga pushed against those in front of her. Then the resistance gave and she hurtled ahead with the others, spear driving forward, a scream ripping from her throat.

Momentum carried them into the enemy's first ranks. Helga held her breath as the warriors in front of her crashed through the mass of enemies. Her spearpoint rammed into chain mail, and her victim screamed and fell. She jerked her spear free, then thrust it into the crowd again. She jabbed in and out, shoving into the thick of the Danish shield wall.

They broke through so suddenly Helga nearly stumbled. Her line swept her around to attack the enemy ranks from the rear.

The Danes were off-balance, having lost precious seconds trying to recover from the breach. Tromøy's warriors maintained their formation and rammed their spears into the crowd, taking their toll before the Danes could regroup. Then the enemy turned on them and the shield walls dissolved into the chaos of battle.

Shouts and screams mingled with the clash of steel. The air reeked of blood, and the grass was slippery with it. Bodies made the footing treacherous, the wounded writhing among the dead.

Having lost her spear in some Dane's mail, Helga drew her short sword and confronted a leering enemy. Weeks of training guided her and she drove her blade upward beneath the Dane's beard. The man's eyes rounded in surprise. Helga tore her weapon from his throat and spun away as he pitched forward. She hacked down the next foe where neck met shoulder, felling him instantly. Pivoting, she bashed her shield into a helmet, sending another Dane stumbling.

Helga stood in a tangle of fallen enemies, catching her breath. Her cheeks were flushed, the joy of battle upon her.

She caught Åsa's eye and grinned proudly.

Beyond the queen, the swan woman loomed, splendid and fierce, hefting a blazing sword. The woman gazed at Helga, a smile on her lips.

Steel flashed as a warrior swung his axe. Åsa screamed a warning. Helga turned to meet the attack, a heartbeat too late. The Dane's axe swung and she felt the blade slice into her neck. Blood sprayed and she stumbled, but there was no pain. She crumpled to the ground, watching her sisters rush toward her, their mouths stretched in screams, eyes full of horror.

The battlefield dissolved in a film of blood. Helga felt herself lifted from the melee.

She was flying through the air in the swan woman's arms.

The Valkyrie smiled at her. "You fought well, daughter. Freyja is pleased. Soon you will take your place in Sessrumnir."

Joy suffused Helga as they soared through the sky. Far below, the battle raged. Her sisters gathered around her fallen corpse. She wanted to shout to them not to mourn. Her dream had come true.

The gods were pleased.

Her Drum

Ernie Xu

I felt I was going to die.

There's little that would make me want to die. But Eira's words were shards of glass, and I was forced to swallow them, and I really felt, as soon as Eira whisked herself away and out of my life, I could never be happy again. The thought sank the shards deeper into my oesophagus. But Eira desired a life among the dead, desired power over those who are doomed, or almost doomed. She has always had this desire – and I knew this – but, until truly made to confront it, how could I possibly know the inevitability of her decision? I might as well be dead, I thought.

But all around me was the smell of the living. Woodsmoke, mead, sweat. Home. How could this not be home? How could this be anywhere but home? Eira gazed at me with eyes that were faraway and sorrowful, and I realised her eyes have never been anything but faraway and the sorrow isn't one of regret but of pity – for me.

"I'm sorry—"

"No. Don't." I couldn't bear to hear her apologise. Her apology was her cue to leave. All she needed was to get her apologies out, and be done with me.

"But I am. I am sorry. But you must understand. This is not the first time I'm telling you this."

"But why are you telling me again? Why are you telling me this now?"

Eira's hand found mine, and her grasp was as firm and strong as ever, but the touch was cool, already half a memory. "This is a greater honour, Astrid. To serve in the Great Hall itself, to welcome the Einherjar…it is a glory beyond any we could dream here. I will wait for you. In Valhalla. When you come, grey and old, after a long life, I will be there. I will pour the mead that heals your aged bones."

The promise was a beautiful, cruel lie. I saw it in the new distance in Eira's eyes. Time would lose all meaning for her. A thousand winters could pass in Asgard, a thousand battles rage on the fields of Valhalla, and Eira would remain as she was now, eternal and unchanged, while I withered and faded into the distant past.

I withdrew my hands from her white-knuckled grip.

"You've already spoken to a Valkyrie," I realised. And my heart, a drum that had beat only for this dark-haired, fierce-eyed woman, stuttered. I already knew Eira's answer. And I hadn't asked a question that needed to be answered, anyhow.

"She spoke to me," Eira said, her voice, unlike mine, firm and unyielding. Her eyes were cold starlight. "That day, when you came home late, and I wasn't hungry. She came to the fjord. Her armour was the winter sky, and her spear a shard of the moon. She promised me that she would return; that my place is forever before a loom, but that I'm sitting before the wrong one."

I knew what I should be saying: that I'm overjoyed for her – wasn't this what she has always wanted? To be recognised by the Valkyries and to be admitted as one of their own into Odin's hall?

How she must be feeling I couldn't even begin to imagine. I didn't have a dream like hers. As intense as hers. Except the dream to be with her. And I have been with her, for four years now – a significant amount of time. How could I not be satisfied with that?

Of course I can't be satisfied with that. Time will soon mean nothing to Eira. I will become a speck in the distance, some faraway person from some faraway time that is not even worth space in her heart. She says she will always remember me, but how can she know that's true when *always* is too long a time to keep promises and she has already started to forget?

Or, if she remembers all we mean to each other, how is it possible to discard me so easily for this desire of hers? Shouldn't *I* be her desire?

Her words hung between us, heavy and final. Hers was a destiny that left no room for a mortal lover in a mortal longhouse. And I knew, I was merely consolation while Eira waited for a better promise, the promise she has been waiting for all her life.

"But…we promised each other… You promised me—" My voice was rough, the words scraping my throat. *How embarrassing.* But what was there to be embarrassed about?

"I'm sorry. I suppose I'm breaking my promise."

Eira should be embarrassed! One should never break their promise! How embarrassing!

But all I could feel was admiration. I admired Eira for her determination, her promises kept to herself – these were promises she made to herself long before she ever met me. Perhaps this made sense. When promises clash, shouldn't one always prioritise the first?

Quite quickly, too quickly, after that, she left. I didn't end up saying anything else to her. No well wishes, but no bitter accusations either. After all, with a slashed-up oesophagus from all her glass-shard words shoved down my throat, how could I speak? And it truly felt like that, for any words that left my dry, cracked lips were hoarse and incoherent anyway.

* * *

Before the first snows melted from the shoulders of the mountains, Eira was gone. There was no body, no grave. Only a rumour from a nearby fjord of a woman with dark hair, her form shifting into that of a great swan, ascending into a storm cloud shot through with unnatural light.

And yet I mourned. I mourned for five years, until I realised that I had been mourning for longer than the relationship had lasted. How ridiculous was that? But I could not help myself.

The warmth of the longhouse that day felt suffocating. I couldn't wait any longer – what was I even waiting for? – and I decided to step outside. I carried upon my hip a basket of woollens. I knew a kindly old man who would allow me to trade them for some more sturdy clothing. Some ring-mail. The sun sat heavy in the sky. It offered no warmth, only a flat, unforgiving light that made the world seem sharp and brittle. The basket of woollens on my hip was a familiar weight, its purpose once so simple: trade for food, for ale, for a new carving knife. Now, it was a disguise, the first layer of a new skin I was pulling over my old life.

The kindly old man was where he always was, outside his sod-roofed hut, his hands busy with a piece of yew wood he was shaping into a bowl. His eyes, milky with age, still saw too much.

He greeted me, his voice like the grind of stone on stone. "You bring the warmth of the loom on a cold day."

"I bring trade," I said, my voice sounding hollow even to my own ears. I set the basket down. "Not for a bowl. Not for bread."

He set his carving aside, wiping his hands on his breeches. He looked at me, then at the basket, then back at me. "What, then, for such fine work? Your fingers have been busy in your mourning."

"Ring-mail," I said, the word foreign and heavy on my tongue. "Or leather, hardened. A helm, if you have one. A spear."

I braced for his response. He was silent for a long time. The only sound was the whisper of the wind through the tall grasses and the distant, rhythmic *thump-thump-thump* from the smithy down in the valley – the steady, heartbeat drum of a hammer on hot iron. It was a sound that usually spoke of ploughshares and nails, of life. Now, to me, it sounded only of forging weapons. Of war.

"This is Eira's path you walk now, girl," he said, not unkindly. "It is a path of shadow and glory, not for those who seek it in grief. It is chosen, not taken."

"I am choosing," I lied, the words ash in my mouth. "I choose to follow."

He sighed, a long, weary sound. "To follow a Valkyrie, one must have the same calling in their blood. It is not a matter of want. It is a matter of *is*. You are Astrid of the loom and the hearth. Your war is against the winter chill, not against mortal men."

"What do you know of my blood?" I snapped, the bitterness I had swallowed for five years finally surging up. "She promised to wait for me. I am merely…taking a shorter road to that promise. And, besides, Eira was also of the loom."

I only realised later that I had referred to Eira in the past tense.

He looked at me with a pity that mirrored Eira's, and it was a knife-twist in a wound that had never healed. Without another word, he rose and disappeared into the gloom of his hut. He returned with a pile of blackened ring-mail, a bundle of oiled leather – a worn but serviceable jerkin – and a simple dented iron cap.

"This is all I have for such a trade," he said. "The mail was my son's. It went to the pyre with him. The spear you must find elsewhere. Perhaps your grief is currency enough for the smith's son. He is young and does not listen to the old stories."

The trade felt like a desecration. My careful, colourful weavings, each thread spun with a memory of a life I was trying to escape, for these cold, dead scraps of a warrior's end.

The smith's son, indeed, did not ask questions. He saw a determined woman with a basket of valuable goods and a dull desperation in her eyes, and he saw a profit. For the rest of my woollens, he gave me a spear with a chipped, but sharp, iron tip. Its haft was smooth and dark from other hands, and I wondered how many men had held it before they died. I hoped it was many. I hoped their fury was still trapped in the grain of the wood.

My preparation was a pathetic pantomime. I knew the stories; the songs skalds sang of the Einherjar. I knew the ideal: a warrior, fallen bravely in battle, sword in hand, a curse on his lips and a prayer to Odin in his heart. That was not me. I had no skill, no rage, no love of battle. I had only a singular, desperate purpose: to fall in a way that would force a Valkyrie to my side. To force *her* to my side.

I practised with the spear in the secluded woods until my palms blistered and my muscles screamed their protest. Every clumsy thrust, every off-balance parry, was a testament to my inadequacy. I was not answering a call in my blood; I was screaming into an empty void, hoping the echo would sound like destiny.

The opportunity came with the first spring raids. A rival jarl, seeking glory and resources, sailed into our fjord. The alarm was raised not by a horn, but by the frantic, thunderous beat of the war drum – a great hide stretched over a hollowed log, pounded with a mammoth's bone. I felt it resonating through me, reverberating under my skin, beating with my heart as one. I recall the promise – one among many – I've once given to Eira – that my heart was hers; it beat only for her. But this was not a heartbeat. It was a summons, a primal pulse that vibrated in the teeth and the bones, demanding violence. It was the antithesis of my gentle world of clicking looms and crackling fires. And I ran towards it.

* * *

The battlefield was a chaos I could never have imagined. The songs spoke of glorious duels and shining heroes. They did not speak of the mud churned to bloody slurry, the stench of opened bowels, the screaming of horses and the wet, ugly thuds of axes finding homes in flesh. The great drum still boomed from the hill, a monstrous, arrhythmic god commanding the frenzy below.

I clutched my spear, my knuckles red. I saw men with eyes wide with battle-joy, singing as they killed. I saw others, like me, wide-eyed with terror, but they fought with the instinct of cornered animals. I just stood, a still point in the storm, looking, always looking, for a sign.

And then I saw her.

Or I thought I did. A flash of impossible light in the gloom, a figure armoured not in iron but in captured starlight, moving through the carnage with an unhurried, terrible grace. Her face was hidden behind a helm, but her hair was a dark river down her back. My heart, that stuttered drum, gave a wild, painful lurch. I did not think. I ran.

I ran not towards the enemy, but towards the spectre. I stumbled over the dead, my feet slipping in the gore. A massive warrior, his beard matted with blood, swung a great axe at me. It was not a skilled move; it was a simple, brutal arc of force. I brought my spear up in a pathetic blocking gesture I'd practised among the trees. The axe shattered the haft, the force of the blow hurling me backwards into the mud.

The air left my lungs in a rush. I lay there, stunned, watching the bronze sky swirl above me. The drum was fading, replaced by a high-pitched whine in my ears. This was it. This was the moment. I had fallen. I had, technically, a weapon in my hand, though it was now just a splintered stick. I turned my head, searching the field, waiting for the winter-skied armour, the moon-shard spear.

Come for me, I begged silently. *Come for me. See me. Take me home.*

The axe-man loomed over me, his shadow blotting out the sky. He raised his weapon for the final blow. And then he grunted, his eyes widening in surprise. A spearpoint erupted from his chest, glistening and red. He toppled sideways.

Standing behind him was not Eira.

It was a Valkyrie, yes. Her armour was the deep grey of a tombstone, her winged helm etched with runes of binding and finality. Her eyes, visible through the slit in her helm, were not cold starlight, but the flat, neutral grey of a midwinter sea. There was no recognition in them, no pity, no sorrow. There was only duty.

She looked down at me, a piece of the battlefield's debris. I had fought. I had fallen. I was, by the strictest terms, eligible.

Her gaze was a physical weight, and in that endless moment, I felt it strip me bare. It saw my pathetic practice in the woods, my traded armour, my complete lack of the battle-joy that illuminated the true warriors around me. It saw my desperate, lonely heart, beating its selfish rhythm out of time with the great war drum. It saw that I was not, and had never been, a warrior. I was a jilted lover, and this was my grand, foolish gesture.

I opened my mouth to speak, to cry out "Wait!" or "No!" or "I'm not one of them!" But just like that day five years ago, no sound emerged. My throat was sealed shut by a terror far greater than the axe-man's.

She did not speak. She simply reached down, her grip like iron on my arm, and pulled me to my feet. The mortal wound I was certain I had felt was gone. There was only a deep ache in my chest. My body was whole, but my spirit was flayed. With a strength that was not of this world, she lifted me onto the back of her spectral steed, its coat the colour of smoke and its eyes burning with pale fire.

The ride was a blur of screaming wind and shifting light. We ascended through the cloud layer, leaving the world of woodsmoke and mead and the fading, never-ending – ending – beat of the war drum far below. I closed my eyes.

The sound that greeted us was the first true shock of my new eternity. It was not a heavenly choir. It was a roar. The roar of five thousand warriors feasting, fighting, laughing. The roar of a perpetual, riotous victory.

The Great Hall of Valhalla was vast beyond comprehension, its rafters made of spears, its roof thatched with shields. The air hummed with power and thrummed with the relentless, pounding rhythm of a hundred drums, beating in a syncopated, frenzied cadence for the eternal battles outside and the riotous feasts within. It was the war drum made infinite, a pulse that promised never-ending violence and celebration.

The Valkyrie deposited me unceremoniously at the entrance to the hall amidst a group of other newly arrived Einherjar. They were clapping each other on the back, roaring with laughter, already reaching for the endless streams of mead carried by silent, graceful figures.

And then I saw her.

Eira.

She moved between the long tables, an urn of mead in her hands. Her armour was indeed the winter sky, a deep blue-black scattered with points of cold light. She was more beautiful than I remembered, terrible and perfect and immutable. She was everything she had ever wanted to be.

She turned, and for a breathtaking second, her eyes met mine across the chaotic hall.

There was a flicker in that faraway gaze. A ghost of a memory, a ripple in the stillness of a frozen lake. She saw me. She recognised me. Her step faltered for a fraction of a heartbeat.

Then the flat neutrality of the Valkyrie returned. The ripple smoothed over. She gave a slight, almost imperceptible shake of her head. It wasn't a denial of knowing me. It was a dismissal. A verdict.

Or, perhaps, she never saw me at all.

She turned away to fill the cup of a laughing giant of a man, her face a mask of serene, eternal duty.

I stood there, whole and strong and young forever, in the midst of the greatest glory my people could conceive. The mead would heal any wound, the feast would never end, the battle would always be glorious.

And I understood the true nature of my punishment. I had gotten exactly what I asked for. I was in Odin's hall with my lover for all time. But I was not a Valkyrie. I was one of the Einherjar, the honoured dead. I would feast and fight and die and be reborn to do it again, tomorrow and tomorrow and tomorrow and tomorrow and tomorrow. And she would be there, eternal and unchanged, pouring the mead that healed my aged bones, pouring and pouring, her eyes already forgetting the woman I was, the love we had, the mortal world we'd both left behind, with no regrets, not looking back.

The frenzied drumming of Valhalla pounded in my skull, a rhythm of endless, meaningless revelry. It was not a heartbeat. It was the sound of my own eternity, a prison of glory I had willingly entered, and it was deafening.

Biographies

Ryaan Akmal
Light as Air, Light as Dawn
(First Publication)
Ryaan Akmal is a hobbyist writer, with previously published poetry and a short story published in the sci-fi collection *Our Dust Earth*. Among all types of writing, he has a deep appreciation for novel structural and thematic ideas. Above all else, he hopes that his work is regarded as interesting and fun.

Don Bisdorf
The Battle of Weaver's Field
(First Publication)
Don Bisdorf is a writer, software developer, and game designer. He and his wife have hidden themselves away in a little house in the woods, where they look after a hoard of books, a stack of computers, and one very good dog. He enjoys baking, drinking tea, and rolling dice while pretending to be an elvish wizard. You can find him online at donbisdorf.com.

Nancy Marie Brown
Introducing The Valkyries
Nancy Marie Brown is the author of *The Real Valkyrie: The Hidden History of Viking Warrior Women*, which tells the story of the warrior woman buried in Birka grave Bj581. An independent scholar, she has been writing about Norse mythology, Icelandic sagas and Viking Age history and archaeology since 2001. She keeps Icelandic horses and considers Tolkien's Eowyn to be a major role model.

Dr Jóhanna Katrín Friðriksdóttir
Foreword
Dr Jóhanna Katrín Friðriksdóttir is a medievalist and author of *Valkyrie: The Women of the Viking World*. Her work focuses on Vikings, medieval

Scandinavia and the reception of these in the modern era. She completed her doctorate in medieval literature from Oxford University in 2010 and held research and teaching positions in Reykjavík, Iceland and the United States before taking up her current position at the National Library of Norway in Oslo. She has also worked as a historical consultant for documentaries and feature films, including Robert Eggers' *The Northman*.

Kay Hanifen

Strike of the Valkyries

Kay Hanifen was born on a Friday the 13th and once lived for three months in a haunted castle. So, obviously, she had to become a horror writer. Her work has appeared in over 100 anthologies and magazines. Her first anthology as an editor, *Till the Yule Log Burns Out*, was published in 2024. Her first novel, *The Last Ballard*, debuted in 2025. When she's not consuming pop culture with the voraciousness of a vampire at a 24-hour blood bank, you can usually find her with her black cats or at kayhanifenauthor.wordpress.com.

Ikechukwu Henry

Fólkvangr

(First Publication)

Ikechukwu Henry is an Igbo Nigerian writer whose writings tackle the issues of environmental and climatic crises, family dynamics, queerness and speculative otherworldliness. He was fifth place in Christian Speculative Fiction Prize, Shortlisted for The Oriire Folktale Prize and has publications in but not limited to *Brittle Paper*, *The Kalahari Review*, *Lampblack Magazine* and others. When not writing, he can be found scouring out the next magazine to submit to.

E.K. Larson-Burnett

The Swan-Helm Thief

(First Publication)

E.K. Larson-Burnett is an award-winning author and professional editor based in Texas. Her published works include *The Bear & the Rose*, *A Madness Unmade*, and *Prickle*. Her fiction marries myth and melancholy with explorations of mental health and the uncanny. When not writing or editing, she enjoys reading, board games, and doting on her rescued animals.

J.B. Riley

Flight School

(First Publication)

J.B. Riley lives in Chicago with her family, which currently includes a dog the size of a bathtub and a six-pound cat that scares the heck out of him. An OG nerd, she enjoys writing both scary and silly stories, and has loved SFF since discovering *The Chronicles of Narnia* at age 8. When not trawling the shelves of local bookstores, she enjoys travel, hockey, beer and cooking.

Laura Shenton

The Confessions of Valdis the Forgotten

(First Publication)

Laura Shenton is probably best known for her music non-fiction, particularly *Dance With The Devil: The Cozy Powell Story* (Wymer Publishing) and *Tommy Bolin: In and Out of Deep Purple* (Sonicbond Publishing). Her fiction books are character-driven with a short, punchy narrative that gets straight to the point – typically novellas and novelettes. Genres include gothic, fantasy, and adventure (mostly, with the occasional diversion). Laura's children's books are simple, accessible, and fun – an excellent choice for youngsters with fertile imaginations who are just beginning their reading journey.

Nina Shepardson

Saving Souls

(First Publication)

Nina Shepardson is a scientist and a lifelong birdwatcher. Her short fiction appears in *Night Shades*, *On Spec*, and the anthology *Between Doorways: Exploration into Liminal Space*, among others. She's an Active Member of SFWA and a member of the Codex Writers Group. She blogs about birds, tea, and books at ninashepardson.substack.com. Nina is currently working on her first novel.

Zac Sherman

The Brightest Star

(First Publication)

Zac Sherman is an Ohio writer of speculative fiction. His work has appeared in *Mythcreants*, *4Horsemen*, and *Penmarks*. After a decade in higher education, he has developed a heart for the ways in which sharing stories connect us to one another and create spaces of belonging and healing. When not writing, Sherman enjoys participating in theatre, composing music, serving as a CASA, and all things *Star Trek*.

D.L. Stille

The Wyrd Sister

(First Publication)

D.L. Stille writes speculative, thriller, and horror fiction. Having grown up both in the New Jersey Highlands and the foothills of the Appalachians, she has a special love for mountains, forests, and autumn. D.L. Stille has been previously published in *Maudlin House*, the Flame Tree Fiction Newsletter, *4LPH4NUM3R1C*, *Tales to Terrify*, and *Cosmic Daffodil Journal*. To find out more and to stay updated on forthcoming projects, visit her website: dlstille.com

Susanna Fraser Stone

Her Terrible Swift Sword

(First Publication)

Susanna Fraser Stone lives in Seattle with her husband and son. Her historical romance under the pen name Susanna Fraser has been published by Carina Press and Entangled Publishing, and her short speculative fiction has appeared in *100-Foot Crow*. If she's not writing (or working at her day job), she's probably reading, singing in her neighborhood chorus, watching the crows and chickadees in her backyard, or fretting over the prospects of her favorite football and baseball teams.

Deborah Tapper

Stone Heart

(First Publication)

Deborah Tapper writes mostly speculative fiction and has been published in anthologies, magazines and online. An occasional stargazer, she collects dictionaries and fossils and is fascinated by folklore and mythology, especially tales that delve into the weird, dark and mysterious. She lives with her understanding partner in an archaeologically rich landscape of barrows and stone circles, drinks too much strong tea and writes at an old desk surrounded by five hundred pet bugs.

Benjamin Thomas
Valhalla Is a Lie
(Originally Published in *Lost Librarian's Grave: Tales of Madness, Horror, and Adventure*, Redwood Press, 2021)
Benjamin Thomas writes from New England where he spends too much time aimlessly wandering around. His short fiction is scattered across print and digital collections, while his medical thriller *Jack Be Quick* is available from Owl Hollow Press. Get in touch at benjiswandering.com

M.M. Williams
A Scream to Split Stone
(First Publication)
M.M. Williams is an author of Norse-inspired fantasy novels and speculative short fiction. She currently lives in Northern Utah, USA, with her spouse, toddler, and tyrannical tortoiseshell cat. When not writing or parenting, she enjoys studying folklore, swimming in the coldest water possible, or translating old handwritten documents. Some of her work can be found in the *Loki* and *Were Wolf* anthologies by Flame Tree Publishing, as well as the recent fourth issue of *Ghoulish Tales* magazine.

Mae Wilmarth
The Death of a Valkyrja
(First Publication)
Mae Wilmarth grew up on a farm in Illinois and studied English at Illinois State University. Over the years and across four states, she has been supported by wonderful writing communities and had the opportunity to serve as a Dogfish Head Poetry Prize first reader for three years. Now she lives in Colorado, where she edits engineering things, haunts her own house and garden, and sometimes wanders the front range of the Rocky Mountains.

Johanna Wittenberg
To Please the Gods
(First Publication)
Johanna Wittenberg is the author of the bestselling *Norsewomen* series, the story of Åsa, a real Norse queen who ruled alone during the early Viking Age. Like her Viking forebears, Johanna has sailed to the far reaches of the world.

She lives on a fjord in the Pacific Northwest with her husband, whom she met on a ship bound for Antarctica. See more at johannawittenberg.com.

Ernie Xu
Her Drum
(First Publication)
Ernie Xu is a Sydney and Shenzhen-based emerging writer and artist, specialising in printmaking (etching and linocut) and painting (gouache). She writes mostly short stories and that one novel that has been in the works for nigh on seven years and has since run way out of control. Her work explores the roles of mythology and speculative fiction, seeking ways to use mythology as a device to describe our own futures through storytelling. You can find Ernie on Instagram @ernie.ink.

Source for the Mythic Tales: Snorri Sturluson

Snorri Sturluson (1179–1241) is the name you will keep reading when learning about the core texts of Norse mythology. This Icelandic scholar, politician, historian and poet is commonly considered the compiler of all or most of the *Prose Edda*, to which we refer in this book, along with being the author of *Egil's Saga* and *Heimskringla*, a collection of Old Norse kings' sagas. Sturluson had the good fortune of being raised by Jón Loftsson, chieftain of Oddi in Iceland and a relative of the Norwegian royal family, and thus benefited from a good education and connections. A favourable marriage bestowed chieftainships upon him, increasing his standing and wealth. He became known as a poet while working as a 'lawspeaker' in the Icelandic parliament, and was also cultivated by the Norwegian royalty, becoming an agent in support of union with Norway. As political events marched on, this relationship turned sour and Sturluson was assassinated by the very nation he had supported – not before penning the enduring chronicles of their kings.

Myths, Gods & Immortals

Discover the mythology of humankind through its heroes, characters, gods and immortal figures. **Myths, Gods and Immortals** brings together the new and the ancient, familiar stories with a fresh and imaginative twist. Each book brings back to life a legendary, mythological or folkloric figure, with completely new stories alongside the original tales and a comprehensive introduction which emphasizes ancient and modern connections, tracing history and stories across continents, cultures and peoples.

Flame Tree Fiction

A wide range of new and classic fiction, from myth to modern stories, with tales from the distant past to the far future, including short story anthologies, **Beyond & Within**, **Collector's Editions**, **Collectable Classics**, **Gothic Fantasy collections** and **Epic Tales** of mythology and folklore.